Eurydice

An epic story of a destroyer's encounters with the
Japanese Navy in the Java Seas in 1942

*This specially prepared edition, issued in 1954, is
for members of The Popular Book Club, 9 Long
Acre, London, W.C.2, from which address par-
ticulars of membership will gladly be sent. This
volume is published by arrangement with Hodder
and Stoughton Ltd., the original publishers*

TAFFRAIL

has also written

Novels

THE NEW MOON
THE JADE LIZARD
TOBY SHAD
CHENIES
THE SHETLAND PLAN
FRED TRAVIS, A.B.
OPERATION M.O.
MYSTERY CRUISE
MID-ATLANTIC
MYSTERY AT MILFORD HAVEN
SECOND OFFICER
SEVENTY NORTH
THE MAN FROM SCAPA FLOW
DOVER-OSTEND
THE SCARLET STRIPE
CYPHER K
THE LONELY BUNGALOW
KERRELL
PIRATES
SHIPMATES
MICHAEL BRAY
THE SUB

Naval History

WESTERN MEDITERRANEAN
THE NAVY IN ACTION
SWEPT CHANNELS
ENDLESS STORY

TAFFRAIL

Eurydice

THE POPULAR BOOK CLUB
LONDON

The characters in this book are entirely imaginary and have no relation to any living person

MADE AND PRINTED IN GREAT BRITAIN FOR
THE POPULAR BOOK CLUB (ODHAMS PRESS LTD.)
BY ODHAMS (WATFORD) LIMITED
WATFORD, HERTS
S1054.SA

FOREWORD

THOUGH some of the earlier events described in this story are more or less true to fact and the names of certain ships are thinly disguised, I wish to emphasize that there never were destroyers called the *Eurydice* and *Anula*, and that they and their officers and men, together with all the other characters mentioned, exist only in my imagination.

I have also taken liberties with geography, and with the movements of convoys and His Majesty's ships, including a destroyer of the Royal Australian Navy.

The book is just a tale—something which might conceivably have happened after the Battle of the Java Sea; but unfortunately did not.

TAFFRAIL

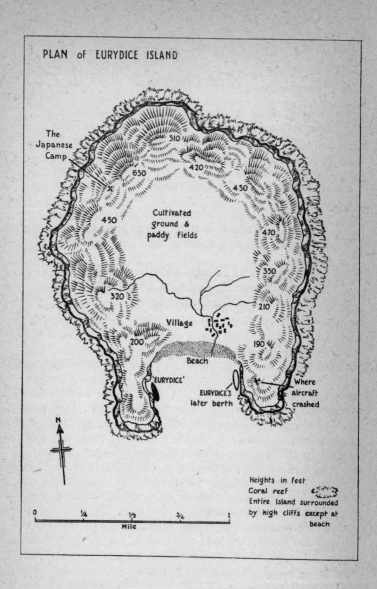

PLAN of EURYDICE ISLAND

The Japanese Camp

510
650
420
450
450
470
350
320
210
Village
200
190
Beach
'EURYDICE'
EURYDICE'S later berth
Where aircraft crashed

Cultivated ground & paddy fields

N

Heights in Feet
Coral reef
Entire Island surrounded by high cliffs except at beach

0   ¼   ½   ¾   1
Mile

1

THE CRUISERS and destroyers of the Allied Striking Force had been ordered to raise steam for full speed with all dispatch, which meant urgency. While the thickening haze of oil-fuel smoke rose from their funnels, white-clad men were busy about their decks preparing for sea—unshackling cables from buoys and reeving slip-ropes; hoisting and turning in boats; casting loose guns and providing ammunition; testing communications and fire-control. Anti-aircraft guns were already manned, as the harbour had frequently been visited by Japanese bombers. A few, pitifully few, submarines were on patrol at sea; with all the available long-range aircraft, sparse and thinly scattered.

Commanding officers had been summoned on board the Dutch flagship for orders, and on the quarter-deck of His Majesty's destroyer *Eurydice* her first lieutenant, George Acton, paced anxiously up and down awaiting the return of his captain, Lieutenant-Commander Robert Stockleigh Pomeroy.

February, 1942, had nearly run its course. There was a feeling of strain and tension in the air. Everyone knew, no one could help knowing, what was in the wind. Neither Acton nor any man of the *Eurydice's* ship's company needed to be told of the situation in the Pacific, the South China Sea or the complicated network of smaller seas and straits and channels which separated the many islands of the Dutch East Indies. The overall picture was perfectly clear in their minds. They had followed events since December 7th, 1941—"the day that will live in infamy"—when the American fleet had been wantonly attacked by the Japanese at Pearl Harbour. Three days later it had been followed by the sinking of the *Prince of Wales* and *Repulse* by enemy torpedo-bombers off the east coast of Malaya while operating without air cover. Ever since then disaster had followed disaster.

Away in the north the gallant remnants of the American troops in the Philippines were still battling fiercely against the enemy at Bataan and Corregidor; but after a seventeen-day siege, Hong Kong, its defenders hopelessly outnumbered and overwhelmed, had fallen on Christmas Day. Landing on the

7

east coast of Malaya, the victorious Japanese had swept down the Malay Peninsula, to secure vast resources of tin and rubber, and to capture Singapore, with its naval base and airfield, on February 15th.

The Allied situation in the Dutch East Indies was crumbling almost visibly. Crippled by the temporary loss of most of her battle fleet at Pearl Harbour, America could not greatly assist. As for Britain—she had been at war for nearly two and a half years; fighting single-handed for her existence for all but nine months of that time against the combined strength of Germany and Italy in the Mediterranean and in North Africa, not to mention the fierce and extending battle against the U-boats in the Atlantic and Home Waters, as well as the air defence of Great Britain and the air offensive against Germany. Bled white by a succession of losses in Norway, at Dunkirk, in Greece and in Crete, stretched to the very limit of her endurance and resources, Britain had neither the ships, the troops nor the aircraft for another war in the East.

With an inadequate fleet, insufficient troops, no more than a handful of obsolescent aircraft, and a native population that was largely apathetic and indifferent, there was nothing the Allies could do in the Dutch East Indies to stem the inexorable Japanese advance to the southward, or to protect every important point in that vast archipelago of rich islands, some of them producing the all-important oil, stretching for about 2,500 miles from Sumatra in the west to New Guinea in the east.

Choosing their own time, the enemy could operate more or less as they pleased. Step by step, unhurried like the deliberate groping of the tentacles of some great octopus, the Japanese fastened upon point after point, here to seize an oil-producing port, there to occupy or to establish an airfield. With carefully-planned caution and infinite cunning their troop convoys, escorted by the necessary warships, never moved beyond the 400-mile range of their shore-based aircraft unless they had the support of an aircraft carrier. The landing of expeditionary forces powerful enough to deal with the slender local garrisons, preceded by air attacks and covered by air power, had pro-ceeded with terrifying regularity. Before the Allies could consolidate any new position they found themselves hemmed in by a system of hostile air bases in front and on either flank. By the beginning of the third week in February Borneo, the Celebes, Amboina, Timor, Bali and Palembang, in Sumatra, were all in Japanese hands. Darwin, in Northern Australia, had been bombed with the loss of much shipping, and the enemy had control of the Sunda and Lombok Straits at the western and eastern ends of Java.

The Dutch Admiral had issued a message to all the ships of his Striking Force:

"I inform all officers and ships' companies that the situation is very serious. I wish to impress upon all of you the necessity for every effort against the enemy to prevent his landing on Java. Every opportunity for offensive action must be seized and sacrifices made to this end. This will be the general line of our conduct in the next days.

"Owing to the experiences during several engagements with the enemy during the last three weeks I fully trust that every man shall understand the earnestness of this message and will realize that we will have to do our duty until the last moment."

They were the gallant words of a gallant sailor; but what could be done?

His Striking Force, the ships of which had already been run almost to the point of exhaustion, consisted of no more than two heavy cruisers, one British and one American, with three light cruisers, one of which was Australian and the others Dutch. For the rest there were ten destroyers—three British, one of which was the *Eurydice*; three Dutch, and four American.

The ships of the three different nations had had no opportunity of working together as a combined force under the operational command of the Dutch Admiral. Little had been prearranged. There was no unified plan, no common code of tactical signals, no common methods. Co-operation, such as it was, had to be achieved by informal collaboration on the spur of the moment. Above all, the Allies had no aircraft carrier, no fighter cover at sea. There were practically no aircraft with which to drive off enemy bombing attacks or the unwelcome prying of the Japanese reconnaissance planes which were able to range with virtual impunity over the whole of the Java Sea.

It was this attenuated and heterogeneous collection of Allied ships, which could not be dignified by the name of a fleet, that had to withstand the victorious, well-trained strength of the Imperial Japanese Navy bent upon further conquest.

Strangely enough no one on board the *Eurydice* seemed in any way downcast. The men bustled about their varied tasks with their usual cheerful energy; noisy, singing, bandying jokes with each other in the highest of spirits. Their tails were well up, which Acton was pleased to see.

Barely twenty minutes earlier, when Pomeroy had duly been piped over the side with all ceremony on his way to the Dutch flagship, the three-badged petty officer of the upper deck, one Hartopp, married with four children and one of Acton's right-hand men, had whispered throatily in the first lieutenant's ear —"What's the breeze now, sir?"

"Breeze, Hartopp? What breeze?"

"All this comin' and goin' aboard the Dutch flagship, sir. What's in the wind?"

Acton was in the middle twenties, and Hartopp nearly old enough to be his father, with much experience of the Navy, particularly in destroyers. The pair were firm friends, and had served together for nearly two years. But for the war Hartopp would long since have taken his pension, and what he didn't know about sailors and their ways wasn't worth thinking about. In proffering good advice he never overstepped the bounds of good manners and naval discipline. If he considered himself Acton's "sea daddy," for which there was some justification, the *Eurydice's* first lieutenant knew himself fortunate to have the counsel of a stalwart who would never let him put a foot wrong and was a tower of strength in any emergency. While Acton knew all about Hartopp's family affairs, which were not uncomplicated as regards two daughters approaching marriageable age, Hartopp was aware that Acton was engaged to be married. Hadn't he seen the photograph of a young lady in evening dress in the silver frame on the chest of drawers in the first lieutenant's cabin?

"What's in the wind, sir?" he asked again.

"That I wouldn't know," Number One replied. "We must wait and see, Hartopp. We'll hear soon enough when the captain returns."

Hartopp grunted. "The lads are all agog, sir," he observed. "They're gettin' fair sick just muckin' around escortin' oilers and transports and what not and never seein' a ruddy thing 'cept a blinkin' Nip aircraft or two, and us with hardly none at all. When d'you expect we'll get a fair crack at these

10

yellow-bellied bastards, sir, if you'll pardon free language?"

Acton laughed and shook his head. He was not to be drawn as to what he thought. "Your guess is as good as mine," he said with a shrug. "Perhaps this is it, or maybe it isn't. Meanwhile, there's rather too much noise on deck, Hartopp. If the ship's company *must* sing, let it be something cheerful, not all this doleful stuff about love in the moonlight. We're a man-o'-war, not a perishing nightclub."

Hartopp grinned, murmured "Aye aye, sir," saluted and went off.

2

EXCEPT for minor changes, the officers and men of the *Eurydice* had been together for a long time and had been welded into a fine ship's company. Earlier in the war the ship had been in action in Norway and at Dunkirk, and apart from screening heavy ships of the Home Fleet as far north as Iceland and the Denmark Straits, had helped to shepherd convoys well to the westward in foul weather in the Atlantic, and up and down the English Channel and the east coast of England, the hunting grounds for German motor torpedo-boats, or E-boats as they came to be called. On occasion she had been detached to Gibraltar for temporary service in the Western Mediterranean.

Destroyers were needed everywhere, and were woefully short after the heavy losses at Dunkirk. They were switched from one job to another with scant time for either refits, rest or relaxation, to carry on so long as officers and men could stand the strain of days and nights at sea, often in fogs and foul weather, and the ships and machinery held together. They were hard driven. There never was a phoney war so far as the Navy was concerned.

The *Eurydice* was no exception. She had been shelled by shore batteries and frequently narrowly missed by bombs from aircraft diving out of the low clouds. Her crew had seen ships torpedoed and ships sunk in minefields, and had rescued survivors in weather which had made the lowering of boats impossible. Her men had seen the "kills" of two U-boats which had attacked a convoy in the Atlantic, and had taken

11

part in a fierce, confused hurly-burly on a pitch-black night somewhere off Yarmouth, with streams of red and green and yellow tracer shooting through the air and the brilliant bluish-white glare of the star-shell flares floating against the dark clouds overhead. Two E-boats, hit in the magazine, disintegrated in great upheavals of orange flame and smoke; but one British merchant ship had been torpedoed and sunk. Fought at a range of no more than a few hundred yards, that little scrap had been even more breathlessly exciting than watching enemy aircraft, flaming and smoking, shot down into the sea.

Apart from some slight damage and half a dozen minor casualties through bomb and shell splinters or bullets, the *Eurydice* had come through without great harm. In course of time her men came to congratulate themselves that they and their ship led charmed lives. Had not fifty-six British destroyers been lost in the first two years of the war, an average of one every eleven days. Only the Admiralty knew how many others had been badly knocked about to limp back into harbour as virtual wrecks. The *Eurydice's* crew saw no reason why their luck shouldn't hold while engaged against a new enemy on the other side of the world.

Pomeroy, the skipper, prime seaman and ship handler, seemed to have the knack of doing the right thing in any difficult situation. A short, thick-set man with reddish hair, bright blue eyes, and a face like an amiable bulldog except when angry, he was a taut hand so far as discipline went, and in those days when thousands of men from shore life were being drafted into the Navy after the briefest of training, discipline mattered more than ever. He chivvied the laggards and had three pet aversions, long hair and the untrimmed beards which seemed to have come into fashion, and any laxity in uniform. Personal cleanliness and smartness were just as important in war as in peace, he was fond of saying. If the sailors fancied themselves in 'face fungus,' otherwise beards, they must first request permission to grow in the proper Service manner, and ever afterwards keep their facial adornments neat and properly trimmed. As for long hair and the sailors carrying pocket combs, he just wouldn't have it. The *Eurydice* wasn't a girls' school. They'd be using powder-puffs next!

The same went for the ship herself. It had rather gone to

the skipper's heart when they had been forced to paint over all the polished brightwork on deck. But that was no excuse for the upper deck remaining unscrubbed, the boats dirty and uncared for, or the state of the mess-decks, storerooms, magazines and other hidden compartments being allowed to degenerate.

Realizing that well-fed sailors were usually contented ones, Pomeroy had acquired the habit of paying unexpected visits to the galley. He was something of a thorn in the flesh to the petty officer cook and his underlings, descending upon them at odd times to taste the soup or the ship's cocoa, or to inspect the men's midday meal. He had an eye like a hawk, and there was the devil to pay if he found pots and pans or kettles harbouring dirt, congealed grease or strange insects, or, as happened on one occasion, when he discovered the assistant cook's working apron and shoes hastily stuffed into a locker with a blackened flue brush, a half-eaten cake on a plate and a bowl of brown sugar overrun with cockroaches. He had given the assistant cook a piece of his mind which, for a time, had caused that young man to regret ever having joined the Navy. Since then the culprit, who in civil life had been a dish-washer in the basement of a Soho restaurant, had mended his ways.

Pomeroy was no believer in official punishment except as a last resort for habitual offenders, when he gave it them hot and strong. The ship's company, over one hundred and forty of them, were neither plaster saints nor hardened sinners. They were just an average decent lot of men, the bulk of them in the middle twenties, living in unnatural, monastic conditions on the crowded mess-decks of a destroyer in wartime, doubly uncomfortable in the sweltering heat of the tropics with the ship darkened at night and ventilation at a minimum. Since the ship was so often at sea they had no regular leave ashore, and when they did land in a place that could be called at all civilised, it is hardly to be wondered at that a few of the livelier characters, bursting with rude health, good spirits, and a sense of temporary freedom, were rather inclined to have their fling. But so long as they did not make nuisances of themselves, and their pranks did not involve breaking up establishments where they catered for thirsty sailors, and consequent tussles with the local police; provided, too, they returned punctually from their leave with the ship under sailing orders; the skipper turned a blind and sympathetic eye to much of what went on ashore. Wherein he was wise.

Pomeroy had a way with him, and thanks also to good officers and petty officers the *Eurydice* was a smart ship and a happy one. The men certainly took a pride in her, and any obstreperous new-comers who thought of throwing their weight about and protesting—"They didn't do that where I came from"—were speedily tamed by their shipmates. There were ways and means of dealing privately with the recalcitrant.

Unmarried, Pomeroy was reputed to be a misogynist after an unfortunate love affair. Not even his best friends knew the truth about that. Undoubtedly he had moods of testiness when he was unapproachable; but on the lower deck, though he knew it not, he was regarded as a sort of lucky mascot. It was inconceivable that anything could ever go wrong with the *Eurydice* with the skipper on the bridge. If he was somewhat feared by the men, the fact that he had no fewer than three nicknames showed they had an affection for him. 'Old Doggo' was understandable because of his face. Nobody knew who had invented 'The Codger' or 'His Worship.'

The men liked his humanity and sense of humour. Though he sometimes had a tongue like a rasp and rated them like a Dutch uncle, he could also talk to the sailors in their own vernacular, and knew every one of them by name. There was none of the anonymous—"Hi, you there!" He knew most of their circumstances and family affairs also. In distress or per-plexity they often sought his advice, particularly the married men with wives and children at home in England.

There was good reason for their anxiety. England was still being bombed, homes devastated and people killed. The mails were irregular, and though the men could listen to the news broadcast by radio, they were avid for more detailed informa-tion as to what was going on in their homes. Some of their wives or girl friends had 'gone into munitions.' Others were not writing as regularly as they should or had ceased to write at all. A few, with their men abroad, had obviously sought comfort and consolation elsewhere. England was full of foreign soldiers, sailors and airmen, all bursting with money.

There were many intimate family problems, and no com-passionate leave from the other side of the world.

Listening to their stories Pomeroy wished he had the patience of Job and the judgment of Solomon. He did his best to be kind and helpful, though anything he could do seemed so futile and unsatisfactory.

Having met Pomeroy and Acton, be introduced to some others of the *Eurydice.*

The second lieutenant, who acted also as navigator besides keeping a regular watch and being responsible for the unenviable job of correcting the charts, was Roger John Melton, a serious-minded young man and the son of a Devonshire clergyman. Tall, dark and not ill-looking, he went by name of 'Lofty' to the men and 'Pontius' to his messmates, because he was the pilot. In the intervals of reading ancient Greek history his principal hobbies were bridge, the Japanese, and ornithology, though when the spirit moved him he was also a competent pen-and-ink caricaturist, usually libellous.

James Draycott, the lieutenant (E), in charge of the *Eurydice's* 36,000 horse-power turbines and boilers, was a man in a thousand, a good messmate and an excellent engineer who was never defeated by any emergency, utterly ignored the word 'impossible,' and somehow contrived to keep the ship running when long overdue for refit and without the help of any dockyard or depot ship. His principal henchmen were Andrew Paulton, the Chief Engine Room Artificer, and the Chief Stoker, William Helpman, monarch of the boiler-rooms— Paulton, chubby and cheerful; Helpman, tall and rather lugubrious, 'like an undertaker's mute at a funeral,' as Draycott sometimes said. They were both good men.

'Pills,' otherwise Surgeon-Lieutenant Donald McInnes, had been a general practitioner in Surbiton before the war. It was a panel practice, and what the young man didn't know about malingerers and how to treat them was not worth talking about. Except for cuts, sprains, bruises, occasional boils and minor ailments the *Eurydice's* ship's company was disgustingly healthy, though when she had had a few wounded, or had rescued half-drowned survivors who had been hideously mangled or scalded or burnt, or were suffering from exposure, McInnes came into his own. He was tireless, working among the maimed and the injured until he was virtually dropping from exhaustion and had to take some of his own benzedrine to keep going.

One knows nothing of his professional skill as a surgeon;

15

but as a good all-rounder on board a destroyer he was very much the right man in the right place. The men liked him, and so did his messmates in the wardroom. In his time off from his more legitimate duties he played the ukulele and ran the ship's very amateur 'band' and concert party; acted as the wardroom caterer; wrote up the wine books and made out the mess bills; besides censoring the ship's company's letters, helping with the ciphering and deciphering, and giving the sub-lieutenant a hand with the confidential books—which filled two sizable steel safes and constantly needed correction. Taking it all in all 'Pills' was a busy man who more than earned his pay.

Another inhabitant of the wardroom was Charles Newton Tracey, Lieutenant R.N.V.R., who in civil life was partner in a firm of tea merchants in the city of London and was blessed with private means. Aged twenty-eight, 'Chas,' as they called him, was the oldest member of the mess apart from Pomeroy himself and the Gunner (T), the grizzled Mr. Blatchington, monarch of the torpedoes, depth charges and gunner's stores in profusion. Newton, a pre-war member of the R.N.V.R., was an enthusiastic yachtsman, and having done some special course in the Gunnery School at Portsmouth was the *Eurydice's* gunnery and fire-control officer. A man of many parts and a good watchkeeper, generously warm-hearted and adaptable, 'Chas' was a great asset to the ship.

The baby of the wardroom was Sub-Lieutenant Caspar Langham Farnworth, almost due for his second stripe. Besides his job as a watchkeeper, he was in charge of all official correspondence and the confidential books, tasks which he hated and sometimes treated with casual levity, greatly to Pomeroy's exasperation.

"Sub, you really *must* pull yourself together and learn to be more accurate!" the captain exclaimed on one occasion, thumping his writing-table in anger. "This is the third time this blasted letter has been typed and it's not right yet. And look at the spelling, for God's sake!" Indeed, there was reason for complaint. The word 'anchorage' had been spelt 'ankerrage.'

"I'm sorry, sir," Farnworth apologized, smiling sweetly. "I know I'm not very good at paper work."

"Good?" Pomeroy groaned. "Merciful heavens! You're a ruddy menace! Just look at this!" he added, underlining the offending word.

Farnworth looked over his captain's shoulder. To tell the truth he had not read the letter through before presenting it for signature. "It certainly does look a bit queer, sir," he had to admit.

"Queer!" Pomeroy snorted.

"I dictated it very carefully to Able Seaman Modin, sir, who does the typing. He's supposed to have done some sort of a secretarial course before he left school. I——"

"Damn Able Seaman Modin! It's your responsibility," Pomeroy broke in.

"I know, sir, and I'm sorry. But you see I've been rather rushed lately, what with one thing and another. I have to leave a good deal to Modin, and his spelling's apt to be a bit phonetic at times."

"Paralytic, you mean! If the fellow can't spell it's up to you to teach him. There's a dictionary in the wardroom library, dammit! Now take this ghastly letter away and rub it in Modin's hair, and never bring me such a thing again, or I'll be really angry. And you can tell Mr. Able Seaman Modin, with my compliments, that if he doesn't take more trouble *I'll* have his guts for a necktie. Is that clear?"

"Quite clear, sir!" said Farnworth.

But it was impossible to be really angry with the sub for very long, he was always so smiling and ingenuous. Moreover, he was in the process of becoming a good officer.

Tall, extremely good-looking, with blue eyes and naturally wavy blond hair, he was what Adolf Hitler would have regarded as a true Aryan. He certainly stirred the hearts of young women. If ever the *Eurydice* stayed more than forty-eight hours in a civilized place Farnworth could always be relied upon to have a bevy of the local lovelies in tow. But his philanderings had to be confined to the shore. There was a strict order that in no circumstances were women to be allowed on board His Majesty's ships in wartime. Farnworth was fatally attractive to the opposite sex, even to those of riper years.

Petty Officer Hartopp, the first lieutenant's principal acolyte on the upper deck, has already been mentioned. Another petty officer, considerably younger than Hartopp, was Percy Huxtable, 'Perce' to his more intimate friends, and a squat, bullheaded little Londoner with a cold grey eye and an incisive manner. He was unmarried. While one rumour had it that he had been left on someone's doorstep as an unwanted child, there were others to the effect that he was a man with a lurid past, and that as a youngster he had played a cornet with the Salvation Army complete with a peaked cap and red jersey embellished with a flaming yellow crown and the motto 'Blood and Fire.' Whatever the truth he was a forceful character. As one of the younger A.B.s expressed it—"Our Perce weren't brought up in the Church Lads' Brigade!"

Chief Petty Officer Robert Harding Wells was the *Eurydice's* faithful and trusted Torpedo Coxswain and one of the staunchest men in the ship, besides being the best helmsman. The friend and adviser of both the captain and the first lieutenant, a seaman of the older-fashioned breed who had spent most of his long service in destroyers, he was a large, cheerful person, with a rubicund face, prominent jaw, bushy eyebrows, and grizzled hair rather thin on top. Responsible for discipline and much else, including the issue of victuals and the all-important rum, he was kindly enough to those who did their job; but a holy terror to the idle, the indifferent or the contumacious.

What with the swarms of young men straight from the training establishments ashore joining the Navy for the duration, the Service, Wells sometimes thought, was rapidly going to the dogs, though in his innermost heart he had to confess that most of the new-comers had 'guts' in plenty and only needed toughening. As he once remarked to his friend Hartopp —and the tale soon percolated to the wardroom—"What do these here new-fangled, long-haired blokes do when they gets ashore, cuttin' a dash in their bell-bottomed trousers with their caps flat aback an' hopin' to be mistook by the gals for real sailors? Why, chum, they don't absorb their pints o' wallop like ordinary humans, they gets sick from stuffin' themselves with ice-cream and chocolates!"

Then there was Able Seaman Fargo, who had dared to complain about the food, which was partly Wells's responsibility.

Taking the air on deck one morning the coxswain came upon Fargo languidly, very languidly, scraping rust off the engine-room casing preparatory to red-leading it. It was one of Wells's testy mornings. He halted and watched Fargo at work, his arms akimbo.

"Able Seaman Fargo," he said ominously. "Come here a moment. A little word in your ear, my son."

It was no pleasant word, Fargo realized. He dropped what he was doing and rose to his feet.

"What were you in civil life?" the coxswain demanded.

"I done all sorts o' jobs, chief."

"What was your last job?"

"Costermonger's assistant," Fargo said.

"Huh!" Wells returned, sticking out his jaw. "Wheelin' the barrow an' shoutin' the wares on Saturday nights in Houndsditch! Sellin' whelks an' winkles and cockles, I don't doubt!"

Fargo quailed. He was a weedy, narrow-chested little runt of a man with a face like a ferret. Wells was huge and menacing.

"No, chief," he stammered. "We worked the Mile End Road. Old iron, bottles an' clothes, mostly, with a bit o' fruit at week-ends."

Wells eyed him dourly. "Bilkin' the poor ruddy populace," he said. "An' how long have you been in the Service?"

"Gettin' on for eighteen months, Mister Wells."

"Ho! An' you, my little merchant, are one o' them who runs the crown an' anchor board on the mess-deck, bleedin' the poor sailors."

Fargo licked his lips and did not reply. It was true that he made a pretty sum out of crown and anchor, and that gambling was strictly forbidden. But how the blazes did the coxswain know, the nosy old porcupine?

"I know everything that goes on in this ship," said Wells, tapping himself on the chest. "An' you're the bloke who has the imperence, the blazin' bleedin' imperence, to think that me an' the chief cook an' the first loo'tenant are crooks an' bloody fools!"

"I never did, chief," Fargo tried to excuse himself. "I . . . I——"

Wells waved his protest aside. "Just you listen here," he broke in. "You're one o' them who went along to the chief cook, Mr. Hubble, and laid a complaint against the meat, sayin' it isn't fit for dogs or Hottentots! Is that right?" he asked, glaring.

Fargo couldn't deny it. He and three of his messmates had dared to complain, and the complaint, as they very well knew, was altogether frivolous. "I did say somethin'," he was forced to admit. "Our Sunday joint was mostly bone an' fat an' gristle."

"Furthermore," Wells continued, "you intimated that me an' Mr. Hubble made a pay-day out o' sellin' the proper meat an' servin' out any old camel bought cheap to the messes forward."

"I didn't mean that, Mr. Wells," Fargo wailed. "Honest I didn't."

"That's what you said," the coxswain insisted. "An' that meat, let me tell you, was the same as what the officers and chiefs got, prime Australian beef!"

Fargo stood there with his mouth open. He hadn't a chance of saying much.

"You'd like to know where that meat came from, so you can tell your pals, would you?" Wells rumbled on. "We'd been down to tinned stuff for three days when we got into harbour, every pound o' fresh meat gone an' the meat screen as bare as a monkey's bottom! So what happens? Routine, just the usual routine. The first loo'tenant sends for me. Mr. Wells, he says, be so kind as to go ashore an' find that bloody contractor, buy up what meat you can get, an' don't come back till you done it, at the same time givin' me the contractor's name an' address. So I goes ashore, rushin' around, sweatin' an' groanin' in the heat, while the likes of you blokes was sleepin' an' sunnin' yourselves on the fo'c'sle or writin' letters to your popsies! I finds the contractor an' the meat comes off to the ship, likewise fresh bread, vegetables, fruit an' canteen stores, all for your benefit. An' instead o' gratitude for me, actin' Father Christmas, what do I get?" He paused, snorting. "Nasty cracks from Mister Able Seaman Fargo! When I was your age we lived on salt beef and pork and biscuit at sea, an' pleased to get it. Nowadays the likes o' you expects to be fed like the Ritz Carlton."

"I'm sorry, Mr. Wells," Fargo murmured.

"Apology accepted," Wells glowered. "And if you know what's good for you, my boyo, don't let it occur again. One little cheep from you, Fargo, an' you'll get such a clip alongside the ear'ole you won't know if it's Christmas or Easter and your own mother won't know you, regulations or no regulations. Now carry on with your work."

Honour was satisfied.

3

THE *Eurydice's* motor-boat, the pendant fluttering in her bows because her captain had been on an official visit to a foreign man-of-war, chuffed noisily alongside.

Pomeroy, immaculate in full whites, was piped over the side, saluted by Acton, Sub-Lieutenant Farnworth, who was officer of the day, and the Lieutenant (E), James Draycott, in brown overalls, waiting to report his engines ready. Sailors in the background, busy about their various tasks, straightened their caps, faced aft and came to attention.

"All ready for sea, Number One?" came Pomeroy's first question, his expression entirely non-committal as he stepped over the gangway.

"All ready, sir."

"Then have the motor-boat hoisted. We'll be sailing in about half an hour. And you, Chief?" the captain continued, turning to the engineer officer.

"All ready below, sir," Draycott replied.

"No further trouble with that number two boiler?"

"No, sir. We've managed to cure it. We'll be all right."

"Good for you," Pomeroy nodded. "We'll probably need every knot you can knock out of her. Number One?"

"Sir?"

"Come down to my cabin while I shift out of my glad rags."

Acton followed his commanding officer below.

Pomeroy's seagoing clothes, life-jacket, a variety of mufflers, binoculars, lined gloves, pipe, newly-filled tobacco pouch and two boxes of matches, had already been laid out on the bunk in his sleeping cabin. Duffle coat, sea-boots, steel helmet, electric torch, with the books he was reading, had already been taken forward to his sea cabin near the bridge. The faithful Jevons, the captain's steward, knew all the drill.

"We British destroyers will be leading out of harbour," said Pomeroy, having divested himself of his white tunic and shoes and standing on one foot while in the process of removing his trousers. "Once outside we'll be stationed five miles ahead of the cruisers in line abreast five miles apart."

"Are we all going to sea?" asked Acton, standing in the doorway.

"The whole shooting match—Dutchmen, Yanks, everyone," the captain returned, standing in his singlet and underpants. "The curse of it is we've never really worked together as a team! There's no real organisation, no nothing! Some of the ships are short of fuel and others have defects. Their men are worn out. What else is to be expected when they've been run off their legs for the last fortnight?" He sat down to put on the old blue uniform trousers he invariably wore at sea.

"Our chaps are pretty fresh, thank God!" Acton put in. "And we're practically bung full of oil. What are we up against, sir?"

"What aren't we!" Pomeroy snorted. "Our air reconnaissance, such as it is, has reported three different lots of Jap troop convoys making for Java, one aiming for the eastern end, one for the centre, and another for the west. It's our job. . . ."

"Gosh!" the first lieutenant broke in. "If only we get in among their transports!"

"Be your age, Number One! The Japs aren't fools. Their convoys'll be escorted by heaven knows what in the way of destroyers, and closely covered by more destroyers and heavy and light cruisers. They've at least four carriers, and probably some battle-wagons as well, lurking in the background. And what have we got in the way of fighter cover? You can call it damn all! No. What it boils down to is that we're up against it. We've got to do our damndest, and that's all there is to it."

Acton looked somewhat startled, as well he might. "At least we'll have a crack at something," he said.

"Several cracks, I hope," Pomeroy grunted, lacing up his shoes. "But what I've told you is for your private ear alone. Don't pass it on. I want no alarm or despondency. I'll talk to the ship's company myself. You'd better clear lower deck now."

The first lieutenant left him and went on deck.

Some minutes later, standing on the after superstructure facing forward, Pomeroy was looking down on a sea of expectant faces.

"Lower deck cleared, sir," Acton reported.

The captain returned his salute.

"Men," he began. "We'll be going to sea in about ten minutes, the whole party of us," he waved a hand towards the other ships. "I've always made it a habit to let you know what's

22

going on, so I thought I'd have a yarn with you now. You've all seen the message circulated by the Dutch Admiral the other day. You know more or less what's been happening during these last few weeks, and that the situation's pretty grim."

He paused for a moment, watching their faces. They gazed up at him in silence which was only disturbed by the steady, humming throb of auxiliary machinery in the engine-room.

"You'll have gathered that something's brewing now," he continued, raising his voice a little to ensure being heard. "Well, it's just this. Japanese troop convoys are moving on Java. They'll be heavily escorted—eight-inch cruisers, light cruisers and many more destroyers than we've got here. There'll be aircraft carriers and probably battleships backing them up from somewhere over the horizon. One of those convoys is coming this way. It's our job to do all we can to stop it."

An angry, growling murmur rose from his audience. Someone coughed.

"I don't want any of you to run away with the idea that we're in for a cushy job," he continued, looking from face to face. "It'll be a very tough job indeed, make up your minds to that. If we're not in action this afternoon or tonight, the chances are a hundred to a halfpenny that we shall be tomorrow. Together we've been through a good deal in this ship in the last two years. We've been places and seen things. . . ."

"An' that's a bloody fact!" a man in the rear of the crowd whispered to a messmate.

"Put a sock in it!" his friend growled. "Let's hear what the old codger's got to say, can't you!"

"You've never failed yet," Pomeroy went on. "I know you can be relied upon to do your damndest when the time comes. Remember what the destroyers have done since the war began. We've a pretty fine tradition. There's something else I should mention. These ships you see in the harbour are all we've got against the Japs in these parts. We're a mixed bag, and only five of us are British; one heavy cruiser, one Australian light cruiser, and we three destroyers. Don't forget that we've been in this war about nine months longer than the Dutch and more than two years longer than the Americans, and that ours is the oldest Navy in the world. We've a reputation, so just let's show the others how the job should be done. Show 'em you've a pride in yourselves, your ship and the Service, and above all show the Japs, who've got their tails well up and think they're the lords of creation, that we know how to fight."

All eyes were fastened on Pomeroy's face.

"That's all I have to tell you," he ended. "God bless you, and good luck to you all. You do your damndest and I'll look after the rest."

He looked round, nodding and smiling, waving a hand. A voice from the back of the throng called out: "Good old Doggo! Give the bar—beg pardon, give the barbarians hell!"

Pomeroy, spotting who had spoken, was quick off the mark. "All right, Able Seaman Worthington," he returned, shaking an admonitory forefinger. "We're trusting largely to you. No misfires this time from that Bofors of yours. No more jammed breech mechanism, if you please."

There came a titter, followed by laughter. 'Old Doggo,' like the elephant, never forgot.

Someone called for three cheers, and cheer they did. There was no alarm or despondency here, the captain was grateful to see. On the contrary, the ship's company seemed to be in the highest of spirits.

Twenty minutes later, with the three British destroyers leading, the Striking Force was threading its way down the seventeen-mile winding channel leading to the open sea.

4

THEY HAD sailed from that friendly harbour late in the afternoon. The short twilight came and soon there was night—dark and brilliant with stars, with hardly a breath of wind to ripple the calm water. The visibility was good and the horizon clear. Even the smallest of ships could have been picked up with the naked eye at two or three miles, easy gun-range.

The British destroyers were spread out ahead of the line of cruisers as they steamed on through the darkness in search of the enemy, first north, then east, then west. The eyes of those on their bridges became tired and strained as they swept the dim horizon through their binoculars. They had no radar. On board the *Eurydice* officers and men were at their night action stations, with guns and torpedo-tubes ready. Two men were up and alert at each of the 4.7's. The rest of the guns' crews might huddle down close to their weapons and sleep if they wished to. The first clanging of the alarm gongs would bring them to their feet. But very few slept. They felt too tense now they were actually at sea, and just lay yawning, sometimes talking in low voices. There were stringent orders against smoking; so they could not seek the comfort of pipes or cigarettes. The night was cold, and their only solace came when mess kettles of viscid ship's cocoa and thick corned beef sandwiches were brought up from the galley at regular intervals. The petty officer cook and his mates were busy through most of the night.

At dawn next morning the clear-cut, steel-blue line of the horizon to seaward was still barren of ships, or any sign of them. The squadron was heading to the westward, retracing its course of the night. Away to the southward the coast gradually showed blue and clear in the gathering light, and beyond it lay a long range of mountains with their summits half hidden in thin, woolly vapour.

Pomeroy, who had been up all night, yawned, stretched himself and relaxed. He was dog-tired. After filling and lighting a pipe, his first for many hours, he went to a telephone on the bridge.

"Captain speaking," he said. "Is that 'X' gun? Yes. I want to speak to the first lieutenant." A pause, and then: "Number One? You can go to cruising stations. Fall out the four-seven guns' crews; but warn 'em to be ready at short notice. Keep all the A.A. stuff fully manned. Yes, the pom-pom and Bofors. Hands can carry on smoking. They'd better get their breakfasts while the going's good. You've already warned the galley, good! No. Nothing much doing this end."

The word was passed and the guns' crews cheerfully secured their weapons and lit cigarettes, chattering like magpies. Someone at 'B' gun, just before the bridge, burst into raucous song. Men started to troop below. The smell of coffee and frying bacon came wafting on to the bridge from the galley.

Jevons, the captain's steward, made his appearance. "Will you be having your bath this morning, sir?" he inquired.

"No," said Pomeroy. "I can't come aft."

"There's hot water, sponge, bath towel, shaving gear, clean socks and underclothes ready in your sea cabin, sir."

"Thank you, Jevons. What about breakfast?"

25

"I'll have it ready in five minutes, sir."

"What is there?"

"Fried eggs and bacon, sir, or, if you prefer it, tinned salmon kedgeree. Tea or coffee, sir?"

Pomeroy chose eggs and bacon and coffee.

Acton came on to the bridge, saluted and said good morning. "What's happening now, sir?" he inquired.

Pomeroy took him to the chart table. "We're roughly here," he said, dabbing a finger at the chart, "steering two-seven-two, twenty knots. Looks to me as if the old boy had decided to return to harbour. I know some of the cruisers are short on fuel. He's probably got that on his mind."

"Then there's no more news of the enemy?"

The captain shook his head. "Nothing beyond what we knew yesterday, Number One. Nothing's come through during the night. There's been a good deal of wireless chattering; but nothing to make sense of."

Acton thought for a minute, looking at the chart. "What's the chance of our being picked up by their aircraft?" he asked. "The visibility's perfect."

"Every possible chance, I should say," Pomeroy returned shortly.

"And no likelihood of air cover for us?"

"Not a hope, Number One. All we've got in these parts are four ancient planes much too short-ranged to be any use to us. If we are attacked, we'll have to beat 'em off by gunfire. That's all there is to it."

The sun had appeared as a blood-red disc over the purple rim of the horizon to the eastward, to set the calm sea sparkling and dancing with flame-coloured brilliance. The day was come.

There was no knowing that enemy submarines might not be in the vicinity. The *Eurydice* was already using her asdic and had started to zigzag.

Pomeroy yawned. "Who's got the proper morning watch?" he inquired.

"Tracey, sir," Acton said.

"Then let him take over. I'm going to my sea cabin for a wash and brush up and breakfast. You'd better do the same while you have the chance. Warn the aircraft look-outs to keep their eyes skinned, and the A.A. guns' crews too. What about the depth charges?"

"They're all ready, sir."

"All right, Number One. Then I'm off."

"Aye aye, sir."

Pomeroy was not allowed much peace. About half an hour after leaving the bridge, simultaneously with the jangle of the alarm gongs calling the men to action stations, the excited voice of Charles Tracey, the officer of the watch, came down the voice-pipe.

"Captain, sir! Enemy aircraft coming in from the north'ard!"

Snatching his binoculars and steel helmet, Pomeroy darted out of his cabin and scrambled up the steep ladder to the upper bridge. Men, still masticating snatched mouthfuls of their morning meal, were rushing to their guns and instruments. The ship was momentarily in a turmoil.

"Where away?" the captain demanded.

"Three of 'em, sir," said Tracey, pointing. "About seven or eight thousand feet up."

Pomeroy brought his glasses to bear. They were difficult to make out; but at last he found them, tiny, almost transparent, like gnats against the pale azure of the sky. They were flying in a tight V-shaped formation, and as the leader banked and the sun glinted on the underside of his wings he had a sudden glimpse of the scarlet, rising sun roundel which indicated their nationality. They were light reconnaissance planes, snoopers, probably from some Japanese carrier. No doubt the strength, course and speed of the Allied Striking Force was already being reported. The bombers would be along presently.

Coming down on the *Eurydice's* starboard bow, the aircraft swerved in the direction of the line of cruisers, five miles astern. The destroyer's bridge was filling up with officers and ratings. Guns were being reported cleared away and ready for action. But the planes were out of range of any anti-aircraft gun the *Eurydice* possessed, and her 4.7's could not be elevated sufficiently to engage.

Farnworth, the A.A. control officer, was itching to do something. "Shall I open up, sir?" he inquired anxiously.

Pomeroy thought for a moment. The *Eurydice* was the nearest ship to the aircraft, and though the range was excessive, opening fire was the quickest way of warning the cruisers. A message had already gone through by wireless.

"Give 'em a short burst from the pom-pom," the captain said hurriedly. "Only a short burst, mind. Don't waste ammunition."

The necessary orders were passed. The gun broke into its stuttering 'poom-poom-poom,' and seconds later, a long way short of the target, a trail of golden-brown puffs dotted themselves against the sky as the little 2-pounder shell burst. They served their purpose.

The leading cruiser, the Dutch flagship, presently sheeted herself in sharp tongues of orange flame and thin clouds of dun-coloured cordite smoke as her A.A. guns came into action. Other ships chimed in, and before long all five of them were sparkling with gun flashes. As the sound of gunfire came travelling across the water the sky became pockmarked with shell bursts, some big, some little—black, grey, white and amber. It was spectacular enough; but the planes flew on unscathed.

"Huh!" Pomeroy grunted disgustedly, watching through his binoculars. "If the big chaps can't do better than that, God help 'em against the bombers!" It was fair criticism. A great quantity of irreplaceable ammunition was being pumped into the sky to no effect whatever.

And the first of the bombers did arrive about an hour later. However, they did not come in the droves that were expected. They arrived singly, keeping to a respectable height and heavily fired upon. There were no more than two quite minor attacks during the whole of the morning. The bombs came whistling down, one stick of seven raising their spray fountains somewhere near one of the destroyers. But that was all. No ship was hit, and the crew of the *Eurydice* thought nothing of the performance as they watched it. It was not to be compared with the work of the German dive-bombers they had met elsewhere.

By about 10.30 a.m., the Striking Force, being then sixty miles to the westward of the harbour from which it had sailed the afternoon before, had reversed its course to the eastward. A signal from the Admiral passed by blinker searchlight intimated his intention of anchoring inside the protective minefields and resuming the patrol that night. Steaming at fifteen knots, the force was just entering the swept channel at about 2.30 p.m., when the Dutch flagship suddenly led round 180 degrees to the northward and increased speed.

Pomeroy and Acton, with Melton, the navigator, were on the *Eurydice's* bridge. They were all weary after many sleepless nights, and nothing but short cat-naps in the daytime to make up for it. Everyone was tired, some even nearing the stage of exhaustion. All hands were looking forward to an hour or two of sleep during the afternoon.

"What the hell's up now?" Pomeroy demanded testily. "What's happening, for God's sake?" The Dutch flagship was steaming at least twenty knots to seaward, a great stern-wave humped up in her wake. The other cruisers followed—a British and then an American heavy cruiser; the Australian light cruiser, followed at the tail-end of the line by another Dutchman.

Nobody on the *Eurydice's* bridge could answer Pomeroy's question; but as she passed the British heavy cruiser a light started winking from the big ship's bridge. The *Eurydice* answered.

"Following received," the yeoman spelled out. "To all ships. . . ."

The precise verbiage mattered little. The gist of the message was that aircraft had reported an enemy force of two cruisers and six destroyers some ninety miles to the northward about fifty minutes earlier. They were steaming south at high speed. A large troop convoy was somewhere in the same vicinity. It was the Dutch Admiral's intention to intercept and bring them to action.

"At last!" Pomeroy exclaimed. "This is it, Number One!"

Acton was peering over Melton's shoulder as he bent over the chart table, busy with dividers, pencil and parallel rulers. The navigator made a hurried calculation.

"If I give the enemy twenty-five knots and we both maintain our present courses we ought to sight each other at about four o'clock, sir," he reported.

The captain grunted. Standing on the compass platform he was watching his leader turning to starboard in the wake of the cruisers. He put his mouth to the voice-pipe leading to the wheel below.

"Starboard ten," he ordered, when the leader's curling wake came close under the bows.

"Starboard ten it is, sir."

The captain recognized the voice as that of the coxswain, Chief Petty Officer Wells.

"Wells?"

"Yes, sir?"

"Carry on. Follow her round."

"Aye aye, sir."

At much the same moment some coloured flags went up to the destroyer leader's masthead and yardarm. Hatfield, the yeoman of signals, needed no telescope.

"Signal to British destroyers, sir," he sang out. "Take up cruising disposition Number One. Speed twenty-eight knots." It meant that they had to take station five miles ahead of the cruisers.

The *Eurydice* repeated the signal to her next astern.

"Answered, sir!" Hatfield called, and then a few seconds later, "Signal's down, sir!"

"All right," said the captain, as the *Eurydice* completed her turn and followed in the wake of the ship ahead. Again he put his lips to the voice-pipe. "Wheel?"

"Sir?" from Wells.

"Revolutions for twenty-eight knots."

"Twenty-eight knots it is, sir."

The rattling sound of the revolution telegraph and the answering clang from the engine-room came up from below. With the creaming white stern-wave mounting in her wake the *Eurydice* gradually increased speed. Very soon she was passing the rear cruiser.

Sub-Lieutenant Farnworth, the officer of the afternoon watch, was allowed to take over for the time being.

Pomeroy lit his pipe. "Number One," he said. "Keep all A.A. guns manned, and warn the hands we'll be going to action stations in half an hour's time. Meanwhile, you'd better broadcast to the ship's company what's happening. Give 'em the words of the signal."

Acton went off to obey.

The *Eurydice* was drawing abreast of the Australian light cruiser, the captain of which was an old friend of Pomeroy's. They waved to each other from their respective bridges as the destroyer crept past.

"Yeoman," said Pomeroy.

"Sir?"

"Make to her: 'Captain to captain, Advance Australia'."

Hatfield hoisted himself on to a locker and flapped his hands in the abbreviated semaphore code with which signalmen of different ships were wont to exchange chit-chat in harbour during dull periods. An arm was waved in acknowledgment from the cruiser's bridge.

The reply came back—"Good luck to you. Happy hunting. Attention is drawn to Nahum, Chapter 2, verse 1."

Hatfield looked puzzled. "I can't rightly make out, sir," he said. "What's Nahum? I never heard of it."

"One of the minor prophets who wrote a book of the Old Testament," the captain told him. "Send down to my steward to bring up the Bible from my bookcase."

It was some time before Jevons appeared.

"Your Bible, sir," he said, somewhat mystified.

"Look up the Old Testament, Jevons. Find Nahum, N-A-H-U-M, in the Index."

"I got it, sir."

"Then look up chapter two and read me the first verse. Come on, man. Get a move on."

Jevons thumbed the pages, cleared his throat and read: "He that dasheth in pieces is come up before thy face: keep the munition, watch the way, make thy loins strong, fortify thy power mightily."

"Thanks," Pomeroy nodded. "You can return the Bible to where you found it. And I'd like the large Thermos filled with coffee and some sandwiches in my sea cabin."

"Very good, sir."

The steward disappeared, still wondering greatly. Was the skipper going nuts, or something? Why had he come over holy all of a sudden?

5

As THE Allied force steamed to the north-westward at twenty-four knots, the calm sea was furred in patches by the gentlest of breezes. Here and there it shone and sparkled in the brilliant sunlight; stretching elsewhere as a great expanse of variegated sapphire and amethyst and veridian to the deeper indigo on the

31

clear-cut horizon. The visibility was extreme. High overhead a few little golden-coloured flocculent clouds sailed lazily across the sky.

Signs of the enemy were not long in arriving, for there came another abortive air attack followed by the appearance of three seaplanes, Japanese snoopers. They dodged around, their radio chattering, twisting and turning and occasionally fired upon; but always keeping outside effective gun-range.

"God in heaven!" Pomeroy exclaimed, exasperated as he watched them. "If only we had a squadron of fighters! Those chaps make one feel so damn naked!"

The *Eurydice*, her men at action stations, was on the star-board wing of the destroyers ahead of the cruisers. Pomeroy, Melton and Tracey, the last-named perched on the director platform and therefore a good deal higher than the others, were all sweeping the northern horizon with their glasses.

"Sir!" Tracey suddenly shouted. "There's faint smoke on the starboard bow!"

"Right, Tracey. I've got it," Pomeroy said a moment later, his binoculars steady. "Yes. It looks like. . . ."

"I see masts and funnels, sir!" Tracey broke in, his voice full of excitement and the glasses still to his eyes. "There's what looks like a . . . yes, a four-funnelled cruiser and a whole bunch of destroyers, they're crossing our bows from starboard to port!" He spoke very hurriedly.

A moment or two later the captain, standing at the standard compass, saw them for himself. "Hatfield," he said, turning to the yeoman of signals. "Pass down to the wireless-room, and they needn't stop to code it: 'One cruiser, unknown number large destroyers, bearing three-three-oh, speed eighteen, course two-two-oh.' Repeat that."

Hatfield did so. "Right. Smack it about and tell 'em to get it off, quick!" Pomeroy ordered, trembling with excitement. "Pilot?"

"Sir?" from Melton.

"Have the word passed. Enemy in sight."

"Aye aye, sir."

The time was about twelve minutes past four.

The hulls of the enemy ships were gradually lifting over the horizon. Their range was 26,000 yards—thirteen sea miles—and rapidly closing. More masts and funnels appeared beyond and to the right of the first group, now plainly to be seen as a light cruiser and seven destroyers. Their foaming bow-waves and wash showed they had increased speed. So clear was the air that their guns could be counted.

The *Eurydice* went on to thirty knots, altering slightly to port to steer parallel to the enemy.

As Pomeroy very well knew, this would be no set and ordered battle. He was aware that the Dutch Admiral's main object was to destroy the enemy's troop convoy. But where was the convoy? Probably somewhere out of sight to the northward, well beyond the warships now in sight.

But the Allies were at a great disadvantage. They had no air cover, no prearranged tactical plan. There was no real overall command, no real means of ship-to-ship communication by wireless, flags, semaphore or searchlight. They had not worked together as a squadron, and except perhaps for the ships of each nationality the captains were strangers to each other and to each other's ideas and methods.

The battle would presently resolve itself into a confused mêlée, a sort of scrambling dog-fight, with each ship working more or less independently and every individual captain taking his own decisions and doing what he thought best. And with ships moving at about thirty knots those decisions, right or wrong, must be made in a matter of split seconds. Hesitation might spell disaster. With part of the Japanese fleet looming up over the horizon, and more ships probably waiting to reinforce, the captain suddenly felt his own responsibility. The lives of nearly one hundred and fifty men were on Pomeroy's hands.

The *Eurydice* had often been in action; but never in an action quite like the one that now threatened. His officers and men trusted him. Most of them were his personal friends, and many had wives and children in England. God grant, he thought to himself, that he did the right thing and didn't let them down.

"Beg pardon, sir," said Hatfield, the yeoman of signals. "Cruisers have hoisted their battle ensigns. Shall we follow motions?"

"Carry on," the captain nodded. "Look out they don't foul the aerials, that's all."

"Very good, sir."

Acton, whose action station was aft, arrived on the bridge —binoculars slung round his neck, steel helmet over one shoulder, and a rubber lifebelt round his waist over his white, anti-flash overalls. He was smoking a cigarette.

"And what in heck are you doing up here, Number One?" Pomeroy demanded, half seriously, half in banter. "We'll be in action at any moment. Get aft to your station, man."

"Just having a look-see, sir," the first lieutenant returned in a tone that was almost casual. "What are we taking on?"

"There you are," said Pomeroy, waving a hand at the northern horizon. "Pay your money and take your choice. Every time a coco-nut. The whole bloody Japanese navy popping up over the skyline one by one for you to shoot at."

"Well, well," Acton observed, using his glasses. "What an array! Destroyers and still more destroyers, and a couple of their eight-inch cruisers just appearing in the background. You can't mistake those funnels."

"Glad you like it," the captain returned, putting his mouth to the voice-pipe. "Wells?"

"Sir?"

"Steer three-one-five."

The *Eurydice* turned slightly to port.

"Ship steady on three-one-five, sir," came up from below. Pomeroy stepped down from the compass platform and took Acton by the arm. "George," he said, keeping his voice low. "You know what to do if anything happens to me?"

Number One regarded his captain with a startled expression. "I suppose I take over the command and carry on with the scrap," he replied. "But I hope to God nothing does happen to you."

"One never knows," said Pomeroy. "But don't let the side down. There's to be no surrendering. If the worst comes to the worst, sink the ship and have done with it. Do your best for the men, that's all."

"I wouldn't dream of surrendering the ship, sir!" Acton replied with some show of indignation. "The thought never..."

The captain smiled. "All right, George," he broke in. "I know you well enough to know that. There's another thing, if I'm knocked out, there's to be no nonsense about my . . .

no, what I mean is just put me over the side with any others. The sea's good enough for the best of us. Well, good luck, old boy," he added, looking into his friend's eyes and patting him on the arm. "Give 'em hell and do your best for the sailors."

Acton hesitated. He felt rather overcome and found it difficult to answer. "I hope you haven't got a presentiment?"

"Presentiment be blistered, George! Now go on. Buzz off to your station. You don't want to miss the opening chorus." And Acton went.

The *Eurydice*'s White Ensigns were streaming in the breeze, one at each masthead and a third at the peak. They were brand-new ensigns, the largest the ship carried.

"Good for you, Hatfield!" said Pomeroy. "A proper dress ship. Does one good to see the old things."

The yeoman of signals grinned. "I've been keeping the good ones for just such a shemozzle as this, sir," he replied. "We must show the chaps who we are."

Herbert Mortimer Hatfield had his own very definite ideas as to how a British destroyer should go into action.

The two Japanese heavy cruisers were hull up over the horizon. They were at extreme range, about 28,000 yards; but even as Hatfield spoke Pomeroy saw stabs of bright orange flame sparkle down their long, lean, grey hulls as they fired their first ranging salvoes. They became momentarily blotted out in clouds of brownish cordite smoke, which rapidly drifted astern. Then more flashes . . . and more. From the direction their guns were pointing they were concentrating on the Allied cruisers, firing ten-gun salvoes.

Meanwhile the enemy light cruiser, leading her line of destroyers, was about 18,000 yards on the *Eurydice*'s bow, steaming hard. Within a matter of seconds she also opened fire, and this time the target was the *Eurydice*.

Many things started to happen all at once. The *Eurydice*, her 4.7's hopelessly outranged, began to zigzag. Another British destroyer came steaming full pelt from the southward to join her. There came the rolling thunder of heavy gunfire, which became louder as the British and American heavy cruisers fell to work with their 8-inch. The three Allied light cruisers, with their 6-inch guns, were still outside effective range.

A cluster of shell plopped into the water round the *Eurydice* and burst on impact—three over, two short, a straddle and a very near thing. Dropping almost vertically the projectiles threw up comparatively small splashes. A few splinters came whizzing overhead; but the ship was not hit.

Pomeroy, leaning over the standard compass, shouted orders down the voice-pipe to the wheelhouse. The reassuring voice of Wells came back. He put the helm over and the *Eurydice* swerved slightly to starboard, steadying on a course which brought her closer to the approaching enemy. She increased to her utmost speed.

Another salvo came shrieking down. The shell plumped harmlessly down, again missing by a very narrow margin. The Japanese shooting was good, far too accurate to be comfortable. Almost automatically, Pomeroy stuffed tobacco into his pipe. His pouch, he noted, was all but empty. He leant down to light a match—two matches.

Melton, seeing his captain bare-headed with his hair streaming in the breeze, had sent someone down to his sea cabin for his steel helmet. "Sir," he said, handing it. "I really think you ought to wear this."

Pomeroy, intent upon what was happening, pushed it aside.

"Sir," Melton insisted. "You really must."

"I hate the blasted thing!" the captain grumbled. "Gives me a headache. But thanks, Pontius. Perhaps I'd better." He put it on.

The range of the nearest ships was about 16,000 yards, and closing fast. They were steaming a good thirty-five knots to judge from their bow-waves, and the *Eurydice* about the same.

Fifteen thousand yards . . . 14,700 . . . 14,200 . . .

The Japanese destroyers were coming in to attack the cruisers with torpedoes . . . 14,000 yards . . . 13,500 . . .

"Tracey!" Pomeroy yelled. "Tracey!"

"Sir?"

"Open fire when you like!"

There came a brief pause, and then the *Eurydice's* guns crashed into a salvo. The ship shuddered. The bridge shook and became enveloped in the hot, sulphurous fumes of burnt cordite, acrid and choking.

Pomeroy couldn't see the fall of shot. Other ships were firing on the attacking destroyers, probably the cruisers. Spray fountains were erupting out of the water all round them; but the range was still very long for the *Eurydice's* 4.7's. Another salvo was fired by the *Eurydice* . . . and another . . .

Now that action was joined he felt the strange exhilaration of battle, that sort of pent-up sensation of sheer excitement. On previous occasions, when being heavily bombed and unable to retaliate, he had felt sick at heart and rather frightened. Any man who said he didn't hate being bombed was a double-distilled liar, to his way of thinking. But this was different. The *Eurydice* was being fired upon and shell were still dropping round, clusters of them, for the enemy destroyers had brought their guns into action. The *Eurydice*, however, was hitting back, that was what mattered.

The battle had become general. The whole of the northern horizon seemed filled with the rushing grey shapes of enemy ships, most of their guns in action. The smaller vessels were dwarfed by the huge silhouettes of the two heavy cruisers, wreathed in smoke and flame of gunfire. They were shooting at their opposite numbers in the Allied line, which were replying. Great geysers were spouting out of the sea round the enemy 'heavies'—some of them a shimmering white, some a brilliant blood-red. It was some time before Pomeroy realized that the American cruiser was using shell containing crimson dye to identify her own salvoes.

Pomeroy could have whooped with joy when he saw a dull reddish glow from the stern of the rear Japanese cruiser, which could only mean a hit. It was followed by clouds of heavy black smoke, and later by tongues of flame. She was on fire; but still continued the action.

One of the enemy destroyers, too, badly hit, had hauled out of her formation and was dropping astern, vomiting smoke and flame.

Then the nearer Japanese destroyers, led by a four-funnelled light cruiser, turned ninety degrees to starboard, fired torpedoes and laid a heavy smoke-screen, behind which they disappeared to the northward.

Incident followed incident with such rapidity, and the *Eurydice* had been altering course so frequently, that Melton, who was trying to take notes, was at a loss to write down everything. He was nothing if not meticulous.

The enemy had first been sighted at 16.12 (4.12 p.m.), and

firing had started about four minutes later. The last scribbled entries in the navigator's note-book for that phase of the action, clarified to make them understandable, were as follows:

16.16—Enemy heavy cruisers opened fire.

16.17—Ship under fire, extreme range, from enemy light cruiser and destroyers to starboard steering 335° approx. Our courses as requisite. Zigzagging. Speed 34 knots.

16.18—Allied heavy cruisers in action.

16.21—We opened fire. Approx. range 13,000.

16.31—Observed apparent hit Dutch flagship. All Allied cruisers in action. Being straddled. Enemy aircraft over cruisers apparently spotting.

16.34—Enemy destroyers altering course to starboard. Engaging on parallel course.

16.35—Observed hit on enemy heavy cruiser. One enemy destroyer apparently stopped on fire aft.

16.40—Approx. Enemy torpedo attack.

16.41—Enemy retiring behind heavy smoke-screen. Ceased firing.

16.45—Altered course to southward. Courses as requisite for rejoining cruisers.

So far the *Eurydice* was unhit and unharmed.

6

To Acton, at his battle station at 'X' gun, the 4.7 mounted on the after superstructure, the action seemed even more confused than to those on the bridge. He was in communication with the bridge by telephone; but couldn't use it with the ship under fire. His view ahead was partially blocked out by the funnels and bridge. He had no more than partial glimpses of what was happening, could only surmise what was in the captain's mind.

He knew from the vibration that the *Eurydice* was steaming at full speed. Dodging the enemy salvoes, she was constantly altering course, and far away to starboard was a four-funnelled Japanese light cruiser leading a line of seven destroyers. The orange-coloured flashes of their guns twinkled through the haze of funnel and cordite smoke which partially obscured them. They were firing at a prodigious rate.

Acton had recognised their silhouettes. He knew that the cruiser had a broadside of six 5.5's and each of the destroyers five 5-inch. The situation was odd, for here was the *Eurydice*, with her four 4.7's, and they outranged, running the gauntlet against forty-one heavier guns. Indeed it was more than odd. It was alarming.

The sailors' remarks were typically pungent and to the point. "Coo'er!" one of them exclaimed. "Just look at the ruddy bastards, an' us doin' the charge o' Balaclava all on our own!" He spoke more in wonderment than fear, no doubt to ease his tension of mind by saying something. There was certainly much to look at.

"Aunt Sally, chum," said another man. "That's wot we blinkin' well are. All the fun o' the fair. Roll, bowl or pitch, the muggers! Havin' it all their. . . . Gawd Ormighty!" he broke off. A cluster of three shells had fallen about fifty yards short. One, if not two more had hurtled noisily overhead to burst harmlessly in the sea.

Acton made no effort to stop the men's chatter. If it eased their minds and made them feel happier, so much the better. Like them he also felt queasy about the stomach, not at all like a hero riding into the valley of death with the gallant six hundred.

It was exasperating and unnerving to be under heavy fire which couldn't be returned. Any one of those dropping salvoes, even a single shell, might put paid to the whole business so far as the *Eurydice* was concerned. It was the suspense of waiting and doing nothing that was so damnably upsetting. It was all very well for people to talk about being cool, calm and collected. What the hell!

Another salvo plumped down . . . another. They were both well over. The Japanese shooting seemed to be getting a bit erratic, thank God!

Range, deflection and bearing were being passed through the transmitters from the control position forward. The order 'Stand by' had been given. The guns were already loaded and cocked up to full elevation.

It was a blessed relief when at last the fire gong jangled and

39

the *Eurydice* shook to her first salvo. At last they were hitting back.

'X' gun flashed, recoiled, ejected the brass cartridge-case from the breech; and ran out again with a thud. A cloud of thick cordite smoke came driving down from forward, the warm, sickly stench of it mingling with the reek of oil fuel from the funnels. The loading tray was swung, and projectile and cartridge rammed home. The breech block slammed to. "Ready!" someone shouted.

The gun's crew worked almost as automatons. They knew their job. They had been drilled often enough.

Acton did not trouble to count; but six or perhaps eight salvoes were fired before the enemy destroyers disappeared behind the dense black pall of their billowing smoke-screen. Then orders came from the bridge to check firing.

The *Eurydice* heeled over as she altered course to port, apparently doubling back to join the cruisers. They, Acton could see, were still in hot action, their guns flashing in the midst of heavy smoke and the towering spray fountains which at times almost hid them from view. He glanced at his wrist-watch. The time, though that mattered nothing, was nine minutes to five.

"Sir!" said the man with a pair of telephone receivers clipped over his head. "You're wanted."

Acton bent down, unclipped his own receiver and put it to his ear. It was Melton, speaking from the bridge.

"Speak up, Pilot! I can't hear you!" The sounds of heavy gunfire and of the *Eurydice* travelling at full speed drowned all ordinary conversation.

"We're joining up with the cruisers!" Melton shouted. "That last little business was a torpedo attack!"

"So I imagined," Acton replied. "What comes next?"

"The captain says the men can stand easy at their guns and carry on smoking, George," came Melton's voice, rather breathless. "He says. . . . Yes, what is it?" in an aside to someone on the bridge. "Yes, of course. . . . Sorry, George, I was interrupted. The captain says they'd better have their teas now, at their guns. It's all laid on, as you know. But they're not to dally. We'll be at it again before long."

"Right! How's it going, d'you think? I can't see much from this end."

"One of their destroyers seems to have bought it and to be on fire, and we think one of their cruisers has been hit! But these cursed smoke-screens of theirs are the devil! Their shooting's pretty good, isn't it?"

"You're telling me!" Acton returned with feeling. "All right, Pilot. If you have the chance give me a shout from time to time and give us the news. We don't see much from aft here."

A respite followed. The guns' crews were allowed to stand easy. Men came aft from the galley with mess kettles of strong tea and sandwiches and biscuits and chocolate from the canteen. It was well organised. Even the cups had been remembered. The arrival of the food and drink was greeted with shouts of 'Lovely char! Lovely grub!' and they certainly were a godsend. They had eaten nothing since dinner at noon.

The men sat or stood around eating and drinking, smoking cigarettes—cheerful, talking excitedly. They might almost have been on a picnic. It was the feeling of sudden relief after imminent peril.

"Get a move on, lads," Acton said. "Don't waste time. We're not through yet."

"Let battle commence," someone remarked. "Who's doctored the tea with rum, or do I imagine things?"

The lull was to last no longer than seventeen minutes.

Turning again, the *Eurydice* took station ahead of the cruiser line with the two other British destroyers, the *Juno* and *Earnest*, to port of her. The trio formed an irregular line abreast, with the ships about half a mile apart.

The cruisers were still firing and being fired upon. Through his glasses Acton could see that some of them were using their secondary batteries, which probably meant that another torpedo attack was developing.

But beyond the haze of smoke to the northward he could see no signs of the attackers. Then he glimpsed a burst of blackish smoke from the second ship in the Allied line, the British heavy cruiser *Norwich*. There was no apparent flash; but the smoke rapidly increased and was soon accompanied by clouds of white steam. It looked as though she had been hit in a boiler-room, for in a few seconds plumes of white vapour were pouring out of her waste steam-pipes. She hauled out of the line, her speed dropping rapidly.

Acton felt sick. If the *Norwich* were badly damaged it meant the loss of six 8-inch guns in an action in which the odds were already heavily against the Allies. Yes. She was damaged! She seemed hardly to be crawling through the water, smoke and steam pouring out of her.

After that all seemed confusion. He saw a heavy explosion and a great upheaval of smoke and spray alongside a Dutch destroyer some way astern and on the disengaged side of the cruisers. It was apparently a torpedo. The ship broke in two, her centre portion dropping into the water and her sharp bow and stern rearing themselves skywards like spearheads. He saw her rudder and propellers come dripping out of the sea, and men struggling in a patch of oily water littered with wreckage.

Meanwhile the Dutch flagship, leading the cruiser line, steamed on to the westward. The *Norwich* was limping off to the southward, and her next astern, the American heavy cruiser *Boston*, followed her motions. So did the next ship, the Australian cruiser *Albany*, and the Dutch cruiser at the tail end of the line.

The enemy's planes were still overhead, reporting every movement. The whole horizon from north to nearly west seemed filled with the smoke of Japanese cruisers and destroyers. Then it was that the captain of the *Albany*, realizing the condition of the *Norwich*, steamed between her and the enemy and started to lay a thick curtain of black funnel smoke which mingled with the greyish vapour of smoke floats dropped in her wake.

Within a few minutes, racing at full speed, the British destroyers were adding to the smoke-screen with the billowing black reek rolling from their funnels.

The sun, low over the horizon to the westward, was blotted out. Steaming through the choking murk it was almost as dark as night with the visibility at zero. Those in the *Eurydice* gasped and choked at their stations. Nobody knew what might come next. Acton was bewildered.

Then the telephone buzzed, and the first lieutenant, his eyes streaming, put the instrument to his ears.

It was Melton again, his voice hurried and excited. "There's a torpedo attack coming in from the west'ard!" he shouted. "We've been ordered to counter-attack! Stand by, old boy." That was all.

"Stand by, lads! Action!" Acton yelled.

The gun's crew sprang to their stations. On orders through the transmitters from forward the guns were trained over to port.

The smoke-curtain, drifting and wreathing fantastically in the gentle breeze, had spread over an area fully two miles long when the *Eurydice* turned and charged through the thickest part of it. It must have taken a full minute before it started to thin, and then she suddenly emerged into clear sunlight.

And there, on an opposite course, clear on the port bow at a distance of about 6,000 yards, steaming at full speed, was a line of three enemy destroyers.

The *Eurydice's* guns were loaded and ready, and this time there was no question of their being outranged. Orders came through the transmitters from the control position, and the guns broke into rapid salvoes, even the pom-pom and Bofors joining in as the range closed at the rate of 2,000 yards a minute. The Japanese replied.

Everything happened very quickly. What with the smoke, the shell splashes, the jarring shock as his gun went off, and the roar of firing, Acton had no clear picture of what was happening. In among the bright flashes of the enemy guns he saw, or thought he saw, bursts of brownish smoke and the deep red glow of hits on the Japanese leader. But still they came on, three against one. The range closed to 4,000 yards . . . 3,000 . . . 2,000, which was practically point-blank.

Then, just as the grey shapes of the enemy began to disappear into the smoke-screen, he felt and heard the crashing thud of a heavy explosion. The *Eurydice* rocked and shuddered. Clouds of escaping steam roared from amidships, to mix with volumes of black smoke and a few streamers of flickering flame, which could only be blazing oil fuel. The fore part of the ship became completely blotted out.

God, thought Acton to himself, we've been hit in a boiler!

"Communication's gone with the bridge, sir!" someone shouted.

"Go into local control!" Acton yelled. "Warn 'Y' gun!"

The enemy had vanished, swallowed up in the smoke-curtain.

The *Eurydice* listed over to port. The familiar throbbing vibration and the pulsation of her turbines ceased. She gradually lost headway, just rippling through the water until she came to a standstill, to lie like a dead and stricken thing.

This seemed the end of everything.

The gun's crew were still grouped round their silent weapon. They were not talking now. There was a look of amazed bewilderment on their faces. They obviously expected Acton to say something.

"All right, lads!" he said, shouting to make himself heard and doing his best to look cheerful. "We're not dead yet. Masters?"

"Sir?" from the gunlayer.

Acton hurriedly told him to take charge, and to be ready for instant action. If the enemy reappeared he was to open fire at once without waiting for orders. He, Acton, must go forward to see what could be done about the damage. "You're to open fire if you see anything Japanese," he added breathlessly. "For God's sake don't engage one of our own ships! Use your discretion. You know what they look like."

"I understand, sir. I'll do my best. Good luck, sir."

"I'll be seeing you," the first lieutenant called back, proceeding to lower himself down the vertical steel rungs leading to the upper deck.

Mr. Blatchington, the Gunner (T), was still at his station by the after set of torpedo-tubes, some of his torpedo ratings with him. The two sets, each of four tubes, were trained out on either beam, practically spanning the whole width of the ship. Acton had to climb over them to get forward. He stopped to talk to the Gunner, who looked, and was, furious.

"This is a bit of bad luck," the first lieutenant said. It was a lame sort of remark; but he had to say something.

"Huh!" the Gunner growled. "Looks like we've copped it in a boiler-room, Number One. A fair bloody mess from the look of it. Think of the poor——" He broke off what he was going to say and added: "Doctor's gone for'ard."

"I'm going to have a look, Guns," Acton said. "If anything happens and I'm away take charge of this end of the ship and carry on." The roar of escaping steam had ceased, though clouds of vapour and smoke still rose from between the funnels.

"I've still got my eight fish," Blatchington grumbled. "Communication's cut with the bridge."

44

"You may get a chance yet," Acton told him.

"Not if this list increases much," came the reply. "We'll be firing uphill one side and downhill the other, blast it! We might have had a crack at those chaps coming in just now; but nothing came through from the torpedo control. Reckon the cap'en was keeping 'em for bigger stuff. Damn my eyes and trouser buttons, Number One, but I'd have given six months' pay to have cracked one of their bloody cruisers! And now . . ."

But Acton, going forward, was already out of earshot. He noticed that the original smoke-screen was gradually dissolving, though what remained of it was slowly drifting towards them. From somewhere beyond the haze, not very far away, there came the throbbing of gunfire.

Though her situation was not hopeless, the *Eurydice* was in a bad way. Hit in number two boiler-room, the explosion had shattered the boiler, severed steam-pipes, and destroyed the telemotor piping leading from the bridge to the steering engine. Steam had been lost because the water had run from number three boiler to the damaged one. All this Acton gathered from one of the engine-room artificers.

Draycott and his people, working like maniacs, were doing all they could. The turbines, thank heaven, were unharmed. Yes. They were already connecting up the secondary steering position on the searchlight platform between the two sets of torpedo-tubes further aft. With any luck they might get the ship steaming again, though at greatly reduced speed.

They'd need all the luck in the world, the first lieutenant realized. The Japanese were still very close, and presently. . . .

There had been casualties below, William Helpman, the Chief Stoker, among them. In one split second of time the boiler-room had become an inferno of flying metal, scalding water, and searing, high-pressure steam, probably mingled with blazing oil fuel. Death must have been instantaneous. Yet one poor wretch had managed to crawl up a vertical steel ladder and fight his way on deck, God only knew how.

On his way forward Acton came upon McInnes and a little group gathered round an unrecognizable, oil-soaked figure laid out on deck. He wondered why the doctor had left his action station in the wardroom and how he had been so quick; but here he was, just rising from his knees with a hypodermic in his hand.

45

"Any hope, Pills?" the first lieutenant asked, dropping his voice.

McInnes shook his head. "Not an earthly, poor devil! He's practically flayed—a goner. I tried to make it easier, that's all."

Acton passed on. There was nothing he could do to help. At the foot of the forecastle ladder he ran into Farnworth, who looked rather shaken, as well he might. Acton himself felt his nerves on edge.

"What now, Sub?" he asked hastily. "Looking for me?"

"Partly, Number One. If an attack comes the skipper wants you to carry on with the after guns in local control. All the bridge communications have gone to hell, and the steering."

"Does he know what's happened? There's a boiler gone."

"He knows. The Chief sent someone up with a report. I'm to let the skipper know when the auxiliary steering's connected up. He won't leave the bridge till then. Then I'm to look out for the pom-pom."

"What about 'A' and 'B' guns?"

"Tracey'll look out for them. What d'you think of our chances?"

Acton wasn't going to say that he thought their chances were very slender indeed. The dusk was coming on, but the smoke was thinning, and the visibility was about a mile. If an enemy destroyer did appear, the *Eurydice* was a sitting duck. However, it would never do to show despondency to young Farnworth. Instead, he tried his best to be cheerful.

"We're not sunk yet, Sub, not by a long chalk!" he said with a laugh that wasn't genuine. "The Chief's doing his damndest. He'll get his old whizzers going again if there's a hope in hell! How's the skipper?"

Farnworth summoned a smile. "Smoking his pipe, chewing sandwiches and cursing blue murder. My word, his language! He surpassed himself, absolutely."

"Always a good sign, Sub," Acton said, patting him on the shoulder. "Now don't stay yarning here. Buzz off and carry on with what you've got to do."

Farnworth went about his business. Acton followed him aft, climbed over the two sets of torpedo-tubes, passing a word or two with Mr. Blatchington on his way, and hoisted himself up to 'X' gun.

The gun's crew took comfort. They were pleased to see him

back, obviously. There were inquiries as to what had happened —what was likely to happen. Acton told them all he knew. He felt most desperately tired all of a sudden. He would have given nearly all he possessed for an hour or two of good, solid sleep.

The haze of funnel and cordite smoke still hung over the sea, drifting westerly on the feeble breeze. The invisible sun, nearing the horizon, showed through it in a nebulous glare of fiery red. The blue of the sky overhead had started to darken. Soon there would come the short tropical twilight, and after that the night. The firing had died away. Except for the voices of men and the gurgling sound as the *Eurydice* rolled sluggishly to the gentle swell, everything was still.

Then, when Acton had half made up his mind that nothing further might happen, a man looking out from the gun position shouted and pointed abaft the port beam. A long grey shadow over the white ruffle of a heavy bow-wave and wash was appearing through the mist. In another instant she was clearly in view—a two-funnelled destroyer, unmistakably Japanese.

"Action!" he yelled, his heart thumping. "Bearing red one-four-oh! Range two thousand! Deflection thirty-two left! Point of aim under the bridge!"

The gunlayer was already on the target. The gun flashed and recoiled. 'Y' gun opened fire. 'A' and 'B' guns chimed in, firing as fast as they could be loaded. The pompom and Bofors opened up, and streams of coloured tracer went hurtling towards the enemy.

But the Japanese were quick off the mark. Before Acton could see his own fall of shot he glimpsed the sparkling flame of her first salvo. In the midst of the thumping roar of the *Eurydice's* gunfire he heard the shrill, high-pitched 'wheew-wheew-wheew' of shell driving overhead. He didn't look to see where they went. The enemy was also using pom-poms. Tracer shell came curving in from the opposite direction, some short, some hitting. He heard the rending crash as they burst.

It was impossible to see. There was smoke and flame every-where; shell fountains spouting up out of the sea; water cascading on board. Something hit the *Eurydice* forward with a crashing shock. It felt as though she had butted head-on into a granite cliff. There came two more stupendous impacts. The ship lurched and shuddered, and then seemed to recover herself, quivering.

47

Glancing forward, his eyes streaming and coughing with his throat full of cordite smoke, Acton had a momentary glimpse of the top of the foremast, with its wireless yard and antennae, swaying in a wild arc across the sky. It seemed to hang for a moment, probably held by its rigging, and then toppled overboard. Beyond, half-veiled in a cloud of brownish smoke, were flashes of orange and scarlet, with virulent green and violet. That could only mean that ready-use ammunition was exploding at 'A' and 'B' guns. The ship must be on fire. He felt stricken with horror.

His first impulse was to rush forward to deal with it. Then he remembered his primary job was to concentrate on the enemy, now almost hidden in her own smoke and gun-flashes and the spouting geysers of falling shell. The *Eurydice's* forward guns were silent; but 'X' and 'Y' were still firing as fast as they could be loaded. Another enemy salvo came shrieking through the air, two or three shell falling short; but one at least hitting somewhere forward. He couldn't look. He felt the shock of it, and the ship tremble to the blow.

Then, in the midst of the smoky turmoil surrounding the enemy he thought he saw the reddish-golden glow of a shell burst . . . then another. He couldn't be certain.

By God, something had happened!

To his intense amazement the Japanese destroyer suddenly ceased firing. A moment or two later clouds of dense, rolling black smoke pouring out of her two funnels darkened the haze astern of her. Her helm went over and she turned away, to disappear behind the pall of her own making, though not before another shell from the *Eurydice* seemed to hit her. He saw an unnatural pinkish burst of flame which could only be an explosion. It was nothing like the flash of a gun.

The sweating gun's crew, realizing their enemy had been hit, whooped with joy as their target disappeared and they ceased firing. Down below at his beloved torpedo-tubes the usually impassive Mr. Blatchington was almost delirious with excitement.

Jubilation was premature, Acton realized. The *Eurydice* was still on fire forward.

It was not until nearly four years later, after the Japanese naval archives had fallen into Allied hands, that an American translator discovered that His Imperial Japanese Majesty's destroyer, bearing, when translated, the poetic name of *Pearly Mist*, had been badly damaged while engaging a disabled British destroyer, name unknown, in February, 1942. She had to be taken in tow by a consort, thereby causing some dislocation to the operation in progress. Her captain, Lieutenant-Commander Osamu Watanabe, fearing censure and feeling he was for ever disgraced in the eyes of the Emperor and his brother officers, bade a ceremonial farewell to his ship's company and shot himself on his bridge.

"Strange guys, these Nips," said the Commander of the United States Naval Reserve—in civil life a professor of languages in Honolulu—after reading the extract to his assistant. "Why must he go shooting himself? Bob, look up the names of the British destroyers in that Java Sea business, February, 'forty-two. You should find it in file fourteen, or maybe fifteen—one of those with the yellow tabs."

7

COLLECTING Mr. Blatchington, Acton hurried forward. He saw at once that both funnels were riddled by shell fragments or the enemy's pom-pom fire, while two of the boats were in splinters. Apart from the large jagged hole in the deck where the shell had gone through to detonate in number two boiler-room, the ship's side was perforated in many places. They were small holes, he noticed, probably nothing to worry about.

Up on the pom-pom platform young Farnworth, rather white-faced, was gritting his teeth with blood from his left arm dripping from his fingers. Acton halted. "What's the matter with you, Sub?"

"Nothing much. A bit of pom-pom shell near the shoulder."

"Any of your gun's crew knocked out?"

"No."

"Then go aft and get yourself looked at before the rush starts," the first lieutenant said. Farnworth was obviously in pain.

"But Number One, it really isn't. . . ."

"Don't argue, Sub!" Acton interrupted. "Get weaving! Do as I tell you!"

The mast, shot away about fifteen feet up by a shell which had gone on to burst and wreck most of the bridge, lay straddled across the port side of the deck with the masthead in the water. Squeezing through a tangle of rigging and up the forecastle ladder Acton saw that the fire was under control, though men were still using foam extinguishers. Petty Officer Hartopp was there superintending.

There had been what looked like direct hits on 'A' and 'B' guns, on the forecastle and forward superstructure, and blazing or exploding ammunition in the ready racks had done the rest. Men, risking their lives, had dragged their dead or wounded shipmates clear of the flames. Acton saw some bodies. From what Hartopp hurriedly told him Tracey and about eleven men of the two guns' crews had been killed, and others wounded.

Sick at heart, Acton couldn't stop to investigate. There were no signs of Pomeroy, and he was desperately anxious about those on the bridge and wheelhouse, which had also suffered a direct hit. He could see the torn and jagged plating. Leaving the Gunner in charge on the forecastle he went into the super-structure and up the ladder. The air in the confined space was full of the sickening reek of high explosive and scorched paint-work, rubber and corticene.

On the wing of the lower bridge, close together, he saw the bodies of two signalmen, both torn and horribly dead. The shell must have burst very close to them, and its other effects were visible everywhere. A veritable shower of splinters seemed to have swept the whole bridge. The steel screen round the upper bridge, the walls of the wheelhouse and charthouse, were discoloured by fire and everywhere riven and gashed and perforated.

Sickened and fearful of what else he might find Acton went into the wheelhouse. It was ghastly enough. A seaman, with arms and legs outstretched almost in the attitude of swimming, sprawled head downwards in a pool of blood near the remains of the revolution telegraph. The wheel, steering compass, and other engine-room telegraph had been blown away, and telephones and other instruments wrenched from their various fastenings. The deck was littered with broken glass and twisted metal. The wheelhouse was little more than a wreck.

Chief Petty Officer Wells, his head drooped on his chest, sat slumped on the deck with his back against the riddled steel wall of the charthouse. There also was much blood, with a broad trail of it reaching to the remains of the wheel. The coxswain must have crawled or pushed himself to where he now lay.

"Wells!" said Acton, touching him gently on the shoulder. "Wells!"

Wells lifted his head, his eyes full of pain. He recognized Acton. "Sir," he managed to whisper, in so low a voice that the first lieutenant had to bend over him to hear. "We . . . we copped it at last."

"I'll send someone up to look after you."

The coxswain closed his eyes and shuddered, clenching his fists and breathing with difficulty. "Mister Acton, sir," he muttered, speaking very slowly with a look of agony on his face. "Don't . . . don't you . . . don't you trouble about me. Reckon I've had it. Go . . . go look after cap'en, Mister Acton. He's the one that matters. Haven't heard his . . . his voice lately. She's been a good ship, Mister Acton . . . I can't say . . . no more. Maybe you'll . . ." The rest of the sentence tailed off into nothing.

He sighed and seemed to choke. A rush of blood came from his mouth. With a last convulsive movement Robert Harding Wells collapsed and died. Acton could have wept. He had lost a much-loved shipmate and a faithful friend.

And the upper bridge, when he nerved himself to crawl up what remained of the vertical steel ladder, was another gruesome shambles.

Pomeroy, with Hatfield, the yeoman of signals, and two ratings lay dead. Melton and another man had escaped with wounds. The navigator, his right side and leg streaming with blood, could just hobble. A seaman, white-faced, lay groaning with his back against the bridge screen.

There were more hideous red pools and splashes amidst the horrid litter on the deck—torn coco-nut matting and corticene; pieces of jagged metal and some glass; the broken remains of the standard compass, the wooden chair that Pomeroy used at sea, and the chart table; telephones and other instruments blown away; loose charts; signal-books and signal-pads; sheets of paper, printed or typewritten; an unbroken plate containing sandwiches wrapped up in a napkin; a smashed tea-cup, and Pomeroy's large Thermos flask still intact.

"Can you manage to get below?" Acton asked Melton.

"I doubt it," the navigator returned. "Not with all the ladders. This right leg of mine's rather giving me gyp—— Anyhow, that poor chap can't," he added, indicating the wounded rating.

The first lieutenant went on the fore-side of the bridge and hailed Mr. Blatchington on the forecastle. Would he send someone for the doctor. There were two wounded on the upper bridge. Bamboo stretchers would be needed, and the men to lower them.

"God! What an awful bloody mess!" the navigator said miserably. "And the poor old skipper! I feel that more than anything."

"Charles Tracey's had it, too," said Acton sadly. "And Wells."

"Poor chaps! Many others?"

"A good few, I fear. Haven't had time to tot up yet."

"And what about the ship? Will she sink or do we have to abandon?"

"I don't know, yet," Acton replied.

"Any prospect of the Chief getting her moving again?"

"I haven't heard since before the last scrap. I believe there was some hope then. If we have to abandon it won't be too good. Most of the boats seem to be hanging in shreds. All we've got are the floats."

The navigator thought for a moment. "What'll you do if the Chief can get her going? You're in command now."

"I haven't even started to think," Acton could only say. "But thank God it's getting dark."

"There'll be a moon later," Melton warned him. "It rises at about 1 a.m."

"Fighting seems to have stopped for the moment," Acton said, looking round the misty horizon. "There's nothing in sight. A good deal of smoke still hanging about, though."

"If we float around here we'll cop hell's delight in the morning, if not earlier," Melton remarked. "The sea's stinking with Japs. Their planes'll spot us for a dead snip."

Acton shrugged. "If the Chief can get her going we'll have a shot at getting somewhere," he said, trying to be cheerful.

"A damn big if!" said Melton, deeply pessimistic. "Anyhow, it's no good going back to the place we came from. The blasted Japs'll be in there in forty-eight hours at the most.

God's teeth!" he exclaimed in sudden passion. "What a muck-up it's been, what an unholy muddle! What chance had we, for God's sake?"

Acton agreed. If Draycott could get the ship running, he said, he was all out for steaming to some island.

"There are plenty of islands within fifty or sixty miles," Melton pointed out. "But what's the big idea?"

"Anchor close inshore, or even run her ashore," the first lieutenant said. "She's no earthly good as a ship without a dockyard, and where'll we find a dockyard with the Japs all over the place? No. We could camouflage her with trees and greenery, and paint her up to look like the natural background."

"What then?"

"Leave a few hands on board to man the two after four-sevens, and the tubes," said Acton, warming to the idea. "Then we could land what remained of the ship's company, with all the lighter guns we can man-handle, the Lewis guns and the rifles, and ammunition and stores. If the Japs do spot us and try smoking us out, we could at least make a fight for it. They'd have to land men."

"Your second name ought to be Hornblower," Melton said wryly. All the same, the idea sounded all right to him. He didn't fancy the idea of scuttling and abandoning the ship with the prospect of being shot at helpless in the water, or spending the rest of the war in a Japanese prison camp. "But it's the getting to this island that matters," he said. "If the Chief can't do the trick, we've had it."

The ladder rattled as McInnes hoisted himself to the upper bridge. Night had nearly fallen.

"How now?" he asked.

"You'd better have a look at them," said Acton motioning him to the prostrate figures of Pomeroy and Hatfield.

McInnes walked over and leant over them in turn, using an electric torch.

"Careful of that light, Pills," Acton warned.

What McInnes did Acton couldn't see; but his verdict was not long in coming. "There's nothing I can do," he said, shaking his head. "Any others?" There was a catch in his voice. He, too, was fond of Pomeroy.

McInnes examined two other bodies, with the same result.

Then he turned to Melton. "You seem to have caught it," he said. "Let's have a look at you."

"There's Johnson," the navigator said, pointing to the wounded man. "Look after him first."

But Able Seaman Johnson was dead.

In all, the *Eurydice* had suffered a loss of twenty-six killed and nineteen wounded, some of them seriously.

But in spite of her battering, the ship was unlikely to sink unless attacked again. Apart from bad leaks in number two boiler-room, and splinter and pom-pom holes in the hull, she had not been greatly damaged below or near the water-line. Only one boat, a whaler, remained serviceable. Practically all of the havoc had been wrought forward by two if not three shell of the same salvo, which had wrecked the bridge and wireless office, brought down the mast, destroyed the galley and canteen, and completely wiped out 'A' and 'B' guns. A few seconds earlier another shell had burst on the upper mess-deck and started a small fire, though this had been dealt with before it could do much harm.

Look-outs were placed, and the two after 4.7's, the pom-pom and the Bofors guns kept manned in case of attack. So far as possible the wreckage was cleared away, and the mast freed of its tangled rigging and dragged inboard. Acton was loath to jettison a spar which might be useful.

The wounded were taken below and made comfortable. The dead, shrouded in hammocks with practice shot at their feet, were carried aft one by one to the gangway. The captain's body was with them.

This dismal task had not been completed when, at about 7.30 p.m., some distance away to the south-westward, they saw the darkening sky suddenly illuminated by the blue-white glare of star-shell or flares from aircraft. They floated slowly to the surface, bathing the sea in brilliance. Using his glasses, Acton could see no signs of any ships. Then, a few minutes later, the orange flashes of heavy guns sparkled over the horizon in the same direction. The firing did not last long. It had ceased before they heard the rumbling growl of it sounding like distant thunder.

It was just after this, when Acton was waiting with a shaded lantern and prayer book, that he heard the voice of James Draycott anxiously asking for the first lieutenant.

"I'm here, Chief. What is it?"

"Good news, George! I've got things moving again! D'you hear?"

Above the sound of lapping water Acton could hear the rhythmic hum of the dynamo and the throbbing of pumps. The miracle had happened! The dead *Eurydice* had come to life! Acton could have fallen on Draycott's neck and kissed him.

"Thank God! Bless you, Chief!" was all he could say. "What about leaks?"

"If you don't mind a bit of a list to port I think we'll be all right. Anyhow, we can get moving."

"What speed?"

The Chief thought for a moment. "I could probably whack her up to eighteen, though I think fifteen would be safer. I'm thinking of that boiler-room. We'd better work up gently."

"Is the after steering position connected up?"

"Connected up, and tested."

"Good," said Acton. "We'll go on presently. I've something to do first. You know all about it, twenty-six all told."

"I know, poor chaps," Draycott replied, his voice strained. "A rotten business, awful, and Helpman and those other fellows of mine among them. Well," he sighed, "perhaps we're lucky it wasn't the whole crowd of us."

"You might hold this light, Chief," Acton said. "Keep it shaded. I've got to read. Hartopp, are you ready?"

"All ready, sir."

And Acton read:

"I am the resurrection and the life, saith the Lord: he that believeth in me, though he were dead, yet shall he live: and whosoever liveth and believeth in me shall never die.

"Man that is born of a woman hath but a short time to live, and is full of misery. He cometh up, and is cut down, like a flower; he fleeth as it were a shadow, and never continueth in one stay.

"In the midst of life we are in death: of whom may we seek for succour, but of thee, O Lord. . . .

"Forasmuch as it hath pleased Almighty God of His great mercy to take unto himself the souls of our dear brothers here departed, we therefore commit their bodies to the deep. . . .

"I heard a voice from heaven, saying unto me, Write, From

henceforth blessed are the dead which die in the Lord: even so saith the Spirit; for they rest from their labours."

Something seemed to stick in Acton's throat. Overcome with emotion, he could read no more.

It was a very abbreviated form of the burial service; but it lacked nothing in reverence, dignity, or feeling among that group of weary, dirty, battle-stained men, some of them wounded, who had clustered aft to witness the last of their friends and shipmates killed in battle. Here, in the solitary gleam of a shaded electric torch, with the stars brilliant in the clear sky overhead and the ship rolling gently to an invisible swell, the scene was intensely poignant.

One by one the shotted hammocks were launched over the side, to disappear in trails of vivid phosphorescence.

Thus were the dead of the *Eurydice* committed to the sea.

Ten minutes later the ship was under way, steaming to the north-eastward. Acton had rescued charts and Sailing Directions from the badly damaged charthouse. He knew where he was going.

Look-outs had been placed forward, and at first Acton had tried conning the ship from the auxiliary steering position in the after searchlight platform. But there his view ahead was restricted. He must go forward and spend the night on the remains of the upper bridge. He ordered a boat's compass to be taken there, and as all communications with the bridge were out of action and even the engine-room telegraph destroyed, Mr. Blatchington, who could improvise anything, had rigged up a temporary circuit and telephones through which orders could be passed to the wheel and on by voice to the engine-room.

Acton heard the Gunner's remarks after he had tested through his instruments. "There," he said, fiercely, handing a pair of earphones to a seaman. "Clip that over your napper, Baltry, listen to all that comes through, and repeat it, pronto. And pay attention, my son. If I catch you mooning I'll bloody well eat you!"

At about half-past nine there came the thud of a distant explosion from somewhere astern, then silence. There was nothing to be seen.

Soon after eleven the silvery spangle of star-shell glittered far away over the horizon to the westward. Before they faded out the orange flashes of heavy gunfire were reflected from the sky in the same directions. They continued for some minutes and could only mean a night action, something more than a mere skirmish, though no sound of it reached the *Eurydice*. Then came a reddish flickering glow, which alternately waxed and waned—a ship on fire, thought Acton. It must have been, for presently there was a great gout of flame erupting skywards, like a volcano. Then darkness. Some ship's magazine had exploded.

After sleepless days and nights, after hours of intense nervous strain and anxiety, Acton felt wearier than he ever had been in his life. He had felt he could have curled up in any corner, to sleep like a dog. To keep himself awake he had sent a messenger down to the doctor for what he called 'dope'. And McInnes had sent him up two little greyish tablets in an envelope, with a chit on which had been inscribed—'To be taken in water.' They were benzedrine. They had their effect.

Soon after midnight someone came climbing up the ladder to the upper bridge. "Mister Acton, sir! Mister Acton!"

"Hullo! What is it?"

"It's me, sir. Jevons. I brought you along a drop o' cocoa and sandwiches, thinking they might be welcome."

"Stout fellow," Acton said. "Thank you, Jevons. I've had nothing since lunch."

"No, sir. I was aware of that," the steward replied, uncorking a Thermos bottle and pouring some of its contents into a tin mug. "Now drink up, sir, while it's hot. I've sweetened it to your taste."

"You think of everything," Acton told him, starting to eat and drink. "What about you?"

"I'm all right, sir."

"Ship's company being looked after?"

"No complaints so far, sir. Now the galley's knocked out the wardroom galley's working overtime."

"It's a cruel bad business about the cap'en, Mister Acton," Jevons continued with sorrow in his voice. "I've been with many officers; but never a better one than Lootenant-Commander Pomeroy. He was always so thoughtful for others. Having been with him for close on three years I shall miss him something dreadful."

"So we all shall," Acton told him. "And Mister Tracey and the others." He went on to ask about the wounded; but Jevons could tell him little, except that Melton and Farnworth were taking nourishment.

"Well, sir, I'll be getting along. I'll leave the stuff up here. I'll be along again later, and if there's anything else you fancy, just send along and let me know. Good night, sir."

Acton thanked him again and was left for his lonely vigil.

By 1 a.m., in consultation with Mr. Blatchington, the only remaining executive officer fit for duty, Acton had made his plans. By the light of an electric torch the Gunner had seen the chart, and knew exactly what he was expected to do. Word had also been passed to the ship's company that they would be required at any time after 3 a.m.

On board the *Eurydice* that night, nobody slept.

8

THE NIGHT was calm and practically windless. The moon was well up over the horizon when, soon after 2 a.m., Acton had sight of the dark outline of a large island to the northward. It was at least twelve miles away and not the island for which he was making. This one, recognizable by its twin peaks, was described in the appropriate volume of the *Eastern Archipelago Pilot* as having a sizeable town and regular trade with the mainland. It was conceivable that it might already have been occupied by the enemy. He altered course ten degrees to the southward to give it a wider berth.

It was far too clear to be pleasant if any Japanese ships were on the prowl; but from any vessel to the north to about the west the *Eurydice* must be up against a dark background. It was from the eastward that the principal danger lay, for from there the ship must be silhouetted against the moonlight.

Acton had already passed an order to the engine-room to increase speed to eighteen knots. According to his rough reckoning they now had another thirty-four miles to go, which made their expected time of arrival about 3.50 a.m. This was rather late for what he intended to do. It would be nearly dawn at 5.0 a.m. He went to the telephone. "I want to speak to Mr. Draycott, please."

After a short delay Draycott's voice came through.

"Chief," Acton asked. "Can you whack her on a bit?"

"I can probably give you twenty-two without straining things," came the reply.

"Then please go on to that. And Chief?"

"Yes."

"Have we been leaking oil?"

Draycott considered the point. "There was probably leakage when we were first hit," he said. "But not since, so far as I know."

"Not even from number two boiler-room?"

"No more than the slightest trickle, if that. We've shut everything off. Why d'you ask?"

"If we've laid a trail across the ocean we might be tracked down by one of their aircraft. Take every possible precaution, old boy. Don't pump your bilges, or do anything likely to give us away."

"Okay," came Draycott's reassuring voice. "I'll see to it. And you want me to go on at twenty-two?"

"As fast as you like, Chief. I want to save time. And no smoke. Be careful about that."

"Right. I understand. I'll try working up to twenty-four and see what happens."

To judge from the gradual increase in speed Draycott more than carried out his word. It felt quite like old times to feel the old ship bustling along at a respectable speed.

It was soon after three o'clock that Acton first had sight of the dark hummock for which he was aiming, a steep, densely wooded peak about 650 feet high running sharply up from the sea bottom. It was really the highest of an overgrown ridge of hills forming the rim of the crater of an extinct volcano; a small island roughly circular in shape and rather more than a mile across. According to the *Pilot* and the small-scale chart, it was fringed by reefs of coral broken in a few places by sandy beaches. But on all sides except to the southward, where the land sloped gently to a small bight with a little village in a valley near the shore, there were sheer cliffs from eighty to a hundred-and-twenty feet high. The land was steep-to, with twelve to fifteen fathoms of water within a hundred yards of the shore.

The island was not normally visited by shipping, the *Pilot* said, though there was occasional native boat traffic with the mainland. The village was 'sparsely inhabited,' whatever that might mean, and the principal occupations of the people were fishing, with the growing of coco-nuts, bananas and other tropical fruits, and small quantities of rice, sugar and tobacco for local consumption. Small quantities of cinnamon and other spices were exported. Mariners were warned that the anchorage was unsafe in southerly winds with a falling barometer, and that during certain seasons of the year there were violent squalls with heavy rain. Steam should be kept on the main engines at all times.

From another official book of reference Acton learnt that, like Java and most of the other islands of the Netherlands East Indies, the island for which he was making abounded with animal life. Wild pig might be found and there were birds and flying foxes in profusion. The large robber or coco-nut crabs (*Birgus latro*), which climbed palm trees to get the fruit, might be seen at all times, as might also the hermit-crabs of the family *Coenobitidae* which lived at considerable distances from the sea to which, however, they returned for hatching out their spawn. "There are many varieties of insects including ants, beetles and flies while mosquitoes are prevalent and particularly noxious at sundown," he read.

So while the island might have its disadvantages, it was unlikely that the ship's company would lack for fresh food.

Acton telephoned for Mr. Blatchington. He wished to see him on the bridge. The gunner arrived.

"You sent for me, sir?"

"Yes," said Acton, pointing ahead. "There's our island. We'll arrive in about twenty minutes. You've got the whaler turned out and ready for lowering?"

"Yes, sir. And the oars muffled, as you said."

"Then I'll just run through your orders again so there's no mistake. I'll turn the ship parallel to the shore as close as I can get in to the beach. Then you'll be lowered in the whaler with twelve men, a signalman with a Very pistol and flashing lamp, and the two boat-keepers. You've chosen the men?"

"Yes."

"Ten men with rifles, not forgetting the bayonets, and two with those Sten guns you stole from the Army some months ago."

"Come, come, Mister Acton," Mr. Blatchington expostulated. "I never stole those six Stens and the ammunition. It was fair barter. Two bottles of Navy rum an' a pound of ship's tobacco. Besides, you knew about it at the time, or very soon afterwards."

"Never mind," Acton laughed. "That doesn't alter the fact that you're a scrounging old rascal, Gunner. You'd pinch the petticoat off your grandmother."

"Only for the good of the Service, Mr. Acton."

"Sez you. But you and your party pull quietly ashore. Leaving the boat-keepers, the rest of you make your way to the village about four hundred yards inland, so far as I make it. With this moon it ought to be light enough to see. You get hold of the leading inhabitants, tell them who you are, and ask if they've any news of the Japanese."

"I've been thinking about that," said the gunner, rather dubiously. "I don't talk the Java lingo, nor they mine. What then, sir?"

"I've never known you at a loss yet," Acton said. "Use sign language, and say you're English. They'll damn soon understand. I want the houses searched, and if you find anything that looks like a wireless transmitter you're to put a guard on it."

"I'll do my best, Mister Acton."

"And remember, there's to be no shooting, no rough stuff whatever, unless you run up against the Japanese. These people are our friends. If the Japs are in occupation, which I don't think they will be, you must use your discretion. If you *do* run into trouble, you're to shoot off a red Very light and make your way back to the beach. If necessary, I'll switch on the searchlight and then open fire with 'X' gun, well over your heads. Are you clear so far?"

"Quite clear, Mister Acton."

"And understand it's *most* important you shouldn't put a foot wrong with the natives. A great deal depends on that. We want them to be with us, not against us."

The Gunner understood. "And if we find no enemy," he went on, "I signal off to you what I do find."

"That's it. The rest depends on what happens. I may decide to anchor, or run the ship ashore, though that'll probably have to wait for daylight. Is there anything else you can think of?"

"Only that if you anchor there'll be no steam on the capstan for weighing again. It'll mean weighing by hand. I'd better detail a party now to get the capstan bars on the fo'c'sle."

Acton, who had not forgotten there was no steam for weighing, agreed. "Yes," he said. "And on your way down please tell Petty Officer Hartopp that I want a few hands on the forecastle and the starboard anchor ready for letting go in ten minutes' time. Anything else?"

"No, sir."

"Then that's all for now, and good luck to you."

Mr. Blatchington was normally a phlegmatic man, taking everything as it came; but for once he felt strangely excited. This was good old-fashioned stuff. He wondered if he ought to carry a cutlass in addition to his automatic pistol.

Easing to dead slow, the *Eurydice* presently glided round a low cliff, passing at a distance of three cables to avoid the outlying ledges of coral. The cliff glimmered palely in the moonlight, and from its upper edge the land rose steeply to the sky. Just beyond lay the little bay.

The air suddenly became filled with a warm, sweet fragrance, a mingled potpourri of flowers and vegetation and spices, mixed with the faintest tang of what smelt like wood smoke. In some strange way it reminded Acton of the perfumer's shop in Bond Street into which he had beguiled his fiancée during his last leave in London, more than a year before. It recalled Fiona herself, and the name of the gloriously extravagant scent he had insisted on buying—Chanel Number 5. He remembered her very words when he gave it to her. "But my dear, silly, extravagant old darling. I can't possibly use scent when I'm driving round London in the blitz and blackout! What on earth would my bosses think, and say?"

Dear Fiona, with all her charm and beauty and tenderness! He had a mortal dread when he thought of her driving a car round London to what she called 'incidents' with buildings ablaze and tottering, and the bombs crashing down. Why couldn't she have joined the Wrens as he had wished her to do? Not that the Wrens were any safer; but because the Navy did look after its people. But no. She had insisted on sticking to

62

the job for which she'd first enrolled herself. She'd feel like a deserter, she said, if she gave it up now. She wrote regularly, though during the last two months or so her letters had arrived erratically and at long intervals. That probably meant nothing, Acton consoled himself. The mails had gone completely haywire so far as the *Eurydice* was concerned. Probably the Japanese were busy sorting through the contents of hundreds of mail-bags at Singapore.

"Port ten!" said Acton to the seaman who had been sent to the bridge to pass orders by telephone. He heard it repeated. "Stop engines!"

The ship slid round a point and into a patch of deep shadow cast by the high land.

"'Midships! Meet her starboard! . . . Steady!"

The little bay was smaller than he had expected, a mere shallow indentation about half a mile wide. As the *Eurydice* moved slowly in towards the land he could see the narrow ribbon of beach, the greater length of it shining like silver in the bright moonlight. On the starboard bow the bight terminated to the eastward in another rampart of low cliff over which the ground rose steeply up to the undulating skyline. Through his glasses Acton could see the V-shaped cleft of the valley between two rounded hummocks, and on the beach near it four or five long black objects which could only be boats or canoes. Except for the moonlight there was no gleam anywhere. But for the hum from the engine-room, the ripple of water and footsteps and hushed voices on deck, the silence was complete.

The *Eurydice* lost her way and was motionless. He ordered another touch ahead on the engines, and then—"Stop both!"

Picking up the megaphone he went to the after end of the bridge. "Mister Blatchington," he said without raising his voice. "Lower the boat down to the gunwale. No noise, please."

"Aye aye, sir."

"And when I tell you. . . ."

At that very moment there came an eldritch screech from the shore followed by an agitated squawking and twittering and an ululating chuckle. Then another piercing scream which sounded almost human.

The sounds were so loud and unexpected that Acton's heart jumped. "God in heaven!" he muttered, thoroughly startled. "What the hell's that?" It was only birds, and the commotion died away as suddenly as it had come.

"Mister Blatchington?"

"Sir?"

"That row was birds."

"I know sir. But it fair gave me the staggers."

"The same here. Now when I tell you, but not before, you're to lower the boat right down into the water and get your men on board. Unhook, don't slip her in the ordinary way. I shall have stopped dead. No noise. No shouting."

"Aye aye, sir. I understand."

The ship, now about two hundred yards from the beach, was still moving slowly ahead. Acton ordered slow astern to check her way. She came to a standstill, with engines stopped. He went to the fore side of the bridge. "Chains!" he called softly to the leadsman on the forecastle. "Get your lead-line up and down and let me know the depth."

He watched the man as he sounded. "No bottom at twenty fathoms, sir," the reply came back in a hoarse whisper.

Twenty fathoms—a hundred and twenty feet within less than a couple of ship's lengths of the beach! The land must slope down into deep water almost like the side of a house.

The whaler, packed with men and their weapons, left the ship and paddled silently to the shore. Acton heard the faint crunch as her bows ran up on the shingle. He watched the men disembark and move up the beach. He could hear the sound of their footsteps and the birds seemed to have heard them too, for there came another deafening chorus from somewhere quite close. He felt apprehensive. Was this discordant cacophony a regular nightly performance, or was it nature's alarm signal?

Still there were no lights ashore, no human voices. He saw the landing-party disappear into the dark background of trees and bush. The scent in the heated air was almost overpowering.

The time was seventeen minutes to four. There was a full hour before first daylight.

While Acton played with the engines to keep the *Eurydice* more or less stationary, Draycott arrived on the bridge to discuss what was to happen next.

He already knew it was Acton's intention to moor the ship close inshore, or even to sink her in shallow water with gun

64

and torpedo-tubes still available, and to fight it out if the Japanese came. There was nothing else for it. Draycott realized better than anyone that the battered *Eurydice* could never be a fighting ship again without the help of a dockyard, and there was no dockyard nearer than Australia, a good two thousand miles away through a sea overrun by the Japanese navy. They might patch up the leaks and make the ship tolerably seaworthy; but she hadn't the fuel for two thousand miles. In short, Australia was off the map.

"It's quite clear there are no Japs here," Acton said, greatly relieved. "If there had Guns would have been in trouble by now. But we can't make up our minds what to do till we've heard what he's found ashore."

Draycott was gazing shorewards. "There's no sign of life anywhere except for those blasted screech-owls!" he remarked dourly. "They give me the creeps. But if the place is uninhabited, or the natives are friendly, d'you intend we shall land and do a sort of Swiss Family Robinson?"

"We obviously can't get away, Chief. You may have to devote your talents to becoming the municipal architect, engineer and surveyor, building palm huts or whatever they use in these parts."

"Listening to those confounded birds all night!" the engineer officer grumbled. "How long's this bloody war going to last?"

"Your guess is as good as mine, Chief. But there's one thing we must think about, and that's making a proper job of wrecking the ship. We mustn't give the Japs any chance of salving her. We'll have to lay everything on, scuttling charges, depth charges or even blowing up a magazine. It'll be your job to make sure of wrecking the remaining boilers and turbines."

"It's as bad as all that, then. But what should the Japs want with a place like this?"

"It's not that, so much. I'm only thinking that we may be spotted by one of their cursed aircraft. If they tumble to the fact that survivors are ashore they'll probably send someone along to mop us up."

Their conversation was interrupted by the arrival of Jevons with provender—tea, this time, with another pile of sandwiches. Acton thanked him, and the steward deposited his burdens and left.

"Help yourself, Chief," Acton said. "The faithful one has

been stuffing me with food most of the night. Where *is* that Gunner?" he went on, his voice fretful with impatience. "He's been gone nearly three-quarters of an hour! I hope to God he's not gone scrambling up the mountain!"

Time, indeed, was passing leaden-footed. Already the first pale gleams of daylight were brightening the clear sky to the eastward.

Then McInnes appeared on the bridge. He was dog-tired. Of the nineteen wounded, he feared, three were unlikely to live. Acton asked their names, and was told. Of the rest, McInnes continued, going into some technical details, seven, with fractures and burns, were 'not so good', as he expressed it. The remaining nine, which included Melton and Farnworth, had escaped more easily. The sub-lieutenant, indeed, with his left arm no more than deeply gashed by a splinter, was virtually fit for duty now. And Melton? Acton asked. McInnes wouldn't commit himself. The navigator had lost a good deal of blood and the wound in his left groin was painful. With luck he might have him hobbling around in a week or ten days, though one never knew.

"Thanks, Pills," Acton said. "It's better than I hoped. There may be a chance of getting the wounded ashore, though I don't know yet. But I believe the place stinks of mosquitoes."

McInnes thought he could deal with mosquitoes.

A minute or two later a dim, shaded light started winking from the shore. It was Mr. Blatchington's signalman. Apart from him all the *Eurydice's* signal ratings had been killed; but a telegraphist was waiting on the lower bridge. Acton heard the click of his light as he answered.

"To—Captain," he read aloud, while someone wrote down. "No—Japs—here—nor—any—seen. Boss—man—Dutch—trader—speaks—slight—English—wife—six—children. Inhabitants—most—friendly. Approximate—total—eight—nine—men—one—five—seven—women—and—girls. Am—pursuing—investigations. Gunner."

Acton, who had overheard, could not help being amused. "Much too verbose," he laughed. "But I thought the old boy was going to say he and his sailors were pursuing the hundred-and-fifty-seven ladies! All right, Travers," he called to the telegraphist. "I heard. Make back—'Should like to see Dutch trader on board as soon as possible.' "

"That's the best bit of news for some time," McInnes remarked, thinking of his wounded. "But what is he investigating, for heaven's sake?"

"Need you ask," Draycott put in, his mouth full of sandwich. "He's separating the sheep from the goats."

"What d'you mean, Chief?"

"He's probably mustering the eligible females by ages, the artful old dodger. You'll see. He'll have the whole thing taped in the proper Service manner."

Ten minutes passed, and the *Eurydice* still lay close inshore. There was no wind and so little current that it was hardly necessary to touch the engines. The light was growing, with a rosy flush creeping up over the hills. And away inland, in the direction of the village, Acton saw through the palms moving lights and the dancing red flames of what looked like a bonfire. A drum started to throb rhythmically, and the birds in the jungle restarted their screeching, chattering outcry.

What on earth was happening now, Acton wondered, stamping with impatience. The drumming sounded like some sort of celebration. What in heck was Mr. Blatchington thinking about?

He hadn't long to wait, for presently the sound of human voices, male and female, joined in in unison with the steady beat of the drum. It was some sort of marching tune, which became louder and louder as the singers approached. A double line of dancing red flares appeared through the boles of the palm trees. It looked like a torchlight procession. It was!

"What's this damned tomfoolery!" Acton muttered angrily to himself. Mr. Blatchington must have taken leave of his senses.

He was quite certain he had when the head of the procession debouched on to the beach and came on, the drum still drumming, the torches flaring and the men and women still chanting. Precisely what they were singing, or in what language, Acton did not know. Nor did any of the *Eurydice's* ship's company, who looked on, goggle-eyed in amazement, as well they might.

The monotonous chant, repeated again and again in marching time, exactly fitted the words later invented by one of the sailors:

(*Men and women*):	Nicky Taylor's long-haired daughter, I kissed her twice and didn't oughter. Nicky Taylor's lovely daughter, Once with her I'll never falter.
(*Men only*):	Wah!—Wah!—Wah! Wah!—Wah!—Wah!
(*Women only*):	Eng—leesh—maan! Eng—leesh—maan!

It was no hostile demonstration. It was a spontaneous mass welcome. The entire population seemed to have turned out, men, women and children—a throng of people.

They marched, and danced, and shuffled, capering in time to the music, young and old. And in their midst were the armed sailors, each sailor, as Acton saw through his glasses and to his horror, accompanied on each side by a bronze-skinned maiden wearing nothing but a brightly-coloured sarong and flowers in her dark hair.

And in the front rank of the procession, now near the water's edge, with two women in sarongs, a paunchy little European in a white suit and helmet, and children frolicking on each flank, marched Mr. Blatchington—with a huge garland of pink blossoms festooned round his neck!

Acton was struck dumb. Discipline had gone to hell!

Some of the sailors aft in the *Eurydice* were cheering, joining in the chorus, waving and whistling cat-calls. If the inhabitants were pleased to see the ship, the sailors were delighted to see the inhabitants. The din was increasing.

Fuming with anger Acton picked up the megaphone to call for order, though nothing he could do would have stopped the excitement on shore. Some of the seamen were embarking in the whaler, in which Mr. Blatchington and the civilian had already taken their places in the stern sheets. Some of the younger men and women, divesting themselves of their scanty raiment, were already wading into the water preparatory to escorting the boat off to the ship!

But Acton thought better of it. Interference would merely make him look ridiculous. It was better to treat this ludicrous business as comic relief. Undoubtedly that was what Pomeroy would have done. All the same, Acton would have something to say to Mr. Blatchington, garland or no garland!

"Wah—Wah!—Wah!" came the men's chorus from the shore. "Wah!—Wah!—Wah!" roared the sailors on board, stamping their feet in time with the drum-beats.

"Eng—leesh—maan!" came the higher voices of the women from the shore. "Eng—leesh—maan!" the sailors echoed in shrill falsetto.

The situation was temporarily out of hand; but the welcome was more than friendly. It was wildly enthusiastic.

Acton began to feel apprehensive as to what might be the results of fraternisation when the ship's company was established ashore.

These cheerful, carefree, tropical daughters of nature had little restraint and few inhibitions, as he very well knew. In particular, a most careful eye would have to be kept on the blond-headed, curly-haired Sub-Lieutenant Caspar Langham Farnworth. The Gunner was no oil-painting; but if he were hung with garlands at first sight, what would happen to the sub?

The whaler left the shore, circled round, and started to pull off to the ship, a train of black heads and golden bodies bobbing and splashing in her wake.

9

Mr. BLATCHINGTON, having discarded his garland and looking rather sheepish, arrived on the bridge. "I've brought the Dutchman, sir," he said, saluting.

"Where is he?" Acton demanded, giving him a fierce look.

"At the foot of the ladder, Mister Acton."

"Well, leave him there for a moment. I want to know first what in heck you've been up to, Gunner? What's the meaning of all this damned riot, with torchlight processions and singing and dancing? Don't these people realize there's a war on?"

The Gunner shrugged his shoulders and tried to look apologetic. "What else was to be done, Mister Acton?" he asked. "I couldn't stop it. They were all over us at once."

"So it seems," said Acton dourly.

"Well, you did say I was to establish friendly relations, sir."

"Friendly!" Acton snorted. "But I didn't anticipate a blasted beanfeast."

"Nor did I, sir. It was all quite unexpected. Came on us like a bombshell, in a manner of speaking."

"Did they serve out any of the local brew ashore?"

"They tried to, Mister Acton. But I wouldn't let our troops touch it, they being on duty in wartime. The fact is, sir, half these natives never seen a ship the size o' this before, and got excited like. Any excuse for a beano."

"You're telling me," Acton said.

Though the chattering crowd still lingered on the beach, the organized singing and drumming had ceased. But aft in the *Eurydice* the men were leaning over the rails whistling or exchanging badinage with a score of merry swimmers floating, splashing and laughing alongside. There seemed to be no language difficulty, and most of the swimmers were girls: pretty ones at that.

"Go aft and keep order among the ship's company," Acton said severely. "They might be sitting in the front row of the stalls at a strip-tease act or a leg show! Those damn women'll be climbing on board next. Get 'em to hell out of it!"

Mr. Blatchington looked dubious. "Short o' throwing things at 'em they won't go till they feel like it," he replied with perfect truth. "Have a heart, sir. The gals are only being friendly."

Acton couldn't help being amused. Mr. Blatchington was so very much in earnest. "A bit too friendly," he laughed. "All right, Gunner. You win. Do your best, and be tactful. But we can't have the ship's company getting wrong ideas and being corrupted."

The Gunner smiled. He was middle-aged and very wise, and here was a young lieutenant trying to act the heavy father. "Nothing you or I can say, or do, is going to alter what the ship's company think, Mister Acton. Sailors are sailors all the world over, poor devils. I know sailors like. . . ."

"I know all about that," Acton interrupted. This argument of good order and naval discipline *v.* the sailors and their girl friends might go on for ever. "Now produce your Dutchman and let me get on with the real business."

Mr. Cornelius Beekman was summoned and introduced.

They shook hands. Wearing crumpled white linen trousers and shirt open at the neck to display a considerable expanse of hairy chest, the visitor was a short, obese little man in the middle forties. He had a round red face, fat unshaven blue jowls and a pair of shrewd bright brown eyes not unlike a robin's. From the look of him, Acton judged it would be difficult to get the better of Mr. Beekman. His English was fluent enough.

"Pleased to meet you, captain," he said with a sort of half-salute. "People here are glad you come. We do all to make you welcome. I," he added, tapping himself on the chest, "am merchant and have property, besides also. . . ." He used some Dutch word which Acton didn't understand; but later discovered to mean he was an ex-officio magistrate. "Our peoples very peaceable, captain. No troubles."

Acton told him they were grateful for the welcome. Meanwhile, Beekman must be aware that the Dutch, the Americans and the British were at war with the Japanese. Had he seen or heard anything of the enemy?

Yes. The Dutchman knew of the war. He had a radio set. But they'd seen nothing except some unidentified warships in the distance four days earlier, and once or twice an aeroplane.

"Were they Dutch or Japanese aircraft?" Acton asked.

Beekman didn't know. They were too far away to be recognizable, and in any case he was no expert. But the island was a very unimportant place. Why should the Japanese trouble about it?

Acton came to the point. "My ship, as you see, has been damaged in battle," he said, going on to explain that the engagement had gone badly for the Allies, and that in all probability the Japanese were already landing in Java. As for the *Eurydice*, she was damaged beyond all possibility of repair outside a dockyard. There was no dockyard within reach. Also there were wounded on board he wished to send ashore.

Acton realized he was on dangerous ground. He would have to be very tactful in explaining his intentions and in securing the co-operation of the inhabitants. He didn't wish unnecessarily to involve the peaceful population in a war which was none of their making, and in which they probably hadn't the slightest interest. Their primary concerns were their own daily lives and welfare. But if they could be induced to help as he

71

hoped they would, the Japanese, if they ever did succeed in occupying the place, might exact their usual ghastly reprisals—rape, wholesale massacre, extermination. They were inhuman fiends. Acton knew how they had used their Chinese prisoners of war for bayonet practice.

But Beekman, apparently, hadn't thought of this, or else he ignored it. He raised no objection when Acton said he proposed landing the wounded and most of his men, and mooring the ship close inshore, or even running her ashore, in a spot where her guns could still be used.

What was really in the Dutchman's mind, though Acton wasn't to know it, was that he regarded a Japanese landing as altogether unlikely. And if they did land, he thought, he and the population could retire to the hills and the bush. Meanwhile the *Eurydice* was a bird in hand. She was probably stuffed full of stores which these Englishmen would be glad to barter for services rendered.

"You have local knowledge," Acton said. "Can you point out some place with deep water very close inshore?"

Beekman could, and did, indicating a low ledge of broken cliff about four hundred yards to the westward of where the boats were drawn up on the beach. A little steamer visited the island at rare and irregular intervals, he went on to explain. She lay there, which must mean there was deep water practically alongside the cliffs. The steamer's lines were made fast to trees on shore, and her cargo, Acton gathered, was either swung ashore on her derricks or laden into boats. The steamer, Beekman added, sometimes brought his stock from Surabaya, and took away what local produce they had for export.

Acton asked some technical questions. Had the steamer anchored down forward and aft? What was the exact depth of water?

Beekman grinned and shook his head. He was no sailor. He knew nothing of such things.

Acton was not worried. He could send someone in the whaler with a lead-line to sound along the cliff-edge. "I want your people to help us," he said.

"How so, captain?"

"I want to camouflage the ship. . . ."

"What is?" Beekman asked, looking puzzled. The Englishman explained. He wished to hide the ship so far as was

72

possible, and intended to splash colour all over the hull, superstructure and funnels to harmonise with the background of cliff and greenery.

Beekman's eyes twinkled. He understood. "I keep shop," he said. "I sell paint, red paint, green paint, yellow paint, all colour. You can have."

They had paint on board, Acton told him; but if more were needed they'd come to him. However, they had no money to pay for anything, not that money was much use now anyhow. What they could do would be to barter some of the ship's stores. They'd pay for labour in the same way. If that wouldn't do—and he wondered what the Admiralty would say if they ever heard of a junior lieutenant gaily bartering Government property—he would have to give signed receipts for everything, repayable after the war. That was all there was to it.

Beekman was agreeable. "You leave all payments to me," he said quite happily. "I organize. You have plenty things in ship I make useful. Canvas, you have?"

"A certain amount," said Acton, thinking of the awnings.

"Goot! You tell me what you want and I organize. I get the people; I pay the people. You trust me. I can arrange."

Full daylight had long since come. The sun was already well up over the high ground to the eastward, and the sky was bright and clear. Apprehensive of being sighted by enemy aircraft, Acton realized the first thing he must do was to get the ship alongside and concealed.

"Have your people any old fishing nets?" he asked.

"Perhaps I can find," Beekman said. "What for?"

Acton explained that he wanted netting of some sort to cover the whole length of the ship, to conceal the tell-tale outline of the deck as seen from the air. The *Eurydice* was more than three hundred feet long. Could netting that length be provided, or shorter sections of net joined together?

The Dutchman scratched his chin and looked rather dubious. The people did use nets for fishing, he said; but their livelihood rather depended upon them. They might be unwilling to part.

"It's extremely important I should have them," Acton pointed out. "And I want them as soon as possible. Old nets will do."

Beekman said he would do his best.

"Then I want a party of your men to cut light bush over by

the cliff there. We spread it over the net to make the ship look as much as possible like the land, to hide the shape of her. Could that be done?"

That, said Beekman, would be easy enough.

"Then my wounded, Mister Beekman. I want to land them, with my doctor."

"How many?"

"Call it twenty all told."

The Dutchman thought for a moment. He could probably put up about ten wounded in his own house, he said, and no doubt the others could be accommodated elsewhere in the village. As for beds, the low, wooden beds covered with matting used by the natives were not uncomfortable. He used one himself.

"My people can bring their own mattresses and blankets," Acton said. "What about mosquito nets?"

Beekman had scores of mosquito nets in his store, he said. He'd bought a job lot in Surabaya as a bargain, hoping to make a profit. But the natives, being immune to mosquitoes, wouldn't have them at any price. Some of the younger girls had cut them up to wear as garments, but the idea hadn't caught on. Yes. He'd be glad to be rid of his mosquito nets.

Acton asked about fresh water and cooking.

A stream tumbling down the mountain-side later passed through the village, Beekman told him. Water was also collected in tanks. There was heavy rain during the present season, the north-west monsoon, November to March, generally one heavy shower a day at least. Sometimes there was bad weather also, when—"the wind he blow very strong," as he expressed it. As for cooking, washing and the usual household chores, there were—"plenty, plenty womans."

"And food?" Acton asked, beginning to feel slightly out of his depth.

There was no trouble on that score, the Dutchman assured him. They had fruit and vegetables, coco-nuts, a certain amount of rice, fish, fowls, eggs, flying foxes, and wild birds in profusion, which the natives either snared or netted while roosting at night; wild pig, too. There was bread-fruit, also. Acton must have heard of bread-fruit.

Acton had. He had read of the mutiny in the *Bounty*.

He thanked Beekman. He was profoundly grateful, he told

him. They couldn't have come to a better spot or to anyone more helpful.

But time was moving on. There was much work to be done, and they had to get on with it. Meanwhile, was there anything he could do for Beekman—a bottle of gin or whisky, perhaps, some cigarettes or tobacco, and chocolates and sweets for his wife and children?

The Dutchman's eyes glistened. He became wreathed in smiles. Ten minutes later, when Acton watched him go ashore in the whaler with Mr. Blatchington, he was heavily laden with a borrowed suit-case.

The whaler returned to the ship with the remainder of the *Eurydice's* landing-party, and then went off to sound along the cliff-edge. The men and women swimming round the ship paddled shorewards with shrill good-byes and rejoined the crowd on the beach, which started to disperse with whoops and shouts after the gesticulating Beekman had harangued them. He seemed to have the natives well in hand, Acton noticed.

There was no depth less than three fathoms close in under the shore, the whaler presently reported by signal, and eighteen feet of water was ample for the *Eurydice*. There seemed to be no outlying snags or pinnacles, with depths of ten and twelve fathoms about thirty yards out.

There was much business and bustle on board before Acton finally worked the ship alongside. He thought it wise to keep the pom-pom and Bofors guns manned in case of the sudden arrival of enemy aircraft; but apart from that the starboard anchor had to be lowered underfoot until the third shackle was awash, with a 'spring,' in the shape of a wire hawser, lightly stopped along the cable. In short, the anchor would touch the bottom at a depth of $37\frac{1}{2}$ fathoms and hold soon afterwards. The cable would be veered and the ship sidled shorewards with her engines. When the bows were close enough the cable would be secured, and the end of the spring taken aft and secured also, to prevent the stern of the ship with one of the vulnerable propellers from actually touching the cliff.

It was not an easy or usual manoeuvre at the best of times; but more complicated now because they were short-handed and there was no steam on the capstan. It involved a good deal of shouting, and pulling and hauling, besides playing with the engines; but soon after 1 p.m., in the midst of a veritable cloud-burst of heavy driving rain which ceased as suddenly as it arrived, the ship, with lines to the shore, was safely moored within about eight feet of the ledge of low cliff, its summit practically level with the forecastle. She lay parallel to the shore, forming, as it were, the base of an isosceles triangle of which the cable and the spring formed the two sides and the anchor the apex.

Acton congratulated himself. He felt that not even Pomeroy could have done it much better. The men were sent to a belated midday meal, very much of a picnic meal since the ship's galley was out of action and all cooking had to be done in the wardroom galley in the after superstructure.

A gang of cheerful islanders was already cutting scrub and bush along the edge of the cliff and piling it into heaps. A broad gang-plank was improvised from the forecastle to the shore, and presently Beekman arrived with another party bringing all the netting he could find. It was in short lengths, he explained, though probably sufficient for what was needed.

McInnes, who had already been told of the arrangements for the wounded, came up to inquire when they should be landed. He was introduced to the Dutchman. Of the nineteen, he said, eight, including the three most serious cases, would have to be carried. Ten others would be able to walk with help if they took it easy, and he proposed leaving the sub-lieutenant behind. Farnworth would have to wear his left arm in a sling for a day or two; but was able to do a job of work and was anxious to help.

"Can we send the wounded now?" Acton asked Beekman.

"Yes, captain. I have arrange. Some in my house. Some in other houses. I go with them, show the way. Anything you take, my boys carry."

Acton watched the wounded carried ashore, and talked to Melton and to all of them who weren't beyond the stage of being spoken to.

"Hurry up and get well," he said to the navigator. "We're desperately hard up for officers, and we've a hell of a lot to do."

"You're telling me!" Melton said. "But the devil of it is Pills says I shan't be fit for a week or ten days. You can bet your life I'll be up and around as soon as I can make it."

"I know," Acton said. "But cheer up! This Dutchman seems

76

all out to do his best for us, and it's a mercy we found him here. I'll be along to see you later; but as you can hobble you might keep a fatherly eye on the sailors."

Melton laughed. "They'll need it," he returned. "I know what went on this morning. Bevies and bevies of beauty, apparently. I shudder to think of what may happen."

The tale of the torchlight procession and of the girls swimming out to the ship had been bruited around. Indeed, no one on board could have avoided hearing the noise.

"*Toujours la politesse*," Acton said.

"Provided it stops at *politesse*," Melton returned.

Considering all things, most of the wounded were wonderfully cheerful, smoking cigarettes and joking, wanting to know what sort of a place this was they had been brought to.

"Is this the human paradise you see in the films, sir; humming-birds and parrots and palm trees around a blue lagoon?" asked a heavily bandaged able seaman. "Do the gals here wear them grass skirts and dance the hula-hula?"

Acton didn't like to say that some of the girls he had seen in the water wore nothing at all. Able Seamen Coggins, who was a married man, must be left to find that out for himself —when he recovered. "The natives are very friendly," Acton said. "You'll be properly looked after, Coggins, and get plenty to eat, with all the home comforts."

"With a nice little bit of brown-skinned fluff to hold my hand when I'm feeling lonesome, sir?"

"I wouldn't know, Coggins. But mind you behave yourself."

"That's all right, Mister Acton. My old woman's broad-minded."

Sailors being what they were, there would have to be a good deal of broad-mindedness in many different directions if they ever got out of this place alive, Acton realised.

With the wireless-room apparently wrecked beyond repair and all the instruments destroyed they were completely out of touch with the outside world, except in so far that they had private radio sets with which they could listen to outside broadcasts. But they couldn't transmit. Outside the island no one could know what had happened to the *Eurydice* beyond the fact that she had last been seen in action and had disappeared. Nobody would be aware of the killed and wounded, or that anyone had survived. Acton could imagine one of those laconic, carefully-worded communiques beginning: 'The Admiralty regret to announce the loss of His Majesty's ship *Eurydice* in action,' followed by a few sparse details and ending: 'The next of kin have been informed.' Probably all the names of the officers and men would eventually be listed, among a number of others, as—'Missing. Presumed killed.'

As Acton saw it there were only two alternatives. If the Japanese discovered the *Eurydice*'s arrival, as they might well do through spies or aircraft reconnaissance, it was more than likely that they would send a ship or ships to make prisoners of the survivors when they had nothing better to do. In that event Acton was fully determined to fight to the last round of ammunition and to destroy his ship. If the enemy did not appear, he and all his men might be condemned to living in this place in the midst of a native population until the end of a war which had only just started and might last for years. How would the sailors respond to that, he wondered? There were no really bad characters among them; but with the free-and-easiness of the natives he'd have a pretty tough time in maintaining some sort of law and order without harshness.

Either prospect seemed dismal. He missed Pomeroy. He suddenly felt his responsibility as frightening.

Until sundown they laboured at trying to make the ship inconspicuous. A party on stages over the ship's side smeared the light grey hull with irregular streaks of darker grey and dirty white and blue. Sizeable trees with good foliage, cut down and dragged on board by gangs of yelling natives, were lashed to the funnels and to the superstructures forward and aft, which were later daubed over with dark and light green. Beekman's fishing nets were stretched well up over most of the deck and scattered with greenery to conceal the outline of the ship and to hide her 4.7's and torpedo-tubes from the air while still allowing them to be fired. Even the pom-pom and the Bofors guns, with the searchlight platform, were partly shrouded in greenery, though not enough to impede their use.

All hands, including the natives, worked with a will, though not everything was completed by sunset when they knocked off for the night. A little earlier Acton and Farnworth had gone off half a mile along the beach to see what the *Eurydice* looked like at that distance. She was certainly a peculiar sight.

"Top part's pretty good on the whole," said Acton, eyeing

her critically. "I like the trees, though I think we'd better build up the green stuff a bit between the after end of the bridge and the foremost funnel. What d'you think Sub?"

"I think the trees and greenery are going to wither after a day or two."

"Then we'll just have to renew them," Acton returned. "But I don't much care for the hull. One can still see the shape of the bow and stern. They're unmistakable."

Farnworth suggested they might try blurring the outline by draping more fishing net over both ends of the ship.

Yes. They might get busy about that in the morning, Acton agreed. However, the camouflage wasn't so bad as a first effort. "How's that arm of yours?" he asked as they started to walk back.

"It's really nothing," the sub protested. "Pills is making a fuss, that's all."

"You're fit for duty?"

"Perfectly."

"Then as I'm sort of acting captain now, you'll take on first lieutenant till Melton's fit again. There's plenty to be done."

"Of course," Farnworth nodded. "I'll do my best."

Acton proceeded to give him orders.

From tomorrow, he said, all officers and men who had khaki should wear it, and there must be no white cap-covers. White was far too conspicuous. Those who didn't possess khaki shirts and shorts, must wear overalls or blues until they could dye their whites.

"What with?" the sub asked.

"Coffee," Acton told him. "But we might see what Beekman can produce in the way of clothing. Anyhow, no whites."

Then as regards the arrangements for the night, the ship must be properly darkened. An officer must be on deck all through the night. The sub and the Gunner could split the time until 4 a.m. when he, Acton, would take over. The ship's company should also be divided into three, with sufficient men on the alert to keep a look-out and others ready to man one 4.7 and the pom-pom if required. A sentry with a rifle was to be posted on the bridge. They would go to general quarters before dawn, and keep all anti-aircraft guns manned from then until dark as a matter of routine.

"Are you expecting anything?" the sub queried.

79

Not necessarily, Acton said, though if any enemy ship did come with the idea of landing men she'd probably arrive at first daylight. The Japanese aircraft were what he really had on his mind, and they might be inquisitive at any time during daylight.

"When we've fixed up everything else," Acton continued, "I intend to land all the Bofors and their ammunition and to mount them ashore in gun-pits. The pom-poms and two four-sevens are more than we'll be able to handle. Then I want men detailed for our forty-eight rifles, equipment ready, and ammunition taken ashore. The same for the Lewis guns and those Stens of the Gunner's. When we've got properly organized, we'll have some of the ship's company living on board and some ashore, taking turn and turn about. Is there anything I've forgotten?"

"We've still got eight torpedoes," Farnworth prompted.

Yes, said Acton, he hadn't forgotten them. He'd consult the Gunner; but it was his idea that the torpedo-tubes should be kept trained out to cover the approaches in case any enemy ships did arrive. Then they might also do something with the depth charges if the Gunner could improvise some method of exploding them electrically. Perhaps they could lay them as mines off the beach. It was worth thinking about.

"Well, that's about enough for the time being, Sub," he went on to say. "I'll leave the details to you. Come to me if you're in any difficulty. Any questions?"

"None at present," Farnworth replied.

"Then I'm going to see how they're looking after our wounded in the village. Oh! There's one more thing. Get busy with the cooks and see the ship's company get a really decent meal tonight. Beekman, that Dutchman, has already sent down baskets of fruit and eggs and fowls, so see it's served out."

"I will."

"And I've already told off Petty Officer Hartopp as Acting Coxswain," Acton said. "You can tell him from me to whack out an extra issue of rum with the men's suppers. They've had one hell of a time, poor chaps. So we'll splice the mainbrace and damn the consequences!"

10

As HAS been said, the island was really an extinct volcano, the old crater having been filled in in the process of time by soil washed down by the torrential rains from the surrounding circle of hills. The only opening lay to the southward, where the valley ran down to the beach.

The village, when Acton came upon it, was much like others he had seen in the Dutch East Indies—a collection of palm huts of all sizes built on piles, with tall, steeply-pointed thatched roofs set in the midst of a wide clearing between two rounded hills covered with thick bush and forest. Every available foot of ground seemed to be under intensive cultivation. There were palms and fruit trees in abundance, with clumps of feathery bamboo, flowering trees and exotic shrubs. The torrid, stagnant air was filled with the heavy scent of sandalwood, cinnamon, blossom, wood smoke, moist earth, and tropical vegetation. A little stream meandered through the valley, and inland, beyond the huts, he could see the dull sheen of flooded paddy-fields.

Scrupulously clean and tidy, the village was thronged with women and girls, some squatting over braziers in the open cooking an evening meal, others crooning to themselves as they pounded some white, sticky-looking substance in large wooden bowls. Still more, the younger girls were busily at work with what looked like net-making with twisted coco-nut fibre, or weaving mats with thin strips of bamboo. There were many children of all ages; but all the men were old, which probably meant the younger men and boys were still working about the *Eurydice*.

As Acton approached, self-conscious in white tropical shirt and shorts, they eyed him with interested curiosity, smiling, calling to him, chattering among themselves. He smiled back and wished them a good evening in English, which was greeted with giggling and shrill laughter. All their eyes were upon him, and a tribe of children gazed up at him open-mouthed in astonishment as though he were some strange and harmless monster from the sea. There was no doubt of their friendliness, particularly when one sloe-eyed young beauty in a sarong, egged on by one of the elder women, rose to her feet, plucked a scarlet hibiscus blossom from her hair and solemnly tucked it under his shoulder-strap, a gesture which evoked loud applause.

"Eng-leesh-mans," she said coyly, fluttering her long eyelashes. "Eng-leesh-mans."

Greatly embarrassed, Acton thought he was about to be embraced. To avoid that ordeal he produced his case and offered her a cigarette, which the girl smilingly accepted. He flicked on his lighter and held it out, whereupon she drew in her breath and proceeded to cough and to splutter with tears in her eyes. He felt covered in confusion. European cigarettes were evidently an acquired taste and he had done the wrong thing, though the onlookers clapped their hands and rocked with amusement.

Beekman's house, approached by a broad pathway of white shingle beaten flat, lay some two hundred yards from the village at the top of a slight rise. With the centre part two-storied, and single-storied wings added, one of which was evidently the store, it was a white-painted wooden structure with green-shuttered windows thatched throughout with the inevitable palm. It had a wide veranda with chairs and tables, and, like the huts, was raised off the ground on short pillars. At the back were various outhouses and what looked like a large water tank. Acton could hear the dull throbbing of an oil-engine, probably for electric light or pumping.

It was the only European habitation in the place, and Beekman must have had an eye for colour, for the fenced clearing in which the house stood had been converted into a garden aglow with blossom and flowering trees, to few of which Acton could give a name. The dwelling itself and the pillars supporting the veranda dripped with bougainvillea in crimson and in pink, mingled with the mauvish-blue of plumbago and a luxuriant creeper with glossy, heart-shaped leaves and clusters of large, trumpet-shaped flowers of brilliant blue which were, in fact, the convolvuluses known as 'Morning Glory.' It was a lovely setting for the simple life if one preferred loneliness and solitude, though no doubt it had its disadvantages.

Acton went up the veranda steps, and hearing voices rapped on the open door. The matted corridor, he noticed at once, was spotless. A woman wearing a flowered cotton frock appeared from the back premises and came forward to receive him. Though light-skinned she was obviously non-European.

From her apparent age and the fact that she wore a wedding ring he assumed she was Beekman's wife.

"Good evening," he said, saluting. "Could I see our wounded, please?"

She smiled and said something he didn't understand; but beckoned him to come in and went along the passage to open a door on the left.

McInnes presently appeared, looking drawn and utterly exhausted. Madame Beekman excused herself and went off.

"I came to see how the chaps are getting on, Pills, and if there's anything I can do?"

"They're as comfortable as possible," the doctor replied quietly. "But I doubt if two of the worst 'll last out the night. I'm doing all I can, God knows! But . . . well, there it is."

"Which two?"

"Scrimshire and Musters," McInnes said, going off into technical details. Apart from their wounds, both men had been horribly burned.

Acton sighed. Scrimshire and Musters were two of the best A.B.s in the ship. "Would they like to see me?" he asked.

McInnes shook his head. "They wouldn't recognize you, poor chaps! I've had to dope them."

"What about the others?"

"I'd much rather you didn't," the doctor said firmly. "Most of them are asleep. You'd only disturb them. You might look in on Melton. He's in a room by himself; but for the others, Number One, I'd be far happier if you made it tomorrow morning."

Acton agreed. "Is there anything you need from the ship?" he wanted to know.

"Plenty. I want more dressings and bandages and all sorts of other surgical stuff, and a couple of bottles of brandy. I'll give you a list before you go. Oh! And they're clamouring for cigarettes, and if the canteen's not entirely destroyed I can do with all the sweets and chocolate and anything else you can think of to give to the Old Trout and the girls. They're doing a fine job, particularly the old 'un."

The girls already, thought Acton, with some alarm. "Then they're all being properly looked after?" he said.

Short of a regular hospital it couldn't be better, McInnes assured him. The Old Trout, as he called Madame Beekman

83

—and she not a day over thirty-five and neither running to fat nor ill-looking—had arranged everything; turning the furniture out of her best rooms; fixing up beds and providing mosquito nets. It was she who'd insisted on having all the wounded under one roof, with one room for the three really serious cases, two large rooms as wards for the others, and a fourth apartment upstairs for Melton and McInnes himself. Nothing was too much trouble. She was a regular Mother in Israel, with a horde of women and girls in the back premises, cooking, boiling the rather doubtful water, washing the patients and doing all sorts of odd jobs besides helping him. Though not one of them had a word of English, they were intelligent and quick to learn—quiet, unobtrusive and always smiling. Some of the more lightly wounded were already beginning to enjoy themselves.

"Now you go upstairs and see Melton," McInnes said. "Turn right at the top and it's the first door on the right. Don't stay too long. I'll give you my list when you come down. Just knock on this door here."

Acton discovered the navigator, sitting up on a low bed in his pyjamas, eating something out of a bowl with a spoon. Close beside him a girl squatted on her heels on the matting floor near a tray of food in more bowls. Undoubtedly attractive, she looked about seventeen, and wore a bright, flame-coloured sarong which glowed against her tawny skin, a short little white jacket open down the front, a string of scarlet beads and the usual flower in her shining blue-black hair. Like all the other maidens he had seen she was gloriously nubile.

The pair were laughing and trying to learn each other's language when Acton entered. On so short an acquaintance they seemed to be getting on extraordinarily well.

"Hullo, George!" Melton exclaimed, looking rather like a small boy caught stealing jam. "I never expected you. This is Lallah, the eldest daughter of the house. She's looking after me."

Acton was amused.

"Lallah," said the girl, looking up with a smile and pointing at herself. "Lojah!" she added laughing, pointing at Melton.

"She means Roger," Melton explained. "Him—George," he added, pointing at Acton.

"George," Lallah repeated, bowing with her large eyes fixed on the visitor's. "George."

84

Acton grinned and bowed back. The girl rose and went across the room to return with a low stool. She was the hostess, and hospitality must be expected.

"You've been quick enough off the mark," Acton bantered. "I certainly admire your taste, Pilot."

"There's no stopping 'em," the navigator excused himself.

"I'm jealous. Well, I just came along to see how you were."

Lallah motioned him to sit down, re-seated herself on the floor, and proceeded to ladle rice into another small bowl. She added other ingredients, poured sauce on the mixture and handed it to Acton with a spoon. He tasted, and smiled his approval. "What is it?" he inquired.

"Heaven knows," Melton said. "It seems like some sort of chicken, mixed up with coco-nut and mushrooms and something else. You'll have to eat the lot, old boy. She'll be mortally offended if you don't."

Talking to Melton, and telling him of the *Eurydice* and what had been done, he did eat the lot. He was hungry, and the food was delicious. He might even have asked for more had not Lallah half-filled another bowl with a pale amber liquid from a bottle and handed it to him. Acton sipped. The drink, whatever it was, tasted rather insipid.

"That's the local brew," Melton told him. "Coco-nuts, rice or something. Go easy, George. It has a delayed action. A little goes a long way."

Acton, duly warned, drank slowly with Lallah's watchful eyes upon him. When he had finished she reached for the bottle and tried to refill his bowl. He excused himself as politely as he could. "I must be going," he said, rising. "I've got a lot to do on board. I'll be here again tomorrow. Is there anything you want, Pilot?"

"Something to read, George."

"Some of the sub's thrillers, or what?"

"Good God, no! You'll find Homer's *Odyssey* and Plato's *Republic* in my cabin bookshelf."

"Nothing else?"

"Half a dozen cakes of soap, cigarettes, and two more suits of pyjamas. I think I've got everything else."

"All right," said Acton, moving towards the door. "I'll be seeing you."

Lallah rose and accompanied him, bowing and smiling as he

left the room. She had perfect manners and was altogether too attractive. If all the other girls were like her he wondered again how long it would be before most of the ship's company became lovesick and demoralized. The island seemed to be a veritable Arcadia.

But what would be the reaction of these friendly people if the Japanese did arrive? That was his chief anxiety, and one that was rather alarming.

He knocked on the door near the foot of the stairs. McInnes came out and gave him the list of what he needed, which was fairly comprehensive.

"D'you want this lot this evening, Pills?"

"No. Tomorrow'll do," said the doctor wearily.

"And look after yourself," Acton said. "It'll never do if you crack up. Can't you get some sleep tonight?"

"Easier said than done, George."

"Is Beekman about?"

"I haven't seen him lately. Why?"

"He knows English. When he returns why not ask him to arrange for some of the women to look out during the night? They could call you if anything happens."

McInnes seemed doubtful.

"Would you like me to send you two or three sailors?"

But the doctor shook his head. He said he could manage somehow.

Beekman was on board the *Eurydice* being entertained in the wardroom by the Gunner when Acton returned. "I want to thank you for all the arrangements you and your wife have made for our wounded," the first lieutenant said. "You've been most kind and helpful."

The Dutchman shrugged his shoulders and said it was nothing.

"There's one thing I particularly want to know, though," Acton continued. "Are you quite sure that this is the only possible landing-place in the island?"

"Nowhere else possible," Beekman said. "I been here long, long time, captain. I know whole place. All other places," and he described a circle with his hands, "much coral, no good for boat, and always wave," moving a hand up and down. "The land, too, what you call, like this?" and his hand was held vertical.

"You mean steep?" Acton asked. "Cliffs?"

"You look," the Dutchman replied, producing a stub of pencil. "You have paper?"

A signal-pad was forthcoming and Beekman drew what looked like a horseshoe, with its narrow opening at the bottom. That, he explained, was all cliff, as Acton already thought. Beekman proceeded to surround the horseshoe with a jagged zigzag showing coral reefs, and inside it put some shading representing hills.

"Here the beach," he added, dotting a line between the two prongs of the horseshoe. "Here the village, and here," pointing to the blank space in the centre, "we use for grow things. This place only, here, we can use for boat," drawing an arrow-head.

His rough sketch, slightly embellished, made it amply clear.

Acton was undecided whether to reopen with Beekman the subject which was uppermost in his mind. One thing that was perfectly clear was if the *Eurydice's* people were to be here for some considerable time they must rely very largely upon the local goodwill and co-operation. But if the Japanese did come, it was his clear duty and firm intention to fight. After all, the Dutch were also at war, and if the *Eurydice* had been a Dutch ship her captain wouldn't hesitate to act precisely as he intended to do.

But how far did these simple, friendly people owe any real allegiance to the Dutch? What would be Beekman's attitude, and that of the inhabitants, if the enemy did put in an appearance? He'd already mentioned it. Moreover, Beekman was aware why the ship had been camouflaged, and that some of the light guns were to be landed. He'd raised no objections. Perhaps he hadn't fully realized all the implications.

Of course it was quite on the cards that the enemy wouldn't trouble their heads about an unimportant island which could be of no possible use to them. They must have more than enough on their hands already. But if they did tumble to the fact that a damaged ship had arrived there, they might spare a cruiser or a destroyer to capture any survivors. In that case Acton must fight, and this inevitably meant retaliation— retaliation in the shape of a probable landing preceded and covered by aircraft attack and bombardment from the sea.

The results of that would be terrible for the inhabitants. And apart from the loss of life and devastation, they would inevitably have it fixed in their minds that the arrival of the *Eurydice* was the cause of all their misery. Undoubtedly they would panic. Away would go their willing co-operation.

It was all very worrying; but the only possible alternative was surrender, which was absolutely unthinkable.

Acton was tired, almost dropping with fatigue; too incapable of consecutive thought to discuss the matter tonight. He needed sleep. He would postpone all talk on the subject for the time being. An opportunity would come later when they had settled down to their new way of life, and much still remained to be organised.

There was one piece of news which pleased him. The petty officer telegraphist, one Scriven, had managed to repair an auxiliary wireless set. Apart from the private radio sets in the ship with which they could pick up voice broadcasts from outside, they would now be able to intercept naval messages over short distances. All they would need was an aerial, which could be made inconspicuous.

"What distance?" Acton asked.

"Seventy or eighty miles, sir. Maybe more."

"Good work, Scriven."

"And I think I'll be able to fix it up so we can transmit, sir."

"Not on your life!" Acton warned him. "Don't touch a wireless key without direct orders from me, Scriven! No transmitting, otherwise we'll be picked up by R.D.F.* for a dead snip and have the Japs buzzing round in next to no time!"

Scriven understood.

The night passed without incident, and at 5 a.m. when Acton, greatly rested, went on deck to relieve the sub-lieutenant, the moon, out of sight behind the land, must have been on the point of setting. It had become intensely dark, though the stars were still brilliant in the deep blue velvet of the sky.

Later, with the first glimmers of dawn to the eastward, came the frenzied screeching and squawking of the birds. One tuneless songster, with a voice like the braying of a trombone, must have its home in a tree within fifty yards of where the *Eurydice* lay.

At daylight two men were sent up to Beekman's house with

* Radio Direction Finding.

packages containing the things needed by McInnes and Melton. They returned with the depressing news that Able Seamen Scrimshire and Musters had died within an hour of each other during the night.

The men not on watch were called at seven o'clock, when the word was again passed that neither whites nor white caps were to be worn on deck.

Presently Jevons appeared with Acton's morning cup of tea, while the crews of the pom-pom and Bofors guns, who had manned their weapons at first daylight, were smoking cigarettes, laughing and chattering. The steward was about to say something, and was in the act of handing the tea, when Acton, gazing round the sky over the trees to the westward, stopped him with a hurried gesture. He could have sworn that he had heard something.

"Silence at those guns!" he shouted. The men looked at him in astonishment. Their talk died away. Then they, too, turned their eyes skywards.

Acton listened. Yes. He was not mistaken. It was the steady drone of an aircraft, which gradually became louder.

At first he could see nothing; but then a man on the pom-pom platform yelled excitedly and pointed. There was no camouflage netting over the anti-aircraft gun positions.

Then Acton saw it, flying at about five thousand feet, heading directly for the island, and looking like a transparent midge against the blue of the sky. His heart pounding, he shouted orders to the guns. Their muzzles were cocked up. Through his binoculars he saw it was a floatplane, probably catapulted from some ship. But what ship?

It was gradually losing height, coming down in a long glide. It banked over, and the sun shone momentarily on the underside of one wing. He had a glimpse of a scarlet disc— Japanese!

He yelled more orders to the guns. "Stand by! Don't open fire till I tell you!"

Jevons had disappeared. Mr. Blatchington, clad in nothing more than a bath-towel and bedroom slippers, and his face still lathered, came rushing forward past the torpedo-tubes, closely followed by the sub-lieutenant in a red silk dressing-gown over bottle-green silk pyjamas.

The plane was perhaps a mile away, and still coming down

in a slant. If it held its course it would just skim over the tops of the trees. It presented an end-on target.

It was all very quick and breathlessly exciting; but Acton still had time to wonder what had brought the aircraft here. Was it mere curiosity, or had the *Eurydice* been spotted? One thing was certain enough, and it made him sick to think of it; if he opened fire and the plane escaped, the *Eurydice's* days were numbered.

Ten seconds . . . and it was within a thousand yards. They could hear the whistling as it dived with propellers idling; then the roar as the engines cut in again and the machine flattened out. . . . Six hundred yards!

He could see the sun glinting on the perspex dome over the cockpit, and behind it could imagine the grinning faces of the pilot and observer.

He shouted orders to open fire.

The pom-pom broke into its deliberate, deafening stutter, to be followed at once by the sharper and more rapid note of the Bofors. Some enthusiast even opened fire from forward with a Lewis gun.

A stream of coloured tracer hurtled up towards the aircraft. It seemed to jerk upwards, as though the pilot, suddenly aware that he was being fired upon, was trying to turn. Then it flattened out again, and screamed on.

Three hundred yards . . . two hundred . . . it was at point-blank range.

Acton, his nerves tense, heard himself muttering. "For God's sake, you bloody fools! Hit the damned thing! Hit it! You can't miss!" The tracer seemed to be sailing harmlessly off into the sky far beyond the target.

Then, quite suddenly, he saw a little puff of greyish smoke and a burst of red flame. Something became detached from the plane and fell clear, turning over and over in the air. He couldn't see what it was. Before he had time to draw another breath the flame expanded, and in another instant, as the plane roared a hundred feet overhead, it was flaring like a comet with a plume of brilliant orange fire ending in a trail of thick black smoke.

He could hardly believe his eyes when it splashed into the sea on the other side of the little bay, and then, lifting again, just cleared the top of the cliff and crashed into the wooded hill above. He heard the rending impact, and the boom of a heavy explosion. A great gout of bright red flame blazed skywards—then a cloud of rolling black smoke.

The men on deck in the *Eurydice*, beside themselves with excitement, burst into wild cheering. People from the village, already streaming down to the beach, were gazing at the burning wreckage.

"That'll learn the bloody bastards!" Petty Officer Hartopp growled in Mr. Blatchington's ear, his voice full of venom.

"Reckon they were flying with the sun in their eyes not knowing we were here," the Gunner replied. "Silly sort o' way to carry on, if you ask me. Just stooging around taking everything for granted, the damned fools! Anyhow, that's one Jap plane the less for having the impertinence to interrupt my morning shave."

He re-hitched the towel round his waist and walked aft with dignity, his bedroom slippers flapping on the deck.

He was a deep-chested, very hairy little man with enormous muscles rather running to fat. It was by no means fit and proper, he thought, that he should be compelled to appear before the ship's company in a state of partial nudity with his face covered in lather. They'd be making ribald remarks next, probably calling him the Wild Man from Borneo!

Ammunition in the burning plane began to explode. They could hear it popping like fire-crackers. It was not for over an hour that the flames finally flickered out and died away, to leave the bush and undergrowth still smouldering.

What *had* brought the plane here, Acton wondered again?

It was a float-plane of the sort used for reconnaissance and artillery observation, a slower machine than any fighter. It might perhaps carry a bomb or two and a couple of machine-guns; but no one but a lunatic would risk running into close-range A.A. fire in such an aircraft. The assumption therefore was that the pilot knew nothing of the *Eurydice's* presence, and for some reason or another, possibly because of engine or other trouble, had been trying to land in the sheltered water of the bay when surprised and shot down. There could be no other explanation, Acton thought, going on to ask himself from what distance the pom-pom shell-bursts and the black smoke might have been seen.

He went ashore, and walked up through the bush and trees

to a little knoll from where he had a view of the horizon to the eastward. The day was clear with full visibility, something over twenty miles. To his infinite relief there was no vestige of anything that mattered—no sign of a ship, no smudge of smoke. All that was to be seen was the dim blue shape of the island they had passed during the night before their arrival.

The wreckage was not cool enough to be examined until late in the afternoon. The aircraft, after colliding with a tree and nearly severing it, had apparently shorn off one wing, disintegrated and plunged to the ground, burying both engines deep in the spongy soil after spraying blazing petrol over a wide area. The place was littered with burnt and twisted debris, with a tangle of wires and a number of unrecognizable instruments and the remains of two light machine-guns. In among the ruin they came upon the calcined body of one man, little more than a skeleton.

Another body, covered in blood, had been flung clear, to land in the fork of a tree about six feet above ground. In the pockets of the flying suit they came upon a note-book, half-filled with Japanese ideographs which conveyed nothing, together with a handkerchief, a woollen cap, and a small box of white tablets, and a leather wallet. It contained a packet of three letters, some paper money, with some visiting-cards printed in English—'Lieutenant Shunzo Kanesaka. Imperial Japanese Navy.' There was also a small photograph, taken by 'Funakoshi. Artistic Photograph,' with an address at Kure, showing an officer in Japanese naval uniform with a smiling Japanese girl and two small children all in national dress. The identity disc round the neck of the corpse bore a number, some more Japanese lettering, and the name—Lieut. S. Kanesaka, I.J.N.—in English.

All the evidence having been removed, the remains were decently buried.

11

It was more than a fortnight before the arrangements were completed for the defence of the little bay on the south side of the island. Twice during this period all work and movement had to cease—once when a Japanese heavy cruiser and four destroyers steaming eastward at high speed passed the island within three miles; and on the second occasion when a flight of six bombers roared about four thousand feet overhead.

However, in close consultation with Draycott, Farnworth, Mr. Blatchington and Melton, who was still on the sick list, Acton had done all he could. The four Bofors guns, taken ashore with their ammunition, had been mounted in camouflaged gun-pits, well separated, sited among the trees above high-water mark and overlooking the beach and landing-place. A hutted camp, hurriedly built of the usual palm by the natives, was established near-by for the guns' crews and two dozen men armed with Sten guns or rifles. In the ship herself there remained the pom-pom and the two after 4.7's, for which latter all the ammunition for the damaged guns had been brought aft from the forward magazines.

The main defence lay in the *Eurydice* herself with her guns and torpedo-tubes. Even so it was no more than a makeshift defence useful only against a landing actually in progress from a ship close inshore, while to be in any way effective fire could not be opened until the enemy were in their boats and on their way to the beach. It afforded little safeguard against any really determined attack by aircraft, and none whatever against bombardment from the sea if the firing ship lay beyond the effective range or out of sight of the *Eurydice's* 4.7's.

A look-out station, manned by two seamen, was established at the southern end of the cliff alongside which the *Eurydice* lay. It gave a clear view from about north-west, through south, to about east; but here again, as in the case of communication between the ship and the Bofors guns, they were greatly handicapped by the lack of telephones. The loudspeaker on the bridge, normally used for hailing other ships, had been demolished.

It was Mr. Blatchington, that prince of improvisators, who had the idea of using the depth charges.

Beekman, as Acton had noticed, possessed an oil-engine used for pumping and running his own electric light. The machine had been giving trouble. Could Acton do anything about it? Acton could, and referred the matter to the expert, Draycott, who went to Beekman's house to investigate. It was quite a minor defect, easily put right, and one of the engine-room artificers had done the job in a few hours.

"Guns," Draycott had said. "You're our electrical expert. The wiring in the Dutchman's house has gone wrong. It's antediluvian. Could one of your gang go up and have a look at it?"

"I'll go myself," Blatchington said. "We've got to keep the right side o' him, the skipper says. Besides, there are our wounded there."

And go he did, again to discover that the job was an easy one, merely the replacement of a few electric leads, which could be done by one of his leading torpedo-men with stuff from the ship in, as he expressed it, 'two shakes of a duck's backside.'

Mr. Blatchington, naturally inquisitive, had made other discoveries. On inquiring how Beekman obtained the fuel for his oil-engine, he was told that it was normally brought by the little steamer from the mainland once every three or four months.

"But the steamer won't come any more," the gunner pointed out.

That, Beekman replied, didn't much matter. He had accumulated a good reserve of oil. With economy, he had sufficient for a year or more.

"What's it come in?" Blatchington asked.

It arrived in the ordinary steel drums of commerce, the Dutchman said, indicating their size.

"You got any empties, Mister Beekman?"

Beekman nodded. Yes, he said. The Gunner might come and have a look.

So the pair went off to examine the contents of a large hut behind the engine-house. Mr. Blatchington went back to the ship, fully satisfied. He sought out Acton.

"That Dutchman, sir," he said. "He's got between fifty and sixty empty oil-drums he's willing to part with."

"What of it?" Acton returned, thinking of something else.

"They're watertight, sir. They'll float."

"Of course, Guns. What's the big idea?"

"Two or three of 'em lashed together'll probably support one depth charge, Mister Acton. We could try that out by experiment."

"And then?"

"We shackle a depth charge by a wire span ten or twelve feet under each lot of oil-drums, the drums being moored to the bottom off the beach with an ordinary wire and sinker. The depth charges are set to explode at twenty-five feet, and we have a line of four or six of 'em moored off the beach."

"You mean as mines?"

"Yes," the Gunner agreed.

Acton asked the obvious question. "But if the drums are floating, with the depth charges ten or twelve feet below them, how in heck are the depth charges going to explode at twenty-five feet?"

Mr. Blatchington's eyes twinkled. "I've thought of that, sir," he nodded. "On the near approach of the enemy we open fire with the pom-pom or Lewis guns. The drums become punctured and sink, being dragged down by the depth charge. She gets down to twenty-five feet and up she goes, thereby creating alarm and despondency!"

Acton laughed. The Gunner's enthusiasm was infectious. "There may be something in the idea," he admitted.

"I'm damn certain there is, Mister Acton! Can I have your permission to go ahead with experiments? I can lay the things from the whaler."

Acton hesitated. Knowing him well, he had every confidence in the Gunner and his ingenuity. Nevertheless, he had visions of the depth charges slipping away and sinking while being laid, and not only Blatchington, but also the boat's crew and the whaler, being blow sky-high.

"You can try one out, using an equivalent weight instead of the actual depth charge," he said. "Then we'll see how many drums it'll take to float it, and how long it'll take us to sink the lot. If that works, we'll decide whether or not to carry on. But I won't have you taking unnecessary risks, Gunner. Is that clear?"

"Perfectly, sir. And I don't want to make Mrs. Blatchington a widow, you mark my words!"

The Gunner's final experiment with his home-made mine was a roaring success; roaring in every sense of the word. Lest they should be alarmed, and already there had been signs of nervousness at the shooting down of the Japanese plane and the sight of enemy ships and bombers, the villagers had been warned through Beekman to expect a great big bang;

but that, if they chose to go out in their boats after the explosion, they might find many fish. So punctually at ten o'clock one morning, when Mr. Blatchington had laid his device from the whaler and returned to the ship, and the *Eurydice's* marksmen opened fire with Lewis guns and rifles on a bunch of floating oil-drums at a range of about 250 yards, a considerable crowd had collected on the beach. In something less than a minute the target disappeared in a bubbling swirl, and a few seconds later there came the thudding shock as the depth charge exploded.

A great hummock-shaped mound of water rose on the surface, to burst upwards in a heavy plume of greyish-white smoke and spray.

There were loud yells from the natives on the beach, who seemed to think that the display had been arranged for their especial benefit. Before even the heavy ripples caused by the explosion had subsided, five boats had been launched and were pulling lustily seaward. The *Eurydice's* whaler, manned by a volunteer crew with buckets and home-made nets and gaffs, joined in the scramble.

"There, sir!" grinned Mr. Blatchington, highly pleased with himself. "Didn't I tell you?"

"You did, Gunner," Acton agreed. "Fried fish tonight, I hope."

And fish there soon were in plenty, dead or stunned, floating bellies-up on the surface—big fish and little fish, fish of every shape and colour, fish to which nobody but the natives could put a name. The crews of the island boats shouted with excitement. In the confusion one of them capsized, to tip all the occupants into the water; but she was soon righted. The whaler returned well laden.

In the intervals of feasting there was drumming and dancing that night in the village, enlivened by a liberal consumption of the local liquor. Those of the *Eurydice's* ship's company who could be spared were invited to the revel, which was kept up until after midnight.

McInnes with his ukulele, and another of the *Eurydice's* instrumentalists with his accordion, were wildly popular. A wonderful time was had by all, and Acton was wise enough not to try preventing the sailors from enjoying a little innocent relaxation. The eating and drinking took place in the open, and the dancing in the large hut with its matting floor which served as the village meeting-house. It was a strange sight to see the seamen, bedecked with garlands, solemnly teaching the local lovelies to dance the fox-trot. The girls were anything but bashful. What happened outside in the darkness was nobody's business.

The news from the outer world, picked up by radio, had gone from bad to worse. From broadcasts, probably from Australia, they heard that the Japanese were in occupation of Batavia, Bandoeng and Surubaya, and later that the whole of Java was in their hands. The enemy had also landed in New Guinea and the Solomon Islands, though the Allies seemed to be hitting back with their aircraft.

After consulting the other officers, Acton had told the ship's company exactly what was in his mind. For the time being, he said, they were completely cut off from England, and he fully realized their feelings and anxiety as regards their wives and families at home. He hoped, though of course he couldn't say for certain, that as there was no definite evidence of their deaths, their allotments and separation allowances would continue to be paid. They must realize there was nothing he could do about it until they returned to civilization.

As for the war, he continued, it might go on for some time, though there wasn't the least doubt in his mind that the Allies must eventually win, particularly when the Americans really got going. Out here, in the Pacific, almost everything depended upon them. It was quite possible, he thought, that the Japanese might never come to the island, which was only one of scores of others. Unless they discovered the *Eurydice's* presence, there was no particular reason why they should take any interest in it. This meant that they, the *Eurydices*, might be marooned here until the war ended, or until this particular area was reconquered. They must just make the best of it and be patient. He knew it meant discomfort and uncertainty as to the future; but as they'd already seen for themselves, they could never starve. If they did make an attempt to get away in boats, they could only reach enemy-occupied territory, where they'd inevitably be hunted down and either shot out of hand or made prisoners of war. Anything was better than that. They'd probably heard how the Japanese treated their prisoners.

If the enemy did come he intended to fight, which they

already knew. No doubt it would be tough, though no tougher than the fighting they'd already had and the fighting thousands of other people were doing all over the world. It was their job, their duty, to do all the damage they could to the enemy. They couldn't just tamely surrender after destroying the ship.

To that statement the ship's company voiced their approval in no uncertain manner.

That was about all he had to say, Acton told them; but if at any time any of them had suggestions, he'd be glad to hear of them. "We're all in this business together," he ended. "And though we're out of the war for the time being through no fault of our own, there are many worse places than this island. So put a good face on it, and be cheerful. That's all."

The men dispersed and went about their business.

It was after this pep talk that Petty Officer Hartopp sought out Acton in his cabin.

"You'll pardon my interruptin', sir," he said.

"Well, Hartopp. What is it?"

"It's the men sleepin' ashore in those huts they put up, sir."

"What's the matter? Mosquitoes?"

"No, sir," the petty officer said, twiddling his cap. "It's them noises in the jungle."

Acton gazed at him in astonishment. "I thought sailors could sleep through anything," he said. "Come, come, Hartopp, they're not schoolgirls. You don't mean to tell me they're jittery?"

"No, sir. Not that exactly."

"Then what?" Acton asked. "We can't do anything about the birds or the frogs."

It wasn't the birds or the frogs, Hartopp explained, though the flying foxes were enough to give anyone the staggers. Indeed, Acton himself had seen flying foxes hanging head downwards from the branches of trees during the daytime with their wings folded around them, and in the evening flying off in groups to feed on the fruit in the village planta-tions. They were great bats, 'kalong' as the natives called them, with bodies about a foot long and a wing-span of four or five feet. On first acquaintance they were rather frightening, though harmless except to the fruit.

"No, sir," Hartopp said. "'Tisn't neither birds nor bats nor frogs, go makin' thuds like someone was droppin' things.

Then there's a clickin' an' a scrapin' noise the men don't know what to make of, an' the last two nights two men swear blind they heard things creepin' and scratchin' across the matting on the floor of them huts, an' somethin' tryin' to pull off their mosquito nets and blankets!"

Acton laughed outright. Hartopp was so intensely serious.

"Most of what they've been hearing, Hartopp, are the land-crabs. Those things with one big nipper and one little one. You've seen them, surely? They're all over the place."

"Yes, sir. I've seen 'em all right."

The lieutenant explained how the crabs climbed palms to get at the coco-nuts, and the thuds were probably the nuts falling. The clicking sound was made by their nippers, and the scrabbling noise when they were climbing or coming down.

"And they crack coco-nuts with their claws?" Hartopp asked, his eyes full of wonderment.

"That's the idea," Acton said. "They're quite friendly really."

Hartopp was unconvinced. "Hardly friendly," he said. "Not when they tries pullin' the bedclothes off of a man to get at the bloke underneath. If they can crack coco-nuts, what'll they do to a man asleep? How would you like havin' one o' them damned things as a bedmate, sir?"

"I shouldn't," Acton agreed.

"No more should I, sir."

"Then make arrangements for the men ashore to sleep in their hammocks instead of on the floor of their huts," Acton said. "If that doesn't work we'll think up something else. And tell the sailors from me they're not a gang of silly old women to go getting the wind up about noises in the night. Let's have no more of this nonsense. We've got other things to think of besides bats and crabs."

"I'll pass the word, sir," said Hartopp, retiring.

In truth there were more important things to think about, for five days afterwards Petty Officer Telegraphist Scriven reported that at 11 p.m. the night before and again at 3 a.m. that morning he had overheard a voice transmission by radio from somewhere very near at hand. The language wasn't English. It sounded like Japanese, and might have come from one of those walkie-talkie sets.

Acton felt perturbed. "How close?" he asked.

"I can't say for certain, sir; but possibly within two or three miles."

"You mean from this island?"

"Either that or from some ship pretty close, sir."

"How far do these walkie-talkie sets carry?"

"I believe about twenty miles in good conditions," Scriven said.

"And were the messages acknowledged?"

"Not that I heard, sir."

"And you've no means of taking the bearing?"

"No, sir."

"Does anyone else know about this?" Acton asked.

"Only Hargrave, sir."

Hargrave was the leading telegraphist.

"Then tell Hargrave to keep his mouth shut. I don't want all and sundry to discuss it. Meanwhile carry on listening, Scriven. Could you fix me up with a pair of earphones?"

"Easily, sir."

"Then I'll be along at eleven tonight in case he pipes up again."

"Aye aye, sir."

If Scriven was right the news was disturbing enough. Acton disliked it still more when, punctually at 11 p.m., he heard the message for himself. The identical short sentence was twice repeated in a clear, staccato singsong. It seemed like some routine report, and there was no answer. Acton knew no Japanese; but both the voice and the language sounded suspiciously like it.

"It's the same man, sir," Scriven said.

"And where the devil is he?" Acton asked.

"I'm certain it's no ship, sir," Scriven returned. "Besides, no ship would be hanging around two nights running at the same time."

Acton agreed. There were various other islands within twenty or thirty miles, though this by no means ruled out the possibility that the broadcaster might be somewhere on *their* island. In that case he was either Japanese, or someone who knew the language.

Soon after three o'clock next morning Scriven reported that what sounded like the same message had been repeated.

A few hours later, seriously perturbed, Acton went off to

see Beekman. Without disclosing his purpose he asked if the Dutchman knew Japanese. To that Beekman replied that he had learnt no more than a few simple words when in business at Surubaya—before he had migrated to the island. Yes. He might recognize it as against Javanese if he heard it spoken.

"Do you think any of the people here know Japanese?" Acton went on to query.

Beekman very much doubted it. Most of the islanders had lived there all their lives. Before the war a few of the men sometimes visited the mainland in their own boats; but beyond that they had no connection with the outer world.

They went on to talk of other matters. Was Beekman absolutely certain that the beach near the village was the only feasible landing-place? By way of reply the Dutchman went to a cupboard and produced a rolled-up, large-scale map of the island which Acton hadn't seen before. It certainly bore out the contention that except to the southward the whole coast of the island consisted of steep cliff with off-lying snags and reefs of coral.

"And all these," asked Acton, running his finger round the circle of hills surrounding the central cultivated depression. "Are they all covered in thick forest, or are there any clearings?"

Beekman seemed puzzled, and Acton had some difficulty in explaining. It finally came out that some of the natives had a few clearings in the hills where they grew fruit and coco-nuts. They were quite small, as most of what the islanders required in the way of food or building materials was grown in the central depression and the foothills surrounding it. The plantations in the hills were more or less private ventures rarely visited by their owners, though hardly ever since the war as there had been no chance of exporting their surplus produce. There were no regular villages in the hills, nothing but a few isolated palm huts on the clearings. Yes, Beekman said, it might be possible for people to live in the forests without the natives being aware of it; but once again he was absolutely certain that there was no other place than the beach to the southward where people could land from boats. Moreover, if anyone *had* landed there they must pass through or near the village. That meant that they would have been seen by the inhabitants and that Beekman himself would have been informed. The people were always inclined to regard new-comers with suspicion.

"Have you been getting anything on your radio?" Acton went on to ask.

Beekman shook his head. "No," he replied. "I listen only to Surubaya and Batavia, and nothing come for many days. All Sumatra, all Java now Japanese, I think. Things very bad for everybody." His voice sounded mournful, as well it might.

Acton had to be satisfied with that. He already knew that Beekman's was the only radio set in the island, and that the Dutchman had no means of transmitting.

What was at the back of Acton's mind was the possibility that enemy parachutists might have been dropped in the island before the *Eurydice*'s arrival and were now living in some hide-out in the hills and using radio. He discussed it with Melton, who was now off the sick list though still slightly lame.

"There are literally scores of islands, George," the navigator said. "It occurs to me that before the Japs brought their fleet into the Java Sea they might quite well have established wireless stations on some of them."

"You mean to give notice of our fleet movements?"

"Yes. And this place is in a fairly likely position."

"But Scriven says he thinks it's a walkie-talkie with a range of no more than twenty miles," Acton pointed out.

"There are various islands within that distance, George. What Scriven's been hearing may come from any of them."

"But he says he thinks the message may be coming from within two or three miles."

"I don't always trust these wireless experts," Melton said. "Radio does funny things sometimes. I've heard of low-powered radio telephony being picked up over abnormal distances."

"Yes. But what beats me is why the Japs should use a walkie-talkie at all. What use was it likely to be to them in this particular island?"

Melton shrugged his shoulders. "Search me!" he replied. "But they're cunning devils, certainly no fools. No. If they did choose this place, and I must confess I see no particular reason why they should, they'd hardly advertise their intentions beforehand by landing a party over the beach with a high-power set. It would have meant a good deal of heavy gear landed from a ship, wouldn't it?"

"Not necessarily," Acton pointed out. "If it's possible to

parachute field-guns and jeeps, why not a fairly high-power set with its generator, oil-engine, fuel and all the rest of it?"

Melton also had an answer to that. Apart from the few clearings, he pointed out, the hilly part of the island was densely wooded. It was one thing parachuting a handful of men with a walkie-talkie and a few days' food; but a very different matter to drop a larger party with loads of heavy gear which might fall widely separated or become hung up on trees. "I'm not suggesting there *are* Japs here," he added. "All the same, it's not impossible."

"If there are," Acton said, "why the devil have they been left here all this time? What's the big idea? We've been here nearly four weeks."

"Don't ask me, George. There's probably some pretty good reason."

"And what are they living on, for God's sake?"

"I suppose Japs can live on coco-nuts and fruit and land-crabs," the navigator returned. "Beekman says the crabs are quite good eating. Anyhow, if the little blighters managed to exist in the swamps and jungle in Malaya, why not here? They're tough, damn 'em, used to living on a handful of rice and the smell of an oily rag! No three full meals a day and cups of tea every time the bell strikes."

Acton became pensive. "And if they are here," he pointed out, "the odds are they'll know of our arrival. They're bound to have seen that aircraft shot down the other day, or at any rate to have heard the gunfire and seen the tracer. And what about that depth charge we popped off?"

"So what?"

"Well, the next time one of their ships comes within range of that radio of theirs they'll whistle up and let her know we're here, if they've not already done it. What about that cruiser and destroyers which went past some time ago, and those bombers?"

"Always supposing there are Japs here," Melton said.

"I'm wondering if we ought to make certain," Acton replied. "We could send out an armed party with native guides."

"With no guarantee of finding out one way or another," the navigator answered at once. "No, George. Not on your life! It would be simple madness to send our sailors crashing up and down hills and through forests to round up a handful

103

of Japs. Our matloes aren't jungle warriors! They'll get lost and go hallooing to each other and be heard a mile off. Even a couple of Japs lying up with tommy-guns could do a hell of a lot of damage."

Acton nodded in agreement. "I think I'll put on an extra sentry or two at night in case they are here and get up to any monkey tricks," he said.

"That's about all that can be done for the time being," Melton returned. "I only hope no trigger-happy sailor shoots up one of the friendlies. That would be just too bad."

"What about a curfew and confining all the natives to their huts from sunset to sunrise?"

"What a hope!" the navigator laughed. "They stroll about at all hours, particularly the girls. There's nothing they seem to like better than . . . well, call it hobnobbing with the sailors after dark. The sailors aren't exactly backward in coming forward, if it comes to that."

"Damn the girls!" Acton muttered.

"Bless their hearts," Melton said. "They're the life and soul of the party."

"But we must keep some sort of discipline, damn it!"

"If we try running this island under martial law or the Naval Discipline Act there'll be a rebellion," Melton observed. "The sailors'll obey orders, of course. But if we try putting restrictions on the inhabitants they just won't understand and we'll be stirring up trouble."

There was truth in that, Acton realized.

12

THE SEASON of the north-west monsoon was nearly at an end, and it was still muggily warm with the air temperature constant at about 80 degrees. For the past thirty-six hours it had been blowing a gale, with hardly a glimpse of the sun through the masses of low, dark cloud driving down from the horizon, accompanied as often as not by sheets of torrential rain. There was occasional thunder and lightning, with frequent violent squalls which whipped the surface off the water and sent it flying to leeward in clouds of scud.

It was the *Eurydice's* first experience of really bad weather, though, lying well under the lee of the low cliff, with the wind shrieking and roaring overhead, she was tolerably well sheltered. But the surf, breaking furiously on the point to the eastward and along the far end of the beach, so heavily as at times almost to obliterate all view of the shore in masses of wind-flung spume, created a confused swell in the little bight which caused the ship to roll a little, to surge to and fro, and to strain and tug at her moorings. There was no real venom in the movement. The anchor, laid in deep water, showed no signs of dragging. If anything, the ship put more strain on her mooring wires to the shore, which they had taken the precaution of doubling.

The strength of the wind during the fiercer gusts was unbelievable. Walking across the promontory to look out to the westward, Acton and Farnworth could hardly stand against it without holding on to something solid. Palms were bending like bows and shedding their foliage. Trees had lost their branches, and as far as the eye could pierce the layer of dense white spindrift the sea was a riot of leaping breakers. Nearer at hand the great waves curled and toppled and erupted against the outlying reefs of coral with a continual booming thunder, to send their clouds of spray hurtling high over the cliff-edge and driving far inland. The lower slopes of the island were shrouded in salt, drifting mist.

So far as the natives were concerned the weather seemed hardly to trouble them at all, as the rain was warm and the village well sheltered from the wind. Even with the sailors work went on much as usual. Most of them had long since become accustomed to wearing little more than khaki shorts with stockings and shoes. Some, with their bodies tanned brown by the sun, were hardly distinguishable from the islanders. It was only from half an hour before sunset, on McInnes's advice, that Acton insisted upon everyone wearing long trousers and adequate body covering. At dusk and throughout the night the mosquitoes were voracious, and though the natives seemed to be immune, mosquitoes meant malaria to white people.

McInnes was a busy man. Except for two seamen with amputated limbs and another who had been badly burned, most of the wounded had recovered and returned to duty.

For the rest, the sailors as a whole were bursting with rude health, probably due to the forced and rather unpopular regular musters for the administration of quinine and certain unpalatable green tablets, and the rigid standing orders that all drinking water must be boiled. It was difficult always to instil into the minds of some of the men that these and other precautions were really necessary and not mere professional fussiness.

McInnes, too, had gradually become absorbed into the communal life of the village as a sort of ex-officio Medical Officer of Health. He had become greatly loved by the islanders, and after overcoming their native timidity and superstitions treated old and young, men and women, even to the extent of bringing two babies into the world, with more to come. His regular surgery hours in the village, attended at first by a mere dribble and then by a swarm, had become a daily function. Patients came flocking in when his fame as a healer was noised abroad. He found much that was distressful and sadly needed doing. Hookworm; beri-beri in one form or another; and those festering, ulcerating sores known as 'yaws' were more or less endemic and accepted as inevitable. The natives were naturally cleanly; but hygiene in the generally accepted sense of the word was practically unknown. Even the water supply was contaminated, though Beekman had done his best to persuade the people to take a few elementary precautions. But the natives, he said, would have none of them. Their grandfathers and grandmothers had lived content and died in the island, and what was good enough for their ancestors was good enough for them.

McInnes did what he could with Lallah and another of the Beekman daughters, with a couple of men from the ship, acting as his assistants; but much had to be left undone. Meanwhile his supply of medical and surgical stores was dwindling and had to be eked out by what simple nostrums he discovered in Beekman's store and what remained of the stock for the *Eurydice's* wrecked canteen. Aspirin and simple purgatives of the fizzy sort, together with water variously flavoured and coloured, were the basis of many of McInnes's cures. The invalids were happy with their harmless bottles, as had been many of his patients in his practice at home in England.

And the natives were grateful, bringing him gifts in return

—fruit and vegetables and coco-nuts; a necklace of highly-prized sea shells; mats; lengths of home-made material; carved wooden images guaranteed to ensure good luck and everlasting virility; once, a live and indignantly protesting wild sucking-pig captured in the jungle. Their generosity was embarrassing; but, as Beekman was at pains to point out, the donors would have been greatly affronted if their gifts had been refused. They were a kindly, simple people.

Within forty-eight hours the gale blew itself out and the sky cleared. The sea became glassily calm with a long, rolling swell, and except during the usual short, heavy shower in the early afternoon the heat of the brazen sun beat down from a cloudless sky. Layers of mist caused by evaporation from the saturated earth shrouded the summits of the hills towards sundown, and later descended to form a thin clammy fog over the lower parts of the island.

The stream running through the village, swollen by the outflow from the paddy-field and reinforced by scores of other rivulets pouring down the hillsides, had become a rushing torrent. Overflowing its banks it discharged itself over the beach into the sea, to stain the usually clear water a dirty, muddy brown littered with leaves and palm-trash. Seeing the inhabitants wading up to their knees, Acton realized why all their huts were raised off the ground. The hastily-erected hutted camp used by the seamen was flooded and had to be abandoned. Flooded, too, were the gun-pits for the Bofors guns, from which the ammunition had had to be hurriedly removed.

The extensive flooding, Beekman said, was unusual, as were the two days of practically incessant heavy rain which had caused it. Only once or twice had he known such things to happen during all the years he had lived on the island. Some days passed before life returned to normal so far as the sailors were concerned.

It was about a week after the gale that Acton and Draycott went up to see Beekman one morning about some unimportant affair which matters nothing to this story. They found the Dutchman, with the white-haired headman of the village, sitting at a table at the top of the steps leading to his veranda, and squatting on the ground in front of them about twenty natives. They were all men of a certain age, and it was rather

107

noticeable that no women or children were present. Some sort of official business was being transacted, for as the Englishmen watched, Beekman and the headman asked questions and members of the audience replied, sometimes breaking out into excited argument among themselves.

"We'd better ooze away and come back later," Acton said hurriedly, turning away. "We don't want to butt in."

"I wonder what all the palaver's about?" Draycott asked casually. "Some of 'em seem to be getting rather worked up." Indeed, Beekman had sometimes to call for silence.

"I hope to heaven they're not laying complaints against our sailors," Acton replied. "That's the last thing we want to happen."

"Why should they?"

"They may have been too free with the girls, James."

Draycott laughed. "From what I've seen it's rather the other way about," he said. "If you ask me, it's the girls who set the pace, and there are plenty of 'em, heaven knows!"

But the conference, as Beekman later told them, had nothing whatever to do with either girls or sailors. It had to do with a case of theft. A locked shed at the far end of the village used as a storehouse had been broken into and two small sacks of rice removed. Since the rice was communal property, the question was who had stolen it?

"I hope you're not suggesting that any of my men may have taken it?" Acton said at once. "You and your people have been kind enough to give us more food than we really need."

Beekman insisted that he suggested nothing of the sort, though undoubtedly the rice had disappeared.

"What's the weight of the sacks?" Acton inquired.

They varied slightly, Beekman said. On the average they weighed ten kilos apiece—say twenty-two English pounds.

"Easily carried by one man."

"One sack, one man, quite easy," Beekman replied.

"D'you mind if I come and have a look at the place?"

"No. You please come along. You see."

Acton's suspicions were aroused. The islanders obviously wouldn't steal their own property. Why should they?

As for the sailors, conservative about their food, they were already growling about a surfeit of rice, which they considered fit only for dark-skinned heathens. In the wardroom the cooks' first essay of curried land-crab and rice had been voted delicious, with one dissentient—Mr. Blatchington, who said that although he could eat crabs that crawled in the sea, he couldn't stomach the outlandish creatures that climbed trees and ate coco-nuts. Farnworth promptly created a diversion by suggesting that sea-crabs were carnivorous, especially favouring corpses, whereas land-crabs were strictly vegetarian. Observing the look of disgust on the Gunner's face McInnes hastily changed the subject.

Served up to the seamen for their suppers, however, the curried land-crab and rice nearly caused a riot. Voicing their grievance through Petty Officer Hartopp they were given a substitute meal of bully beef and pickles, and were satisfied. Nor on other occasions could the sailors be persuaded to eat flying foxes, which were esteemed by Beekman and rather resembled hare. Acton began to realize that there would be some difficulty in inducing the ship's company to take kindly to an unorthodox diet. The tinned provisions in the *Eurydice* wouldn't last for ever.

But rice, as Acton very well knew, was the staple food of the Japanese. Did the forcible entry into the storehouse mean that Japs were on the island and were running short of food? For more than ten days Scriven had overheard no further spoken radio messages.

The storehouse, which Acton hadn't seen before, lay about a hundred yards away from the village, not far from where the paddy-fields started. It was a fair-sized, single-storied, solidly-built wooden structure with shuttered unglazed windows and a corrugated-iron roof, standing off the ground on the usual wooden piles. A short flight of steps led up to the door, which was secured with a long steel hasp and padlock. Beekman pointed out where the fastening had been wrenched away, which was no very difficult matter.

Inside there was a smooth wooden floor, clean and polished through long use, with piles of the little filled jute sacks carefully stacked up at one end and along one side. As the Dutchman explained in answer to Acton's question, the rice was first boiled in metal cauldrons in the open before the skin of the grain was removed. After being dried in the sun it then was brought into the shed in closely-woven baskets to be winnowed, graded and stored in sacks ready for use. He pointed out a gap where two sacks had been removed from one of the lower tiers, together with a long knife-slash in another sack from which rice had spilled out on to the floor. That must have been done, Beekman observed, to make certain what the sacks contained. A trail of confused, dusty footmarks, which looked like those of bare feet, led across the polished floor from the doorway. They might have been anyone's. There were no other signs, no clues, that Acton could see.

As Beekman said, the loss of forty-four pounds of rice mattered nothing. They had more than enough anyway. What was worrying him was who had taken it, for such a thing had never happened before. "The people," he explained. "They do not like it. They are frightened. They think bad men do this."

"What bad men?" Acton inquired, anxious to know if Beekman had any suspicion that Japanese might be in the island.

"I do not know, Captain. That is what the people say."

"Then what do you intend to do?"

"We have decided. A man shall watch at night."

"Will he be armed?" Acton queried.

"No gun. He shall have a parang," which, as the Englishman knew, was a heavy sheath-knife used for cutting cane.

"You wouldn't like me to put an armed sentry on the place?"

Beekman thought not. Someone who didn't know the language wouldn't be much use.

So they left it at that.

Five nights later, at 1.15 a.m., Able Seaman John Spencer, armed with a Sten gun, was on duty as sentry by the Bofors gun-pits facing the sea, it being his two-hour spell from midnight until 2.0 a.m. There was no moon, and the sky having clouded over it was unusually dark with chilly breaths of air fanning in from the sky. Frankly bored, Spencer had tired of walking his beat and leant against a palm, longing for a cigarette. But smoking was strictly forbidden. There would be the devil to pay if he were caught on duty with a lighted cigarette.

But this sentry business, which he supposed was necessary, was monotonous to the last degree. Nothing ever happened.

There was nothing to look at, nothing to which to listen except the swish of shingle and the lapping of the ripples on the beach, with the nightly twittering and stirring and rustling of birds in the trees and undergrowth, and the occasional scrabbling sounds of land-crabs. Spencer's thoughts were far away—on his wife and two children in his mother-in-law's home at Petersfield, where they had migrated after much of Portsmouth had been burnt or obliterated by German bombers. He had had no news of them for nearly two months. And now he was stuck on this accursed island for an indefinite period, heaven only knew when he would hear from them again. Well, there were worse places than the island; as Mr. Acton had said when addressing the ship's company. He, Spencer, might even have been dead, like so many of his shipmates. There was always something for which to be thankful.

Whistling softly between his teeth Spencer had resumed his tramp to and fro when he heard a shout from the direction of the village. He stopped in his tracks, listening. Then came a scream, followed by a short, quick burst of fire from what sounded like a light machine-gun. There was a moment's silence, and then the confused hubbub of many voices as the villagers streamed out of their huts.

The sentry's orders were precise. He was in no circumstances to leave his post; not to open fire unless he was approached and his challenge ignored, or unless he saw ships or boats approaching or men landing on the beach. His principal duty was to rouse the men sleeping in the camp near-by, who on this particular night were in charge of the sub-lieutenant. Accordingly, Spencer blew his whistle.

The noise from the village increased to a babel. He heard the seamen calling to each other as they left their huts and armed themselves. Then Farnworth's voice, shouting: "Sentry! Sentry!"

"I'm here, sir," Spencer answered.

"What the blazes is going on?" the sub demanded, approaching.

"Did you hear the shooting, sir?"

"No. What shooting?"

"In the village, sir. I heard shots, sir, and then this rampage. It sounds like. . . ."

Farnworth didn't stop to listen. Hastily collecting four sailors

111

he disappeared in the direction of the village, to find it deserted except for a few women and children chattering outside their huts. It was very dark, but running on with his men at his heels he saw the glare of flaming torches beyond. A crowd of people, men and women, were gathered outside the storehouse. They were in a ferment of excitement, and he heard the buzz of angry conversation. In the flickering light he saw brown faces distorted with fury. Some of the men carried parangs or bludgeons. The throng made way as the armed party arrived, and Farnworth saw Beekman, in pyjamas and rubber boots, kneeling beside the body of a man lying at the foot of the steps leading up to the doorway.

"What's happened?" he asked breathlessly, flicking on the electric torch which he always carried at night.

Beekman looked up. "This man our watchman," he said. "He have been shot. You see?"

Farnworth did see—four or five neat little purple-ringed, blood-oozing punctures in the man's bare brown chest and stomach. His eyes were closed.

"Is he dead?" he asked.

"I think dead," Beekman replied. "I think no breath."

The sub-lieutenant turned to the nearest of the sailors. "Clarke," he said. "Give me your gun. Go to the ship as quickly as you can. Tell the doctor he's wanted here at once, and inform the captain there's been shooting! As fast as you can, Clarke. This chap's life may depend on it!"

The A.B. handed over his weapon and disappeared.

"I think something else happen," Beekman said.

A blood-stained parang lay on the ground close beside the body, and about two feet away was a patch of blood. Using his torch Farnworth saw a trail of blood-stains leading off into the darkness.

The assailant, whoever he was, must be badly wounded, and from the look of it couldn't have gone far. There were no signs of his gun, which probably meant he was still armed.

Farnworth had been fully briefed as to the possibility of some Japanese being on the island, and the previous raid on the storehouse seemed rather to confirm it. They were probably hard up for food. Added to that, none of the islanders had firearms so far as he knew. The chances were that the killer was a Jap.

The sub didn't stop to calculate the risk. He *must* get that man before he managed to escape, though for all he knew the fellow might not be alone. It was useless to delay the pursuit until daylight. He had three seamen with Sten guns—four men counting himself. They should be able to put up a pretty good show even if they did run into trouble.

It was not without a feeling of queasiness that he slung the weapon over one shoulder and told the three sailors to come with him—one beside him, and the others close behind. "Have your guns ready," he said. "But for God's sake don't shoot me! All set?"

"All ready, sir."

"Then come on. If anything happens, lie down."

He moved off, stooping, following the trail of blood with his torch, shielded with his fingers over the reflector. Though the night was very dark the stains were not difficult to follow. They led along a track of dry, trodden mud on one bank of the stream leading to the paddy-fields. About fifty yards on they came across a patch of blood where their quarry had apparently rested. After stopping for a moment to examine it Farnworth led cautiously on.

Before long he saw the dull sheen of the flooded paddy-fields on the right, and to the left what looked like a patch of thick reeds or bamboo. He could hear the soughing of the breeze through the foliage, and felt the excited pounding of his own heart. "Keep your eyes skinned, Morgan!" he whispered to the seaman beside him.

They crept on for perhaps twenty feet, when Morgan suddenly clutched him by the arm. "Look out, sir!" he hissed. "Get down! I heard something!" He flung himself prone, his head raised, his eyes watchful, his gun ready.

Farnworth had heard it too—a sort of rustling, splashing sound as though someone or something were forcing a way through the reeds, very close on their left front. Switching off his light he instantly dropped to his knees, hastily unslung his weapon and lay down. With a round ready in the breech and his finger on the trigger he waited, listening intently, all his nerves on edge.

He could hear Morgan's heavy breathing beside him, and the whisper of the wind, rising and falling. But the heavy rustling had stopped. It might have been caused by an animal, perhaps one of the wild pig with which the island abounded, though if it had been an animal surely they would have heard it for longer. No. He felt in his bones that something lay hidden, and quite close, in that belt of reeds or bamboo. He had the uneasy feeling that they were being watched.

For how long they waited, hardly daring to breathe, Farnworth never knew. Though it seemed like minutes, it was probably only seconds. He was just about to say something to Morgan when he heard a clicking sound, and saw a dark shadow beside the pathway about fifteen feet ahead which he could have sworn hadn't been there before. It seemed to be moving.

There was no time to think. It all happened in split seconds.

Simultaneously with the spitting reports of a hand machine-gun he saw the little spurts of reddish flame and heard the shrill 'whew—whew—whew' of bullets driving overhead. Morgan opened fire, traversing his gun muzzle from side to side. Farnworth squeezed his trigger and felt the kick of his Sten as it responded. There was a stench of burnt cordite, and amidst the rattle of the shooting the sub thought he heard a scream. Half-blinded by the flashes he could see nothing.

The firing ceased as suddenly as it had started. "Got the bastard!" he heard Morgan grunt, his voice full of fury as he scrambled to his feet and darted forward.

"Careful!" Farnworth shouted, rising. "There may be others!"

The two remaining sailors hadn't fired a shot. Telling them to accompany him and to stand guard, the sub joined Morgan.

There were no other raiders, or, if there had been, they had fled. The man they found lay sprawled face downwards with the upper part of his body on the path and his legs trailing in the ditch. His weapon lay beside him. Switching on his torch Farnworth couldn't restrain a gasp of horror. The back of the man's khaki tunic and trousers were drenched in blood.

Morgan wasn't squeamish. "Let's have a look at him, sir," he growled, reaching down to drag the limp body on to the pathway and to turn it over on its back. "Huh! I thought so," he added gruffly. "He's a Jap all right, sir, and a deader. Gosh! He hasn't half copped it."

Looking down at that hideous yellow face with its high cheek-bones and the lips drawn back in a snarl to show the teeth, Farnworth shuddered. He felt quite sick.

114

"What'll we do now, sir?" Morgan asked.

"I suppose we'd better see if he carries any papers or an identity disc," Farnworth told him.

The able seaman sensed the sub's fastidiousness. "Right, sir," he said. "You leave that to me. Let's have your torch, sir."

Farnworth gladly handed it over and looked away.

"Not a blinkin' thing 'cept a wrist-watch, a handkerchief, an' a spare clip o' cartridges," Morgan said at last, having looked for an identity disc and examined all the man's pockets. "Not even a packet o' fags or a love letter. No name or number on his clothing."

"Then bring his gun and leave him," Farnworth ordered. "We'd better be getting back. They'll be wondering what's happened."

"Shall we put a sentry on the corpse, sir?" the seaman queried. "Supposin' his pals return?"

"We don't know that he had any, Morgan. Anyhow, we can do no more till daylight."

On their way back to the village in the darkness they were suddenly challenged by a loud—"Halt! Who goes there?"

"Friends!" Farnworth shouted.

It was Mr. Blatchington, rather breathless, with another small party of armed seamen. He demanded to know what had been happening. The captain, he said, meaning Acton, had heard the firing and had sent him along in case the sub had run into trouble.

Farnworth explained briefly. "If you go another ten yards along this path you'll find a dead Jap," he said. "He's not a pretty sight. I shouldn't worry if I were you."

"So you got him then."

"We finished him off," the sub explained. "I think he'd have died anyhow. He'd been horribly slashed by that night watchman. Is he dead, by the way?"

"He is, poor devil," the Gunner said, "and the folk in the village are kicking up a fair song and dance about it, specially the females. I reckon they've got the wind up, not knowing what's coming next."

They found Acton, McInnes and more armed seamen in the village, and Farnworth had to tell his story a second time. He exhibited the captured hand machine-gun and ammunition.

The weapon itself, still messy with the blood of its late owner, was of small bore and very light, hardly larger than a pistol. It bore Japanese lettering, with the official chrysanthemum sign which marked it as a government weapon.

"This'll have to be looked into," Acton remarked, his voice serious.

"Meaning what?" Farnworth inquired.

"We'll have to organise a mopping-up party, Sub. There's nothing else for it. The people here are all of a hoo-hah. They're rattled. Confound these bloody Japs!"

13

IT IS not an easy task to plan a mopping-up expedition if the whereabouts of the objective is unknown. The Japanese, for there must be several others apart from the man who had been killed, might be lying up anywhere in the undulating ridge of hills which practically encircled the low-lying, cultivated depression in the centre of the island.

Its most prominent feature was the steep, 650-foot hummock in the north-western corner, though there were other ridges running up to 550 and 500 feet. From what Acton could see with his binoculars, corroborated by Beekman's large-scale map, they were all covered with bush and densely wooded. The map showed the few small clearings the Dutchman had mentioned, with here and there dotted lines indicating tracks through the jungle and forest. But these paths, said Beekman, were rarely used and could not always be relied upon. With the rapid growth of the tropics they soon became choked and tangled with bush and great netted masses of hanging liana almost as thick as a man's arm.

As Acton explained at a conference in the *Eurydice's* ward-room attended by all the officers, something had to be done to round up the Japanese. Since the shooting of the watchman the natives had become more jittery than ever. But how, he asked, were they to set about the task of beating every square yard of some five miles of wooded, hilly country varying in width from a half to a quarter of a mile on the off-chance of discovering a possible Japanese hide-out? Had anyone any ideas of how it should be done, he went on to query, looking first at Melton.

"As I said before, I rather think we're asking for trouble," the navigator replied at once. "It's practically all forest and thick scrub and bush. We can't expect the sailors to be expert jungle fighters, particularly in this heat. It may take days."

"So you're against it, Pilot?"

Melton nodded emphatically. "Yes," he said, "unless we can make a quick job of it with native guides."

Acton looked doubtful. The natives might know their way about the island, he observed; but if nobody had any idea of where the Japs might be, what then? From what he'd seen the islanders were rather easygoing and indolent, by no means the sort of people willingly to run their heads into danger. The Japanese would fight to the death, let there be no doubt about that. "What are your ideas, Chief?" he asked, turning to the engineer officer, always a man of strength and sage counsel. "We'll have to draw on some of your engine-room ratings."

"I agree with the Pilot," Draycott said. "I'm no expert; but it does seem to me that hunting out Japs is like looking for a needle in a haystack. How many d'you think there are?"

"I don't know, Chief; but probably no more than half a dozen."

"Even half a dozen can do a hell of a lot of damage," Draycott remarked. "If we could locate the blighters more or less, well and good. If we can't . . . well . . . honestly, I don't know what to suggest. I agree they ought to be wiped out so that we can feel more or less secure from the land, and to pacify the natives; but beyond that. . . ." He shrugged his shoulders.

"And you, Pills," Acton asked. "What's your medical opinion?"

"I don't like it," McInnes replied without hesitation.

"Meaning malaria, dysentery and so forth?"

"Yes, though if we can do the job inside a day I'm all for it. If it means camping out in the jungle for several nights I'm dead against it. We don't want half the ship's company on the sick list."

Acton agreed. "Any bright ideas from you, Sub?" he went on to ask.

Farnworth thought for a moment before replying. "I think

117

it would be better if we let the Japs come to us," he said. "They've done it twice already, probably because they're hard up for food, and we've wiped out one of them. . . ."

"And they've killed one of the villagers," Acton put in. "We want to guard against that happening again. We can't have the Japs just raiding the village when they feel like it. We'll have the whole place in an uproar. Something's *got* to be done. Any remarks from you, Gunner?"

"I wouldn't mind leading a party to go hunting through the island," Mr. Blatchington said.

"None of us would shirk that," Acton returned. "The question is what good would it be? We'd be hunting blind."

They had borrowed Beekman's map, which was laid out on the table. Melton had been examining it and measuring distances with a pair of dividers. "I've been trying to imagine myself as the O.C. Japs," he said, looking up. "I have a wireless set. . . ."

"Which hasn't been heard for some days," Acton put in.

"Never mind," the navigator said. "I'm in charge of a party of Japs with a portable radio. I've been landed here, no matter how, with orders to transmit at regular intervals. . . ."

"Exactly *why* d'you imagine they've been landed here?" Draycott asked. "What's their job?"

Melton shrugged his shoulders. "All I can think of is that they had orders to establish some sort of a look-out station," he replied. "They must have been here before we arrived."

"In which case it's deuced strange we've seen nothing of them before this; nor, so far as we know, have the natives," the engineer officer put in again. "It doesn't make sense to me."

Melton agreed. "They can only be lying doggo on purpose," he said. "They must know we're here and that they're outnumbered. They merely raided the village because they were short of food."

"The point is we *know* they're here," Acton said. "*Why* they're here doesn't matter a hoot. Go on, Pilot."

"Well, all I was going to say was that if I were landed in charge of a party I'd probably make for high ground with a good all-round view, preferably the top of a hill."

The others agreed.

The highest hill in the island, Melton went on to say, was the 650-foot hummock to the north-west, and the next tallest the 510-foot knoll about a quarter of a mile to the north-east of it.

"Hill Six-Fifty," he said, "is just about a mile from the village as the crow flies, and there's a dip of sorts between it and Hill Five-Ten. To the sou'-west of Six-Fifty is a ridge, Four-Fifty, with another dip in between them, after which the hills run down to Three-Twenty and Two Hundred and less." He indicated the various spots with his pencil. "You can ignore the east side of the island."*

"What are you getting at, Pilot?" Acton asked.

"The Jap that was killed last night, or rather early this morning, was making his way *left* after leaving the village, along a path leaving the paddy-fields on his *right*. That's correct, Sub, isn't it?"

Farnworth agreed.

"Then I think it's a pretty safe bet he was trying to get back to his friends on Hills Six-Fifty, Five-Ten or Four-Fifty," Melton continued. "Personally I'd back Six-Fifty, as probably having the best view."

"So what?" Acton queried.

"I'm just suggesting we needn't waste time beating the whole jungle," Melton said. "Let's concentrate on the three hill-tops to start with, and be blowed to everything else. There must be some sort of a way up to each of them, and I'll bet Beekman could cough up native guides if we really put it to him." He went on to elaborate his plan, recommending that a party of ten or a dozen men, each led by an officer, should make a simultaneous ascent of each of the three hills by the most direct route.

"What time of day d'you suggest the parties should arrive?" Acton asked at once. "I don't fancy letting them loose at night in the bush, so a dawn arrival on each hill's out of the question."

"I agree," Melton nodded. "But if we can get native guides we could move out across the paddy at night, be concentrated at the foot of each hill by dawn, and then start the actual show at daylight."

"And if there are no tracks up the hills, Pilot, what then? We can't hack our way through thick jungle."

Melton was not to be stumped. "The Japs have found a

* See plan on page 6.

119

way to the village from somewhere," he insisted. "If they can come stealing sacks of rice and getting away with them can't we discover how they came and went?"

"But how, for heaven's sake? We're not police dogs! If it comes to that I haven't seen a dog in the village."

"I'll bet there are native trackers if we can get hold of 'em, George. If they can hunt wild pig, why not Japs?"

"Because the Japs are infinitely more dangerous," Acton said.

"Not if we're with the hunters."

"That's true enough. What it boils down to is that we've got to ginger up Beekman into persuading the natives that they've darned well got to help us if we're to mop up the Japs. If they don't, the raids on the village'll continue and more people may be shot up. Is everyone agreed on that?"

Everybody was.

"Right," said Acton. "Then you and I, Pilot, will go along and see Beekman, and the sooner the better."

"That's okay by me," Melton nodded.

Mr. Blatchington cleared his throat. "May I say a word?" he asked.

"Fire away, Guns."

"I've been looking at the map, sir. Unless I'm mistaken these two hills," and he indicated 'Five-Ten' and 'Six-Fifty,' "are in sight of the ship. The range is a bit more than a mile. If the mopping-up party runs into trouble, what's the matter with giving the Nips a dose from 'X' gun and the pom-pom?"

"In other words, covering fire."

"Yes, sir."

"It's worth thinking about if the worst comes to the worst and we're pushed back," Acton replied. "But it's no good using guns unless and until the Japs are definitely located. We can't just go blazing off into the countryside on the off-chance of hitting something. You see that, Guns, don't you?"

"Perfectly, sir. I was only pointing out that the crests of those hills were in easy range if we wanted to open fire."

"I know," said Acton. "And thanks for the idea. You might get on to working out the exact range of both targets in case we need it." He didn't wish to be discouraging; but preferred to pin his chances of success on a surprise assault when once the enemy were located.

Beekman was definitely helpful when Acton and Melton went to see him later in the morning. Yes. He thought he could provide trustworthy guides and trackers. But what about himself? He knew every yard of the island and would gladly accompany the main party. He possessed a shot-gun and an antiquated sporting rifle he sometimes used for shooting pig.

Acton jumped at the idea and thanked him.

"When do you start?" the Dutchman asked.

"We have our preparations to make," Acton said. "We don't want to rush it. What d'you think, Pilot? Shall we aim at leaving the village at 3 a.m. the day after tomorrow?"

Beekman's face showed his disappointment. "No sooner, Captain?" he inquired anxiously. "You see, since that man he been kill, the people much, what you call . . . frighten. Plenty women, and they not like it."

Acton had already sensed the feeling of tension among the villagers. Those he had seen were no longer the merry, carefree, smiling folk he had met before. Their laughter and cheerful chatter had ceased. They seemed gloomy and full of apprehension; wondering, waiting for they knew not what. Even Melton's particular friend, the lively Lallah, was depressed and unhappy. So was Beekman's wife.

Acton explained the difficulties of leaving any earlier, pointing out there would be three parties each of ten or twelve men led by an officer. There were various arrangements to make, routes to be decided upon, and so on.

Melton corroborated.

Beekman seemed to understand, and cheered up a little when Acton reassured him. Extra sentries would be mounted in the village that night and the next, he promised. The people would be well guarded, and could rest in peace. In return, could Beekman ensure that the villagers, men, women and children, kept strictly to their huts between nightfall and sunrise? He wanted no regrettable incidents; nobody shot by mistake.

The Dutchman agreed. He would see to that.

They spent over an hour discussing further details with the map spread out in front of them. It was nearly one o'clock by the time they had finished and the two Englishmen got up to go.

"We must get back to the ship," Acton said. Lunch in the wardroom, which was always at twelve-thirty, must be nearly over.

"No, no, please," Beekman protested, waving them back to their chairs. "You please to eat with me. My wife have make ready."

Acton did his best to refuse. Dutch hospitality was often prolonged, and he was in a fret of impatience with much on his mind. But Beekman was persistent, and Melton, who knew the family well, was nodding and frowning, obviously indicating acceptance.

"Well, thank you very much," Acton surrendered, reseating himself. "It's kind of you."

Beekman disappeared for a moment, and presently Lallah and another of the daughters came out on to the veranda with a tray of bottles and glasses.

Tiffin followed, at which the three men were waited on by the girls. Beekman's wife could be heard in the background, but did not put in an appearance. The meal was a gastronomic treat compared with the food in the wardroom—little slivers of salt fish, with some small shell-fish like oysters, and a salad of young coco-nut buds served as hors-d'oeuvres; followed by curry and rice with all the trimmings; and mangoes as a sweet.

The time was two-fifteen, and coffee was on the table, when they heard clamour from the village. They could see people flocking out of their huts, gesticulating, shouting.

Beekman half rose from his chair, and then, in deference to his guests, sat down again. "I think," he said, "something happen."

The two Englishmen stood up at once.

"Come on, Pilot, we'll be off," Acton said. "Thank you for a very nice lunch," he added to his host. "Please tell Mrs. Beekman how much. . . ."

But Beekman wasn't listening. A man had come running up the pathway. Seeing the group on the veranda he halted at the foot of the steps and broke into a torrent of words, waving his arms, pointing, beside himself with excitement.

Beekman replied. There was some rapid conversation, question and answer. The Dutchman himself was perturbed. "Someone been kill!" he exclaimed hurriedly starting off down the steps. "You come with me?"

Startled, not knowing what to expect, but fearing another islander had been shot, Acton and Melton had no option but to follow.

They passed rapidly through the village, to where a group of chattering natives were clustered outside the headman's hut. In the midst of the circle stood a brown-skinned, muscular fellow, naked except for a loin-cloth and sandals. He had a murderous-looking parang in his belt and a blood-stained cloth in one hand. On the ground at his feet lay a recently severed human head, gruesome and ghastly to gaze upon.

"Good God!" Acton muttered, shuddering with horror. Melton's expression showed his disgust.

Beekman meanwhile was speaking to the man with the parang, who was replying and occasionally pointing away across the paddy-fields. The grinning native seemed very pleased with himself, and his friends with him. The conversation went on interminably. The Dutchman appeared to have forgotten his companions until Melton asked him what had happened. Then the story came out.

It seemed that the previous evening, before sundown, the man, one Paku, set out from the village to cut bamboo near a trail through the jungle in the foothills, over on the far side of the paddy-fields. His chosen spot was no great distance from one possible path leading up to Hill Six-Fifty, Beekman explained. Anyhow, Paku had spent the night in some hide-out of his own in the bush, and started his work soon after daylight. He had made his bamboos into a bundle and was resting after his labour, well hidden in the undergrowth, when he heard something or someone moving along the trail. Peering out, he saw a figure, dressed in khaki and wearing a peaked cap, carrying a gun.

Acton's interest quickened. "Japanese?" he asked, looking at the horrible object at his feet.

Beekman nodded.

"Moving up or down?"

Beekman translated the question, and Paku answered.

"He was coming down, Captain."

"And what happened next?"

It was a grisly deed, done by stealth and cunning in the dank, dim green twilight of the forest.

Recognizing the stranger as an enemy, Paku had crept from his lair and followed, parang in hand, unseen and unheard by his quarry. The Japanese had seemed entirely oblivious to any danger and walked on, smoking a cigarette with his weapon slung over one shoulder. At a place near where the trail twisted the man had stopped to relieve himself. Seizing his opportunity Paku had run up from behind and slashed at his victim with his keen-edged blade. The Japanese had uttered what Beekman called 'a peculiar cry' while stumbling and falling to his knees, desperately wounded. Paku had finished him off, afterwards dragging the body into the undergrowth and hacking off the head to bring back as evidence.

That was all there was to it. Though it meant one Japanese the less it was a gruesome story. Paku and his loin-cloth were still spattered with blood. Acton could hardly bear to look at him.

"Did he bring back the gun?" he asked Beekman.

The Dutchman said something, and the weapon was produced from the headman's hut. Still messy with blood, it was the same pattern of light automatic rifle as that carried by the Japanese killed early that morning. Acton unloaded it and handed it to Beekman.

"You'd better take charge of this," he said. "We don't want any of your people shot by accident." He went on to ask if Paku had examined the corpse; if anything had been discovered in the pockets?

All that had been found were two spare charges for the gun, a packet of cigarettes and a box of matches.

This new development necessitated a change in Acton's plans. Judging from the spot where Paku had killed his man, it was now fairly certain that the Japanese, in unknown strength, were established somewhere near the top of Hill Six-Fifty. By following the jungle trail uphill they would probably find the enemy hide-out, though there was the risk of being ambushed on the way. Native trackers might be able to help there.

Meanwhile the Japanese would be aware that two of their number were missing. What would be their reaction? They would probably come down the jungle trail to find out what had happened, and according to Paku's account of what he had done there must be blood on the trail. The Japs, who weren't fools, would discover this. Searching further, they would discover a headless corpse. What then? The chances were they would revenge themselves by taking reprisals in force against the village, probably that night.

For the hundredth time Acton asked himself if the enemy

could fail to know of the *Eurydice's* arrival. In view of all that had happened it seemed hardly credible. They *must* be aware of it.

"We'll have to get busy at once," he said, after mentioning all these points to Melton. "We *must* send our mopping-up party right away and finish the job by dark, if possible. D'you agree, Pilot?"

The navigator looked at his watch. "It'll be one hell of a rush," he replied. "But I couldn't agree more."

They told Beekman, who understood and asked how soon would they be ready?

In about an hour or an hour and a half, Acton said. And would Beekman come with them, and bring what native trackers he could produce? The man Paku would be useful.

The Dutchman agreed.

The two officers hurried back to the ship to make their arrangements.

They were met by Scriven, the petty officer telegraphist.

"That wireless, sir," he reported. "It's been in use regularly every hour since ten this morning."

"Spoken?" Acton asked.

"Yes, sir. The same voice; but a different message. He talked quicker and sounded urgent, as if he was calling for help."

"Any acknowledgment?"

"No, sir. No reply that I heard."

"You think the speaker had the wind up?"

"Not knowing the lingo, sir, I couldn't say for certain; but it sounded to me like he was properly rattled."

14

THERE had to be some very hurried organization on board the *Eurydice*.

Acton had no pretensions to being anything of a tactical expert. Staking everything on a few Japanese being ensconced somewhere on or near Hill Six-Fifty, his plan was probably too simple to be orthodox. The main consideration was speed, and immediate action, otherwise there might be trouble with the inhabitants.

Melton would be left in charge of the ship in case it became necessary to open fire on certain specified targets if pre-arranged red, white or green Very light signals were used by any of the assaulting parties.

The navigator, disgruntled and somewhat rebellious, raised his voice in protest. Why, he demanded, should he be confined to the ship, thereby missing all the 'fun'?

Acton, backed up by McInnes, had to explain that, having been wounded, Melton was in no fit condition for scrambling up hills through thick bush and jungle. He was still more or less convalescent and under the doctor's orders, so let there be no nonsense about it. The pilot said no more; but if looks could have killed McInnes was a dead man.

Farnworth and a dozen riflemen—Party F.—keeping as far as possible under cover, were to work their way along the undulating ridge to the northward through Hills Two Hundred and Three-Twenty to Hill Four-Fifty. On reaching Four-Fifty they would await the arrival of Mr. Blatchington and another twelve men—Party B.—who would climb that hill from the level ground to the eastward using a track shown on Beekman's large map. Having linked up, F. and B. would await developments. Hill Six-Fifty was no more than about four hundred yards away, and if Acton's party ran into trouble Farnworth and Blatchington must use their own discretion about reinforcing. Yes, said Acton, in answer to Farnworth's natural question, Beekman had promised to provide native guides. They would have been told exactly what was expected of them, so the language difficulty shouldn't arise.

Acton himself would command the assaulting party of twenty men—Party A.—some with rifles and the others with Stens, for the main attack on Hill Six-Fifty. They would use the trail leading up through the foothills from the paddy-fields, and McInnes, with stretcher-bearers, would go with them.

For the rest, there must be no unnecessary noise and no smoking. All hands would carry food for twenty-four hours and must go easy with the contents of their water-bottles, which might have to last for the same time. Since no water-proof sheets were available, they must carry rolled-up oilskins and blankets in case they had to spend the night in the open.

Dress would be khaki shirts and long trousers, no shorts because of mosquitoes, with boots and gaiters. Steel helmets need not be taken. They would only be an encumbrance and an added weight. The men could wear any headgear they pleased provided it wasn't white.

The three parties were well on their way by half-past four, and a little later, with the man Paku ahead and Beekman at his side, Acton was leading his men up the jungle trail to Hill Six-Fifty. The narrow, twisting path was fairly well defined and trodden. According to Paku, it must have been in regular use by the Japanese, probably to replenish their water supply from the stream below.

They came to the spot where Paku had killed his man and the trail was blackened with congealed blood, crawling with flies and insects. The headless corpse still lay sprawled in the undergrowth where the native had dragged it—bloated and hideous, alive with great red ants and with a cloud of flies buzzing over it. A few land-crabs, disturbed in their grisly work, scuttled away to disappear in the undergrowth. It was over-poweringly hot; a damp, stifling, airless heat which was utterly enervating, like the inside of a greenhouse. Mingled with the strong odours of damp earth and decaying vegetation Acton thought he smelt the loathsome stench of something worse.

"I think," said Beekman casually, glancing at the body, "he not stay long. Very soon, all gone."

Sickened, Acton turned away. They resumed the ascent. The jungle was eerie to those who didn't know it. As the ground rose the thinner bush and undergrowth of the foot-hills gave way to patches of thick, spongy moss, and low tree-ferns with their barrel-shaped trunks and spreading foliage. The boles of the taller trees were swathed and twisted around with great woody creepers; some twisted like veritable cables; some gnarled and knotted; others flattened like ribbon. The all-conquering liana drooped down from the branches in thick single tendrils tufted with leaves; hung looped in great festoons from bough to bough; or stretched tightly from tree to tree like the rigging of a ship. On the ground it lay twisted in huge serpentine coils, knotted and entangled in impenetrable masses.

In places, as Beekman had said, the narrow trail was almost choked. Here and there were the unmistakable signs of a way having been hacked through, and quite recently.

In the stagnant air and the deep blue-green shade of the forest Acton had a nightmarish feeling of claustrophobia. Occasional thin shafts of golden sunlight filtered through the dense mass of foliage overhead, sometimes to strike a flash of brilliant colour from a cluster of blossom, or to glint from a bird's wing. Otherwise the sky overhead was practically obscured by the thick green canopy of the tree-tops, mingled with the luxuriant leaves of the liana reaching and growing upwards towards the light. Beneath this horizontal curtain it was dark and uncanny. Surrounded by the fantastic shapes of the trees and the creeping, hanging liana, Acton had the peculiar sensation of being entrapped in some underwater cavern with the tentacles of giant decapods groping on all sides.

The jungle was alive. Birds screeched and twittered. Monkeys, hanging like acrobats, peered down from the tangle aloft and fled, chattering in voices that sounded nearly human. Fearful that the sounds might attract attention, Acton asked Beekman if they were anything unusual. The Dutchman seemed to think not. Noises, he said, went on all the time.

The track led over a little muddy ditch with a trickle of water and then on and up a steeper slope where the ground became clear of jungle or thick undergrowth and the trees were smaller and more widely spaced. Daylight could be seen through their serried trunks ahead. They were nearly at the summit, Acton realized, and on the other side the ridge sloped sharply down to the cliff-edge and the sea.

Paku said something in Beekman's ear.

"I think we stop here," the Dutchman whispered. "Paku he go look. Best make no noise now. Perhaps Japanese near."

Paku, bending low, wearing nothing but khaki shorts, ran silently on, flitting from tree to tree and bush to bush like a brown shadow, stopping every now and then to gaze ahead.

Acton had fully expected to meet some sort of a sentry on the way up. The enemy, if they had their hide-out anywhere near the summit of Hill Six-Fifty, seemed surprisingly casual and incautious. However, the well-trodden trail, the passages cut through the encroaching liana, and, above all, the body lower down, all pointed to the fact that they *did* use that route.

Puzzled, Acton passed the word for the men to come into the open, to spread out, lie down and keep still. Tired and soaked with perspiration the burdened sailors were thankful enough for the respite. Here, at any rate, the air was cool. Many drank from their water-bottles.

"Petty Officer Hartopp!"

"Sir?"

"Warn everyone to go easy with their water. We don't know when we'll get more. And no smoking, Hartopp."

"Aye, aye, sir."

McInnes flung himself down beside Acton. "That damn jungle gave me the creeps!" he said. "What happens next, George?"

"The native's gone on ahead to have a look," Acton said.

"Have we drawn blank?"

"Your guess is as good as mine, Pills. But they *must* be somewhere about here. If they're not—well, we'll have to hunt around until we find 'em."

"With about an hour-and-a-half of daylight left," McInnes grunted. "I don't like the look of the weather if we've got to spend the night in the open."

He was right. Here, near the top of the hill, they could feel the fresh breeze from the westward. The lower sky in the same direction had begun to cloud over with dark, purplish nimbus. The sun would presently be obscured. From the look of it there would be heavy rain before long.

Paku had been gone for nearly ten minutes, and was nowhere in sight. The inaction was beginning to get on Acton's nerves.

"Where on earth's that fellow of yours got to?" he asked Beekman.

"I think soon he come back," was all the Dutchman could reply.

Acton glanced at his wrist-watch. "I'll give him two minutes," he said. "If he's not back by then we'll . . ."

He didn't finish, for at that instant there came the sound of a single shot from somewhere on their left front . . . then three more reports, followed by the stuttering bursts of automatics.

"God!" Acton cried, scrambling to his feet. "That's the sub's party! Come on, Pills. Come on, men!" he shouted. "Keep spread out. Don't get bunched up!"

There came the first drops of heavy rain as he led them off uphill towards the sounds of combat.

The firing died away into single shots. Men could be heard shouting.

Then silence.

Between them Farnworth and Mr. Blatchington had most of the excitement.

Led by their native guides, Parties F. and B. had climbed to the top of the ridge known as Hill Four-Fifty from their two different directions without incident or any great difficulty. There they had joined up and moved to the north-eastern end of the ridge, where the men were halted and told to lie down under cover.

Immediately in front of them the ground sloped gently down to a shallow valley about three hundred yards wide dotted with patches of low scrub and bush, beyond which the slope of Hill Six-Fifty rose steeply to its partially wooded crest. Using his glasses Farnworth could see nothing moving; no signs of Acton's party on the hill opposite.

"Not a darned thing," he observed.

"It's early yet," the Gunner said. "I reckon Number One had the longest job, and the toughest one."

The wind had risen. To the left they could see part of the western coast of the island and the blue-grey sea flecked with white horses.

"It's breezing up," Mr. Blatchington remarked. "And look at those clouds. There'll be some wet shirts before we've finished."

Ten minutes passed . . . a quarter of an hour.

The sub suddenly plucked at Blatchington's arm.

"Guns," he said, pointing. "D'you see that clump of low, dark green bush this side of that little sort of gully coming down the hill opposite—about two-fifty yards from us?"

"You mean that bit o' bush with the cloud shadow passing over it, about two fingers right of the tree?"

"Yes," Farnworth replied, handing over his binoculars. "Take a look through these and tell me if you see anything unusual."

The Gunner, sprawling uncomfortably on his stomach and breathing heavily, put the glasses to his eyes and fiddled with the focusing—"I don't think much of these glasses of yours!" he grumbled after a lengthy scrutiny. "It's like trying to look through a blinkin' jellyfish. What you been doing with 'em, wearing 'em in your bath? What's it I'm supposed to be looking for?"

Farnworth was about to reply when Blatchington spoke again. "Half a mo'!" he exclaimed. "I did see something just then . . . no, damn it, it's gone. . . . No. There she puffs!"

A streamer of white smoke which the sub could see with his naked eye rose over the clump of bush and curled away to leeward, dispersing as it went.

"That's a wood fire, Guns!"

"The Nips cooking their supper!" the Gunner said, handing back the glasses. "Can't be anyone else. What'll we do, rush 'em?"

The excitement had caught on. The men had also seen the smoke and had drawn the inevitable conclusion. They were fingering their weapons, whispering to each other, glancing at their officers, wondering what was to happen next.

For the moment Farnworth was undecided. There were still no signs of the other party on the hill opposite, and he didn't wish to run the risk of hampering Acton's plans by acting prematurely.

The smoke had thinned to a barely perceptible haze when a sailor away on the sub's left suddenly drew his attention to another quarter.

"Sir!" he called, pointing at the crest of Hill Six-Fifty, a good four hundred yards distant. "I saw something moving among those trees on the skyline!"

"A man?" Farnworth demanded, putting up his binoculars.

"I couldn't rightly say, sir. It was just something moving."

Others corroborated the statement.

Farnworth's glasses had a magnification of twelve. In spite of the Gunner's strictures, probably because the Blatchington eyesight wasn't the same as the sub's, every detail on Hill Six-Fifty stood out with amazing clarity. He could even pick out the pink and white blossom on some of the trees and the greyish strands of the creepers coiled round their trunks. They might have been twenty yards distant instead of four hundred.

For a full thirty seconds he saw no signs of any movement. Then, in a flash, as several people exclaimed at once, he had sight of a crouching brown body flickering in and out among the trees. The man ran through a patch of bright sunlight and then flung himself prone and disappeared under cover.

In that fleeting instant Farnworth saw that he wore nothing but khaki shorts, and carried no weapon.

"That fellow's no Jap," he said to the Gunner. "He looks like one of the natives. But what the blazes is he doing dodging about up there?"

"Maybe it's that guide with Number One's party," the Gunner returned. "The chap who killed the Jap and brought back his head."

"You mean Paku, Guns."

"Aye, that's it."

"But if we saw the smoke why hasn't he?" Farnworth asked.

"Maybe he will in a minute," Mr. Blatchington said. "That's to say if he *is* Number One's guide. Perhaps he isn't."

Farnworth made up his mind. "We won't wait any longer," he decided. "Something's making that smoke. Come on, Guns! Let's get cracking."

Orders were passed and the men rose to their feet, relieved at the prospect of action. There were twenty-four of them, divided into four sections of six. Led by the two officers, well spread out, they started to move down the hill towards the clump of bush, their rifles ready. The going was easy enough except where patches of scrub had to be circumvented.

The denser thicket in the valley for which they were making was about forty feet long and well over the height of a man. Tendrils of smoke still rose above it. It was Farnworth's intention that one party, led by himself, should work round the right edge of the clump to see what lay behind it. Another, with the Gunner in charge, would make for the left edge and remain there, hidden if possible, in case the fire-makers were Japanese and they bolted that way on Farnworth's appearance. The sub had a lurking suspicion that they might, after all, be islanders.

Nothing happened as they moved downhill, though by the time Farnworth and his men were nearing their objective spots of rain were already falling. Drawing his pistol he signalled his sailors to stop and went on alone, crouching as he silently skirted the edge of the clump and finally dropped to his knees to peer cautiously round the corner, his heart throbbing. His men, watching his movements, were close behind. What he saw caused him to wave them on, motioning them to keep low and to circle to the left.

Within thirty feet of him, close under the shelter of the bushes, were four men squatting round a wood fire, cooking something in a tin hung from a tripod. Unshaven and hollow-eyed, they wore dirty khaki uniforms with faded red sleeve and collar badges. They were unmistakably Japanese. Beyond them was a low tent of what looked like waterproof sheeting, camouflaged with branches and greenery.

A leading seaman, one Jordan, crawled up on Farnworth's right and lay down, breathing heavily. Beyond him were several others, lying prone, their rifles beside them.

They could all see the group round the fire.

"Shall I let 'em have it, sir?" Jordan whispered, oozing his weapon forward.

"Hold on a second," Farnworth breathed. "Are the others all up?"

"Looks like it, sir," the seaman replied.

"Then cover that fellow facing us, the one with the cap on. But don't. . . ."

He didn't finish the sentence, for at that moment a fifth Japanese, carrying a tommy-gun in his left hand, appeared from behind the tent and trotted hurriedly to join his companions, jabbering excitedly and pointing to his right, towards the hill down which the sailors had come. He was evidently a sentry, and had either heard or seen something, probably one of the Gunner's party.

"Go on, Jordan!" Farnworth exclaimed, firing his pistol.

The seaman's rifle cracked.

Both shots must have missed, for the tommy-gunner, with a look of amazement on his face, turned in their direction and pressed his trigger, moving his weapon from side to side to spray the bullets.

Farnworth heard the snick of Jordan's rifle bolt as he reloaded, and the report as he fired again. Other rifles cracked, and the tommy-gunner dropped his weapon, collapsed and fell. His companions must have had their weapons close by them, for they scattered, flung themselves down and opened fire. The sub could hear the bullets zizzing through the air and snicking twigs and leaves from the bush overhead.

At that moment he would have given a year's pay for a

couple of Sten guns. At close quarters the sailors' rifles were clearly no match for the Japanese light automatics. But all the Stens were with Acton's party.

Hell, he muttered to himself! Something must be done. They couldn't, they mustn't, be held up by four Japs!

There came a lull in the enemy's fire, probably as they reloaded.

Nerving himself, Farnworth rose to his feet, shouted to the others to come on, and dashed forward, pistol in hand. Jordan, who had fixed his bayonet, was close beside him. Other men followed, shouting.

It was all very savage and horrible. So far as the enemy were concerned there was no thought of surrender. And the seamen, wild with excitement and mindful of what they had heard of the atrocities inflicted upon British wounded and British women in Hong Kong and Malaya, were in no mood for showing mercy, even if it had been asked for. Their hatred for the Japanese far exceeded the loathing in which they held the Germans.

Three men were hit during the rush, none of them seriously. They all made light of their injuries and only one, with a bullet through the thigh, would have to be carried when McInnes and the stretcher-party arrived. Meanwhile they were bandaged and made comfortable.

Farnworth had been rejoined by Mr. Blatchington and his party when Acton and his men appeared on the skyline to come sliding and scrambling hot-foot down Hill Six-Fifty. The rain, driving in from seaward, seemed to have settled down into a steady downpour which was rapidly converting the softer ground into a quagmire.

"What'll we do with the deaders?" the Gunner asked, eyeing the corpses with a look of disgust on his weather-beaten face. "'Tisn't hardly decent to leave the poor bastards out here in the open," he added. "But we've nothing to bury 'em with."

"Leave them," the sub said. "Number One'll be here in a minute. He'll decide. Collect their guns and ammunition. Detail a couple of hands to search them for papers and identity discs. I'm going to have a look in that tent."

Crouching to enter, Farnworth had no time for anything but the most cursory look round in the semi-darkness inside.

The low shelter, with its canvas floor, revealed nothing un-expected. Large enough to have accommodated at least ten men, it contained bedding-rolls, clothing and other personal belongings; haversacks; several light wooden boxes of what looked like ammunition; cartons of provisions; two small sacks of rice; some oblong tins, like petrol tins, which might hold water; a few bottles and other oddments. So far as he could see in the dim light, the interior was clean and neatly stowed. There was nothing anywhere which gave any immediate clue as to *how* the Japanese had come to the island, or how long they had been there.

Once again, however, Farnworth found himself wondering how the enemy had allowed themselves to be surprised in the way they had. It was true that their hide-out in the dip between the two hills was well concealed by clumps of thick bush on three sides. All the same, they surely *must* have been aware of the *Eurydice's* arrival, if only because of the aeroplane that had been shot down. Had it not occurred to them that sooner or later they would be hunted? Their actions were as mysterious as they were unintelligent.

Bending low to pass through the tent, the sub entered a covered alcove at the further end. There he found the radio set, which was unlike any such apparatus he had seen before. Mounted on a light wooden platform, with four handles for carrying, it had the usual box-like arrangement with dials, knobs, transmitter and receiver, and at one end what looked like a small motor-bicycle engine driving a generator, together with a saddle and a pair of pedals. Only Petty Officer Tele-graphist Scriven could give an opinion as to how the contrap-tion worked and he was not present. Farnworth was no expert.

He was still examining it when he heard Acton's voice outside, and Acton in a hurry from the sound of it.

"Sub! Farnworth! Where the blazes are you?"

"Here!" he called, moving back into the main tent.

Acton, dripping wet and plastered with mud, was outside. The men, Farnworth noticed, were starting to move off.

"I've found their wireless set," he explained.

"Excellent, and good work wiping out this lot," the lieuten-ant replied, breathless and visibly excited. "But we can't stop now! Drop everything, Sub! Back to the ship as fast as we can make it!"

"What's up?"

"There's a small ship coming this way! She might be a landing craft. We saw her from the top of the hill, five or six miles off."

"Gosh! Japanese?"

"She can hardly be anything else. Come on. Let's get moving! She'll arrive before dusk if she's coming here."

"What d'you intend to do?" Farnworth inquired as they hurried off.

"Do?" Acton grunted. "Sink her, of course, if she comes in close and tries landing anyone. We shan't welcome her with song and dance and bunches of orchids!" Tired and wet, he was not in the best of tempers.

"I only thought she might be passing," the sub put in. There was no need, he thought, for Acton to be quite so snappish.

"Maybe; but don't forget those wireless signals that Scriven heard this morning. The odds are they were sent off by the party you've just mopped up."

"But Scriven said there was no acknowledgment, Number One."

"Hell!" Acton exclaimed. "How you will argue, Sub! What Scriven told me was that he'd *heard* no acknowledgment, and that these chaps here were pumping out what he thought was an S O S. Who's to say it wasn't picked up by the ship that's making this way? Anyhow, there it is. If she does arrive, we'll let her have it."

The distance back to the ship was little more than a mile as the bird flew, though considerably further with all the twists and turns in the devious trails through the jungle. It was lucky they had Beekman and the natives to guide them. Taking the shortest route they had no sight of the open sea to the westward; but the seamen, fully aware that a ship had been sighted, needed no encouragement to hasten. Leaving McInnes and his stretcher-party and the three wounded to set their own pace, the others hurried on, sliding and tumbling downhill in places where the track had been converted into an oozy glissade. The warm rain was still pouring down in torrents.

They reached the *Eurydice* before dusk—drenched through, tired, dirty and blasphemous.

Melton, bubbling over with excitement, met Acton as he

arrived on board. He reported that the look-out on the far side of the little promontory alongside which the *Eurydice* lay had sighted a small ship approaching the island. The two after 4.7's and the pom-pom were already manned and ready for action.

"We saw her from the top of the hill and came back hell for leather," Acton said. "What about the Bofors along the beach?"

"I hadn't enough hands for them until your people came back."

"Better have 'em manned at once, Pilot, though I expect the gun-pits are filled up with water again. Blast this rain! I'm fed up with it."

Melton passed the necessary orders, and Farnworth, whose job it was, went off with the Bofors guns' crews.

Acton called for Mr. Blatchington.

"Sir?"

"Are your torpedoes ready for running?"

"Yes, sir. All topped up and ready for six feet."

"Then train one set of tubes outboard. You may have a chance of using them."

"Aye, aye, sir."

"What happened up topsides, George?" Melton asked. "We heard some shooting."

"My party never fired a round," Acton said disgustedly, taking the pistol out of its holster and unloading it. "The sub had all the luck. It was a bloody business. They went in with the bayonet, scuppered five Japs, and found their radio."

"Five. That makes seven of 'em killed all told. Is that the lot, d'you think?"

"I sincerely hope so. We've three wounded, by the way, none really serious, I believe. They're coming on behind with Pills and his stretcher-party. When ought this ship to arrive?"

Melton thought for a moment. "She was about three miles away when last reported," he said. "If she *is* coming here she ought to be rounding the point in about fifteen or twenty minutes."

"Right," Acton said. "I'll go ashore and have a look at her. I won't be long."

The faithful Jevons, always solicitous for Acton's welfare,

had been lurking in the background. "Sir," he asked, coming forward. "Would you like your bath now?"

"No time, Jevons," the lieutenant laughed, divesting himself of his accoutrements. "But you can take this little lot down to my cabin."

"Is there nothing else I can get you, sir? What about sandwiches, or a nice cup o' strong tea?"

"I think nice cups of strong tea for all the hands who've been ashore, Jevons. Tell the cooks."

"Be ready in a few minutes, sir. It's already on order."

The rain was gradually ceasing, and as Acton hurriedly left the ship and walked up through the scrub and the trees to the point where he had a good view to the westward, the darkening sky overhead was becoming clearer. Stars had already started to twinkle, and twilight had come. Though a few lingering gleams of rose-pink and pale orange from the departed sun still showed over the purple-cloud masses piled up over the distant horizon, night would soon be upon them with all the suddenness of the tropics.

But Acton's main attention was riveted upon the approaching ship, little more than a mile away. She was a dark grey landing-craft with a long, low fore-deck and a curious-looking superstructure with mast and funnel in the stern. Rolling sluggishly in the following sea kicked up by the fresh westerly breeze, she was steaming leisurely to pass quite close to the point about a quarter of a mile to Acton's left, which could only mean she was making for the little bay, the sole anchorage the island afforded.

Using his glasses Acton could see what looked like covered vehicles massed in the fore part of the ship, with some men apparently clearing away the anchor. There were more figures on the bridge, and a few light guns, with their muzzles cocked up in the air, mounted on the after superstructure.

There was an ensign of some sort at the short gaff on the solitary mast. Half-hidden by the funnel, and hanging limply up and down with the breeze almost dead astern, it was impossible to distinguish it. Bursting with impatience Acton watched it until a freakish puff of wind caused it momentarily to flutter clear.

"My God!" Acton muttered, turning to run back to the *Eurydice*.

It was the chance of a lifetime. The strange vessel was steaming blindly on oblivious to any danger. No doubt her crew would be looking forward to a run ashore for what looting they fancied and a free-and-easy among the native girls.

That brief glimpse of her flag had shown him the red rising sun with its red rays on a white ground—the ensign of the Imperial Japanese Navy.

15

AGED THIRTY-SIX, and therefore old for his rank, Lieutenant Hikaru Makoto was neither a regular officer of the Imperial Japanese Navy, nor had he been brought up in the traditions of that service through the strict discipline and hard training of the Naval College at Etajima. The son of a small shopkeeper, Makoto had joined the Merchant Service as a young man, and with regular periods of training as a reservist had served for fourteen years as an officer in that steamship line known as the Nippon Yusen Kaisha. Early in 1941, when war against America and the British Empire was a matter of months and the navy was being largely expanded, Makoto, somewhat to his chagrin, had been called up to fulfil his naval obligations.

Comfortably married, with his home at Kobe and a wife and two children whom he had seen at fairly frequent intervals during peace, he had voyaged to America, Australia, India and England in passenger steamers and had met many foreigners. He spoke tolerably good high-school English, and having lived outside the narrow and orthodox caste system of the navy did not regard all foreigners as rivals and potential enemies. Indeed, there were many he actually liked, and they liked him. He was a soft-spoken, polite and friendly little man.

Like most Japanese he glorified in his country's greatness, and believed in the 'Greater East Asia Co-Prosperity Sphere' and the popular saying 'The peace of East Asia means the peace of the World.' He believed that Japan was destined to bring about that peace. It never occurred to him that the Japanese idea of 'peace', as dictated by her ruling class, was precisely the same as Hitler's and entirely contrary to that of

139

other nations. It meant complete control, military, political and economic, of all other oriental nations, a control exercised by force and terror if not abjectly accepted by its victims.

Makoto was no warrior. He had none of the fighting instincts of the old Samurai class upon which the code of the army and navy was so largely based. He by no means subscribed to the shibboleths 'If you are born a Japanese, then die on the battlefield'; 'Dedicated to the Emperor, our lives are glorious as the morning sun'; 'To die is to live in the great soul of the Emperor.'

As a loyal subject he revered the Emperor, though he loved his wife and children far more than an impersonal deity he had never seen. He did not hold with the Imperial Rescript addressed to all those in the fighting services: 'Be resolved that honour is heavier than the mountains and death lighter than a feather.' Honour was certainly worth striving for; but the statement about death left him cold. He wished to live in peace and quietness, to love his wife and bring up his children.

Whatever the high-and-mighty ones might say, Hikaru Makoto could see no sense in committing hara-kiri, or suicide by disembowelment, as an alternative to the so-called disgrace of defeat or surrender. Why, he asked himself, should being made a prisoner-of-war after having fought against great odds be regarded as an irredeemable disgrace? It struck him as nonsense. He did not wish to die violently, and saw no particular glory in it. He preferred to live to a ripe old age and to die peacefully in his bed.

As an officer of the reserve and a qualified navigator, Makoto had been appointed to the command of Landing Craft 4903, which was principally used for carrying stores. It was a monotonous sort of job which had meant long periods at sea in the crowded discomfort of a small ship, often in bad weather. After the Japanese landings in the Lingayen Gulf, in Luzon, in late December, 1941, Makoto's flotilla had been sent on to join up with the fleet covering the transports carrying the occupation force for Palembang, the important oil centre in Sumatra, in the middle of February, 1942. Thence they were ordered on to Batavia, in Java, for more fetch-and-carry jobs.

So far as Makoto was concerned the war up-to-date had been rather dull and unexciting. He had seen the Japanese cruisers and destroyers bombarding, and the carriers flying off their aircraft on bombing expeditions; but the whole business had been rather one-sided. There was practically no retaliation. Neither a bomb nor a shell had ever fallen near L.C. 4903. Yet the work suited him. He preferred his dull routine to the more strenuous action enjoyed by those in the regular fighting ships. He was not athirst for glory and renown.

About a week before the elimination of the last Japanese in 'Eurydice Island,' as we may call it, since the Dutch and the old native names mean nothing to this story, Makoto had been summoned to present himself at the Japanese naval headquarters at Batavia to receive further sailing orders.

Saluted by an armed bluejacket sentry outside the front door the visitor was taken on by an orderly to the office of the Assistant Sea Transport Officer, one Lieutenant Kondo, a reservist from the mercantile marine like Makoto himself. The pair knew each other. They had foregathered ashore, and were friends. Kondo rose from his littered desk and bowed.

"What have you for me this morning?" Makoto asked after the usual polite salutations.

"The honourable old gentleman wishes to see you personally," Kondo said, nodding towards the inner doorway. He had used a form of speech in referring to a senior officer that he would never have dared to employ except with a close friend.

"And how is the health of the honourable Commander?" Makoto inquired, judging from Kondo's wry expression that all was not well.

Kondo intimated that the honourable Senior Sea Transport Officer, Commander Yaichi Tanaka, was in a worse temper than usual. He was as cross as two crabs, bristling like a porcupine, after his morning interview with the Chief of Staff. Something had gone wrong, though Kondo knew not what. But he, Kondo, had borne the brunt of it. "Be wary, my friend," Kondo warned. "Speak softly to the bear, or you will be scratched also."

Makoto knew Commander Tanaka as a testy, dour-faced officer who had somehow missed his promotion and bitterly resented being relegated to shore duty while most of his contemporaries were winning new honour and glory as captains of fighting ships at sea.

He, Tanaka, wearer of the Order of the Golden Kite* given only for gallantry in action, with a whole string of other decorations and medals for faithful service to his Emperor, was tied to an office desk during what was probably the greatest war in Japanese history!

He came of ancient Samurai stock—those warriors who in older times attached an almost holy veneration to the swords which they alone had the distinction of wearing, and never drew their blades without using them. He still treasured as a precious heirloom the long, heavy, two-handed weapon with its razor edge, laboriously fashioned by hand by a celebrated sword-maker of the seventeenth century and bearing his mark, which had belonged to his father and his remote ancestors. An almost incredible value was set upon a rare blade, and to test the sharpness of their finished products with their finely-tempered, carefully-honed edges, it was said that the old swordsmiths held their weapons horizontally and slantwise in a stream and floated a handful of wool against it. If the wool slid off the point without bisection the sword was considered imperfect.

True to his caste and its narrow outlook Commander Yaichi Tanaka despised all merchants and traders and those who dealt in goods or money. He also regarded with a lofty disdain officers of the reserve who had been drafted into the Imperial Japanese Navy from the mercantile marine as a wartime measure. They might be seamen; but they were not fighting seamen. Clothed in a little brief authority, at heart they were little better than hucksters and sutlers who traded for money.

Kondo stood in awe of his formidable chief. He walked across to the inner door, knocked and listened. An answer came from inside. He opened the door, bowed, hissed between his teeth and announced: "Lieutenant Makoto, sir. Commanding Officer L.C. 4903."

"Send him in,'" came a growling voice.

Makoto was ushered into the inner sanctum, and the door closed behind him. He bowed and introduced himself.

Tanaka, seated at his desk in front of a huge chart on the wall dotted with different-coloured flags and symbols indicating individual ships and convoys, bowed without rising. From

* The equivalent of the British Victoria Cross.

his expression Makoto realized his superior was in a foul temper, and his first remark made it painfully evident.

"You are late in obeying orders!" the commander snapped, glowering. "I do not await the convenience of junior officers. Why?"

Makoto blinked. "Sir," he explained, standing rigidly to attention. "I came as soon as I received your message."

"Excuses. Always excuses! My signal was sent off nearly two hours ago."

"I am sorry, sir. It reached me half an hour ago, and I came at once."

Tanaka grunted. "Do you know why I sent for you?"

"To receive sailing orders, sir."

"Your ship is ready for sea?"

"Yes, sir."

"All the stores are on board?"

"Yes, sir."

"What stores?"

Makoto thought for a moment. "Ammunition, aircraft bombs, six light anti-aircraft guns, spare parts for aeroplanes, and some motor vehicles on deck, sir," he said.

"You have seen to it that your cargo is properly stowed and secure?"

"Be certain of that, sir."

"Then here are your detailed sailing orders in writing," Tanaka said, handing over a sealed envelope and rising from his chair. "You will open them when you get to sea. But I may tell you what they contain," he added, going to the wall chart. "You will proceed to Macassar," pointing to the port of that name in the south-western prong of the Celebes Islands. "There you will receive further orders, probably for Kendari Bay or Amboina, here and here. You have the necessary charts?"

"Yes, sir," Makoto said. "My ship goes alone, sir?" he asked.

"That is so," Tanaka nodded. "You will have no escort. Since our great victory the Java Sea is now finally cleared of all enemy warships."

"I see, sir."

"We have submarines patrolling here and here," the commander continued, again sweeping a finger over the chart.

143

"Their precise areas are shown in your detailed orders. They will be warned that you pass through their patrol grounds and instructed to make touch with you by radio or otherwise."

"I understand, sir."

"And in the event of bad weather you are at liberty to take shelter in any convenient anchorage, reporting your movements to the Senior Naval Officer, Macassar. Any questions?"

"None, sir," Makoto replied.

"Very well, Lieutenant. You will sail at seven-thirty to-morrow morning. And the next time you come to see me make it your convenience not to keep me waiting. You may go, Lieutenant Makoto."

Dismissed, Makoto bowed low and said 'thank you' with all the politeness he could muster. He was glad to leave the presence of Commander Tanaka.

Punctually on time next morning L.C. 4903 cast off from the jetty and proceeded to sea. Makoto felt proud as he took his ship out of harbour with his small crew fallen in on deck, the Rising Sun ensign fluttering at the peak, and his pendant flying at the stumpy masthead. It was the first time he had been entrusted with an independent mission, and, he judged, an important one. Hitherto he had always been at sea in company with other ships. Commander Tanaka, for all his boorishness, must think well of him. Indeed, Kondo, who knew everything that went on in the office, had hinted that Makoto's name was on a list for consideration for promotion to the rank of temporary lieutenant-commander.

The distance to Macassar from Batavia was roughly 900 miles, which meant about four days' steaming at L.C. 4903's economical speed. The weather promised to be fine. Makoto, with Hirata, his sub-lieutenant; Nakamura, the deck warrant-officer; Fujita, the engineer warrant-officer in charge of the twin Diesels, and all the men of the small ship's company were in the highest spirits at the prospect of a leisurely amble across the calm blue sea free for the time being from the trammels of superior authority. Strict discipline would be relaxed. The voyage would be more or less of a picnic.

And so they moved eastward along the green coast of Java with its golden beaches shimmering in the sun, the dim mauve shapes of the cloud-capped mountains always in the back-ground, and the spicy scent of vegetation drifting seaward

144

from the land. The dusk came down and the shore faded away, and at dawn next morning the mainland was out of sight. A cluster of small islands, darkly silhouetted against the glow of the rising sun, appeared over the horizon on the port bow. L.C. 4903 plodded on and passed them by, to endure a day of blazing heat with a cloudless sky and a glassy sea just heaving and undulating to a slight westerly swell. The ship was little more than a steel box, and the cramped, comfortless living quarters below were not unlike the inside of an oven. The crew, discarding everything except their scanty loin-cloths, slept and ate and lazed on deck under the shade of improvised awnings. Except for the sight of another island or two the day passed without incident and the second night darkened to an indigo sky brilliant with stars.

Then dawn again, with clouds banking up to the westward and a breeze which freshened as the morning wore on. By noon there was a regular little breaking sea from astern which caused the heavily-laden landing-craft to roll and to wallow sluggishly. But the crew were used to that. They were thankful for the breeze which mitigated the tropical heat.

At about 2 p.m., soon after the hump of a large island had been sighted over the horizon to the northward, Makoto, dozing in a deck-chair close to the bridge, was roused by a seaman sent by Warrant-Officer Nakamura, the officer of the watch. A submarine, the sailor reported, had suddenly surfaced about a mile ahead. Would the honourable captain kindly come to the bridge?

Mindful of what appeared in his sailing orders about friendly submarines being on patrol somewhere along his route, Makoto was in no way perturbed. The newcomer couldn't be anything but Japanese. According to his information all the British, American or Dutch ships in the area had long since been sunk or had fled.

The pair exchanged signals and identified each other. The submarine was one of the older class of 655-tonners, armed with four torpedo-tubes, and a single 4-inch gun. They were presently moving close abreast of each other with the two commanding officers shouting through megaphones and the crews grinning and waving.

"Have you anything to report?" demanded the man on the submarine's conning tower.

"No, sir. Nothing."

"Have you sighted any ships or aircraft?"

Once more the answer was in the negative. "Have you any orders for me?" Makoto went on to ask. "I was told to make touch with you."

"I have no orders for you," the submarine captain shouted back. "I was warned you would be passing, that is all. Have you intercepted any radio signals?"

"No. Nothing, sir. Why do you ask?"

"No matter. Can you spare us any fresh fruit or vegetables, cigarettes also? We have been three days on patrol, with another five to go. We are running rather short. We should be most grateful."

It was a request that could hardly be refused, and it so happened that L.C. 4903 was amply stocked. Moreover, in about thirty-six hours or so she would arrive at Macassar, where they could replenish.

"Yes, sir," Makoto said. "I can spare you something. If you will stop, I will send it across by boat."

There was no need for that, the submarine commander replied. If L.C. 4903 would go ahead a little and then stop, he would bring his ship alongside. He was greatly obliged.

The manoeuvre was carried out, and some laden rattan baskets and sacks, together with six bottles of saké and a large cardboard container of American cigarettes found in a canteen at Batavia were safely handed across.

It was a deadly monotonous job having to spend most of the day submerged in the heat of the tropics and only coming to the surface at night to recharge his batteries, Lieutenant-Commander Takagi told Makoto. He had a crew of more than forty, and the heat and the stench inside his boat were unbelievable. There had been no excitement to keep them going. It irked his soul to be so idle, particularly when great events were about to happen far away to the eastward.

Makoto pricked up his ears. "To what great events do you refer, sir?" he asked.

"Have you not heard that part of our fleet and many transports are concentrating at Rabaul, in New Britain, and in the Solomon Islands?" Takagi inquired.

"I heard a rumour," Makoto said.

"It is true," the other told him. "There will be some excitement there, without a doubt. Alas that it is two thousand five hundred miles away, and not here."

"What of the Americans, honourable commander?" Makoto inquired.

Takagi seemed amused. "The Americans!" he scoffed. "What can they or the British do against our invincible navy?"

"The Americans bombed Tokyo," Makoto ventured.

Takagi snorted. "For which impertinence we shall soon be revenged a hundredfold!" he returned. "You shall see. Well, I thank you for your kind gifts, which are of great service."

"It is nothing," Makoto said. "We are happy to be of help."

"I wish you a very good voyage," Takagi said.

"And the same to you, sir," Makoto answered, bowing and saluting.

The two crews waved to each other and shouted 'Banzai!', the patriotic Japanese cheer which means 'May you live ten thousand years!'

The lines were cast off and the submarine backed astern. The engine-room telegraphs of L.C. 4903 clanged and she started to move ahead. A few minutes later the men disappeared from the submarine's deck. Moving ahead again she dived in a little flurry of foam and spray and was soon out of sight.

Makoto was watching through his glasses. "I am thankful," he observed with deep feeling, "that I do not serve in a submarine. It is no fit life for dogs, let alone for honourable gentlemen."

With which possibly unpatriotic remark both Sub-Lieutenant Hirata and Warrant-Officer Nakamura most cordially agreed.

By four o'clock the wind had freshened and the following sea had increased to a regular breaking lop. The sky was clouding over with leaden-coloured nimbus. There would be rain before long—heavy rain from the look of it.

The steep peak of a small wooded island gradually hove itself up over the horizon on the port bow as L.C. 4903 lurched on. Makoto, on the bridge, was in the act of taking a compass bearing when he felt a sudden vibration from below. It lasted for no more than a few seconds; but the familiar throbbing rhythm of the engines seemed to have changed. Then he noticed the ship's head was falling off to starboard.

"Mind your steering, Hosaka!" he shouted to the quarter-master at the wheel. "Be careful! You're off your course!"

"The ship is not steering, sir," Hosaka grunted, putting his wheel over. "I am unable to . . ."

There came a ring from the engine-room telephone. Makoto picked up the receiver. "What is it?" he demanded. "Is something wrong?"

Fujita, the engineer officer, answered. "Is that the captain?" he asked. His voice was agitated.

"Yes. What is it?"

"I beg to report," Fujita said. "I have had to stop the star-board engine, sir."

"Stop the starboard engine!" Makoto exclaimed in sudden anger. "Why?"

"I fear we have a piston seizure."

Makoto cursed under his breath. He knew little about Diesels; but visualized wreck and destruction in the engine room, and his ship lying stopped and helpless in worsening weather. "Can you repair it?" he wanted to know.

"I hope so, sir. I have spare parts."

"And how long will it take?"

"I cannot say, Captain. It may be a cracked or broken piston ring, or perhaps a fault in the lubrication system. I must examine before I can say for certain."

"Then get on with your repairs!" Makoto snapped. "It is most important we are not delayed. I hold you responsible. Can we go on under the port engine?"

"Sir," replied the engineer, and his voice was miserable. "I do my utmost. I will ascertain the damage and report to you in person."

"I asked if we could proceed under the port engine?" the captain demanded.

"Yes, sir. We can."

"Then do so," Makoto said, putting back the telephone receiver.

L.C. 4903 moved slowly on with the helmsman doing his best to keep her on a steady course. It was not easy with only one engine in use and the rising sea kicking her stern this way and that. The following wind also had its effect, for the high stern of the ship, light compared with the heavily-laden fore part, acted like a sail. She yawed widely as Hosaka struggled at the wheel with the sweat running down his face and naked torso.

Fujita arrived on the bridge twenty minutes later to find Makoto still fretting and fuming. The little engineer was nearly in tears as he reported that the ship might have to struggle on with one engine for perhaps six or twelve or even twenty-four hours. There was no knowing how long the repair would take, if it could be repaired at all with their own resources. The damaged engine must be partially stripped, which took time. What with the sweltering heat and restricted space in the engine-room, and the ship tumbling and rolling, the work was extremely difficult. His men were working like demons. The cause of the stoppage was incomprehensible; but was certainly not due to any lack of supervision on his part.

Makoto relented. He knew Fujita was not the sort of man to magnify molehills into mountains. Since commissioning he had nursed his machinery as a mother nurses her first-born, and had often pulled them out of tight corners when things went wrong. Like other craft mass-produced under the emergency war programme L.C. 4903 had been hurriedly constructed, almost slapped together, and sent to sea at once without any chance of getting over her teething troubles.

"Take comfort, Fujita," the captain said gently, patting his subordinate on the shoulder of his oil-streaked overalls. "I know the breakdown is no fault of yours."

Fujita felt happier. He smiled.

Nevertheless Makoto was perturbed. It had been impressed upon him that his cargo was of great importance, and its safe delivery was the first independent mission with which he had been entrusted. His reputation depended upon it, and now all his hopes might be shattered by this exasperating breakdown.

He had the idea of waiting until dusk, by which time the submarine they had already met would have come to the surface to charge her batteries, and then using his wireless to ask for assistance. She must have Diesels for running on the surface, and a swarm of skilled artificers who would willingly lend a hand. Lieutenant-Commander Takagi had seemed a likeable sort of man, and certainly owed them a good turn in exchange for the fruit and saké and vegetables and cigarettes. To accelerate the meeting, Makoto might even turn his ship round and steam back towards Takagi's patrol area.

But on considering all the implications of this notion he

149

turned it down. A wireless signal would probably be intercepted at Batavia, and if that happened it must inevitably come to the ears of the fiery Commander Tanaka, who would rage and swear and tear chunks off poor Kondo while calling him, Makoto, an incompetent, double-distilled fool. He might even send a peremptory signal ordering L.C. 4903 to return to Batavia, and give the job to someone else. This would mean much shame and loss of face for Makoto, and he had his pride. For the same reason he refrained from using his radio to inform the Senior Naval Officer, Macassar, of his predicament. He hoped again to be on his way without too much delay. Also, if he asked for help from Takagi's submarine, Fujita, who likewise had his pride, might take umbrage because he might think his captain considered him incompetent to do the necessary repairs. It would never do to estrange Fujita.

On the other hand, the green island ahead was drawing nearer every minute, and was now no more than five miles away. At the present reduced speed they should reach it just about dusk. Makoto read the sailing directions and examined the chart. The island, he saw, was sparsely inhabited, while there was a small bay or inlet on its south coast which afforded some sort of anchorage sheltered by a low promontory against any wind and sea from the westward. It looked a hospitable sort of place. A few spots of rain had started to fall, and from the look of the sky they would soon develop into a regular downpour. Undoubtedly the wind and sea were still increasing.

"Fujita," Makoto asked. "How would it be if we anchored in calm water for the night? Would it help you and your men?"

"Honourable captain," the engineer replied, "it is the opportunity for which I could have wished to complete our task." He bowed.

"Then so it shall be," said Makoto. "Sub-Lieutenant Hirata?" he continued, addressing his second in-command, who was the officer of the watch.

"Sir?"

"Be ready to anchor in about an hour. The water is deep, fifteen to twenty fathoms."

"It shall be done, sir," the sub-lieutenant said. "Permission to leave the bridge for a few minutes to arrange?"

"Permission granted," Makoto said.

Able Seaman Tamotsu Hosaka, intent upon the steering and still wrestling with his wheel to keep the ship steady on her course, had overheard the conversation. He also thanked heaven at the prospect of a quiet night in harbour. He accounted himself a pretty good helmsman, as indeed he was— probably the best in the ship; but steering L.C. 4903 in present circumstances was like trying to direct a lumbering and very recalcitrant water-buffalo through a narrow village alleyway by pulling on its tail.

Time drew on, and towards dusk, after a period of drenching rain, L.C. 4903 was slowly approaching a low, wooded promontory to the left of which, over a coastline of sheer cliff, the ground rose steeply to a tier of undulating hills covered in jungle and dense forest, steaming with the haze of evaporation. Beyond the point of land Makoto had sight of the far end of the bay with its calm, unruffled water and beach of golden sand, and beyond that again a bolder wooded hummock marking its eastern extremity.

It was all very quiet and peaceful; beautiful in its way. As they moved on Makoto could smell the mingled scents of trees and flowering foliage and wet earth. He was a sentimental soul and had a sudden feeling of nostalgia, for in some mysterious way the scene now opening out before him reminded him of his own beloved Japan and some of the lovely islands of the Inland Sea. He said as much to Nakamura, who was on the bridge with him; but the warrant-officer, more prosaically-minded, and thinking mainly of his evening meal, what remained in the saké bottle in the locker in his tiny cabin, and the prospect of a night in his bunk, did not seem impressed. He merely grunted. Scenery had no message for him.

Hirata was forward with some of the men standing by to let go the anchor when ordered. Makoto was alternately using his glasses, taking bearings with the compass, and examining the chart, which was on a very small scale.

"Ring down for 'slow'," he ordered, as the ship sidled slowly round the point at a distance of about four hundred yards, and more and more of the bay came into view. It had become much darker; but he could see a few figures on the beach, which could only be natives. "Hosaka!" he called, as the engine-room reply gong clanged.

"Steer ten degrees more to port."

"Ten degrees to port, sir," the quartermaster repeated, putting his wheel over.

The ship slowly started to swing.

"Stop engines," Makoto said, reaching down for his megaphone. There was a leadsman on the upper deck, and the captain was about to tell the man to get an up-and-down cast when all hell broke loose.

Simultaneously with the bright golden-red flash of a gun from about two hundred yards away to port there came the deafening roar of the discharge followed by a shuddering concussion and another explosion as L.C. 4903 was hit and the shell detonated. Stricken with terror Makoto heard men screaming. Then another gun crashed, another and another. At so close a range they could not miss. The ship reeled and shook and quivered. Makoto realized this was the end. He had four little anti-aircraft guns mounted abaft the bridge, and they were not even manned.

Then a pom-pom chimed in, and he saw a line of small splashes zipping towards him across the water. Ahead, from somewhere in among the trees over the line of the beach, he saw more flashes and the streaks of converging brilliant red tracer.

Hit in the engine-room, hit everywhere, the ship was already a smoking shambles. She was on fire, badly down by the bows, and listing heavily to port. The noise was shattering.

The enemy's lighter guns seemed to be concentrating on the bridge. Hit through the body, Hosaka collapsed by the wheel, kicked and lay still in a widening pool of blood. The next instant Nakamura fell, dead before he touched the deck.

Makoto was left alone on the bridge, his ship destroyed and himself helpless. Still unaware of whose were the guns firing upon him, he had had time to realize his folly in assuming the island to be innocuous. It was too late to consider that now. He had failed most dismally and no longer wanted to live. If there had been a pistol on the bridge he would have used it to shoot himself, to die alongside his shipmates and friends, Nakamura and Hosaka.

Makoto went to his death about thirty seconds later, when a shell struck close under the already riven bridge and the whole structure disintegrated into flying fragments.

Only those of the *Eurydice*, and the natives clustered on the foreshore, actually saw the end of L.C. 4903.

The stricken ship, wrapped in red flame and black smoke, had toppled over to port with her bows nearly under water. Bulldozers and jeeps and what looked like guns and covered vehicles broke away from their lashings and cascaded into the sea.

All except one of the *Eurydice's* guns, and that a 4.7, had ceased firing. In the din of battle the gunlayer had heard no orders and again pressed his trigger with his sights full on the target.

His shell drove home, to burst in a glow of rosy pink and the usual puff of blackish smoke. The result was spectacular beyond expectation. The detonation must have touched off part of the cargo, for a split second afterwards, with a reverberating explosion and a blast which shook the air and sent waves surging across the water, the smoking wreck erupted in a great geyser of orange flame and thick, yellowish-black smoke mingled with flying debris. The pillar of fire leapt a full two hundred feet skywards.

The *Eurydice* reeled and shuddered and shook herself as the terrific blast struck her. It felt as though depth charges had exploded alongside. Wreckage rained down into the sea, and there came a clanging thud from somewhere near the funnels as one heavy fragment struck the upper deck and embedded itself.

Draycott, the engineer officer, who had been watching from the upper deck, scuttled below like a startled rabbit. The *Eurydice* had no diver, and with all his ingenuity he had not been able to stop all the leaks caused by the damage sustained in action more than two months before. Some of the athwartship bulkheads, particularly those at each end of number two boiler-room, were buckled and weeping, while other small holes well below the water-line could not be satisfactorily dealt with from inside the ship. She had regularly to be pumped dry, and Draycott was fearful that this new shattering concussion might have opened up more of the side plating.

By the time the smoke had cleared away only the blunt stern of the stricken landing-craft, with the rudder and one propeller, was visible in the growing darkness. It hung momentarily at an angle of forty-five degrees and then reared itself vertical, finally to disappear in an upheaval of spray and the hiss and gurgle of escaping air. The water swirled and eddied. A scum of thick oil, littered with floating wreckage, crept over the surface in a widening circle.

"Poor devils!" said Acton, smitten with sudden compassion. He felt rather sick. War was war; but this was no great victory. It was more like the massacre of unarmed men. The wretched Japanese, suspecting nothing, had walked blindly to destruction.

"Mr. Blatchington!"

"Sir?"

"Collect a crew for the whaler and see if you can find any survivors."

They found no one alive—nothing but four dead bodies in lifebelts floating in the oil among the splintered wreckage and the shattered remains of two boats floating bottom upwards.

At sunset, about twelve miles away to the westward, Commander Takagi had brought his submarine to the surface to recharge his batteries.

He duly fixed his position by bearings of two islands, a large one away to the northward, and the tall peak of another smaller one to the west. The Diesel engines throbbed as the ship moved slowly ahead.

The wind and sea had dropped, and the sky had partly cleared. Stars were already scintillating overhead.

Soon after dusk, having eaten their evening meal before retiring to sleep, Takagi and some of his officers were idling and smoking on the conning tower. Most of the crew were clustered round the 4-inch gun on the fore-deck, enjoying the fresh air after being cooped up for most of the day in the vile, stinking stench of oil and the stifling heat of their submerged steel hull. They were chattering and cheerful. Some, reclining full length on the saddle-tanks and holding on, were enjoying the wash of the warm sea as the water hissed over them.

The shapes of the two islands gradually faded away and disappeared, presently to leave the submarine alone and isolated in the gathering darkness. Darkness came down; moonless. The rigid circle of the horizon vanished. There was no telling where the sea ended and the sky began—no gleam or blink of light from any ship or island.

Takagi was thinking about nothing in particular when his attention was suddenly attracted by a flickering, orange-coloured glow far away to the westward. It waxed and waned, and was reflected from the sky. Some of the men pointed, calling to those on the conning-tower. The glare, Takagi noticed, came from practically the same direction as that of the smaller island which had been in sight before dark.

He stubbed out his cigarette and lifted his binoculars. "It's a fire ashore," he said casually to his first lieutenant. "Probably one of those fool natives has set alight to his palm hut."

A few seconds later he realized his mistake. The fire suddenly gushed upwards into a tall, trumpet-shaped column of brilliant red flame, not unlike the eruption of a volcano. It hung momentarily and then disappeared.

"That," he exclaimed at once, "was an explosion!"

It was a heavy explosion from the look of it, and it certainly came from the direction of the island, much the same direction in which Lieutenant Makoto's landing-craft had finally disappeared over the horizon some hours earlier. Had something untoward happened?

Through his glasses Takagi thought he could see a cloud of smoke against the lighter darkness of the sky, though it was too far away for him to be certain. He waited, half expecting to hear a sound like a distant clap of thunder. But the breeze still blew steadily towards the island. He heard nothing but the rhythmic mutter of his own Diesel engines and the splash and gurgle of the water alongside.

Takagi's sailing orders were fairly elastic and left much to his own discretion. He was at liberty to leave his patrol area if anything unusual occurred and he considered the circumstances demanded it. The powers that be would certainly regard an unexpected and undoubtedly heavy explosion as 'unusual'. So he made up his mind.

"I shall proceed to investigate," he said to his first lieutenant. He had already examined the chart.

"You will remain on the surface, sir?"

"Yes. Warn them in the engine-room that I intend to increase speed to ten knots. Keep the gun manned."

"Yes, sir."

"And Hamamoto . . ."

"Sir?"

"There is no moon tonight?"

"No, sir."

"Then I shall make no close approach to the island before dawn," Takagi said. "The chart is small, and the survey an old one. The island, I see, is fringed with reefs of coral."

Lieutenant Hamamoto, who also acted as navigator, agreed. Takagi's suggestion, he considered, though he did not venture to say so, was both wise and seamanlike. "Will you report our movements, sir?" he asked.

Takagi thought for a moment. He didn't wish to risk a scare about nothing. "I shall make the usual routine signal at eleven o'clock tonight," he replied. "Tomorrow morning, when we've investigated, I may make a further report."

Whatever he thought, Hamamoto did not question the decision. Takagi always knew best.

16

DRIVEN from his usual sleeping billet on a camp bed on deck by a heavy shower soon after midnight, Acton had taken refuge in his cabin. Now, with no more covering than a thin sarong and his naked torso beaded with perspiration, he lay sound asleep on his bunk.

Able Seaman Jordan stood undecided. Three times he had tried to call the captain, which he supposed Mr. Acton really was, and three times there had been no reply. Mr. Acton's eyes remained tight shut and his mouth wide open. He snored and puffed gently, not at all a pretty sight to Jordan's way of thinking.

Faint daylight filtered in through the row of small circular side scuttles over the bunk. They were wide open and draped with mosquito netting; but being within fifteen feet of the cliff-face admitted little fresh air. The *Eurydice's* ventilating fans were not running and the cabin was oppressively hot. The ship, little better than a steel box, seemed to absorb all the glowering heat of the sun during daylight, and to give it off at night.

"Sir! Mister Acton!" said Jordan for the fourth time,

shaking the recumbent figure by its bare shoulder. "Wake up, sir, please!"

Acton grunted and sat up, rubbing his eyes. There was a vile taste in his mouth.

"What is it?" he demanded, blinking. "What's the time?"

"Getting on for half after five, sir. Mister . . ."

"I left orders to be called at half-past six," Acton broke in.

"Yessir. But, Mister Farnworth says I'm to tell you there's what he thinks is a submarine in sight."

Acton became galvanized into sudden activity. "A submarine!" he exclaimed, swinging his legs over the side of the bunk, dropping to the deck, whipping off his sarong and hurriedly starting to dress himself. "Whereabouts, Jordan?"

"I don't rightly know, sir. She was reported by the look-out ashore. Mister Farnworth's gone off to have a look."

"Has anyone else been told?" Acton asked, struggling into his trousers.

"Not at present, sir."

"Then call all officers and get the hands to action stations, at the rush! I'm going ashore to have a look."

Jordan disappeared.

The dawn had started to break as Acton landed and hurried across the low promontory to where the look-out man was stationed on a little knoll overlooking the sea. To the eastward the horizon was already beginning to brighten with bands of pale colour from the still invisible sun. To the west the cloudless sky was still a deep purple-blue spattered with the faint silver pin-points of fading stars. The wind had died away to a little breeze, which just furred the deep indigo of the sea. There were no longer any white-caps.

And there, beyond any doubt whatever, was a submarine—barely a mile away and apparently steering straight for the island. Having forgotten his own glasses in his hurry Acton borrowed the sub's. He could see the long dark hull with its heavy-looking conning tower and superstructure, and in front of it what looked like a gun with some figures clustered around it. He could make out no ensign. To judge from the white bow wave and wash the submarine was travelling at about ten knots, which meant that in about six minutes she might be abreast of the point and in full sight from the *Eurydice*.

There was no time to be lost. Acton felt himself trembling with excitement.

"She can only be a Jap," he said, handing the binoculars back to Farnworth. "She probably saw that explosion last night and is snooping round to see what caused it."

The sub-lieutenant agreed. "She may have sighted that landing-craft on her way here," he went on to suggest. "Perhaps she's come to look for survivors, in which case she'll probably try landing a party. The whole bay's still covered in oil. It's probably drifting out to sea. If she sights that and follows it up. . . ."

Acton had to do some quick thinking. "You stay here, Sub!" he broke in hurriedly. "Watch her movements, and send your man back to the ship to report. We can't see her from the ship until she's clear of the point. I'll send another hand along to act as a second messenger. Let me know everything important. Understand?"

Farnworth nodded, and Acton rushed off.

He tried to put himself in the position of the submarine commander. The flash of the explosion the evening before must have been visible for quite twenty or thirty miles. Assuming that he, Acton, *had* seen it, he would instinctively have taken its compass bearing and laid it off on the chart, to discover that it coincided exactly with the bearing of the island. As the sub-lieutenant had said, there was also the possibility that he *might* have sighted the landing-craft earlier in the day and have been in actual communication with her. What would be his natural reactions?

The answer was fairly obvious. He would approach the island on the surface at daylight to search the area for possible survivors and to discover what had happened. Heavy explosions didn't just occur without some very good reason. He would find no survivors; but would most likely sight floating wreckage and that tell-tale slick of oil. Naturally, he would follow the trail into the bay.

Still finding nothing, he might see three groups of oil-drums floating innocently on the surface about three hundred yards out from the shore and more or less in line with the natives' boats drawn up on the beach above high-water mark. He might mistake the drums for more wreckage, and could close them to investigate. Anyhow, he would probably take his submarine fairly close inshore and land someone to question the inhabitants as to what they knew of the explosion or any survivors.

Submarines carried no ordinary boats. Men, a few at a time, would have to paddle themselves to the beach in some sort of collapsible canoes or rubber dinghies. What it really boiled down to was that if the submarine entered the bay at all, she *must* pass within three or four hundred yards of the *Eurydice's* 4.7's, and at that range, except by some wild mischance, they could hardly miss.

Twenty-five feet beneath each of those three groups of floating oil-drums was suspended a depth charge; Mr. Blatchington's improvised mines. Once the drums were punctured by pom-pom fire, and they were by no means difficult targets, the depth charges would sink to their set depths and explode. Acton hoped they were fool-proof.

All the same, it was quite on the cards that a submarine manned by fully-trained personnel would not come blundering into the bay in quite so free-and-easy a manner as had the landing-craft. It was not full daylight; but rounding the promontory the Japanese commander, searching through his binoculars, might recognize the camouflaged *Eurydice* as a ship. The disguise, Acton thought, was pretty good. It had been greatly improved as time went on, and at any distance the outlines of hull, funnels, superstructures, guns and torpedo-tubes blended very well into the background of greyish cliff and the green of the scrub and the trees above it. However, one never knew. Something had to be left to chance.

Acton found the ship's company at action stations when he got back, with the two 4.7's, the pom-pom and one set of torpedo-tubes ready for use. Melton had already sent the crews to man the Bofors along the beach. Everybody knew what was in the wind. The *Eurydice* was buzzing with excitement.

"I want all hands warned to lie down and to keep still till I give orders to open fire," Acton told the officers. "Pass the word to everyone. Any movement on the upper deck may attract attention."

"When's she due?" Melton asked.

"At any time after five minutes. I want both guns trained just clear of the point. I'll be at 'X' gun," Acton added, referring to the 4.7 on top of the after superstructure. "You, Pilot, had better look out for 'Y'. We'll have to judge the range."

Melton nodded.

"And don't open fire until I do!" Acton went on to warn him. "Unless she spots us first and takes action, I shan't bang off until we're certain of hitting! If she once spots us and gets away, she'll whistle up a cruiser or destroyer and that'll be the end of us. We *must* make a quick job of it. You know your drill, Gunner?"

"I hope so, sir," Mr. Blatchington nodded. "We've rehearsed it often enough." He had four torpedoes topped up with air and set for six feet, with permission to fire if he had a fair chance.

"Good! And I hope the darned things run straight and don't dive. Is there anything I've forgotten, Pilot?"

Melton thought not. The men at the pom-pom knew what to do, he said, and so did the crews of the Bofors guns mounted ashore.

"Right," Acton said. "Then we'll go to our stations and pray for luck." He hoped none of the others had noticed his nervousness. The tension of watching and waiting for what was to happen was becoming almost unbearable.

Every few minutes Farnworth's two messengers came running to the ship with the latest information.

The submarine was within half a mile, and seemed to be steering to pass the promontory at a distance of eight hundred or a thousand yards. . . .

She had reduced speed. . . .

She had stopped near what looked like floating wreckage. . . .

The sun was nearing the horizon, and away to the eastward merging layers of luminous rose-pink, orange, citron, and a pale greenish turquoise, were already encroaching on the blue of the upper sky.

Then more reports. . . .

The enemy was moving ahead again, and seemed to be altering course to starboard. . . .

She was on a steady course, moving dead slow. . . .

And a minute later. She was turning to port, evidently making for the bay. . . .

Hot-foot after this last report came Farnworth and his other messenger. The sub didn't come on board; but shouted his news from the cliff-edge.

The submarine should be in sight at any moment. She was flying a small Japanese ensign, and had most of her crew on deck. . . .

"Right!" Acton called back. "Go and take charge of the Bofors along the beach! Keep out of sight, and don't open fire until we do!"

Farnworth waved a hand, shouted "Aye aye" and set off, running.

A minute or two later Acton had sight of a hump-shaped grey bow creeping slowly into view round the point of land, and about a thousand yards astern of the *Eurydice*. Through his glasses he could see the bow-cap of a torpedo-tube right forward as she rose to the slight swell and then dipped again in a little flutter of whitened water. Some men were clustered forward.

He passed an order to the guns, and heard the usual sounds as they were loaded, followed by the slam of the breech mechanism. In the still morning air with his nerves all on edge the noises sounded startlingly loud.

"Quiet! For God's sake quiet!" he burst out, as the loading number at 'X' gun reported the weapon ready in his normal voice. "Don't shout, man! You'll be heard a mile!"

The guns, laid practically horizontal, were following their target.

More and more of the submarine came into sight as she moved silently on with the blue water creaming round her blunt bows and washing aft along the curve of the saddle-tanks. He saw what looked like a 4-inch gun forward of the conning tower, then the upstanding tower itself with its housed periscopes, and the short superstructure abaft it with a thin wireless mast and aerials and a stumpy staff from which fluttered a dingy, tattered Rising Sun ensign. Finally she was in full view, with knots of men on deck and a little cloud of greyish smoke from exhausts rising from her stern. To his infinite relief Acton noticed that the gun was not manned, while one group of men in blue dungarees were engaged in extracting something out of the torpedo-hatch further forward. It was probably a collapsible boat.

It was clear enough that for the moment the Japanese suspected nothing, though watchful eyes on that grey conning tower must be searching and scanning the land through their binoculars.

The *Eurydice's* guns still followed their target as the range fell to eight hundred yards and then, slowly, to six hundred. Acton, his heart throbbing, watched with breathless expectation. Should he open fire at once, or wait until he was offered a still better target? He was undecided.

The enemy was approaching at an angle, steering, it seemed, direct for the floating oil-drums and the boats drawn up on the beach beyond them. If all went well, her course should bring her within four hundred yards of the *Eurydice*. There were no natives to be seen ashore.

Acton's mind was so concentrated upon the guns that he had temporarily forgotten about the torpedoes. But Mr. Blatchington hadn't. They were his pets, almost as cherished as his children. For months the Gunner (T) and his satellites had nurtured and looked after them—oiling, greasing, adjusting and polishing; topping them up with air; seeing to their gyroscopes and complicated engines and other internal mechanism. Each of those 'fish' had its history sheet which carried full details of their performance and any modifications since the original date of manufacture and issue. In the eyes of the torpedo-men their weapons were practically human, and every bit as temperamental as ordinary people.

Like the guns, which had female names painted upon them, a custom permitted by Pomeroy because it seemed to please and amuse the men, the torpedoes also had their pet names. The set of four at the foremost tubes were known as 'Amelia,' 'Jane,' 'Maggie' and 'Sally'—Amelia being Mrs. Blatchington, and the others the names of some of the torpedo-men's wives, children or best girls. It was accounted something of an honour to have a gun or a torpedo christened after the lady of one's choice.

Crouched on his wooden seat at the foremost set of tubes, which were trained as far aft as safety permitted, Blatchington was watching the submarine move slowly towards the line of sight set on his director. He, too, usually so imperturbable, was beginning to feel the strain. He was all keyed up, his nerves as taut as a fiddle-string. He felt himself trembling.

He was being offered the chance of a lifetime unless something went wrong. The enemy had no more than two hundred yards to travel before his sights came on, and was still moving ahead . . . a hundred and fifty yards. . . . It was a tense moment.

The sun must be rising behind the headland on the other side of the bay, for the sky was aglow with brilliance. To him it was inconceivable that in the fierce light the enemy hadn't already sighted the *Eurydice*, draped though she might be in fishing nets covered with branches and greenery renewed at frequent intervals, with whole trees and palms lashed here and there to funnels and superstructures to heighten the illusion. Some of the foliage was already very withered: a complete give away, one would think. The Japs must be keeping a very poor look-out. It amazed him to think they hadn't spotted the lips and gaping orifices of the four 21-inch torpedo-tubes. Carefully camouflaged though they were they must be very conspicuous.

But what in heck was holding up Mr. Acton? Why hadn't he opened fire? The enemy was already at point-blank range, virtually a sitting target. Was he waiting for the submarine to make the first move? One thing that was certain was that as soon as the first torpedo was fired the tell-tale thud of the discharge and the heavy splash would inevitably do away with any further chance of concealment.

The enemy still moved slowly ahead. About another hundred yards would bring her in line with the director sights . . . eighty yards . . . fifty. . . .

Seconds seemed magnified into minutes as the gunner watched. Bursting with pent-up emotion he was sweating profusely.

He was startled by the sudden discordant blare of a Klaxon horn sounding a series of short, meaningless blasts. 'Whoop! . . . Whoop! . . . Whoop! . . . Whooooop!' it screeched, and went on screeching.

"Bloody hell!" Henry Blatchington growled to himself. "What's the bastard up to now, for God's sake?" Then it occurred to him. The Japs must be trying to attract the attention of any natives ashore.

Then he noticed a swirl of whitened water under the submarine's tail. She was going astern to check her way. He watched, mouthing profanity. Was he to be balked of his target at the very last moment?

163

No. The white water subsided to leave the enemy still creeping slowly ahead, foot by foot. She had twenty yards to travel before he could have a fair shot . . . ten yards. . . .

She was still blaring away on that accursed Klaxon.

Then some freakish puff of wind from the westward, acting on the *Eurydice's* high bow and bridge structure, caused her to tauten the forward wires and to swing her bows away from the cliff. The movement was only temporary and the ship would soon swing back again; but Blatchington, with joy in his heart, watched his director sight moving slowly to the right.

"Stand by!" he ordered breathlessly.

The sights came level with the submarine's humped bow; then with the gun, then with the conning tower. . . .

"Fire one! . . . Fire two!"

With a thud, a hissing 'w-o-o-o-sh,' and the smell of burnt cordite, the torpedoes known as 'Sally' and 'Maggie' dived overboard in flashes of silver and whirring propellers to splash noisily into the sea.

"Fire three!" the Gunner shouted, determined to give full measure.

Standing up in his excitement he was vouchsafed a fleeting glimpse of two, no, three, oily-looking bubbling tracks streaking out across the shining irridescent sea at something like forty knots. They seemed to be running straight enough.

He saw little else. The ship shook as one of the 4.7's opened fire, closely followed by the other and the pom-pom. Successive waves of thick brown cordite smoke obscured Mr. Blatchington's view from the upper deck. In its warm, suffocating acridity he found it difficult to breathe. But through the rifts in the murk, as it thinned momentarily, he had a fleeting sight of lines of red and yellow tracer shooting seaward from two different directions. The pom-pom was using tracer, and the Bofors guns ashore must also have joined in.

The noise of gunfire became deafening. The Gunner, trying to say something to a leading torpedo-man, shouted to make himself heard. Even then his remark was inaudible.

"What's that you say, sir?" the man yelled, a hand to his ear.

Blatchington made no reply, for at that moment the air was suddenly filled with the deep-toned, thudding reverberation of a shattering detonation, almost as loud as that when the landing-craft had exploded skywards the evening before. Almost simultaneously it was followed by another heavy concussion like a clap of rolling thunder.

"God Almighty!" the Gunner murmured.

Two torpedoes, at any rate, had gone home on something, though on what he couldn't see. The guns were still in action and his view was blotted out by the yellowish smoke drifting eastward on the breeze. He was filled with doubt. Though unlikely, it was always possible that his torpedoes had dived to the bottom, or overrun their target to detonate on hitting the coral reef fringing the point of land beyond.

Then came a third heavy thud, duller and more muffled than those which had gone before.

Next he heard the shrill blasts of a whistle. In the absence of other communications they were Acton's signal for ceasing fire.

Another round crashed from 'Y' gun, after which the *Eurydice's* weapons became silent. From the left, Blatchington could still hear the staccato, popping reports of the Bofors mounted above the beach. Then they also died away.

He heard hoarse cheering from somewhere aft . . . then the smoke curtain rolled aside, dissolving.

"We done it, lads! We done it!" he cried, wild with excitement as a succession of heavy ripples travelling across the calm water came slapping against the *Eurydice's* side and caused her to lurch heavily. There was more cheering, louder than before.

With the others, Blatchington saw a spectacle he could never forget—the up-ended bow of the submarine standing at a steep angle out of a broad patch of oily sea. It slid slowly backwards and downwards, finally to disappear in a heavy uprush of air and swirling, bubbling spray. The turmoil gradually subsided, to leave the discoloured area dotted with floating wreckage and the black heads of a few men swimming for their lives.

"God in heaven!" he muttered, wiping his dripping face. "Poor bloody bastards!"

At heart Henry Arthur Blatchington was a humane sort of man. Though he hated and despised the Japanese for their callous barbarity and their complete disregard of most things he considered decent, he felt a certain pity for the poor devils cooped up in that shattered steel hull to die horrible deaths by drowning or slow suffocation. Some of them, like himself, must have a wife and children.

Acton came climbing down from the after superstructure and made his way forward. He was delighted.

"Guns, you old devil!" he exclaimed, clapping Blatchington on the back. "Congratulations. Damn fine work! I could almost kiss the lot of you!"

"So we hit her then?" the Gunner asked.

"I should damn well think so."

"Never saw a thing down here, Mr. Acton, nothing but smoke. What happened?"

"I could see over the smoke," the lieutenant explained. "The guns started hitting almost at once and knocked a few chunks off her. Then your two fish came along and finished the job. She seemed to break in two in a great burst of smoke and spray, and the bits went under."

The Gunner didn't look particularly satisfied. "I fired three," he grumbled. "What happened to the other?"

"God knows," said Acton. "I never saw it."

"Huh! More than three thousand pounds o' the taxpayers' ruddy money gone down the drain for no result! But what made you hang on all that time before opening fire? I couldn't imagine what was up, and it seemed ages before my sights came on. I thought we'd never get a crack, to be honest. Well, perhaps two's better than nothing, but I'd like to have done the hat trick."

"Don't be so particular," Acton laughed. "As for the guns, I just waited to make certain. But in the excitement I clean forgot the ensign. I believe it's illegal to open fire without it." He pointed aft to 'X' gun-deck, where a brand-new White Ensign flapped lazily from a boat-hook stave. The *Eurydice's* mainmast had long since been removed as too conspicuous.

The ethics of naval warfare were beyond the ken of Mr. Blatchington and did not really interest him; but the sight of the old flag greatly pleased him. "Looks good to me," he said. "Grand to see it up again after us masquerading as a blinkin' Christmas tree all this time."

Acton left him to give orders about the whaler. Always unemotional, the Gunner concealed his real feelings by turning on his torpedo-tubes' crews. "Come on, lads," he ordered tersely. "Don't go goofin' around like a lot o' schoolgirls 'cos we've sunk another bloomin' submarine! Get the tubes trained inboard an' everything cleaned up an' shipshape!"

In all, about fifteen Japanese had struck out for the beach, though no more than five reached it. The others, struggling desperately through the thick, treacly scum floating on the water, gave up and sank one by one. Once more the *Eurydice's* whaler, sent to search for possible survivors, found nothing but a few corpses drifting slowly seaward on the current.

Later, Farnworth, with Petty Officer Telegraphist Scriven, half a dozen sailors, and Beekman with a gang of natives, were sent up to the site of the Japanese camp in the hills to dispose of the corpses and bring back anything useful, including the portable radio set. Hot and tired, they returned during the afternoon after what the sub-lieutenant described as a thoroughly disgusting job. He didn't like dead bodies in the sweltering heat, though the natives had done the actual job of burial. However, it was just as well they had gone when they did, he added. Some natives, aware of what had happened and scenting loot, were already on the scene when the official party arrived. Caught in the act, they had been searched and made to give up most of the stolen property.

Of the five Japanese who successfully made the beach three, including a junior officer, were badly injured and died before sundown. Only two seamen, mere boys, still suffering from severe shock and half-suffocated by the viscid oil they had swallowed, remained alive. McInnes took a poor view of their condition. As usual he was doing all he could; but had to admit there was little chance of their survival.

17

THAT evening Acton called an informal council of war in the *Eurydice's* wardroom, which was attended by all the officers. Uneasy in his mind, he wanted to tell them what he thought and to hear their ideas.

In the first place, he said, the arrival of the landing-craft and the submarine within twelve hours of each other couldn't be mere coincidence. It was useless to try guessing what had brought the L.C. to the island. Her commanding officer might either have fancied a night in harbour on passage from A to B, or she might have put in for repairs. Anyhow, she was laden with ammunition, and the submarine had probably seen the flash of the explosion when she blew up, and had come along to investigate.

The important question was, had either vessel reported her movements by wireless? Scriven and his telegraphists, who spent most of their time listening, had picked up nothing in particular on the air. They knew the Japanese wavelengths, though of course it was quite on the cards that they might have missed any particular signal.

One couldn't say, he continued, whether enemy ships kept wireless silence at sea, or whether submarines on patrol, for instance, transmitted at routine times. However, if any signal had been sent off connecting either of the two sunken ships with the island, had they stirred up a hornet's nest? "In other words," Acton asked, "will the Japs tumble to the fact that something's happened here and send some ship to blast hell out of us?"

"Or aircraft," Melton suggested.

"They're bound to discover they're missing within a day or two," Draycott said after a moment's thought.

"That's true enough, Chief," the sub remarked. "But will they necessarily link up their loss with this island?"

The engineer officer shrugged his shoulders. "God only knows!" he replied. "As Number One—I beg your pardon, the captain, said just now, it's no damn use guessing."

Acton mopped his streaming face with a sodden handkerchief. The heat below was stifling. In spite of the fans and the mosquito netting over the side scuttles, a cloud of flies and other winged insects buzzed and banged against the electric lights. Singed, they sometimes fell to the table. Mr. Blatchington, using a match-box, obliterated a healthy-looking beetle with a scrunch, and consigned its remains to a glass ash-tray.

Acton looked round. He felt desperately tired, almost exhausted.

"The fact is," he said wearily, "we're up against it. We may get the Japs here in strength, or we may not. They may try bombing us as more economical. There's no telling. It's our job to carry on till we've fired our last round of ammunition.

No undue heroics; but I'll be damned," he continued, his voice rising, "before I listen to any nonsense of surrendering to the Japanese because it's one way out. I know that goes for all of you," he added, looking round the faces of his shipmates—Melton, Farnworth and Mr. Blatchington on one side of the table, Draycott and McInnes on the other. All their eyes were fixed on his. "We're here to fight, and I want that impressed on the men, every chance you get."

There were sounds of approval.

"Hear, hear!" Melton exclaimed, thumping the table in his eagerness to support his friend.

"To hell with the bloody Japs!" Mr. Blatchington growled under his breath.

Acton smiled and nodded. "Thanks," he said. "You might remind the men, I'll do it myself next time I talk to them, what the C.-in-C. Med., Andrew Cunningham, said during the evacuation from Crete about this time last year when the Navy was getting hell from the Luftwaffe and was losing men and ships every day. He pointed out, if you remember, that the evacuation *must* continue and that the Army mustn't be let down. He said, I believe—'If it takes three years to build a ship, it takes three hundred years to build a tradition!' We've no Army here; but that goes for us," he added. "Tradition. No mock heroics. We're here to fight."

"You can rely on all of us," Melton said. There came another murmur of approval.

"Good! That's settled," Acton continued. "Now there's something else I want to discuss, and this is where you come in, Pills. As you all know, I've done my best to let the ship's company know what's going on, mainly by putting two and two together from what Scriven has been able to pick up by wireless. Have any of you noticed any alarm or despondency among the men? I've no doubt. . . ."

"I haven't," Melton broke in. "They're. . . ."

Acton held up a hand to silence him. "Wait, Pilot!" he said. "Listen to what I've got to say. I've no doubt, like ourselves, there are times when they all feel fed up and depressed and they ask themselves what's going to happen. They wouldn't be human if they didn't. It's the damned uncertainty that's so trying. Here we are, locked up in a sort of backwater, cut off from practically everything, and unable to get away. We've had our excitements; but what I particularly want to know is if anyone round this table has noticed signs of any of our people wanting to chuck their hands in? You first, Pills," as Melton was about to reply. "You're our psychologist."

McInnes thought for a moment before answering. In his ministrations to the ship's company, he said, and he inspected every man twice a week, he'd noticed a certain amount of strain and weariness. That, he said, was only natural. It was brought about by the trying climate, the unusual food and way of life, and, most important of all, the fact they were cut off from home and anxious about wives and families in England. Some men, of course, were worse than others. It took all sorts to make a ship's company. There were a few chronic grumblers who raised rather frivolous complaints, and an odd malingerer or two. But these, he observed with a grin, could usually be dealt with.

"With what?" Melton laughed. "A Number Nine pill?"

McInnes withered him with a glance. "Don't interrupt a serious conversation, Pilot," he chided. During his bi-weekly medical examinations, he continued, he often had the opportunity of talking confidentially to people as man to man. He'd frequently been asked what he thought of their chances. He'd noticed no signs whatever of anything approaching defeatism. On the contrary, when anything exciting happened, like the shooting down of the aeroplane or the mopping-up expedition, the men's tails were well up and wagging. The sinking of the L.C. and the submarine, he added, would have an even greater effect. The sailors liked to have the chance of feeling proud of themselves. It was boredom and inactivity that got them down.

Acton thanked him and turned to Melton. "And what from you, Pilot?" he asked.

"I agree with Pills," the navigator replied. "I've nothing much to add, except that we're damned lucky in our petty officers. I'm not handing out bouquets when I say they're the salt of the earth."

Mr. Blatchington nodded.

"Anything from you, Chief?" Acton asked.

"I agree with the others," the engineer officer said. "There's nothing really wrong with my chaps apart from the usual boredom. They grumble a bit about the heat, the food, the flies, the land-crabs, the lack of beer and a good deal else; but on the whole they're pretty cheerful. I find it pays to keep 'em busy. If there's nothing special to be done on board, and they're not wanted for guard or other duties, there are plenty of useful jobs in the village. We've refitted all Beekman's pumps, and his antiquated ice machine, cleaned out the tanks, and laid on a supply of piped water. We've built an incinerator to burn the village garbage instead of allowing it to rot in the sun, and the Chief E.R.A. and I have various other schemes on hand. Whether our dusky friends are really grateful for the benefits of civilization is quite another matter. Personally I rather doubt it."

"Thank you, Chief," Acton nodded. "Any remarks from you, Sub?"

"I think it would be a good idea if we organized a wild-pig hunt every now and then," Farnworth replied. "I'm perfectly serious," he added, as Draycott and McInnes raised their eyebrows, looked at each other and tittered. "I've seen wild pig in the hills. They'd give us a change of diet, anyhow. The natives trap them. Why shouldn't we?"

"How d'you propose to set about it?" Melton asked.

"A couple of decent shots with rifles, and native beaters. I've already had a talk with Beekman. I don't mind organizing it."

"Is pork fit and proper food in this sort of climate?" Acton asked the doctor.

McInnes saw no reason why it shouldn't be.

"Right, Sub. You'll be O.C. pig hunt," Acton said. "Now, Guns. Have you any suggestions?"

"Meaning are the men happy or discontented, and is there anything more we can do to keep 'em up to the mark?" Mr. Blatchington asked.

"Yes. That's about it."

"Then I agree with what the other officers have said. Keep 'em busy. Give 'em too easy a time, an' they'll get into mischief. If you ask me, sir, some of 'em are already enjoying themselves a bit *too* much."

"Meaning what, precisely?"

The Gunner considered his reply. "It's the gals, Mister Acton. They're free-and-easy like, or should I call it forth-coming?"

171

"I was already aware of that," Acton said, glancing at Melton and thinking of Beekman's daughter, Lallah.

Melton looked elsewhere. So did Farnworth, the susceptible, who had another maiden on his mind.

"Yes, sir," the Gunner continued. "But some of our lads have got themselves entangled."

"Good God!" Acton exclaimed. "You don't mean. . . ."

"You can't blame the sailors," the Gunner broke in, quick to defend his own kind. "They're only human. Gals are gals the world over, as we very well know, and I've seen some. But here they're hot-blooded, red-hot, you take my word! What d'you expect the sailors to do when gals twine themselves round their necks an' put flowers in their hair? 'Tisn't in human nature to resist. An' what happens?"

"What does happen?" Acton asked, aware that Mr. Blatchington had the ear of the lower deck.

"Ask Able Seaman Wiley, sir. He's only one who's got himself mixed up."

Acton demanded an explanation.

It was a long and rather rambling story.

It had come to Mr. Blatchington's ears, through Petty Officer Hartopp, that Wiley, a nice lad of twenty-two, expected in due course to become a father.

McInnes pricked up his ears. Wiley, he observed, must have been pretty quick off the mark.

Aye, said the Gunner; but the girls were quicker.

"You mean the girl's in an interesting condition?" the doctor asked.

"That's what's said," Blatchington replied.

"Who says it?"

"The gal's mother an' all the female witch-doctors in the village. A proper lot of old battle-axes all hangin' in heaps!"

"Am I expected to give an expert opinion?" McInnes asked with a look of horror on his face. "If so, I refuse point-blank to be let in for a gynaecological argument with the local Mothers' Union!"

"What's the point of all this?" Acton demanded. "Why the blazes should we be bothered with Wiley's love affairs? Is the girl insisting that he should make an honest woman of her?"

The Gunner shook his head. It wasn't that, he explained. The girl, a seventeen-year-old peach, already possessed one baby. She didn't give a hoot about marrying young Wiley. No. The fact was, young Wiley wanted to marry the girl. Beekman, it seemed, being a sort of a kind of a magistrate, had some powers in that respect. Failing that, Wiley thought he could be married according to the usual tribal ritual, which apparently involved payment of some sort to the bride's parents.

"And if we ever get away from here does the damn fool propose to take his peach home to England and live happily ever afterwards?" Acton asked. "What'll his people think? How will he fit into life at home with this . . . this trollop of his?"

"Don't blame me, sir, please," Mr. Blatchington protested. "I'm merely repeating what Petty Officer Hartopp told me. Wiley's an orphan. It seems he says he doesn't care if he goes home to England or not. He wouldn't mind living the rest of his life in this island."

"The bloody fool!" Acton exploded. "I'll have a word with Mr. Wiley and put a stop to this damned nonsense!"

Petty Officer Hartopp had already had a word with Wiley, the Gunner explained, several words. But Wiley, it seemed, had fallen head over ears in love.

"Love, my foot!" Acton burst out.

"Well, sir," Mr. Blatchington continued. "Petty Officer Hartopp says to Wiley: 'Look you here, my lad,' he says, 'you're a young man, an' I'm damn near old enough to be your pa. Don't you go actin' stupid an' spoilin' the whole of your life on the spur o' the moment. Your gal's a good-looker,' he says. 'She's got flashin' eyes an' one o' them curvin' figures an' a sweet smile as would tempt a graven image. But if you want to know what your peacherino'll look like in a few years' time, just you take a peep at her mother, who's such a fat old wobblin' bag o' guts you can't tell whether she's comin' or goin'.' That's what Hartopp tells young Wiley, sir."

Carried away, Mr. Blatchington had excelled himself. There was laughter round the wardroom table.

Acton yawned. "Well done, Guns," he said. "And good for Hartopp, if he really said what you've just told us."

"He said all that, an' a good deal more," the Gunner insisted.

"I sincerely hope so," Acton returned. "But to tell the truth

I'm a little bit weary of Wiley. Pilot, we'll have to put our heads together and take some rather drastic measures to put a stopper on these . . . 'er, well, promiscuous love affairs. Boys will be boys; but we can't have the ship's company. . . ."

The conversation was interrupted by a loud knock on the wardroom door.

"Come in!" Acton called.

It was Petty Officer Telegraphist Scriven, in a state of considerable excitement and carrying a signal-pad.

"Well, Scriven?"

"There's news, sir! Good news! We've just picked up bits of an American broadcast, very faint. I think it came from Australia. We didn't get the lot."

"Australia! That's a hell of a way!"

"Well, anyhow we heard it, sir. The Jap fleet's had a hammering from the Yanks!"

There were exclamations of joy all round the table. Acton sprang to his feet. "Are you certain, Scriven?"

"I can only say what we heard, sir, and it was faint, with a good deal of fading out. It sounded like an American broadcasting. . . ."

"But what did he say, man?" Acton demanded, bursting with impatience.

Scriven referred to his signal-pad. "That there'd been a sea and air battle lasting several days, sir," he replied. "The Japs lost a carrier, a heavy cruiser, a light cruiser, some destroyers and other ships sunk, and more damaged. Transports and supply ships were mentioned. When last seen the Japanese fleet was retiring northward."

The sudden news was startling. For a moment there was a tense silence, then a buzz of excited conversation.

"Anything about American losses?" Acton wanted to know.

"Nothing was said, sir."

"Where was this battle fought?" Melton inquired.

"The Coral Sea was mentioned, sir."

"And that's the lot?" Acton asked.

"That's all for the moment, sir. I'd best be getting back if you'll excuse me. Perhaps more may be coming through. Can I inform the ship's company?"

"You may, Scriven, and thanks for the best bit of news we've had for months. I only hope to heaven it's true."

The petty officer telegraphist grinned happily and retired.

Melton had left his chair to examine the chart pinned to a board on the after bulkhead of the wardroom—a small-scale chart covering an enormous area, from the Indian Ocean some eight thousand miles eastward to a point fully two-thirds of the way across the Pacific.

"Here's the Coral Sea," he said, dabbing a finger on the spot. "To the south of the Solomon Islands."

The chart presented a depressing picture. Its centre portion was dotted with an almost unbroken chain, doubled in places, of little home-made Japanese flags showing territories and islands already occupied by the enemy. Malaya and Singapore, Sumatra and Java, parts of the Philippines, Borneo, the Celebes and the archipelago of islands to the eastward, the north coast of New Guinea, New Britain, New Ireland, and certain of the Solomon Islands already showed the hideous Rising Sun emblem of Japan, the tide of Japanese conquest.

Melton had done his best to keep the map up to date through intercepted broadcasts. Acton hated the very sight of it. It was too dismal a record and a reminder. The pattern of thickly-clustered Japanese flags got on his nerves and made everything seem so hopeless. Only here and there, in isolation, were stuck the friendly flags—the Union Flag of Britain and the Stars and Stripes of the United States. The Dutch flags had long since been removed.

Melton was still gazing at the chart with a rapt expression when they heard the sounds of frantic cheering from forward. Scriven had imparted the news.

"I'm glad they're pleased," Acton observed. "It'll help to keep 'em cheerful."

"D'you know what I think this means, George?" the navigator suddenly asked over his shoulder.

"What?"

"The Jap effort to the southward," Melton said, pointing with his pipe-stem. "You see all these islands where the stinkers have already landed and dug themselves in?"

Acton nodded.

"Well, we heard on the wireless two months ago that they got a bloody nose when they had a shot at taking Port Moresby —here, on the south coast of New Guinea. They were well pasted by aircraft from American carriers. That probably

175

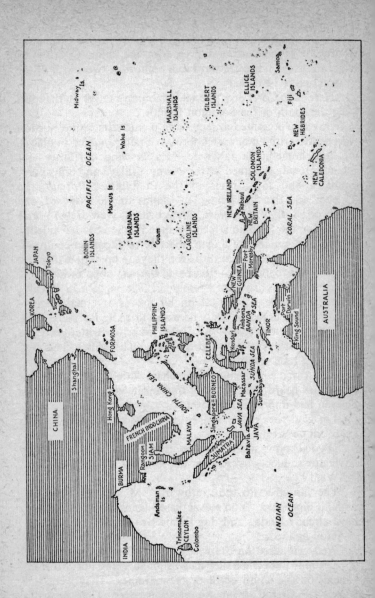

scared 'em, and showed 'em they couldn't expect to have things exactly their own way." He paused.

"Go on," Acton prompted.

Melton continued. It was his idea, he said, that in their latest effort the Japs were probably having another crack at Port Moresby, or else at landing in force in Northern Australia, in Queensland, to be precise. If that had come about they would have gone on to the eastward, as they'd done all along, occupying more islands and establishing air bases, first New Caledonia and the New Hebrides, then Fiji and Samoa, which he indicated one by one on the map.

"With what object, Pilot?" Draycott asked, somewhat mystified.

"To isolate Australia and New Zealand. They'd have had a complete barrier of islands with air bases to the northward, and have been able to occupy Australian and New Zealand ports and harbours more or less at their leisure.

"You may think I'm talking through my hat!" he went on to say, noticing looks of incredulity on some of his listeners' faces. "But it's plain common sense. You may say that if Australia and New Zealand fell to the Japs, we'd just have to turn 'em out again. God!" he continued, his voice rising as he warmed to his theme. "What sort of a job would that have been, even with the Americans, and us fighting the Germans and Italians in North Africa, U-boats swarming all over the Atlantic, and the Japs in the Indian Ocean? We must be pretty well scraping the bottom of the barrel as it is. Where could we have found the ships and the sailors and the troops to fight another full-size war this end of the world? One day, too, we'll have to land in Europe to finish the Nazis and the Wops."

"Good for you, Pilot!" Acton approved.

"Thank you, George. What I'm really trying to point out is that if Australia and New Zealand went, we'd have probably lost the war. That's my opinion, anyway."

"You may be right," Acton said, concealing a yawn. "I won't argue about it."

"And if this latest news about the Coral Sea battle is true, and I hope to God that some of our ships and the Australians were in on it, it's my belief they've saved Australia and New Zealand," the navigator declared. "I've studied the Japs. I don't think they'll try smashing their way southward again

177

after two bloody noses. They'll probably have a crack in some other direction."

Only time was to show how right Melton was. No one in the *Eurydice's* wardroom that sweltering evening could realize that the battle of the Coral Sea was to be Japan's last threatening stretch towards Australasia.

Opening one of their last bottles of whisky in celebration, they sat discussing the situation until nearly midnight.

18

IT WAS the late afternoon of May 9th, 1942. For the first time since the opening of the war in the Pacific by the bombing of the American fleet in Pearl Harbour five months earlier, the Flag Officer, Java Sea, Rear-Admiral Isoroku Yamaguchi, at his headquarters ashore in Surabaya, had feelings of disquietude.

A short, stocky, shaven-headed seaman brought up in the strict line of his profession, the Admiral was ruthless in his pursuit of efficiency and devoid of all sentimentality. Cloaked in reserve and dignity, he was blunt-spoken and not given to showing his feelings, even to his most trusted subordinates. He was a fierce little martinet; his the responsibility of giving orders which it was the duty of others to obey without question. He would accept no discussion or argument. Except as regards operations with which a junior was intimately connected, Yamaguchi seldom delegated authority. He was not even on really intimate terms with his Chief of Staff, a senior captain, and would never have dreamt of accepting his advice. Nobody really knew the Admiral's innermost thoughts, not even his harassed flag lieutenant.

Like most of his compatriots Yamaguchi had blind faith in the sublime virtue of the Emperor and supreme confidence in Japanese leadership. It was Japan's divine task to rule the Orient—China, the Philippines, Malaya, Borneo, and the whole of the rich Dutch East Indies with the other islands stretching east as far as Fiji and Samoa. If the British and Americans objected, then let them fight for it.

Mighty conquests had already been achieved with comparatively trifling loss. French Indo-China and Siam were under Japanese 'protection.' Hong Kong, Malaya and Singapore had been taken from the British, Burma overrun, and the Andaman Islands occupied as an advanced base in the Indian Ocean. The Dutch East Indies had fallen to the victorious Japanese arms, and the last remnant of the Americans battling at Corregidor, in the Philippines, had been forced to surrender on May 6th.

And what of Yamaguchi's own Service, the Imperial Japanese Navy?

Its record, with success after success, had been even more glorious than that of the Russo-Japanese War: first the smashing blow against the American battle fleet at Pearl Harbour; then the battle of the Java Sea, followed by daring strikes by Japanese carrier-borne aircraft against Rabaul, Amboina, Darwin in Northern Australia, and off Java.

Japanese carriers, battleships, cruisers and destroyers had even penetrated boldly into the Indian Ocean and the Bay of Bengal, where for a time they had complete control. British warships and many merchant vessels had been sunk, and Colombo and Trincomalee heavily bombed. Japanese submarines were operating off the west coast of India and the east coast of Africa. India feared invasion, and what the British had been able to scrape up in the way of a fleet had been forced to withdraw to East Africa. It was Yamaguchi's idea that Britain's weakness was further shown when she occupied the harbour of Diego Suarez in Madagascar because she feared it might be used as a base by Japanese submarines.

The first five months of the war had added many triumphant pages to Japanese naval history, the little Admiral believed. If they had the will to fight, the Allies seemed to have neither the ships nor the men with which to stand up against the mighty power of the Imperial Japanese Navy. It was ubiquitous, omnipotent and invincible. Yamaguchi felt immensely proud. Most of what Japan was fighting for was already in her grasp, hers to keep and to develop in her own interests. A fig for the vaunted strength of the British Empire and the United States of America!

But on May 9th the Admiral was not quite his confident self, a fact of which none of his staff could fail to be aware. He was even more morose and testy than usual, gazing for minutes on

179

end at the large wall chart in his operations-room without saying a word. There was much on his mind.

For the past three days bits and pieces of information about a great naval battle in the Coral Sea, nearly 2,500 miles to the eastward, had been filtering into his Intelligence Centre. Some of it came through intercepted wireless signals, some through spoken broadcasts, Japanese, American and British. Carrier-borne aircraft had been in action on both sides. The Admiral had nearly exploded with rage when his intelligence officer had shown him the text of a translated broadcast in which the Americans had the effrontery to claim a great victory with many Japanese ships sunk.

"Impossible!" he exclaimed, banging his desk in anger. "American propaganda to bolster up their own defeat! All Americans are liars!"

He was only partly relieved when Tokyo broadcast a message contradicting the American statements.

Though not immediately concerned, Yamaguchi was aware of the broad outline of the Japanese plan, which had as its object the landing of an expeditionary force at Port Moresby, on the south coast of New Guinea, preparatory to a further advance to other islands to the eastward, all with a view to isolating Australia and New Zealand. If the earlier stages of the plan succeeded, it might be the prelude to the Japanese invasion of both those British Dominions.

But as the hours passed into days and more and more news came over the air, it became clear that something untoward had happened. The Japanese fleet had retired northward, according to the Americans, to which Tokyo responded with the assertion that two American carriers, with a battleship and a heavy cruiser, had all been sunk. This the Americans had flatly denied.

The Admiral did not know what to believe. Were the Americans really lying, or had the Japanese suffered their first serious reverse at sea?

Yamaguchi was a worried man. For nearly two months convoys of transports and supply ships, lightly escorted by what small craft and aircraft were available, had been passing east through the Java Sea in an almost unending stream. Troops from Singapore, Borneo, Sumatra and Java, their work there ended, were being ferried in battalions and brigades to the

180

new theatre of war farther east. With the soldiers went all their guns, ammunition, vehicles, food and masses of miscellaneous war material. It was the Admiral's responsibility and the navy's duty to see to it that the men and their supplies got through unscathed.

In spite of his repeated protests, the higher authorities had gradually and consistently whittled away his surface escorts and aircraft for what they considered urgent duty in more important areas. The Java Sea, with the Sunda Sea and the Banda Sea to the eastward, they argued, were virtually Japanese lakes, safe from any enemy interference. To this Yamaguchi, after a cautious interval, had tactfully mentioned American submarines, which, according to his information, were having successes in other parts of the Pacific. The answer he received to this, by secret cipher, was terse and to the point. He was informed, in so many words, that it was the business of others who knew the overall picture to allocate the ships and vessels of the Imperial Japanese Navy to their respective tasks and areas. He must do the best he could with what ships and aircraft he had. No more could be spared. If and when the situation changed the matter might be reconsidered.

So apart from a few of the smaller submarines used for patrol work, with some rather antiquated flying-boats and half a dozen obsolescent naval fighters, the Admiral was left with no more than a handful of older destroyers, torpedo-boats and a few aged sloops for use as surface escorts. Greatly overworked, they were insufficient for the task. His convoys were too weakly escorted for what he considered was safety. Some of the faster transports, supply ships and landing-craft had to sail singly and unescorted.

About a fortnight earlier, one crowded transport, after an explosion in the early dawn, caused, it was thought, by a drifting mine, had been forced to beach herself in a sinking condition on a solitary coral islet in the Sunda Sea, and had wirelessed for immediate assistance. It was blowing hard from the westward with a very heavy surf, and many troops had been drowned while trying to get ashore. By the time the rescuers arrived the ship herself had broken up and become a total wreck.

That incident had evoked an acrimonious inquiry from Yamaguchi's superiors demanding to know the exact circumstances of the loss. Merchant shipping was desperately short. Why had that particular vessel, which was a comparatively new one, been selected for the voyage? Who had been responsible for sailing her unescorted and issuing her route orders?

The Admiral had ordered a Court of Inquiry when the necessary witnesses could be assembled. He knew the verdict beforehand. The court would inevitably find that the accident was one of the usual hazards of wartime navigation, and that, because the ship was a fast one and urgently required, she had been sailed alone and unescorted because sufficient escorts did not exist. That, though literally true, would not enhance Yamaguchi's prestige in high circles.

Then, some days later, had come the unfortunate business when Commander Kamimura, commanding the submarine flotilla used for patrol duties, came post-haste to the Admiral's office to report to the Chief of Staff.

"Sir," he said, visibly agitated as he made the usual low bow on being shown into the Chief of Staff's room. "I regret to report. One of our submarines has failed to make the usual routine signals. We have lost touch with her."

The captain pushed a box of cigarettes across his desk and motioned Kamimura to help himself and sit down. "Explain, Commander," he said tersely, without any change of expression.

"It was the submarine in Number Three patrol area," Kamimura replied, "commanded by one of the most competent officers, Lieutenant-Commander Takagi."

"I know Takagi," the senior officer nodded. "Go on. What has happened?"

"All submarines on patrol, sir, are ordered to send a short message while on the surface at night recharging their batteries. It is a matter of routine. They normally transmit between eleven and eleven-fifteen, only at other times in case of sighting the enemy or in emergency."

"Yes."

"They listen between eleven-thirty and one o'clock a.m., and again for an hour before diving at dawn."

The Chief of Staff nodded.

"For two nights now, sir, Takagi has made no report," Kamimura continued. "For two nights he has acknowledged none of our signals."

"And the others have, Commander?"

"Yes, sir."

The Chief of Staff rose from his chair and examined the chart on the wall behind him.

"Area Number Three," he observed, his face inscrutable. "That is the one to the eastward."

"Yes, sir."

"And you fear something may have happened, Commander?"

Kamimura hesitated. "I don't know what to think, sir," he replied. "It is unlike Takagi not to be punctilious in. . . ."

"I understand," the captain broke in, shrugging his shoulders. "Come with me. We had better see the Admiral."

Rear-Admiral Yamaguchi was informed, and, for him, took the news philosophically. He ordered a couple of the precious flying-boats to search area Number Three from dusk to dawn, while Kamimura was to continue calling up Takagi's submarine at the usual routine times.

So far there had been no results.

Misfortunes rarely happen singly, or even in pairs. They usually come in threes.

Landing Craft 4903, commanded by a reserve lieutenant, one Makoto, vanished into the blue. Makoto didn't greatly matter, nor did his ship or the couple of dozen other officers and men who served in her. They were all expendable. What was of real consequence, and what infuriated an already worried Admiral, was the fact that L.C. 4903 carried a full cargo of ammunition and other important military stores for which he, Yamaguchi, was ultimately responsible.

She had sailed from Batavia for Macassar in fine, clear weather and was more than two days overdue. She had made no wireless signals reporting her movements or anything amiss. The Senior Naval Officer, Macassar, no doubt spurred on by the Army, was sending almost frantic inquiries to know when the ship might be expected. The air was humming with messages about L.C. 4903—Macassar communicating direct with Batavia and Surabaya; and Yamaguchi, at Surabaya, with the Senior Naval Officer and Sea Transport Officer at Batavia, neither of whom had a clue as to what had happened except that L.C. 4903 had sailed punctually on time. More aircraft had to be ordered to continue a widespread search, this time by day.

Then, shortly before dusk one evening, there came an emergency report by radio-telephone from one of the Japanese flying-boats:

> TWO LARGE SUBMARINES SURFACED IN COMPANY SQUARE 95z. PROCEEDING 260 DEGREES SPEED 15 KNOTS.

And a minute later:

> SUBMARINES PREVIOUSLY REPORTED HAVE NOT REPLIED TO CHALLENGE. EVIDENTLY HOSTILE.

Then a short pause, followed by:

> ENEMY OPENED FIRE. AM ATTACKING.

Admiral Yamaguchi's worst fears were realized. American long-range submarines *had* penetrated to the Java Sea!

He longed to send an 'I told you so' message to his immediate superior who had refused to accept the counsel of the man on the spot, the man who knew all the circumstances. Instead, he drafted a priority signal:

> MOST SECRET. URGENT. TWO ENEMY SUBMARINES SIGHTED SQUARE 95z 1850 TODAY. HAVE CANCELLED CONVOY SAILINGS UNTIL SITUATION CLEARER. REQUEST IMMEDIATE REINFORCEMENT PATROL AND ESCORT FORCES, INCLUDING ADDITIONAL AIRCRAFT. F.O. J.A.S.*

"Perhaps that will make them see sense!" he observed to his Chief of Staff, his lips pursed and his face grim. "What convoys have we at sea?"

"One of eight ships left Batavia for Amboina and Kendari last night, sir. They're due to be joined by another three ships from here some time tomorrow evening."

"Is the Batavia convoy escorted?"

"Yes sir. Three destroyers."

The Admiral gazed at his wall chart. "Order the Batavia party to return, and cancel the Surabaya sailing," he grunted.

*Flag Officer. Java Sea.

"Use everything we have to search. Have all mine-sweeping forces warned. The enemy may be mine-layers."

"Yes, sir."

"You understand our programme is dislocated until they send us reinforcements," Yamaguchi continued. "These submarines *must* be hunted down and destroyed, and there may be others. Their destruction is our first duty."

"I understand," the Chief of Staff agreed.

The situation was certainly disturbing.

First had come the loss of that transport filled with troops, which might well have been brought about by an American submarine. Then came the conflicting news of the battle in the Coral Sea, which was still being claimed as a great American victory, in spite of Tokyo's rather unconvincing efforts to deny it. Next had followed the disappearance of Takagi's submarine and L.C. 4903, of neither of which there was any further information. Both the Admiral and the Chief of Staff had made up their minds that they must probably be written off as lost—American submarines again.

To cap it all, the flying-boat which had first startled everybody with her enemy report had failed to return from her patrol, and a consort, sent out to search the area, had found nothing.

19

EVER since the *Eurydice* had reached the island about ten weeks earlier, George Acton, snatching what opportunities he could, had sat himself down to write to Fiona in London. His letters, in the form of a personal journal describing all that had happened, intermingled with a reflection of his own innermost thoughts and feelings, now covered more than thirty closely-written sheets of quarto typewriting paper.

Sometimes, when tired and feeling utterly depressed and disconsolate, he wondered what was the use of writing at all. Would Fiona ever receive the outpourings of his heart? He might never get away from the island, and even if he did his narrative might ruthlessly be censored by some little man in an office who might be beyond the bounds of human kindness or comprehension.

Added to that, the *Eurydice* and all on board had probably long since been officially announced as lost in action. He knew that Fiona had loved him, and she certainly meant all the world to him. But giving up all hope of his survival she might have steeled herself to forget. She had many friends, and might quite well have decided to marry someone else. Driving her car through all the fiery perils of the blitz on London, she might even be dead.

He would never forget the last sad time they had dined together in that intimate little French restaurant in Soho—Fiona's choice—where one sat side by side on red velvet settees, and, in spite of the bombing and the rigours of war and of rationing, the food and the cooking were still good and there was no distracting music. He had spent the last few days of his leave with his people in Sussex, and coming up to London earlier in the day was due to rejoin the *Eurydice* at Devonport next morning, which meant catching a late train from Paddington and travelling through most of the night. They had tried their best to be cheerful; but it had been a miserable meal. They hardly noticed what they were eating.

"Fiona, darling," he had said. "God only knows how long I'll be abroad, or what may happen."

"I know, my lamb," she replied, trying to smile and be cheerful. "Don't think I'm not feeling pretty wretched. But you'll be back. I know it, feel it in my bones, so cheer up." She squeezed his hand under the table.

"I'll be most horribly worried about you," he returned. "Can't you get some equally useful job to driving that car during these beastly air-raids?"

Fiona shook her head. "We've had all this out before," she said. "I've got a job to do just as much as you have. What would you think of me if I chucked in my hand now?"

"I don't know," he replied gloomily. "But every time I hear of an attack on London I'm frightened stiff in case something awful's happened to you."

"There are times when I'm scared myself, old pet. But if no one ran risks in wartime where would we all be? It's just as bad for me knowing that you're knocking about at sea in a destroyer. That makes us quits, doesn't it?"

"Maybe," George Acton had to admit. "Lord! I wish we'd been married six months ago when the ship was smashed up and I had that fortnight's leave. Fiona, darling! Why didn't we?"

"Heaven knows!" she sighed. "Perhaps we were a pair of fools, I don't know. We hadn't much money; but if your people and mine hadn't objected we might have pulled it off, regardless. Why must parents interfere?"

"We could have scratched along somehow," he said. "Oh, Fiona! And now it's come to our parting I can hardly bear it. You mean such an awful lot to me."

"My dear, I know what *you* mean to me," she replied gently. "I love you, darling."

"You'll never change your mind?"

"No. Never, *never!*"

"If you ever do think better of it, I don't want you to feel tied. Just let me know, that's all."

"I shan't think better of it, my pet," she answered. "I *want* to be tied to you, so that's all about it. Don't fret. I'm not going to change my mind." She spoke in all sincerity.

The last time George Acton had seen Fiona was on the darkened platform at Paddington, just before his train pulled out.

"God bring you home safe, my precious," she had murmured as they hugged and kissed.

A whistle blew. Acton tore himself away, too overcome to speak. There were tears in Fiona's eyes.

. . . And that had been months and months ago on the opposite side of the world. Looking back, it seemed almost unreal. So much had happened since.

Though the mails had been woefully erratic and letters frequently arrived in the wrong sequence, they had written regularly. The last air-mail letter George had received a day before sailing from Surabaya had been dated two months earlier—Christmas Eve, 1941.

But to George Acton, Fiona was still very tangible and living. Even though she might never receive his letters the mere act of writing was a solace. It seemed to bring her closer, and gave him something intimate and personal to think about; something very precious and sacred—what the French, with all their facility for apt expression, might have called *la vie d'intérieur* in which no one else but their two selves could share.

Late one evening towards the end of May, in the dank steaminess of the cabin which had been Pomeroy's, Acton sat himself down at the desk to add to his letter to the girl he loved. The electric fan whirring and swaying on the bulkhead merely served to disperse the heat, not to dissipate it. He wore nothing but a sarong.

"Darling, Beloved Fiona," he wrote. "You're so much in my heart and mind that I feel I must write a little more to you before turning in. It's close on 10.30 p.m., and after a day of glaring brazen sun without a vestige of breeze the heat is still sweltering. Down here in my cabin it's like being in the hottest chamber of a Turkish bath with the door hermetically sealed. Jevons, my steward, has managed to produce a large jug of iced water and unsweetened lime juice, though it's not much use. I'm dripping everywhere, so forgive the smudginess of my writing.

"What have I to tell you? Very little, I fear. We've had no further excitements comparable to wiping out that party of Japs and sinking that landing-craft and submarine that I told you about some time ago. Oh! I forgot. Two days ago, just after sunrise, we sighted a formation of heavy bombers going east. They were too far off to the southward to be really distinguishable. I thought they were Japs. But others, including Melton and Farnworth, and the pilot's a wizard at aircraft identification, swore they were American, probably flown off a carrier and returning from a raid on Surabaya or Batavia. I hope to heaven they were! You'll have heard, of course, of the Americans giving the Japs a bloody nose in the Coral Sea earlier this month. Scriven and Hargrave, our telegraphists, managed to pick up bits and pieces from outside broadcasts, and I've no doubt the Japs had a worse tonking than they'll ever admit. The news certainly put new heart into us.

"Speaking of Japs reminds me of that party we mopped up. Well, we went through the contents of their camp with a fine tooth comb and discovered seven complete parachutes neatly folded up and stowed away, with the remains of several others. There were ten or a dozen in all. So there's no longer any doubt as to how the blighters came in the first instance, or that they landed before our arrival, though precisely what for I don't know. Why the natives knew nothing about it, and why

188

Beekman, the Dutchman, didn't get to hear of it, I just can't imagine. Perhaps some of the natives did know and thought it advisable to remain mum. Anyhow, the parachutes are pure silk, so Beekman says. Some are pale blue, others a sort of lemon colour, and a couple bright red. I've given Beekman one for his wife and daughters, served out five more for the ladies of the village to disport themselves in, and divided the rest among our officers and men. I've pinched a complete pale blue one for you, knowing that pale blue is one of your colours, you being blue-eyed, blonde and altogether adorable. I shall take it to pieces, and some day, perhaps, you'll be able to use it for undies! God! How I hope so, though how we're ever to get away from this island I can't see. All told there are 117 of us.

"I told you of that Jap wireless set we found in their camp. It's a sort of super walkie-talkie, and Scriven, the P.O. Telegraphist, who has been experimenting, says it's of far longer range than anything of the sort he's ever seen before. Some nights ago, when he was playing around, he heard English being spoken, or rather, American. He said it certainly wasn't aircraft, and must be two ships talking to each other, and from the strength of their messages put their distance at fifty miles more or less. By the time I'd been routed out of bed and tried to listen, the speakers had gone off the air. Question is, if Scriven is right, and he isn't given to making wild statements, what ships could they have been? They can't have been surface ships, and it occurs to me that they might have been American submarines.

"I don't honestly know what to think; but if American submarines are operating anywhere near here we might catch their wavelength and get into touch with them. If we could, at least they'd be able to get news of us to the outside world, or to take a few of our people away. They could never lift the whole 117 of us, and in any case I'll have to remain here until the last of our men has gone.

"The only thing we can eventually do with the poor old *Eurydice* is to take her out and scuttle her in deep water. I see nothing else for it. We could steam for as long as our fuel lasted; but haven't enough to reach Ceylon, on the one hand, or Australia on the other. At the same time Sumatra, Java, and all the islands to the eastward are held by the Japs, which means we'd soon be spotted by their aircraft and bombed to shreds. To make matters worse Draycott, the Chief, tells me he hasn't been able to deal with all the leaks we sustained in action, while the terrific explosion when that landing-craft blew up bulged in several plates below water and did other damage we can't compete with.

"I'm left in a very ticklish predicament, and whatever I decide to do may be considered wrong. We could of course make up our minds to remain here until the end of the war, though this has the disadvantage of keeping 117 perfectly good officers and men more or less idle until the Japs are finally defeated, which may take years, though I'm fully confident they will be defeated in the end.

"If there's any chance of rescue for the whole lot of us, in driblets, I think it's my duty to regard the ship as expendable and sink her in deep water before the last of us leave. After all, 117 sailors are of more importance to the war effort than one badly damaged destroyer which can't be made seaworthy outside a dockyard which there isn't a dog's chance of reaching. I've therefore made up my mind to this if the chance of rescue comes, and hope to heaven I'm doing the right thing. It's a difficult problem, and of course there's always the chance that the Japs will tumble to the fact that we're here and send some ship along to knock hell out of us. I'm rather surprised they haven't done so already. They must know by this time that a landing-craft and a submarine have disappeared somewhere about here.

"As for me, I've practically got over the touch of dysentery I mentioned in my last instalment. I must say, though, that this climate with its damp heat is very trying. So is the food. But McInnes, our doctor, is a marvel, and keeps us all as fit as may be. Some of the sailors are a bit grumbly and restive. One or two of the younger ones who've become rather too attached to the local girls want to marry and remain here for life! Can you beat it? I must say, though, that the girls are very attractive, though not so their mothers. I've tried to reason with them, the sailors who want to marry, I mean, though I don't know if they're really convinced how foolish they are. Their line of thought seems to be that because we've probably all been reported as missing, presumed killed in action, they're no longer subject to naval discipline and are free to do as they like. One sometimes needs the patience of Job and the wisdom of Solomon, though the bulk of the ship's company, particularly the petty officers, are splendid.

"It's past midnight and time I turned in. The heat's still sweltering, and in spite of the mosquito netting over my scuttles a cloud of flies and insects still buzzes around my electric light. Good night, Fiona darling. To the end, however it happens, *you* have all my love and heart."

20

FORTY-EIGHT hours of intermittent drenching rain pouring vertically down in one deluge after another had converted all the hillside streams and gullies into tumbling, muddy torrents which again had flooded the lower parts of the island. The rain had ceased, and after another two days of intense heat with no breeze the summits of the hills had become wrapped in layers of heavy mist. They crept lower and lower, while streams of woolly vapour, creeping slowly down the valleys, coalesced into a thick steaming blanket which finally enveloped the whole island.

Farnworth was keeping the morning watch, and at first daylight, when Acton was called and went on deck, as was his habit, there was thick, blinding fog. The visibility was down to twenty yards, certainly no more. It was impossible to see the fore part of the *Eurydice* from the stern.

"You can fall out the duty gun's crew," he said, glancing at the murk overhead and then to the eastward where the invisible risen sun was staining the thick shroud of vapour with the first faint blush of orange and rose. "It won't lift yet awhile."

"Not till we get a breeze," the sub agreed. "D'you notice the smell? It's much stronger than usual."

Acton sniffed. "It's rather pleasant," he replied, savouring the heavy fragrance mingled with the strong, clean odour of sodden earth. "A cross between a heated conservatory and a scent shop; anyhow, a darned sight better than the fug in my cabin." He lit a cigarette.

Farnworth yawned and stretched himself. "I'd give a hundred pounds for the sight and smell of a proper old pea-soup fog in London, with me, having dined well, just coming out of a theatre, and going on to a night-club. . . ."

"Alone?" Acton queried.

"Have a heart, Number One! Certainly not alone. What 'ud be the sense of it?"

"Proceed," Acton said. "What's on your mind?"

"Well, imagine all the illuminated advertisements in Piccadilly Circus twinkling through the fog, and you trying to charter a disengaged taxi to take you on to the 'Naughty Ninety' . . ."

"Never heard of the place. One of your low haunts, I suppose."

"On the contrary," the sub replied. "Most select, I assure you. No signing on as a member at the door. No, *sir*! You have to be properly proposed and seconded, and wait at least a month. It's a good spot. Dim lights and soft music. Caviare and champagne. Hot bacon sandwiches and lager beer at three a.m., and a doorkeeper dressed up like a Peruvian field-marshal, all very posh and proper. Good old London!" he sighed. "Shall we ever see it again?"

"Of course we shall. Don't be so damn mournful," Acton returned, amused. "All right, sub, fall out the gun's crew, and you can go below. If there's any cocoa brewing you might tell one of the stewards I'd like a cup. I shan't be turning in again."

Farnworth and the men disappeared below, and Jevons presently arrived with a cup of thick ship's cocoa and a plate with two biscuits carefully balanced on a tray.

"I've sugared it according to your taste, sir," said he with an air of mild disapproval. "But if I may suggest it, cocoa's hardly the sort o' drink for this temperature. It lies too heavy on the stomach. For myself, I prefer a nice cup o' tea with a slice of lime or lemon to start the day on."

Acton smiled at the faithful one. He took the cup and sipped. Jevons always looked after him like a mother. "No doubt you're right," he agreed. "Cocoa is a bit cloying. We'll try tea in future. And how's that toothache? I hope you had a decent night's sleep in spite of it?"

The steward touched a slight swelling at the side of his jaw. "Fair to middling, Mister Acton. The doctor gave me some dope. He says he's no great shakes as a dentist; but'll have a shot at yanking the darned thing out if there's nothing else for it. What time'll you be taking your bath, sir?"

"Usual time, Jevons. Seven-thirty."

"Today being Sunday I've laid out your best khaki shorts and shirt, with the new shoulder-straps," Jevons continued. "Which reminds me, sir, all your shoes are in desperate condition. If we can't find a bit o' leather and someone to do a bit o' cobbling Gord Ormighty knows where we'll be at the end of another month."

"We're all in the same boat," Acton pointed out. "I've already passed the word that shoes must be regarded as a luxury, only to be worn on special occasions. As for mine, I don't give a damn. The native-made sandals'll have to do. There's nothing else for it."

The steward pursed his lips. "I might see about getting some canvas uppers made," he said, scratching his unshaven chin. "I'll ask that Dutchman. There's another thing, sir."

"What?" Acton asked, gulping the last of his cocoa and handing over the cup.

"Soap's beginning to run short, sir. That gang o' female pirates ashore who do the dobeying seem to eat it. If you ask me, Mister Acton, we were too lavish when we first came here, giving stuff away right and left with a free hand."

"Don't forget the islanders have done a lot for us, Jevons. They've helped us no end."

"I know, sir. But fair's fair," the steward returned shaking his head. "These natives are a lot o' sharks when they get the chance, specially the women. We've been too generous. We give them extra bits of this and that for doing our laundry; but what's to be done when the soap's all gone I tremble to think of. I can't have you looking like a scarecrow. 'Tisn't fit nor proper. We've our reputation to consider." Jevons was very much in earnest.

"Don't worry," Acton consoled him. "We've pulled through up to date, and we'll go on contriving somehow. Shoes and soap are the least of our difficulties, worse luck. We've a good deal else to think about."

Jevons still lingered. Like everyone else he was avid for the latest news and anxious to hear what Acton thought of things in general.

"I know, sir," he said. "But what d'you *really* think of our

193

chances of getting away, you being in the position to put two and two together?"

Acton shrugged his shoulders and shook his head. He was not prepared to give an opinion.

As Draycott came on deck Jevons disappeared.

The two officers passed the time of day and reviled the fog, which, though full daylight had come, was as dense as ever.

"Coming ashore, Chief?" Acton asked.

"Ashore! Whatever for?" the engineer officer asked in surprise.

"I feel shut in and uncomfortable under this darned camouflage netting," said the other. "Let's walk out to the point and see if it looks clearer to seaward."

"Provided we don't lose our way."

"We shan't if we stick to the cliff-edge. The track's pretty well marked. Come on! A little spot of exercise'll do you good."

They made their way forward, went ashore by way of the gang-plank from the forecastle, and walked on, chatting.

Before they had gone thirty yards the *Eurydice* was out of sight. Close on their left was the low buttress of vertical cliff, with the sea gurgling gently among the tumbled coral boulders at its base and great masses of kelp and trailing seaweed swaying to and fro as the ripples surged in and out. There was thick undergrowth to their right, then taller bush; and beyond, the ghostly shapes of trees and palms. Acton had used the path a hundred times and could almost have followed it blindfold. Weeks before it had been marked with little white pegs in case it had to be used at night. The fog was thicker than ever, a dense white blanket of steaming opacity.

Acton, who was leading, suddenly stopped, listening. He had heard what sounded like the regular 'phut-phut-phut-phut' of a motor-engine, now fairly loud, now fading away to practically nothing. As sound is always capricious in fog it was impossible to judge its exact direction; but it was not the familiar throb of the *Eurydice's* auxiliary engine used for running the lights in harbour.

"Beekman's running his pumping engine at a peculiar hour," he said casually. "He doesn't usually start it up till the afternoon."

Draycott, with a hand to his ear, was also listening intently.

"That," he said, "isn't Beekman's engine. I know the sound of it."

"Then what, Chief?"

"Sounds to me like an old-fashioned, two-stroke semi-Diesel," the engineer replied.

"A ship?"

"Probably a sailing craft of some sort with an auxiliary engine. Yes, and I'll swear she's coming towards us," Draycott added, pointing to the southward. "D'you hear?"

Acton did hear. The regular throb was becoming louder, more resonant. Whatever was causing it couldn't be more than a few hundred yards away. "Damn this fog!" he muttered, and then, in an afterthought, "She can't be another Jap, surely?"

"She might be anything," his friend said, "but I'll bet my bottom dollar she's a sailing craft with an auxiliary engine. What about one of those coastal schooners? We saw dozens at Batavia and Surabaya."

The explosive 'phut-phut-phut' became louder, still approaching. Then they heard the sound of men's voices: someone shouting and another man evidently answering. The rhythm of the engine slowed to a gentler beat. The vessel, whatever she was, must be within two hundred yards.

Then the engine stopped. Acton, his nerves tense, could hear the gentle splash of parted water, then more voices. To seaward the murk was as opaque as ever, though overhead it seemed to be dissolving. Through the wreathing haze he could see the pale blueness of the sky. He didn't wait.

"Come on, Chief! Back to the ship!"

Back on board the men were called away from their breakfasts; the crew of the pom-pom and X gun to be sent to their weapons, and a party of a dozen, with rifles, sent ashore along the beach to cover the most probable landing-place near the village. Melton, already dressed, went off in charge. Acton had given him hurried orders. There was to be no shooting except in retaliation. If anyone attempted to land they were to be rounded up. Inevitably there was some noise as the ship's company went to their stations.

Acton waited. Minutes passed, and there was still no sign or sound of the approaching vessel.

Then, quite suddenly, came another babel of voices from somewhere astern of the *Eurydice*, followed in a few seconds by

195

the rumbling roar of a re-started engine. It was obvious what had happened. Whoever was in charge of the oncoming vessel had sighted the cliffs and was hauling off into safety. Faint breaths of air came fanning in from the eastward. The heat of the sun was increasing, and the fog was gradually thinning. The visibility had lifted to about fifty yards.

The engine settled down to its regular throbbing. Then more voices, and the sounds of a ship rippling through the calm water and rolling to an almost imperceptible swell. They could hear the creaking of blocks and running gear and the noise of slatting canvas as sails alternately filled and emptied themselves in the errant breeze.

Then, standing on X gun-deck with Draycott and Mr. Blatchington, Acton had his first sight of the stranger as a dim grey shadow sliding slowly through the murk on the *Eurydice's* starboard quarter. She was passing at an angle, steering more or less for the middle of the bay.

"Target in sight, sir!" the gunlayer reported, training his weapon.

"Shall we load, sir?" Mr. Blatchington asked excitedly. "She'll be out of sight in a moment!"

"No, no!" Acton hurriedly ordered. "Do nothing, for God's sake!"

In the brief glimpse afforded him he had recognised the ship as a sizeable, two-masted, black-painted schooner with her sails still set. So far as he could see she flew no ensign. She was too indistinct for him to notice whether she carried any unusual number of men. But there was no mistaking what she was: one of the local trading vessels common enough in Java and all over the Dutch East Indies. She vanished in the haze, her engine pulsating slowly.

"You were perfectly right, Chief," Acton said. "The question is who's she manned by?"

"Heaven knows," Draycott returned. "And why's she come here? Can she be the craft that used to bring Beekman's stores and take away his copra and whatever else he exported?"

The noise of the engine died away, and then ceased altogether. They heard more shouting, then the cheeping of blocks as sails were lowered. A few minutes later the curtain of fog started slowly to dissolve and roll aside, presently to disclose the schooner and the dim outline of the shore beyond.

"God in heaven!" Acton exclaimed in horror. "Just look what the damned fools have done!"

He might well be alarmed. The schooner, presumably manned by friendly natives, had a rope over her bows and had made fast to the nearest of Mr. Blatchington's most carefully moored bunches of oil-drums, which had been hoisted half out of the water.

"Strike me blazing well pink!" the Gunner ejaculated, the eyes nearly popping out of his head. "That sinker o' mine or the moorings'll never hold her! If a puff o' wind comes and she starts dragging and cuts away the drums or parts the wire up goes the bloody depth charge and her with it!"

The risk was obvious.

"Call away the whaler!" Acton ordered.

"I'll go, sir," the Gunner volunteered at once. "I know exactly how those things are moored."

"You'll do no such thing, Gunner. I'll go myself," Acton returned. "No. No argument!" as the other opened his mouth to protest. "You'll obey orders!"

Mr. Blatchington knew that tone of old. Protestation was futile. "Very well, sir," he said resignedly, a look of sorrow in his faithful eyes. "But for heaven's sake be careful, Mister Acton!" he added with great earnestness. "If anything happens to you we're up a bloody gum-tree!"

Acton reassured him.

Within a few minutes the whaler was away and pulling lustily shoreward, bearing Acton, with his pistol, and three extra hands armed with Sten guns, besides the regular boat's crew. Haste was necessary. The breeze had risen, and the schooner seemed to be see-sawing and tugging sharply at her temporary moorings. Though the sun had not completely broken through, the fog had thinned. Melton and his party, with Beekman, conspicuous in a white suit, and some natives, could be seen on the beach.

Those on board the *Eurydice* watched the whaler as she circled preparatory to boarding the schooner, which seemed to be manned by no more than six or eight dark-skinned natives clustered aft and staring in wonderment. Every available telescope or pair of binoculars in the destroyer was focused upon what was happening. The bowman tossed and boated his oar and stood up with his boat-hook. They could almost hear the order 'Way enough!' as the boat dashed alongside and her starboard oars went fore and aft and were lifted inboard.

Followed by his boarding-party, Acton hoisted himself over the schooner's bulwarks. Seeing their weapons, three of the native crew promptly dived overboard and started swimming for the beach. The remainder flung up their hands in token of surrender. Acton could be seen pointing and gesticulating as he tried to make himself understood. It was evidently beyond him, for leaving one man on guard he went forward with the two others and cautiously cast off and unrove the schooner's bow-fast. The oil-drums splashed into the sea and the ship drifted clear.

There were audible sighs of relief from the men congregated on the *Eurydice's* upper deck. Mr. Blatchington removed his cap and mopped his sweating brow. "He's done it! He's ruddy well done it!" he exclaimed, clapping his hands and almost dancing in his relief.

The whaler presently left the schooner's side and pulled in to the beach, where she was met by Melton, whose men had already collected the three dripping swimmers as they landed. Beekman and some of the natives joined the party at the water's edge, where there was more talk and gesticulation before the Dutchman was carried pick-a-back into the water and deposited in the stern sheets of the boat, which backed away from the shore and returned to the schooner. Assisted on board, Beekman held further conference with Acton and the native crew. Then the schooner's engine was re-started, and the whaler came hustling back to the *Eurydice*.

"Mr. Farnworth, sir!" the coxswain hailed as she drew near. "Yes!"

"The Cap'en says he'll be mooring the schooner alongside the cliff close ahead of us, sir! He wants a berthing-party with heaving lines!"

The sub-lieutenant waved a hand in acknowledgment.

They made quick work of it, and by 8.30 a.m. the *Agung*, with one anchor off shore, was safely moored alongside the cliff ahead of the *Eurydice*.

She was a schooner about 100 feet long with a low poop and forecastle and roomy holds now empty of cargo. So far as Acton could discover through Beekman, who had inspected

198

what books and papers had been found on board, she had been built for her native owners eight years earlier. From Acton's own rather cursory inspection, carried out with Draycott and various others from the *Eurydice*, her hull was in sound condition. Her standing rigging and running gear, with the sails, were in good order, and so was the engine.

When the Japanese overran the island of Bali, at the eastern end of Java, it seemed that the *Agung* had been lying in an anchorage called Benua, and the regular crew, seeking safety, had fled to the hills, leaving their ship in the harbour. For one reason or another the ship had not been requisitioned by the enemy, and had finally been seized by some natives described by Beekman in his halting English with many shakings of his head as 'most bad mans.'

Acton asked what he meant, and it came out that most of the *Agung's* present crew were escaped prisoners, two of whom had been serving long sentences for murder. When the Japanese arrived in Bali, they had rounded up all available males for forced labour, and had emptied the prison. Many of the men had been shipped to other islands for the construction of airstrips. The long and short of it was that a party of malcontents had managed to escape, to seize the *Agung*, and sail away. According to Beekman, they had been wandering round the islands for weeks overawing the natives, interfering with the women, and helping themselves to what they needed.

Ideas were simmering in Acton's mind. "If these men stole the ship," he asked, "who does she legally belong to now?"

Beekman couldn't say for certain. He supposed the schooner was still the rightful property of her native owners, though as the whole of the Netherlands East Indies had been conquered by the Japanese, private ownership was no longer of any account. He gathered that the enemy just helped themselves to what they fancied as the legitimate spoils of war.

"You're the head man here, Beekman. You're an official magistrate, aren't you?"

The Dutchman nodded.

"If we hadn't happened to be here what would you have done about this schooner?"

Beekman had no answer to that one. He hadn't considered the matter.

"Put it this way," Acton insisted. "Would you have tried

199

to seize the ship as stolen property, or would you have allowed the crew to remain in possession?"

The Dutchman thought for a moment. "There is not much I can do," he replied. "We have no guns."

"Are these men armed?"

Beekman thought not.

Acton made up his mind. "I intend to requisition the *Agung*," he announced. "I shall take possession of her in the name of the British Government and give you a formal receipt."

The Dutchman seemed taken aback. His eyelids flickered. It was possible, Acton surmised, that he hoped that the schooner might somehow become his property. For a moment he did not reply. Then he asked: "You pay money, Lieutenant?"

"We have no money, and if we had it would be useless," Acton pointed out. "Whoever the ship belongs to will have to wait for compensation until after the war."

Beekman shrugged his shoulders. Protests would be useless. There was nothing he could do. This young Englishman had the whip hand—sailors, guns and everything. Already he was the virtual ruler of the island.

On the other hand, Beekman had heard the rumour that the *Eurydice* was in no fit condition to put to sea. If these English sailors had a chance of leaving the island by some other means, they would probably sink their ship before departure to prevent any chance of her falling into the hands of the enemy. But there would be no sense in destroying everything the *Eurydice* contained, and there were plenty of useful pickings in the way of fittings, stores, furniture, rope, canvas and other useful odds and ends that might be had for the asking if he went about it in the right way. After all, these Englishmen owed him something in return for all his help and hospitality. He felt he deserved a substantial *quid pro quo*.

By the end of the second day after her arrival the *Agung*, duly camouflaged with nets and greenery like the *Eurydice*, had been taken over as His Majesty's ship *Fiona*. They re-christened the prize, which Acton so considered her, with a little ceremony and some Navy rum, now rapidly running short.

Seamen and natives were sent on board for repairs, alterations and cleaning, while another party from the engine-room, under the direction of Draycott and Paulton, the Chief Engine-Room Artificer, stripped and overhauled the old-fashioned engine, which sadly needed it. By great good luck the fuel tanks were still three-quarters full, and six more drums of Diesel oil were obtained by barter from Beekman. Even so, the engine must be used sparingly. "I don't know what's in your mind," Draycott warned Acton, "but this darned machine'll simply eat oil! If you're considering a longish run they'll have to go very easy with the fuel."

The two holds were thoroughly scoured, scrubbed out, whitewashed, and fitted up as living spaces for sixty men with bamboo bunks manufactured by local labour. Even this would be a tight squeeze, and no room could be found for any more men. There were innumerable colonies of cockroaches in the forecastle, galley and the living quarters aft which had to be eradicated by chemical means devised by McInnes. The galley itself had to be enlarged, and an extra water-tank removed from the *Eurydice* and installed on the *Fiona's* upper deck. A single Bofors gun was mounted in a collapsible deckhouse amidships, admittedly an awkward place but the best that could be provided at short notice. Apart from two Lewis guns, a couple of the Gunner's precious Stens, and ten rifles, there was no room for any further armament.

There was much to be done. It took twelve full working days before the little *Fiona* was ready for sea. They were uneventful days of intense heat and undiluted toil, disturbed by nothing more exciting than the sighting, on two different occasions, of flights of unidentifiable aircraft to the southward. Apart from the usual routine news broadcasts, Scriven had picked up no further spoken messages from close at hand, no more friendly American voices exchanging information by radio-telephony. So far as the outside world went, Eurydice Island might never have existed.

21

TWO EVENINGS before the *Fiona's* completion Acton had a heart-to-heart talk with Melton in his cabin. A chart, with the Sailing Directions and other books of reference, together with parallel rulers, dividers and pencil, lay on the table before them, at one end of which was a tray with one of the last bottles of Pomeroy's whisky with tumblers and a jug of iced water.

"We've discussed this before, Pilot," Acton started by saying. "What do we do with the *Fiona*? Something's got to be decided. Help yourself to a drink, meanwhile."

"What I've thought all along," Melton returned without hesitation. "One of us should make a break for it with about half the ship's company." He uncorked the precious bottle.

"The more I think of it, the less I like it, Pilot. It's such a risk with these goddam Japs in every island."

"No more risk than staying here," the navigator said. "One way or another the whole crowd of us are in it up to our necks. Whisky for you, George?"

"A very tiny one."

Melton poured out two small nips, added water and handed Acton his glass. "Here's fluff on your eyebrows and hair on your chest," he said, sipping.

"I look towards you, Pilot," his friend returned. "Well, I've been thinking. If we decide the *Fiona* is to be sent off on her own, and I haven't fully made up my mind, who's to go in command? *I* can't. It's my job to stay here till the last man's gone."

Melton, cramming tobacco into his pipe, nodded in agreement. "Obviously," he said.

"Which means the choice boils down to the Sub, the Gunner, or yourself."

"I suppose so."

"I like Farnworth," Acton continued. "He's got plenty of guts; but is rather inclined to run haywire and lacks experience. Old Guns, too. I'd trust him anywhere in a tight corner, though at times he's a bit bull-headed. But does he know much about navigation?"

"Hardly enough for the sort of job we've got in mind," Melton replied. "It'll be a bit tricky."

"A bit!" Acton exclaimed. "It'll be most damnably tricky if you ask me! Well, Pilot, much as I dislike the idea of losing you, I fear you're the obvious choice if we *do* decide on it."

"I was hoping you'd say that, George, though I hate the idea of leaving you if it comes to the point. But if some of us *can* get through to civilization, we might stir up someone to have a shot at rescuing the chaps left here."

"And how?"

"Aircraft, submarines or a combination of both."

Acton looked doubtful. "I wonder," he said. "Who's going to worry about sixty or seventy of us marooned on this God-forsaken island?"

"Anyhow, I'm game," Melton returned. "It's our only chance. I've been looking into details. I believe we've at least a fifty-fifty chance of pulling it off. If we don't," and he shrugged his shoulders, "it'll be just too bad."

"Which way," Acton asked. "East or west?"

"It's no good going west, George. That means the Indian Ocean, and probably running short of food and water long before we get anywhere. Granted we'd probably have a fair wind all the way, the South-East Trade, and that we might have a shot at making the Seychelles or Mauritius. Well, they're both something like three thousand five hundred miles. Even if we averaged six knots, which I very much doubt, it would take the best part of four weeks, probably longer. I'm not saying it *couldn't* be done; but I'm thinking mainly of food and water. Also, if the Japs are still busy in the Indian Ocean, a solitary sailing craft runs a pretty good chance of being spotted."

"So what?" Acton wanted to know.

"My idea's to go east, to Australia; to be precise, to King Sound in the north of Western Australia, distance roughly thirteen hundred miles as the seagull flies. It's nearer than Darwin." Melton pointed out both places on the chart.

"Thirteen hundred!" Acton observed. "That's still a hell of a long way. And don't forget, it'll be considerably further by the time you've done a lot of tacking and zig-zagging against a foul wind. King Sound's practically dead to wind'ard, and, don't forget, you'd have to go very easy with the engine."

"I know. All the same, I'd much prefer to have a crack at going that way."

"Not forgetting that all the larger islands which you'd have to pass are stinking with Japs and their bloody aircraft," Acton pointed out. "Look at 'em, stretching over miles and miles!" He swept his finger over the thousand-mile chain from Bali, in the west, to beyond Timor, in the east, a formidable-looking barrier broken by about half a dozen narrow channels giving access to the open ocean.

Melton proceeded to elaborate his plan in greater detail.

It was unlikely, he said, that the Japanese had stopped all the local traffic between the islands, though in all probability they'd issued permits or licences of one sort or another for small sailing craft to be at sea in certain areas. They might even have instituted patrols of motor-craft and so on to enforce their traffic regulations. But had the Japs sufficient craft to cover the whole area, and to stop, board and examine every little sailing craft? He very much doubted it.

"I think you're an optimist," Acton broke in. "What about aircraft, flying-boats and so on?"

Melton said he had considered that. It had struck him as peculiar, to say the least, that their island had been visited by no more than a solitary Japanese fighter, which had luckily been shot down. Also, after the disappearance of a landing-craft and a submarine, wasn't it damn strange that the island hadn't been closely examined from the air for any traces of survivors? What was the answer to that? Either the Japs were woefully stupid or slow off the mark, which he didn't believe, or else they hadn't sufficient aircraft to do all the more important jobs, like escorting convoys.

"I still think you're an optimist, Pilot," Acton interjected.

The navigator shook his head. He didn't think so. On the contrary, he thought they had a fair chance of getting through if they went about it the right way. If the *Fiona* project came off under his command there were plenty of small islands covering the first part of the journey. Depending on the breeze, he'd make for the Allas Strait, between the large islands of Lombok and Sumbawa—which he pointed out on the chart— or else the Sapi Strait, about a hundred and fifty miles farther east, between Sumbawa and the next island, Flores.

"Have you got me so far?" he asked Acton.

His friend nodded.

There were many small islands on the way, Melton continued. He would sail only by night, using the engine as little as possible, and anchoring before daylight each morning close in under the lee of the land, camouflaging the ship as best he could. He would push on again at dusk. Once through the straits, he'd stand on to the southward until the land was well out of sight, and then make the best of his way to Western Australia. He was very eager and persuasive.

"You seem to have thought of everything," Acton had to admit.

"I hope I have, George. I've had this trip in my mind ever since that schooner turned up and we took her over."

"But *I* don't much care for the responsibility of letting you go."

"Hell!" Melton exclaimed hotly. "You're not asking me to go, or even suggesting it! I'm volunteering, George. Get that into your noodle."

"I know that, Pilot. But you're not the only one concerned. Anyhow, there's no need to fly off the handle."

"I'm sorry," the other apologized. "We've known each other for so long I was forgetting you were my commanding officer. You've the final say, of course, and I obey your orders, whatever happens." Melton did not add that he and Acton were practically the same age, and that Acton was only three months his senior.

"For heaven's sake forget I'm supposed to be C.O.," Acton protested. "I'm merely trying to consider all the pros and cons, to satisfy myself that if I do let you go on this jaunt I'm doing the right thing. If Pomeroy had still been alive," he added, "what d'you think he'd have done?"

"Allowed one of us to have a crack at it," came the immediate reply. "The risks are no worse than many others we've been through together, the whole blinkin' crowd of us! They're no worse than staying on this island, so far as that goes. What are risks in wartime, for God's sake?"

Acton seemed to be weakening. "And suppose I agree and say you can have fifty men to try this scheme of yours. How do we set about choosing them?"

"Call for volunteers."

"And all our best men'll volunteer for the sake of the excitement, and I'll be left with the others. I'm not playing on those lines."

"Then what?"

"Volunteering tempered by selection. I'll give you a list of the people I won't spare, the key-men, and you can take your choice of the others."

"That suits me," said Melton with a shrug. "But I *must* have a fair proportion of the older toughs, say one petty officer, Huxtable, and a couple of leading seamen."

Acton nodded. "I'll see to that," he replied. "But in your party, anyhow, there'll be those five or six young chaps who've fallen for the native girls. I'm. . . ."

"Five or six!" the other laughed. "Now it's you, George, who's being the optimist."

"How so?"

"There are a good many more than five or six who've been . . . what shall I call it, well, who've felt the biological urge, as I once heard it called."

"Our men?" Acton demanded, showing signs of alarm.

"I shouldn't wonder," Melton returned with an air of mystery. "No names, no pack drill. But you'd be surprised!"

"Hell!" Acton exclaimed. "I'm not going to preside over a matrimonial bureau serving out affiliation orders in this blasted island, nor do I intend to be honorary god-father to a whole tribe of coffee-coloured little love-tokens! I've plenty enough to worry about without that. Give me some more whisky, for God's sake!" He handed his tumbler across.

Melton laughed and refilled the glass, and his own also. "Be your age, George!" he remarked. "You'll be an honorary god-father several times over in six or seven months, like it or not." He held up a tumbler to the light to gauge the depth of its amber-coloured contents and lowered it again to add water. "Anyhow, let's hope we're all clear of this place before anything happens. All the same, from the ethnological point of view, a little new blood now and then among people like these isn't altogether a bad idea. They've been intermarrying for far too long, and there's a superfluity of women, unless they go in for polygamy. I'm not at all certain our visit won't have done a considerable amount of good if you regard it scientifically."

"Huh!" Acton grunted, regarding his friend. "You and your science! What a cold-blooded devil you sometimes are."

"Not at all, George. It's mere common sense."

As Acton was well aware, Melton, though the son of a clergyman and seriously-minded, was also a gay and giddy bachelor. One couldn't be messmates with a man for so long without knowing that. The only photograph in his cabin was that of a female cousin to whom he wrote about once every six months. His messmates had thought him engaged until he disabused them one Saturday night at sea, after they had drunk the toast of 'Sweethearts and Wives.'

"What, me marry old Aggie?" he laughed. "Good Lord, no! Give us a chance. I merely write to keep her happy and give her something to talk about. She's got a face like a horse and looks as though she'd been pulled backwards through a blackberry bush. She's practically booked for a curate." All of which was rather unkind, though judging from the photograph the description of the lady was not inapt.

However, having heard Melton's remarks about the advantages of introducing new blood among the islanders, Acton found himself wondering if he had any *arrière-pensée*. Could it be possible that he was anxious to leave the island because of something which might have happened between him and Lallah, Beekman's beautiful dark-eyed daughter? He knew they often saw each other, and that Melton had given her various little odds and ends, including a fountain pen, his silver cigarette-case, and a moonstone brooch in the shape of a butterfly bought during an irresponsible evening ashore at Colombo. No. Perish the ungenerous thought! The presents must have been mere acknowledgments for what Lallah had done for Melton when he lay wounded.

The hard-boiled McInnes, Draycott and Mr. Blatchington were beyond suspicion, though Acton wasn't so certain about Farnworth. That young man, with his roving 'come hither' eye and undoubted good looks, had a message for the girls. It was noticeable that whenever he was around the pretty dears with the flowers in their dark hair coyly fluttered their eyelashes and smiled and sidled in his direction.

There were times when Acton felt rather overwhelmed by what might be called these domestic difficulties. Never in his wildest dreams had he imagined he would ever find himself in charge of more than one hundred sentimental and susceptible sailors marooned on a tropical island largely inhabited by lovely and nubile young women! What would Pomeroy have done? Such unlikely problems were not dealt with in 'The King's Regulations and Admiralty Instructions,' or in the equally voluminous 'Admiralty Fleet Orders,' confidential or otherwise.

However, before they retired to their respective bunks that night, it was decided that Melton should undertake the prospective voyage.

"You'll have to make it official, George," the navigator said.

"How d'you mean? Sailing orders?"

"No. Some official document appointing me in command of the *Fiona*. If we're copped we don't want to be hanged as pirates."

Acton looked puzzled.

"I'll draft it out if you like and have it typed in duplicate," said Melton cheerfully. "All you'll have to do is to sign on the dotted line. It'll be something to send to the Admiralty when I put in a claim for command money."

"Ho!" laughed Acton. "So that's what you're thinking of, you old money-grubber! There'll be a good dollop of back pay due to all of us if and when we ever get home. All right, Pilot. Do your worst. I'll sign."

The document produced by Melton next morning with some pride was a masterpiece of phraseology.

"To Lieutenant Roger John Melton of His Majesty's Ship *Eurydice* hereby appointed Lieutenant-in-Command of His Majesty's Ship *Fiona*.

"By virtue of the power and authority given to me, I do hereby constitute and appoint you Lieutenant-in-Command of His Majesty's Ship *Fiona*, authorizing and requiring you forthwith to repair on board the said ship and to take charge of her in that rank, strictly commanding all the company of the said ship, subordinate to you, to behave themselves jointly and severally in their respective employments with all due respect and obedience unto you their superior officer; and you likewise to observe and execute such orders and directions for His Majesty's service as you shall from time to time receive from me or any other your superior officer. Hereof, nor you, nor any of you, may fail as you will answer the contrary at your peril. And for so doing this shall be your order.

"Given under my hand on board His Majesty's Ship *Eurydice*
          this the..............day of..............1942.
          .... Lieutenant-in-Command."

Acton read it through in amazement. "Where on earth did you dig out the official language?" he inquired. "And have I the power and authority to appoint you etcetera etcetera?"

"No one else has, George. You're the senior officer on the spot. Anyhow, it's official enough."

"You're telling me, Pilot," Acton laughed. "I particularly like the bit about you answering the contrary at your peril. You'll have to watch your step, old boy. But where did you get all the jargon?"

"Practically word for word from my Commission. I think it covers everything."

Acton took up his pen. "I thought it sounded dimly familiar. Well, here goes. I suppose it's all right, and I wish you the best luck in the world."

He filled in the date and signed his name in full.

Five evenings later, in the last glow of a flaming sunset, with a fresh breeze from the eastward ruffling the sparkling sea and the sky overhead deepening to a star-spangled indigo, the *Fiona* slipped from her moorings, weighed her anchor, and moved slowly seaward under her engine.

Apart from Melton, she carried fifty-eight men including six natives, these latter having been embarked in case the ship came to be closely inspected by enemy patrols or aircraft, when a crowd of men on deck would inevitably arouse suspicion. The seamen would be concealed below and in the collapsible box-like wooden structure housing the Bofors gun, and the natives would represent the normal working crew.

It had been impossible to keep the departure a secret. The news had spread around, and practically the whole population of the village, men, women and children, flocked down to see the *Fiona* sail. Some brought baskets of fruit and vegetables which were passed on board, together with garlands of flowers and at least two large openwork bamboo crates containing live fowls.

To start with they were a silent crowd. The lamentation really began when the *Fiona* cast off and weighed her anchor. Some of the girls, Acton noticed, were weeping unrestrainedly, and one shrill young voice kept calling "Jon-ie! Jon-ie!" though which particular Johnnie was being called he didn't know. Then one of the men broke into a song, which was taken up by voice after voice until the whole crowd had joined in. It sounded inexpressibly sad and mournful.

Beekman was standing with Acton and the other officers on the *Eurydice's* battered bridge with all the ship's company that remained clustered on the upper deck.

"What's that they're singing?" Acton asked.

"They make what we call the farewell song," the Dutchman explained. "They say these people who go much good friend. They very sad they go away, and much hope they soon come once more. They very sorry, I think."

The *Fiona's* engine was started up and Acton called for three cheers as she gathered way. The roar of the men's voices drowned the chorus from the shore, and was answered from the *Fiona*. Men shouted and waved to their departing shipmates as the schooner slid by, and the *Fiona's* men called back.

Acton took up his megaphone and shouted above the din: "Good luck to you all! A happy voyage!"

Melton waved a hand, and another roar of cheering came back.

And so the little ship started off on her long journey, stopping her engine and hoisting her sails when clear of the land. They watched her heel over with her canvas bellying out to the freshening breeze. She shaped course to the southward, soon to fade to a dim silhouette, finally to disappear into the misty darkness of the moonless night.

Acton watched her until she vanished, and so did the others. Everything depended upon Melton and the *Fiona*.

"Well, that's that!" he said to Draycott, putting down his binoculars. "There goes our forlorn hope! God!" he sighed, "I hope we've done the right thing." There was doubt in his voice. Had Melton undertaken, had he himself sanctioned, an altogether impossible task?

"Don't worry, George!" the engineer officer consoled him. "I know what you're feeling; but if I'd been in your shoes I'd have done precisely as you did. If there's anyone who can pull it off it's the Pilot, bless his heart!"

Acton wasn't convinced. "All I know is we may have lost some damned good shipmates," he returned. "Heaven knows if we'll ever hear of them again."

Draycott was about to remark that they didn't seem to stand too rosy a chance themselves; but thought better of it.

THE STORY of Melton's voyage in the *Fiona* would make a book of its own if related in all its detail.

The first days, during which the schooner sailed from island to island during darkness, sometimes making a good seven knots in a stiff breeze with every stitch of canvas set and drawing, sometimes just ghosting along in light airs fanning in from the eastward, were not uneventful. Always during daylight Melton took the precaution of lying as close up under the land as the depth of water permitted, and on occasion had to use the engine to reach his chosen anchorage before dawn.

The first excitement occurred soon after midnight on the second night after leaving Eurydice Island, when Melton, who invariably slept on a mattress on deck beside the wheel and compass, was suddenly roused by the petty officer on watch, Huxtable, with the news that a vessel was approaching from the westward. "She's a big ship, sir, darkened!" the man said in a state of considerable excitement.

It was a clear, dark night with a fresh breeze, and using his glasses Melton could see the black shape of the vessel at a distance of just over a mile. She looked like a medium-sized passenger liner, with two masts, a built-up superstructure amidships and low squat funnel. To judge from the size of her phosphorescent bow wave she was travelling a good sixteen knots.

"What'll we do, sir?" Huxtable asked.

"Nothing," Melton replied with an assurance he didn't feel. "She'll pass clear of us."

"Is she a Jap, sir?"

"Can't be anything else, Huxtable. Probably a transport. I doubt if she'll worry about us. She'll be in a hurry to get somewhere."

All the same, Melton felt far from happy. He looked to the southward, where the horizon was banked up with dark cloud. That was lucky. There was just a chance that the *Fiona* might not be sighted. Even if she were, a solitary small schooner might not be worth attention.

Nevertheless, the three or four minutes that elapsed from the time the ship was first sighted until she passed some six hundred yards under the *Fiona's* stern was agonizing. They could hear the muffled throbbing of machinery and the hiss and splash of parted water as she drove by without a light showing. The *Fiona* gave two or three deep lurches as her heavy wash came rolling down from astern. Then the air became filled with the tang of oil-fuel as the ship moved on to the eastward, and in a few minutes was almost out of sight.

Melton couldn't help sighing with relief. "So that's that, Huxtable. I thought she wouldn't bother."

"She fair scared the guts out of me, sir," the petty officer admitted wryly.

"No wonder. Well, keep your eyes skinned, and don't hesitate to call me if you sight anything. How's she steering, quartermaster?"

"Steady enough on sou'-east by south, sir," the able seaman at the wheel gave answer, his eyes on the dimly-lit compass card. "She's carrying a bit o' starboard helm."

"Tush, man!" Melton laughed. "We're in a sailing ship now. You mean *weather* helm."

"These new-fangled orders take a lot o' getting into, sir," the seaman said. "An' steering this ship isn't like a destroyer. This one's all over the shop. She keeps pulling up to port."

"We'll soon cure that. Huxtable?"

"Sir?"

"Are your head sheets well home?" Melton asked, referring to the fore-staysail and jib.

"Flat aft, sir."

"Then we'll pay out another few feet of the main sheet and see if that makes the steering easier."

It did.

With the breeze and little breaking sea broad on the port bow, the *Fiona* was travelling well, plunging a little with occasional whiffs of heavy spray bursting over the low bulwarks forward. For a crowd of complete amateurs in sail, Melton thought, they weren't doing so badly. Apart from the possible interference of the King's enemies he was rather enjoying himself.

"Huxtable, keep a good look-out for a conical-shaped island fine on the port bow. That's where we'll be spending the day. Unless it gets much darker to the southward you should see it soon after 3 a.m."

"Ay aye, sir."

They duly sighted the island with the unpronounceable name, and as dawn was breaking the *Fiona* anchored in five fathoms close inshore under a little promontory with a stern rope made fast to a convenient tree. The ship's company spent the forenoon cleaning ship and fishing, with ill success, later bathing from a small, palm-fringed cove with a sandy beach as white as a hound's tooth.

A few natives gathered around, timid and gazing in wonderment at these strange beings, with deeply-tanned legs and torsos and white midriffs disporting themselves mother-naked and whooping and splashing about like schoolboys in the clear green water. For months the seamen had worn little but khaki shorts. There were a few boats hauled up on the beach with nets hung up to dry. Those of the men who had cigarettes to spare exchanged them for newly-caught fish. There was a village somewhere nearby; but Melton had posted a sentry with strict orders that no one must leave the beach to wander off inland.

Fresh water, or the lack of it for so many men, was one of Melton's principal anxieties. It had to be strictly rationed for drinking and cooking purposes only, though even so, with the prospect of a long ocean voyage ahead, it was being used much faster than was desirable. They had hoped for rain and had devised means of collecting it in canvas funnels; but no rain had come. So having established friendly relations with the inhabitants, partly by sign language, partly with the help of one of the natives in the *Fiona* who had acquired a smattering of English and knew what was wanted, they were shown a stream of clear water tumbling down the hillside. The *Fiona* carried spare casks for just this contingency, and Melton had brought rope, canvas and odds and ends of clothing for barter. For a very small consideration a gang of islanders, under Huxtable's eagle eye, had been glad enough to take the casks ashore, fill them at the stream, carry them to the beach and ferry them off to the ship in one of their own boats. With this job done Melton felt easier in his mind.

It was during the early afternoon, when many more natives had appeared with their women and children, and most of the *Fiona's* men were stretched out asleep after the midday meal, that they sighted a flying-boat bearing the blood-red Japanese

213

roundels. The crowd ashore and the little ship lying close in must have attracted the pilot's attention, for three times he came circling over the cove.

The natives had dispersed with shrill cries the moment the aircraft appeared, and when, on her third circuit, the machine came roaring over the *Fiona's* mastheads at a height of no more than a hundred feet, Melton himself became seriously alarmed. The Bofors gun crew were already standing by their weapon, and he all but gave orders for the collapsible wooden screens to be dropped and the gun to open fire. But he hesitated. The weapon was very awkwardly placed with camouflage netting overhead. It would have been difficult and very lucky shooting at a fast-moving target, and if they had opened fire and missed, if the aircraft had been only lightly hit and managed to get away, it must have meant trouble for the *Fiona*. He was thankful he hadn't obeyed his first instinct. Apparently satisfied, the flying-boat boomed off to the westward and disappeared.

From this, their last island anchorage, they could see the dim, blue-grey peak of a great mountain over the clear-cut line of the sea to the southward. Clearly marked on the chart, it was a good fifty miles away, a volcano over twelve thousand feet high on the island on the western side of the strait for which Melton was making, the channel which finally led to the Indian Ocean some forty miles beyond.

As usual, the *Fiona* weighed at dusk, and at about 10.30 p.m. on the third evening after leaving Eurydice Island, the night being clear and starlit with good visibility, the dark loom of high land was in sight across the southern horizon. The breeze gradually died away, and the air became hot and stagnant with an almost overpowering scent of spice and sandalwood. The sails flapped, idle and useless. They lowered them, and started up the engine.

About an hour later the *Fiona* was passing through the five-mile gap between two little groups of low, scrub-covered uninhabited islands at the northern entrance to the channel. There were no navigational difficulties. The Admiralty chart showed every shoal and reef, and there was deep water close inshore. With a strong tide or current setting to the southward Melton stood in towards the western coast to keep well in under the dark shadow of the land.

214

They had sighted various sailing craft—schooners, a few native 'praus,' which were really enlarged canoes with their peculiar V-shaped lateen sails. Some showed lights and others did not; but their mere presence showed that the local coasting vessels were still engaged on the normal business upon which the livelihood of their crews and owners depended. The *Fiona* showed no lights at all; but even if the Japanese were patrolling the channel with motor-craft, which seemed rather unlikely, one small schooner might not attract attention. But it was wise to be prepared for any eventuality. The ship's company were at action stations, with the Bofors gun cleared away and the Lewis guns, Stens and rifles on deck.

The sea was glassily calm, and the flickering lights from a few scattered villages glowed redly along the fore-shore to starboard and were reflected in shimmering streaks across the water. Dominating everything else brooded the great volcano, with a thin trail of smoke drifting from its summit and its lower slopes partly shrouded in horizontal layers of mist. Its sharp outline, with those of some lesser peaks, looked as though they were carved in ebony against the luminous velvet-blue of the starry sky.

The passage through the channel, which, after entering, widened out to ten and fifteen miles, was accomplished in less than five hours with the current in the *Fiona's* favour. There were masses of low, dark cloud banked up to the southward, and once, far away over a point of land, they saw a bluish-white flicker which might almost have been the reflection from a searchlight. It was twice repeated.

"Did you see that, sir?" Huxtable asked breathlessly.

"Yes," said Melton. "It looked to me like lightning. There's thunder in the air. D'you notice the heat?" Indeed, it was sweltering, the hottest night they had experienced.

"I hope it's not them bloody Japs," the petty officer remarked.

Melton tried to reassure him. "No," he replied. "I'll swear it was sheet lightning. Look at all that black cloud. It's a thunder-storm, miles away."

They didn't pursue the subject.

At half-past four in the morning, by which time the sky was heavily overcast and there had already been two showers of heavy rain, the *Fiona* had reached the southern exit of the channel. There was no wind, and the little ship rolled and pitched crazily in a long ocean swell from the south-eastward. Uninured to the violent corkscrew motion, softened perhaps by their long sojourn at Eurydice Island, most of the seamen were soon groaning in the misery of seasickness. Even Melton and Petty Officer Percy Huxtable felt squeamish and unhappy.

Shaping course along a buttress of dark cliff against which the great rollers could be seen and heard breaking and roaring in whitened fury, Melton was steering for an inlet a few miles to the westward in which he intended to spend the day. It was a two-mile-long fissure in the rocky coast and easy of access, and far away from any roads or civilization. As shown on the chart and described in the sailing directions, which duly warned mariners of the heavy swell off the entrance, it provided good deep-water anchorage and shelter for small vessels. 'There is no village,' the sailing directions said in as many words. 'There are a few isolated huts; but no supplies are obtainable. There are sandy beaches with occasional steep low cliffs, and a shore which is marshy in places.'

The wind was rising and the swell starting to curl over and break by the time the *Fiona* approached the entrance. In the grey half-light of early dawn and the sky heavily overcast with low, leaden-looking cloud, the shore looked bleakly forbidding. A blinding rain-squall came down as Melton turned to starboard with the little ship lurching and staggering drunkenly in the confused, toppling sea which seemed to be running in all directions at once, caused, no doubt, by the backwash from the cliffs. Five minutes later, under the lee of the land, wind and sea gradually subsided until it became almost flat calm. The rain-squall passed and the light grew.

"Thank God!" said Melton, as the harbour gradually opened out before them. "Now we can see."

"Huxtable."

"Sir?"

"Have the starboard anchor ready for letting go."

"Aye aye, sir. Shall we secure the gun?"

"No. Leave everything till we've anchored." It was in Melton's mind that after the spray and rain the Bofors and all the small arms on deck would need careful cleaning and oiling.

The petty officer went forward to collect men for anchoring. Glancing at the chart spread out on the covered table near the wheel, Melton looked over the helmsman's shoulder at the compass.

"Steer north a half-west," he said.

The seaman repeated the order, and the *Fiona* slewed slightly to starboard, and steadied.

Full daylight had not yet come; but more and more of the little haven slid into view as the *Fiona* moved on under her engine. Using his glasses Melton could see the sandy beaches, the little stretches of low cliff, and a few desolate-looking huts ashore. It might have been the end of the world. There were no signs of life except those derelict habitations. Everything looked grim and arid and inhospitable, with none of the luxuriant greenery to which they had become accustomed.

They had about another half-mile to go before anchoring when Huxtable came aft to report everything ready forward. They were passing a low tongue of land at the time preparatory to altering course to port, when, over it, Melton suddenly saw the twin masts of a schooner lying in a little bight. A moment or two later her hull came into sight.

Using his glasses he gasped in horrified amazement. His heart jumped. And well it might. The schooner was roughly the same size as the *Fiona*, and though native-built, was no ordinary trading vessel. The hull was grey painted, with some sort of white lettering on the bow. Her bowsprit had been removed, and so apparently had all the sails, for there were no signs of any booms or running gear. There were short signal yards crossed on each mast, and stretched between the masts themselves what looked suspiciously like wireless aerials. There was a large deckhouse amidships, and on deck forward and aft what seemed to be a couple of small guns with their covers on. There was another unusual erection on the low poop, with a bridge overhead and something else which might have been a covered searchlight. He could see no one on deck.

She was a native-built schooner; but had evidently been taken over and refitted for war purposes, just as hundreds of yachts and other small craft had been requisitioned at home in England. What on earth she was doing in this solitary little harbour unless she had run in for shelter Melton could not imagine.

"Good God!" he exclaimed. "Huxtable! D'you see that ship?"

"Yessir!"

"She's a bloody Jap or I'm a Hottentot!"

"Christ!" the petty officer muttered, thoroughly startled. "What'll you do, sir?"

Melton had to do some very quick thinking. He could hardly turn the *Fiona* and take her out to sea again without exciting suspicion. On the other hand, the Japs, if they were Japs, might quite easily mistake the *Fiona* for a native craft.

"I shall board her, port side alongside, if I can make it," he said, making up his mind.

"Suffering cats!" Huxtable murmured.

"Get the hands to action stations, quick, and no noise about it!" Melton went on. "Drop a bit of the mainsail over the Bofors to keep it hidden as long as possible, and keep the men out of sight. Wait," he added, as the petty officer started off to obey.

"Yessir?"

"I want men for'ard and aft with hook-ropes or something to make fast when we're once alongside! Send two men up here with rifles or Lewis guns! There's to be no shooting unless she starts in on us, or until I give orders."

"I understand, sir," Huxtable grinned. "Is that the lot?"

"Where's the White Ensign?"

"In my place, under the bunk, sir."

"I'll be damned if I go into action without it," Melton observed. "Have it bent on ready for hoisting at the main truck. We'll show it as we go alongside or when we open fire, whichever happens first. And I want the pistol and a spare clip or two from the drawer in my cabin. I'll lead the boarders. You, as my number two, will remain in charge of this ship."

The petty officer opened his mouth to protest; but Melton cut him short. "No argument," he said. "That's an order. Now go to it, Huxtable. Action stations! We've no time to waste!"

Huxtable hesitated with a peculiar expression on his face. It would be much better, he thought, if he led the boarders. How the merry hell was he expected to take the *Fiona* to Australia if anything happened to Mister Melton? He knew little about navigation, and Australia was a long, long way across a trackless ocean.

"Go on, man!" Melton broke in. "Get cracking!"

Huxtable saluted and hurried off. This was neither the time nor place for discussion. It was an emergency. Every minute was precious.

23

THE *Fiona's* engine, noisy at any time, was throttled down to slow. Full daylight had almost come when she circled and approached the strange ship from nearly astern. Here, under the lee of the land, it was glassily calm, and hanging up and down from a short gaff on her mainmast Melton could see the unmistakable red and white of a tattered Japanese ensign. Except for some smoke rising from what looked like a galley-stove funnel at the forward end of the deckhouse there were no signs of life on board; not a man on deck. To Melton it was incomprehensible. He had expected a certain degree of vigilance. The Japanese were either very lax or very sure of themselves.

The *Fiona* moved on, her engine just ticking over; her men, their weapons ready, crouching behind the low bulwarks, and the Bofors amidships still partially hidden under the drooping canvas folds of the mainsail. But whatever happened now the gun was useless. With the other ship fine on the port bow its line of fire was masked by the fore rigging.

They had another hundred yards to go . . . seventy . . . fifty . . . and still there were no signs of activity on board the Jap. It was almost too good to be true.

"God!" said Melton to the helmsman, beside himself with excitement. "We've caught her with her breeks off!"

The able seaman, intent on his steering to take the ship alongside, grinned and grunted some reply to the effect that it served the yellow-skinned bastards bloody well right.

On the low poop, not far from the wheel and compass, lay two men with Lewis guns waiting for what might happen. But if the enemy did come to life now, all they would see was Melton and the man at the wheel. They were both bare-headed, deeply tanned and unshaven. Both wore dirty white plimsolls and the helmsman was still in his oilskin. Melton had discarded his, and wore a disreputable pair of grey flannel trousers and above it a faded blue shirt beneath a tattered old uniform monkey jacket with the stripes and brass buttons removed. At any distance both might have been taken for natives.

Twenty yards to go . . . ten. . . .

Melton, his heart throbbing, stopped the engine, put it to astern to check the way, and then stopped it again. The *Fiona* rubbed alongside with a gentle nudge, scraped a little and came to a standstill. After that everything seemed to happen at once.

A door was suddenly flung open in the other ship's deck-house. Two startled figures emerged, the first in a seaman's uniform with a belt and clutching a rifle, and a second in a dirty white singlet and apron, obviously the cook. The pair must have been hobnobbing in the galley over an early cup of tea. For a moment they stared in amazement, and then the sailor yelped and rushed to the ship's side, brandishing his weapon. He was much too late.

A new White Ensign had already gone up to the *Fiona's* mainmast head. Melton, pistol in hand, leapt down from the poop, and with a cry of "Come on, lads!" rushed across the deck, balanced himself on the bulwarks and jumped for the other ship. The boarders followed shouting, while men forward and aft secured the *Fiona* alongside. The Japanese sentry, or whoever he was, was knocked sideways with a rifle butt and fell senseless to the deck before he could fire a shot, and his weapon hurled overboard.

It was all over in a few minutes. Melton, throwing open another door in the deckhouse, found himself in the wireless-room, which was unoccupied. He tried the next door abaft it, which seemed to be locked. Wrenching at the handle he heard a report from inside, and a bullet whizzed through the panel close to his head. There came a second report, followed by a third.

"Stand clear, sir!" yelled a seaman with a Sten gun. "I'll settle the bastard!"

Melton sprang aside, and the man discharged his weapon through the door from a range of a few feet. He fired ten or fifteen rounds, splintering the panelling and shattering the lock, then tugged at the handle and pulled it open.

It was an officer's cabin, with a bunk and drawers under-neath, writing-table, bookshelf and washstand. Some clothing and a uniform cap lay on a chair. The occupant, who had evidently just leapt out of his bed and wore no more than a pair of white drawers, sat bleeding on the deck with his back to the bunk. As Melton peered inside the wounded man feebly lifted his automatic and fired. His bullet missed. Melton retaliated with four shots from his pistol, and the Japanese dropped his weapon and toppled over sideways. Beyond stepping inside to take his enemy's pistol, he didn't stop to investigate. The whole incident had taken less than a minute.

There came shouting, with a short splutter of firearms, from both ends of the ship. As arranged on the spur of the moment the boarders had divided up; one party to round up anyone in the forecastle, a second to investigate the living quarters aft, and other men to go below to the engine-room to prevent sabotage, and to go through what in normal times were the cargo holds, but had now probably been fitted out as extra living accommodation.

In less time than it takes to describe it His Imperial Japanese Majesty's auxiliary patrol vessel Number 5017 was in British hands, and her terrified, sorry-looking crew, most of them in their night attire and one or two wounded, were being herded on deck by armed bluejackets. It took some time before all of them were hunted out from where they had hidden themselves.

Petty Officer Huxtable appeared, armed, for want of a better weapon, with a formidable-looking, home-made bludgeon.

"I thought I told you to remain on board," Melton said, half scoldingly.

Huxtable saluted and grinned. "Yessir," he grinned. "But seeing as how things have gone so well I thought I'd come along. These prisoners, sir," he added, eyeing the miserable group with fierce disfavour. "What's to be done about them?"

The prisoners certainly presented a complication which Melton hadn't really considered. There seemed to be a con-siderable number, and how eventually to dispose of them was a problem. "Have 'em all searched for weapons to start with," he said. "Then make 'em sit on deck with their hands on their heads. Keep a guard on 'em; but there's to be no unnecessary rough stuff. Have we any casualties? I heard some shooting."

"I dunno, sir. I've only just come aboard."

"Well, let me know, Huxtable. Oh! And have that damned Japanese ensign hauled down. I hate the sight of it. Preserve it. We may need it later."

During a rough-and-tumble in the forecastle two of the *Fiona's* men had been hit by pistol bullets, one in the left shoulder and one through the thigh, though neither wound was dangerous. There had been more shooting during a scrimmage in the accommodation aft, though no British were hit.

In all, five Japanese who refused to surrender had been killed and another four wounded. One of the killed, Melton's victim, was the reserve lieutenant in command. They found themselves left with thirteen prisoners of war.

Melton looked over the scowling, miserable-looking group squatting on deck. Probably they expected to be shot out of hand.

"What are we goin' to do with 'em, sir?" Huxtable growled in his officer's ear. "We've no room for the bastards in our ship. If I had my way I'd take 'em out to sea an' dump the whole bleedin' lot over the side arter what they an' their pals've done to some of our poor chaps!" he added fiercely.

"None of that, Huxtable!" Melton returned sharply. "We're not murderers, and if it came to the point you'd no more dump them overboard than you would your own grandmother."

"Do any of you speak English?" he went on to ask, looking along the row of abject faces. "English," he repeated. "Anyone savvy?"

Nobody answered. Melton repeated his question. Finally one man bowed and lifted a timid hand.

"Me," he replied, searching for the necessary words. "Me one time learn Engleesh."

"Can you understand what I say?" Melton demanded, speaking very deliberately.

"I tink, yess," came the answer, with another bow.

"Are you an officer?"

After great difficulty Melton gathered the spokesman was a junior engineer, some sort of petty officer, it seemed. His knowledge of English was trifling, though with patience and much explanation and repetition it sufficed.

"Are there any officers here?" Melton asked.

One of the seamen from the *Fiona* broke in. "Beg pardon, sir," he said, pointing to one of the wounded. "I reckon that bloke's an officer." The man indicated, shot through the chest and dripping blood, was on the point of collapse.

"What happened?"

"I found 'im in a cabin aft, sir. He had a gun an' had a shot at me. I had to give 'im one."

Melton told Huxtable to send someone for the first-aid bag and to have the poor wretch looked after. He was carried off. Further questioning of the engineer elicited the fact that the badly wounded man was a warrant-officer, second-in-command of the ship.

"Now listen to what I say," Melton continued, speaking very slowly and enunciating every word. "You can tell your friends that though they are prisoners of war, we shall not hurt them if they make no trouble. Any resistance or disobedience of orders will be treated with severity. Do you understand?"

The engineer looked puzzled. "Plis to say again," he asked.

Melton repeated what he had said even more slowly. "Now do you understand?"

"I tink, yess," the engineer nodded, his expression brightening. "I tank you." He bowed.

"Then translate."

The little man gabbled something in singsong Japanese. A few of the prisoners glanced at each other with grins of relief, though the expressions of most of them remained surly and inscrutable.

It took some time before Melton managed to make them understand all he thought it necessary to say for the moment. All weapons, firearms, swords or knives, must be handed over. The Japanese must look after their own wounded, and, again, all orders must be strictly obeyed.

There was much to be done.

The *Fiona*'s two wounded were taken back to the ship and attended to. The five dead Japanese were brought on deck and sewn up in weighted canvas preparatory to burial at sea. There was some bother over this. Their shipmates wished to take the bodies ashore for cremation so that the ashes could be sent to Japan. As Fukuni, the engineer petty officer, explained with

223

much hissing and bowing: "It iss Japanese custom. Wife, mudder, farder, childs, like to have."

Melton was tired and his patience was exhausted. "You can tell them there'll be no cremation ashore!" he said angrily. "No one is going ashore! No ashes will be sent to Japan! If they don't like it they can lump it, and be damned to them!"

Fukuni couldn't have understood what the Englishman had said; but his tone, his expression and gestures were more than sufficient. There was no further nonsense.

Leaving a guard over the prisoners, Melton, with Petty Officer Huxtable and the young engine-room artificer from the *Fiona*, inspected the prize with Fukuni.

Number 5017 was a wooden, Batavia-built schooner slightly larger than the *Fiona*, and in some respects a better ship. As armed and refitted by the Japanese, she carried a couple of 6-pounder guns, besides machine-guns, rifles, pistols and a good supply of light depth charges apparently for use against submarines. She had a small searchlight, auxiliary generator and wireless, and had been fitted with a fairly modern Diesel engine which, according to Fukuni, gave a speed of about nine knots. Further prolonged questioning, during which it became more and more difficult to make Fukuni understand, produced the reply that at full stowage 5017 carried enough fuel for about five hundred miles, though at the moment the tanks were half empty. Yes. They normally refuelled every three or four days.

This at once ruled out Melton's first idea of transferring the whole of the *Fiona's* ship's company, and her six islanders, to the prize with the prisoners, and then, after scuttling the *Fiona*, taking 5017 on to Australia under her engine. But Australia was at least eight hundred miles away. Even if they topped up 5017's tanks from the *Fiona* they could never make it, and the prize had no sails if the fuel ran short.

He was in something of a dilemma. However inhospitable and desolate the little harbour might be, and no natives had appeared ashore, it might at any time be visited by enemy aircraft. From what he gathered from Fukuni, who became more and more reticent, it seemed that 5017 frequently used the anchorage during the daytime. Was she in the habit of reporting her whereabouts by wireless, and, if an aircraft did appear and sighted *two* ships alongside each other, would it excite suspicion and closer investigation? There was certainly the risk of that. On the other hand, the sight of the two ships might perhaps cause a snooping aircraft to imagine that 5017 was herself examining a suspicious vessel. This thought caused Melton to give orders for the signal locker of the prize to be rummaged and for the largest Japanese ensigns available to be hoisted in both ships.

Weighing up the pros and cons Melton decided on his course of action. They spent the daylight hours transferring everything useful from the prize to the *Fiona*, hardly stopping to eat. This included what Diesel oil could be pumped out; provisions and fresh water; all the machine-guns, small arms and ammunition; together with mattresses and blankets; some codes and signal-books and bundles of Japanese paper money from the small steel safe in the dead captain's cabin; a few charts and instruments; a collection of fishing lines and books which might come in useful; signal-flags and a good deal else. The two six-pounders had to be left behind. They were difficult to move, and there was nowhere they could be mounted in the *Fiona*. Nor could any room be found for the auxiliary generator, without which the searchlight was useless.

Beyond the death of the Japanese warrant-officer, the day passed without incident. No aircraft appeared, no natives were seen ashore. The few huts seemed to be unoccupied.

Before dusk all the twelve prisoners and the dead were transferred to the *Fiona*, a most unwelcome addition to an already overcrowded ship; but to which there was no alternative. As darkness fell the *Fiona* put to sea with 5017 in tow, and once clear of the harbour entrance and in tolerably deep water the shrouded, weighted bodies were launched overboard in the presence of their shipmates. They showed little emotion.

The strong wind of the day before had dropped to a steady breeze, and the rain had ceased. The sky was clear, though a long, smooth swell still rolled down from the south-eastward. Number 5017 sheered from side to side and plunged heavily in the *Fiona*'s wake as she closely skirted a low barrier of sheer cliff to leeward.

It was with a heavy heart and all a seaman's reluctance that Melton had decided he must destroy a perfectly good ship taken in lawful prize; but there was nothing else for it. So they towed 5017 to within a few hundred yards of the line of heavy surf and cut the hawser. With the rocky coast close under her lee her destruction was inevitable, though to hasten the process Melton circled round and opened fire at close range with the Bofors.

Number 5017 listed heavily over to starboard with a few tongues of red and orange flame flickering from her wooden hull and deckhouse. There came the flash and thump of a small explosion, followed by a cloud of black smoke. Then the flames died away, and when last seen the wreck appeared as a dim shape heaving and wallowing in the rioting welter of surf breaking furiously along the iron-bound shore. Nobody saw her actual dissolution.

The *Fiona* turned her bows seaward, and presently shut off her engine and made sail with a fair breeze from the eastward. As she drew clear of the land the really heavy swell subsided.

The night was starlit and peaceful with a thin sickle moon after midnight. At daylight next morning there was nothing in sight except the dim blue shape of a mountain-top far away to the northward.

Drinking his early morning cup of cocoa on the poop, Melton felt pleased with himself. The *Fiona* was sailing well, curtsying easily to the long, smooth swell without shipping a drop of water. Before her stretched the limitless horizon. They had a long, long way to travel and anything might happen; but what was undoubtedly the most dangerous part of the journey, the passage from island to island and then on through the straits, had been safely accomplished.

Huxtable came aft, saluted and said "Good morning."

"Lovely yachting weather," Melton remarked. "What could be better?"

The petty officer didn't seem too cheerful. "Them Jap prisoners, sir," he grumbled.

"What, giving trouble?"

"No, sir. Not yet. We got 'em locked up safe in the fo'c'sle. It's their food an' water I'm thinkin' about, and are they to be allowed on deck?"

They discussed the situation. Twelve possibly recalcitrant Japanese who must be guarded and watched over day and night were certainly a responsibility.

"They must produce their own cook to boil their rice and

226

whatever else they live on," Melton finally ordered. "As for water, one quart per man per day for drinking and tea-making, the same allowance as the rest of us. If they want to wash there's plenty of sea."

"What about 'em coming on deck, sir?"

"Two hours on deck forenoon and afternoon, half at a time, properly guarded. You can put 'em on to scrubbing decks or any other odd jobs, Huxtable. *Make* 'em work. Keep 'em busy. We're carrying no passengers this trip."

During the days that followed the prisoners gave little trouble. According to Fukuni practically all of them were ex-fishermen and boatmen hastily conscripted and put into uniform just before the outbreak of war. With a minimum of naval training they were imbued with none of the fighting tradition and fierce discipline of the regular Japanese navy. From being cowed and frightened they became almost cheerful, even helpful and useful.

On the third day after sailing the sky clouded over and the wind started to rise. In a few hours it was blowing with almost gale force, with intermittent thunder-storms accompanied by fierce squalls and torrential driving rain. Staggering and plunging in the heavy breaking sea the *Fiona* drove on under reefed canvas, with her decks awash and the spray sweeping over her in sheets. The foul weather lasted for forty-eight hours, to make life supremely wet and uncomfortable in a little ship overcrowded with seventy people.

Twice, with the storm at its height and the wind roaring like the wrath of God, Melton hove to with a small piece of the close-reefed mainsail showing to keep wind and sea on the bow. They made one attempt to lay out a sea anchor improvized from a spar and old canvas; but had to give it up as hopeless when the *Fiona's* violent movement snapped the hawser like a piece of string.

The foresail split and the half-drowned cook slid out of his galley on deck with most of his pots and pans. Men had narrow escapes of being washed overboard as they clawed their way along the reeling deck with the seas coming over waist-deep. . . . Those forty-eight hours until the gale blew itself out, the sea subsided, the sky cleared and the sun reappeared, were hours of undiluted misery. They snatched what food and drink they could. Nobody slept.

Then Huxtable came aft with a tale of woe. Four of the six extra casks of fresh water lashed on deck had worked adrift in the gale and were leaking hopelessly, he explained with a face of gloom. The other two, he hoped, were not damaged.

"Oh God!" said Melton, horrified.

Shortage of fresh water, that most precious commodity, was the most dreadful calamity that could happen. True, they had fitted extra tanks in the *Fiona* and there were other water casks below; but with seventy men on board heavy inroads had already been made and there was still a long voyage ahead of them. It had rained heavily during the storm; but with the spray sweeping over the ship in sheets any attempt at collecting fresh water to the exclusion of the salt had been out of the question.

Consulting together they came to the conclusion that with the normal ration they had sufficient fresh water to last for about ten days.

"We must pray for rain, this time without a gale o' wind," Melton said, looking at the almost cloudless sky. "From now on," he added, "all cooking's to be done in sea water. Fresh water for *all* purposes will be reduced to one pint a man a day, and not a drop more without direct orders from me."

"Aye aye, sir," Huxtable replied.

Holy mackerel, he thought to himself, scratching his bearded chin. One blinking, perishing pint, the contents of *one* of those foaming tankards served out by Lottie, the barmaid at the Golden Lion in Fulham! At home on leave he often sank three full pints of wallop in a single evening between half-past eight and closing time. And now, one pint of tepid, musty-tasting water every twenty-four hours . . . suffering cats! Who'd have thought it?

"We'll put a guard on the water," Melton continued. "It's just *got* to last. And you can pass the word that if anyone's found stealing water I'll make his life a misery and a torment. Is that clear?"

"Yessir."

There followed three days of brilliant weather, with a blazing sun, full visibility all round the horizon, a smooth, rolling swell and gentle favouring breeze. They would have welcomed dark clouds to windward as heralds of rain, but none appeared.

Fish could be seen following the ship through the clear green water. With home-made spinners and hooks baited with white rag, or pieces of the silvery skin of the fish themselves, some of the Japanese were put on to fishing and managed to catch sufficient for several meals for all hands. Though no one could give them a name, they were not unlike large rather coarse mackerel, which served as a welcome change to the everlasting biscuit, rice and tinned food. The fresh fruit and vegetables and fowls had long since been eaten. Someone suggested that a lantern hung in the main rigging after dark would attract the flying fish. It worked. As many as twenty or thirty a night would come sailing in to hit the mainsail and drop flapping to the deck, eagerly to be pounced upon for breakfast.

But in the torrid heat nothing could make up for the lack of fresh water. Their throats were parched. Men became dull and listless, lacking even the energy to draw and pour buckets of sea water over each other each morning and evening in the hope of alleviating their terrible thirst. A meagre pint of water a day, and that evil-tasting, went nowhere. Some treasured it in bottles, sipping it drop by drop. Others, less provident, drank half their allowance at a time and by the end of the day were clamouring for more. It was sweated out again almost as soon as drunk.

Quarrels and bickering broke out, and falling-in the ship's company on deck Melton talked to them. The nonsense must stop, he said in very plain language. They must pull together and not behave like children. The measures he had decided upon were for the good of them all, and he hoped, with God's help, to bring them safely to Australia. He knew what they were suffering, for he was suffering the same. Thirst was a hellish thing. No. Unless rain came, and it didn't seem likely at the moment, the water ration would remain at *one pint* a day, and that was all there was to it. He didn't tell them that with the lime juice exhausted, and in the absence of fresh meat, fruit and vegetables, he had scurvy on his mind.

Two of the Japanese wounded died, and a third committed suicide by hanging himself in the forecastle. The bodies were committed to the sea in weighted canvas.

On the tenth day out Melton, as usual, was on deck before dawn. The light burgeoned, and the eastern sky gradually became suffused with the aureate flush of approaching sunrise over a rolling sea of deep indigo furred by the steady breeze.

To the west the sky was still dark, with a few stars twinkling like burnished silver.

The sun rose and full daylight came. A few minutes later, sweeping his glasses all round the clear-cut horizon, Melton suddenly had sight of what looked like a faint trail of smoke far away to the south-west. It vanished almost at once and he thought his imagination was playing tricks. . . . But no, in another few minutes, clear and distinct, he saw the masts and funnels of a ship still hull down. Her upper-works gradually hove into sight, finally her hull. She looked like a large merchant ship, grey painted, and steering directly towards the *Fiona*. A little later she altered course to starboard. Melton realized she was zigzagging.

He felt himself shaking with suppressed excitement. What was a solitary merchant ship doing here, hundreds of miles from anywhere? Could she be British? It seemed much more likely that she was Japanese. She might even be German, perhaps one of those merchant ships they were known to be using as raiders. It was a sickening thought. She could not avoid sighting the *Fiona* against the glaring sky to the eastward, and if she came close to investigate could Melton pull off the pretence of being a native-owned schooner from Java? What should a native schooner be doing in mid-ocean? Where was she going? If it came to being boarded and questioned they must inevitably be found out. That meant the end of the *Fiona*, and himself and all the men spending the rest of the war as prisoners. The tables would be turned with a vengeance, and he could imagine the triumphant joy of his Japanese captives, blast them!

The suspense became intolerable as the minutes passed. Then, again, the strange ship swerved towards the *Fiona*, much clearer this time and steaming fast, to judge from the heavy white plume of her bow wave. Then more ships appeared beyond her, two of them large liners like the first, and the third an unmistakable cruiser.

"My God!" he muttered, gazing at the cruiser in blank amazement. He was hardly able to believe his eyes. There were no other cruisers of that type in the world.

She was neither Japanese nor German. Her great hull, her three large funnels and two masts, proclaimed her to be a British cruiser of the 'County' class. It was nothing short of a miracle. The last thing he had expected to tumble across was what looked like a fast troop convoy, escorted by a British cruiser, foaming eastward at a good twenty knots!

Melton put down his glasses, his heart throbbing with relief. The men of the watch on deck had seen the oncoming ships, and were gathered along the lee bulwarks, pointing and gesticulating. Bare-chested, bronzed by the sun and bearded, they looked thin and hollow-eyed. The helmsman's eyes wandered from his compass. The foresail flapped and shook as he allowed the ship to stray off into the wind.

"Watch your steering, Coggins!" Melton warned. "Keep that fors'l full, dammit!" He went on to hail the leading seaman of the watch.

"Mathers!"

"Sir?"

"Tell Petty Officer Huxtable one of our cruisers is in sight. . . ."

The men gave vent to their feelings by loud cheering. Melton had to hold up his hand for silence before continuing.

"I want everyone on deck for shortening sail, and the engine warmed up ready for starting! Tell Huxtable. And I want the ensign and the Very pistol and cartridges up here at once. D'you understand?"

"Yessir."

"And tell the cook he can brew all the tea he likes, and all hands can help themselves to fresh water."

There were more cheers at that.

Huxtable appeared on deck and the White Ensign went up to the *Fiona's* main masthead. Her engine gave its usual preliminary coughs and rumbles, then broke into its steady pulsation. The men were in the highest of spirits, shouting and laughing, patting each other on the back, as cheerful as a gang of schoolchildren released for an unexpected holiday. Only the Japanese, clustered in the bows, looked supremely miserable.

The convoy came on, zigzagging; but never out of sight . . . ten miles . . . eight . . . four . . .

The sails were lowered and secured, and the *Fiona* lay motionless, heaving to the long swell.

Melton started firing Very cartridges to attract attention, and the red, white and green balls of fire went soaring up into the air to curve over and fall. All eyes were on the cruiser. They watched her, silent and breathless. Then a light flashed from her bridge, and a moment or two later she altered course and came steering straight towards them.

There was an audible sigh of relief. "She's comin', sir! She's comin'!" the usually phlegmatic Huxtable exclaimed, his voice hoarse with emotion. "Holy Maggie! What a bit o' luck!" He clutched Melton by the arm.

In less than ten minutes, with her turbines going astern to check her way, the cruiser was within thirty yards and moving parallel to the *Fiona*, her great grey hull with its rows of scuttles, surmounted by the twin 8-inch gun turrets, the tall bridge structure and three huge funnels towering high overhead. Her upper deck was crowded with men, all gazing curiously down at the schooner.

An officer with gold oak leaves on the peak of his cap, evidently the captain, leant over the bridge. He lifted a megaphone.

"What ship is that?" he hailed, noting the White Ensign and the tatterdemalion, bearded crowd on the *Fiona's* deck.

"The *Fiona*, sir," Melton shouted back. "A captured schooner. There are fifty-two of us from the *Eurydice*. . . ."

"From the what?"

"The *Eurydice*, sir, a destroyer!"

"The *Eurydice*, d'you say?"

"Yes, sir. We got knocked out in that battle in the Java Sea on February the twenty-eighth; but managed to get to an island, and have been there ever since! I was sent off with some of our men to see if anything could be done about rescuing the rest of our party, left behind."

"And who are you?"

"My name's Melton, sir! I was the *Eurydice's* number two lieutenant and navigator. There are fifty-two of us here from the *Eurydice*, six natives and ten Japanese prisoners. We managed to. . . ."

"Explain later," the cruiser's captain interrupted. "This is the *Lincoln*. We're bound for Australia with a convoy. D'you want us to take you on?"

"Yes sir, please!" Melton shouted back.

"You've an engine, I see," came back. "I'll turn and give you a lee from the swell, so come alongside when we're ready. We'll have a boat-rope and jumping ladders."

"I've three wounded, sir!" Melton hailed, as the cruiser's

helm went over and the water started to boil under her stern. Her port propeller was going astern.

"Right. We'll hoist 'em in! And Melton?"

"Sir?"

"I can't afford to hang about, so look slippy and don't bring masses of gear. We'll look after you."

"Aye aye, sir!"

Within ten or twelve minutes everyone from the *Fiona* had been transferred. They took with them a precious mail-bag containing letters home from the *Eurydice*'s officers and men; a copy of the destroyer's log and Acton's official letter of proceedings, together with nominal lists of those killed or wounded, and the others who had survived.

It was a rush job, with the *Lincoln*'s commander exhorting everyone to 'smack it about' and 'get a move on.' But Melton did manage to save the *Fiona*'s White Ensign, his own sextant and a suit-case of uniform clothing, some bundles belonging to the men, with the rifles and small arms. The Japanese ensign, with their code and signal-books and a few of the captured weapons, including a sword found in the captain's cabin, went with the rest. Given time, he would like to have taken much else.

Melton was the last to leave. He felt a pang of regret as he looked round the *Fiona*'s deck for the last time before pulling himself up the jumping ladder hung over the *Lincoln*'s wall side. The *Fiona* was his first command, and she had served them well.

He had hardly reached the cruiser's deck and was introducing himself to the commander, one Charteris, before she started to move ahead and the schooner was cast off and drifting astern.

The big ship circled. A 4-inch gun opened fire at close range. The *Fiona*'s mainmast toppled overboard as the first shell hit and burst in a shower of debris. Six rounds sufficed. Riven and battered, the schooner's stern dipped under and her dripping bows lifted, her bowsprit pointing skywards like a finger-post. She hung for a moment or two and then slowly disappeared in a little swirl of whitened, bubbling water, to leave a scum of oil littered with floating wreckage.

The *Lincoln* increased to full speed to overtake her convoy, now several miles ahead.

"Rotten bad business having to sink a perfectly good ship," Commander Charteris said, bringing down his glasses. "It goes against the grain. And now, Melton, I expect you'd like to see the captain."

"Yes, sir. But how about my men? I'm sorry to inflict such a crowd on you."

"Don't you bother yourself," the other laughed. "We'll take care of 'em. They look pretty well all in, poor chaps. Are you the only officer?"

Melton said he was.

"I counted sixteen heathen, Melton. How come?"

"Six are friendly islanders and the rest Japanese prisoners," Melton told him, going on with a brief explanation of what had happened.

"Some people have all the luck," the commander observed. "But one of your people had better tell us which are which. They all look the same to me. How are the Japs, mutinous or amenable?"

They had better be kept under guard, Melton said. Otherwise they were as tame as rabbits. They were conscripts, not proper naval seamen.

A petty officer, the captain's coxswain, came up to Charteris and saluted. "The cap'en's compliments, sir," he said, glancing at Melton, "and he hopes the officer'll make use of his spare cabin and bathroom aft. The valet's"—he pronounced it 'varlet'—"been warned. Also the cap'en says, sir, he hopes the officer'll give him the pleasure of his company at breakfast in his sea cabin in about half an hour's time."

"So he doesn't want to see Mister Melton now?"

"No, sir. The cap'en's about to shave. After that he'll take his bath."

"Well, Melton. There are your orders."

"And I haven't a rag fit to wear," Melton said. "Nothing but an ancient monkey jacket and trousers and some khaki."

"That," the commander replied, "will be looked after. Now come along. We'll see about that cabin of yours."

It was joy indeed to be shown into a spotless cabin with the smiling 'varlet' waiting with a pot of tea, milk, sugar, cup and plate of biscuits on a silver tray, and clean underclothes with a tropical white shirt, shorts and stockings laid out on the bunk. The valet hoped they would fit. Captain Jeffreys had given orders they should be provided, though possibly the captain was a shade stouter than his guest.

"The bathroom's here, sir," the young man continued, opening a communicating door. "I've run you a warm bath. I think you'll find everything."

"And what's your name?" Melton asked, noting the soap, towels and sponge, with a new toothbrush, shaving gear, nail scissors and other oddments on the rack in front of the mirror. Nothing had been forgotten, even to a pair of bedroom slippers, comb and hairbrushes.

"I'm Walters, sir."

"And have you been long at sea?"

"Ever since the outbreak, sir. I looked after Captain Molyneux in the *Cerberus* until we got sunk in Norway and he was killed."

"Nasty business, war," Melton said. "What were you doing beforehand?"

"I had a job at the Savoy Hotel, sir, when I *volunteered*, my father being a sailor. I wanted to be a seaman, but my eyesight wasn't up to scratch. So I joined up as officer's steward."

"Stout fellow!" said Melton, gazing at his own reflection in the mirror. He had something of a shock. For the first time in weeks he was seeing himself as others saw him. "Gosh!" he exclaimed, regarding his hollow eyes, his drawn, tanned face, ragged growth of beard and long, tangled hair. "I'm a horrid sight!"

Walters, himself immaculate in clean whites, coughed discreetly. "You'd certainly do with a bit of a trim, sir," he observed judicially. "I'll get the barber along later. If there's anything else you need now, sir, just press the bell marked pantry and I'll be along. I'll take you up for'ard for breakfast when you're ready."

Melton thanked him, and the valet took himself off. Walters was most attentive. Captain Jeffreys had drawn a winner.

To soap oneself, lie back and wallow full length in warm fresh water for ten minutes was unalloyed bliss. Emerging dripping, Melton felt a new man. The beard, he decided, after a few ineffectual efforts with the nail scissors, must remain for the time being. The barber could remove it later.

Captain Jeffreys was a good host. Breakfast in his sea cabin near the bridge was a pleasant meal, quite apart from the fact that it was months since Melton had seen porridge, a choice of real kippers or bacon and eggs, with hot rolls, fresh butter and marmalade, and coffee which tasted as coffee should. With her large refrigerators, bakery and well-stocked canteen, the *Lincoln* was amply provided.

They soon discovered mutual Service friends and acquaintances, and when the steward had retired they came down to real business. Melton told his story, Jeffreys sometimes breaking in with a question. Their sitting was a long one.

The *Lincoln* and her convoy, carrying Australian troops, was bound for Melbourne unless they received other orders in the interval. Meanwhile, because of the Japanese, there was strict wireless silence which couldn't be broken unless the enemy actually appeared and action became imminent. Nothing could be done about reporting to the Admiralty until they arrived in harbour.

"What it boils down to is that sixty-five people are left in the *Eurydice* at the island, and they haven't a dog's chance of getting away unless something's done?" Jeffreys asked.

Melton agreed.

Then as he saw it, the captain continued, the first and most important thing was to have those sixty-five rescued if it were humanly possible. That was outside his province, and how it could be done, heaven only knew! It mightn't be possible if the Java Sea was still under close Japanese control. Anyhow, he, Jeffreys, could take steps to inform the Admiralty and the local naval authorities that the *Lincoln* had picked up the *Fiona's* people, and that others from the *Eurydice* were marooned on an island in Latitude X, Longitude Y. He presumed Melton had a nominal list of all the survivors?

"Yes, sir. And a list of the killed and wounded."

"Then I'll make myself responsible for getting all the names to the Admiralty. Whether or not they inform the next of kin straight away is up to them. I imagine they'll probably decide to hold up *all* news to the relatives for the time being. That includes your people. If it once gets about that we picked you up it might spoil the chance of getting the others away."

"I see that, sir," Melton said. "I can only leave it in your hands. You know best."

Jeffreys went on to ask if it was possible to communicate with the *Eurydice* by wireless, to which Melton replied that she could receive, but not transmit. Anyhow, they had thought of that, and he had brought a paper from Scriven, the petty officer telegraphist, giving wavelengths, times of listening, what cipher might be used, and so on. And mentioning codes reminded him that he also had the code- and signal-books from the Japanese patrol schooner they'd captured. "I'd better hand them over to you, sir," he said.

The captain nodded. "Yes," he agreed. "They may be useful for breaking enemy ciphers. I'll send them to the Admiralty, or whoever's most concerned out here. Then I understand you've a bag full of private letters home from the *Eurydice's* people," he added. "Have they been censored?"

"Up to a point, sir," Melton explained. In the circumstances ordinary ship censorship was difficult. They could hardly prevent the men saying that the *Eurydice* had reached an island and that they themselves were alive and well.

Jeffreys thought for a moment. "I quite see that," he smiled. "But we've got to think of security and getting these other chaps of yours away. I'll have the bag properly sealed, Melton, and send it direct to the Admiralty by the quickest possible route, whatever that may be. It's for them to decide how your private letters are dealt with; but it's my guess they'll hold them up until . . . well, until it's been decided whether or not they have a shot at rescuing the sixty-five from the island."

"Yes, sir. I understand."

There must be other precautions, the captain went on to say. The *Lincoln's* ship's company would be warned that nothing was to be said in their letters, and above all that nothing must be mentioned on shore, about the island or the *Lincoln* having picked up the *Fiona*. The *Fiona's* men must also be warned. It was vitally important.

"I'll see to that, sir," Melton promised. "But how about my six natives and the Japanese prisoners?"

"The Australians'll look after the prisoners," Jeffreys said grimly. "As for the friendly natives, I don't know; but we can't have them running around saying what they like. I expect the police'll look after that, though. Do any of 'em speak English, by the way?"

"Not more than a few words, sir."

The captain went on to explain. "If the news of your rescue and of the others left behind once leaks out into the newspapers or gets broadcast it'll be all round the world in less than no time," he said. "You've probably all been reported as killed in action. Now, after months on an exotic island in the Java Sea, largely inhabited by lovely young women, a hundred and seventeen British sailors suddenly pop up again, rather incredibly. It would make a fine romantic yarn for the newshounds. Imagine the headlines!"

"Yes sir," Melton said, stubbing out a cigarette. He hadn't really considered all the complexities of the situation, and found it difficult to think. He felt abominably tired. Having eaten well he wanted to sleep.

"Tell your chaps," Jeffreys warned him again. "Tell them to keep their mouths tight shut when they get ashore, which ought to be in four days' time if the weather holds. They can say they're shipwrecked sailors picked up in open boats off the Cape of Good Hope, any old yarn provided they all say the same. We'll hash up a likely story. If the real truth gets around, if it's broadcast and the Japs get to hear of it, it may mean farewell and adieu to your shipmates."

Melton understood.

The captain had realized Melton's weariness. "Well, that's all for now," he said, rising. "I expect you'd like to get your head down. We'll draft out our signals to the Admiralty later. There's plenty of time. Meanwhile you have the run of the ship, so ask for anything you want. They'll make you an honorary member of the wardroom, which'll be more matey than having your meals alone in my cabin aft. I don't leave this end of the ship at sea; but come up and have a yarn whenever you feel like it. All right?"

"Thank you, sir," said Melton, his voice full of gratitude. "Thank you very much indeed."

Jeffreys grinned, patted him on the shoulder and pushed him gently out.

Melton felt overwhelmed. He couldn't say all he wanted to say. He hadn't the words. So much had happened in the last few hours.

At this very time the day before they had been suffering the torments of extreme thirst, with every prospect of their fresh water becoming exhausted. They had prayed for rain; but no rain had come.

And now. . . .

24

AFTER THE *Fiona's* departure, life in Eurydice Island went on much as before, except that one night the roar and thudding shock of a heavy explosion shook the ship and brought everyone rushing on deck in the sketchiest of night attire. The villagers were reduced to a state of babbling terror, and as a few solitary aircraft had been sighted in the distance during the past three days, some of them, imagining that the big bang was the prelude to an air-raid, promptly took to the bush with their wives and children.

As usual, men were sleeping round the *Eurydice's* guns when the explosion occurred at about 1.45 a.m. Farnworth was keeping the middle watch, and when Acton, closely followed by Mr. Blatchington, Draycott, McInnes and most of the men arrived breathless on deck, Acton found the sub all but speechless with laughter.

"What the hell?" Acton demanded, gazing seaward. The night was hot and airless, dark; but perfectly clear. There was nothing unusual to be seen.

"Sorry you've been troubled," Farnworth managed to splutter. "It was only one of old Guns's depth charges going to glory! The darned thing must have slipped from its moorings."

Mr. Blatchington seemed to take the remark as a personal affront. "I'll swear the bloody things were moored all right!" he declared angrily. "Think I don't know my job as a seaman! It must 'a been that damn schooner muckin' about with it the other day!"

The Gunner had to be pacified before they went below; but the next morning, after warning the villagers, the oil-drums floating the other two depth charges were duly sunk by gunfire and there were two shattering detonations. Mr. Blatchington, to solace his injured feelings, went away in the whaler and returned with the stern sheets full of fish, quantities of them.

"Anyway, Mr. Farnworth," he said at lunch, with an old-fashioned glance at the sub-lieutenant. "You got me to thank for a change of diet from the everlasting sweet Fanny Adams,* flyin' foxes an' those bloody land-crabs."

* "Fanny Adams"—Tinned corned beef.

"A pity you can't blow up a few spuds, you old wizard," Farnworth retorted with a friendly grin. "Then we could have fried fish and chips for every meal."

Mr. Blatchington glowered.

Acton looked up. "That's enough from you, Sub!" he broke in sharply. "Let's hear no more about it, if you please."

The change in the prevailing wind to the south-east sometimes brought a moderate swell running into the bay, so that the *Eurydice*, in her exposed position, occasionally rolled so heavily as to make life on board supremely uncomfortable. Tugging and straining at her single anchor from the cable forward and the wire spring aft, there was also the danger that she might damage herself against the sheer face of the low cliff if it came on to blow really hard.

A new berth had to be found, and on Beekman's advice and after soundings had been taken from the whaler, Acton made up his mind to shift billet to a place alongside the cliff on the opposite side of the bay. There, at any rate, the ship could lie under the lee of the land and out of the swell.

Unwilling to move during daylight in case it attracted the attention of some prowling enemy aircraft, they carried out the operation at night. It meant a good deal of detailed preparation, and was not just like taking the ship from A to B in a well-lit and charted harbour. Steam had to be raised on the main engines, and as the capstan engine had been destroyed, the starboard anchor must be weighed by hand, a straining, back-breaking job, particularly in the darkness.

This done, Acton took her stern-first to seaward, preparatory to coming in again to let go the port anchor with a spring on the cable off the new billet, and finally securing alongside the cliff. They had shaded lights to guide them and a party of men ashore to take the mooring lines. Farnworth was in charge on the forecastle and the Gunner aft; but with the *Eurydice* short-handed and both forecastle and quarter-deck a tangle of slippery hawsers, the job was by no means so easy as it looked. There was considerable delay.

Damaged and leaking though she was, it was good to feel the *Eurydice* alive and throbbing and under way under the thrust of her own turbines. Acton brought her on dead slow and let go the port anchor before starting to sidle the ship alongside.

They were steering the ship from the auxiliary position in the searchlight platform abaft the funnels, with Acton himself on the remains of the upper bridge forward for a better view. His orders to helm and engine-room were being passed by telephone. It was not easy to see, and it was while he was going astern on the starboard engine that he misjudged the distance from the shore.

Quite suddenly there came a muffled, grinding scrunching from aft, followed by heavy vibration. The ship jarred and shook to the ominous sound of underwater scraping before the propeller was stopped, apparently from the engine-room. The revolving screw had touched an outlying fang of coral!

Cursing himself for over-confidence, Acton felt physically sick. Rudder and helm were still in working order, he discovered. That was a consolation; but heaven only knew what damage had been done to the propeller!

He sent down word 'Finished with engines' and was still securing the ship alongside when Draycott arrived on the bridge. Dawn was starting to break.

"You've come to tell me that the starboard whizzer's all chewed up to ribbons," Acton said disgustedly.

"I'm afraid so," Draycott returned. "But it might have happened to anyone going alongside a place like this."

"Huh! It was all my cack-handedness. I thought I knew how to handle her. I let the stern come too close in and tried to kick it out, too late, blast it! What's the damage?"

"I can't tell you exactly until we have a look over the side at daylight, if the water's clear enough. But the screw's had it. I shouldn't wonder if we haven't bent the shaft. It sounded rather like it."

"Any more leaks?"

"Shouldn't wonder," the engineer replied. "I'll know for certain presently. But another leak or two won't make much odds. This old ship's just about had it so far as going to sea's concerned."

Acton didn't answer. The thought that he'd helped to complete the damage to the *Eurydice* through what he considered was an unpardonable case of mishandling and bad seamanship was painful. He had been too sure of himself. What would Pomeroy have thought? What would the officers and men think?

"Cheer up!" Draycott consoled him. "She's a wreck, any-how. And it might have been much worse."

"Worse!" Acton muttered.

"We've still got the port propeller, which means we can move if we want to. And thank God the rudder wasn't bashed! If that had been knocked endways or carried away we'd have been in a proper ruddy mess."

"Mess enough already," Acton muttered. "I could kick myself for being such a B.F."

When daylight came and they were able to look over the side through the clear green water they could see the propeller, each of its three blades bent over and their scored, jagged edges shining like burnished gold. The propeller shaft, though they could detect no damage, was immovable.

So that was that. There was nothing they could do. They spent the rest of the day camouflaging the ship as before.

Though the *Eurydice* could not use her wireless for trans-mission, Scriven, the petty officer telegraphist, and Hargrave, his assistant, were still able to receive over long distances at night. And before Melton's departure in the *Fiona*, Scriven, as already mentioned, had given him full written details of his regular times of listening, wavelengths, the cipher for use, and so on and so forth.

It was during the small hours of the morning on the twenty-eighth day after the *Fiona* had sailed that Acton asleep in his bunk, was roused by loud knocking on his cabin door and someone calling his name. It was Scriven, wild-eyed with excitement.

"Sir! Sir!" he exclaimed, signal-pad in hand. "There's a cipher message come through addressed to us! It was repeated twice."

Acton was out of his bunk in a twinkling. "What's it say?" he demanded.

"I wouldn't know, sir. The ciphers are locked up in your steel chest. But it was addressed to us by our proper call sign!"

"All right, Scriven. Leave me the pad. I want the doctor and the sub-lieutenant at once. Tell them it's urgent. They needn't trouble to dress."

Scriven's agitation was infectious. Acton's hands were trembling as he found the key of the steel chest in his day cabin and opened it. It was almost unbelievable. A cipher signal addressed directly to the *Eurydice* after all these weeks and months could only mean one thing. At last the outside world realized that she still existed. Melton must have reached civilization! What now?

He was in a fret of impatience until McInnes and Farnworth arrived together. They were sleepy-eyed and tousle-headed. "What's this I hear about a cipher message?" the doctor demanded.

"It's true," Acton replied, handing over the signal-pad. "You two are the experts, or used to be, so get busy!"

"Lord! Does it mean the old Pilot's turned up somewhere?"

"It *can't* mean anything else, Pills. How else would anyone know this ship's still afloat?"

Farnworth, scrabbling in the steel chest, produced two quarto-sized brown books with weighted covers and put them on the table. They set to work.

It was by no means a simple business. The message had to be deciphered word by word, sometimes, when words were spelt, letter by letter. McInnes read out each group on the signal-pad and waited with pencil poised, while Farnworth flicked over the pages of his book and read out the meaning. Acton, fidgeting and bursting with impatience, lit a pipe and watched them. The pair seemed confoundedly slow and deliberate, as they had to be. Accuracy meant everything, and sometimes they were hung up.

"Check that last group again, Sub," McInnes sighed, frowning and running the point of his pencil through his sandy hair. "It doesn't make sense."

"Letter E," Farnworth repeated. "E for Edward."

"Certain?"

"Absolutely."

Acton, unable to bear it any longer, left the cabin and went on deck, where he sent a seaman off to tell Jevons that he wanted tea and biscuits for three in his cabin. Mr. Blatchington was keeping the middle watch. He had 'heard the buzz' from Scriven and knew that McInnes and Farnworth had been sent for in a hurry.

"Is it true that Mister Melton's fetched up?" he asked, avid for the latest news.

"It seems so, Guns. Why else should there be a cipher signal addressed to us?"

"Holy Maggie!" the Gunner exclaimed, delighted. "Any idea of what it says, sir? Does it mean we're going to be taken off this perishin' island?"

"I just don't know," Acton replied. "It'll take our decoders the rest of the night to sort it out. They can't rush it."

It took the best part of two hours before McInnes and Farnworth had finished, with Acton spending most of the time peering over the doctor's shoulder and all three of them becoming more and more excited as the message was slowly transcribed. It was startling enough. With a few unimportant omissions it read:

ADMIRALTY TO EURYDICE REPEATED AUSTRALIAN NAVAL BOARD, FLAG OFFICER COMMANDING ROYAL AUSTRALIAN NAVY ————. M-E-L-T-O-N ARRIVED MELBOURNE. FOLLOWING ARRANGEMENTS MADE BY AUSTRALIAN NAVAL BOARD. WEATHER AND OTHER CIRCUMSTANCES PERMITTING IT IS INTENDED THAT H.M.A.S. ANULA SHALL OPERATE JAVA SEA FIRST MOONLESS NIGHT WHICH IS TWENTY-SEVENTH. FAILING THAT DATE TWENTY-EIGHTH OR TWENTY-NINTH. ATTEMPT WILL BE MADE REACH YOU ONE THESE THREE NIGHTS. BE PREPARED TRANSFER ALL EURYDICE SURVIVORS UTMOST DISPATCH. EURYDICE TO BE SUNK REPEAT SUNK DEEP WATER. DESTROY CONFIDENTIAL BOOKS BUT TRANSFER CIPHERS SIGNAL BOOKS TO ANULA. ANULA DISGUISED FUBUKI CLASS DESTROYER MAY FLY JAPANESE REPEAT JAPANESE COLOURS. MAINTAIN WIRELESS WATCH USUAL TIMES. THIS SIGNAL WILL BE REPEATED FURTHER NIGHTS SAME TIME. ANULA WILL COMMUNICATE EXPECTED TIME OF ARRIVAL. MOST URGENT SHE IS NOT DELAYED. ENDS.

"God bless the Australians!" McInnes muttered, having read and re-read the signal in its entirety. "Lord! D'you think they'll pull it off?"

Acton shrugged his shoulders. "Your guess is as good as mine," he replied. "It's a hell of a long way and she's taking a big risk. Hence the Japanese colours and the Japanese disguise in case she's spotted from the air by daylight."

"What *is* the *Anula*?" the sub queried. "It's a new one on me."

"Obviously an Australian destroyer as she's being disguised as a 'Fubuki'," Acton told him. "I seem to remember reading somewhere that the Aussies were building 'Tribals', all same as our 'Cossack' and the rest of them. Eight four-sevens, thirty-six and a half knots."

"Gosh, what a frolic!" Farnworth exclaimed delightedly. "Coming in disguised and all. What a show, what ruddy nerve!" He was lost in admiration.

"D'you notice they say it's 'intended that *Anula* shall operate Java Sea first moonless night,' etcetera?" McInnes put in quietly. "From that wording it looks to me as though she's combining lifting us with something else."

"Yes. I'd noticed that," Acton said.

"What sort of operation can it be?" the doctor wanted to know. "Have you any ideas?"

Acton shook his head. "Several ideas," he replied. "But it's no good making wild guesses. What concerns us is that today's the nineteenth and she may arrive on the twenty-seventh. We've eight days."

Farnworth asked if the men were to be told.

Acton considered the point. Yes, he said. From what he'd heard on deck from the Gunner, the fact that a cipher signal had arrived out of the blue was pretty well known already, and would be all over the ship by morning. He'd talk to the ship's company, omitting all reference to Japanese colours and so forth, and merely telling them that an Australian destroyer *might* be arriving to rescue them on such and such a night. It was no good trying to conceal the main facts. That would only give rise to a crop of silly rumours. The men might even take it into their heads that the news received was *bad* news, which was the last thing he wanted.

The others agreed.

When Acton addressed the assembled ship's company later in the day the first part of his talk was received with wild acclamation. However, he took care to end on a note of caution.

"Hope and go on hoping," he said, after holding up his hand for silence. "But *don't* be too optimistic. If our rescue doesn't come off, if we're left here, we've just got to go on making the best of things as we have up to date. At any rate you'll know that the effort's been made and that we're not forgotten. As I told you, Mister Melton and the others must have reached Australia, and by this time all our names should be with the Admiralty. I hope that all our families at home will have been told we're still alive, somewhere."

There were more cheers before Acton could resume.

He had orders to sink the ship in deep water, he continued. When the time came for them to be transferred to the *Anula*, *if they were*, it would be a rush job, so all hands must make an evolution of it. There would be no time to move piles of gear or clothing, so that must be left behind. Each man could take one small suit-case or bundle with what he needed most, no more than he could conveniently carry. No hammocks. Nothing bulky. But nothing which might be of use if they had to remain on the island must be given to the natives until they had definite news that the *Anula* was coming. Then they could give away what private possessions they pleased, and the islanders certainly deserved their gratitude.

"That's all for now, men," he ended. "I'll let you know if I have further news. All right, Mister Farnworth. You can pipe down."

The ship's company dispersed, to stand around in knots discussing the situation. As could be seen from their varied expressions some were elated, some rather dubious, and a few, with girl friends in the island and no real ties at home, definitely glum.

Life on shore was effortless and easy. Why shouldn't they remain behind and go native? Where was the joy in returning to civilization, presently to be sent to other ships to be herded together on some overcrowded mess-deck, to live in stark discomfort in torrid heat or arctic cold and wetness, with broken nights and never a pretty girl to speak to for weeks and months on end? They were only temporary sailors enrolled for the duration. To hell with a bloody war which might continue for years! Let the old sweats get on with it.

Petty Officer Hartopp, busy as ever, shouldered his way through the groups. "Get a move on, lads," he said, grinning. "Break it up! You've got jobs to do. Don't stand around chewin' the fat all the forenoon! You've heard the news, so carry on."

"Silly old buzzard!" murmured one young A.B. "Who the blazin' hell wants to go home? The last I heard o' my gal

246

she was runnin' round with a Canadian corporal drawin' six times my pay!"

It was as well Hartopp didn't hear the remark.

The next few days passed with wearisome monotony. On two nights the cipher message was repeated; then silence except for the usual spoken news broadcasts, which were sometimes difficult to intercept. Suspense grew, anxiety mingling with expectation. Even Acton felt the strain, and became nervous and irritable.

The 25th came and went, then the 26th, with still no news of the *Anula*. The cipher signal had mentioned the night of the 27th as the first probable time of arrival, so uncertainty became intensified. Nothing came through.

It was at about 1 a.m. on the night of the 27th, or, more correctly, the early morning of the 28th, that Acton, hot, restless and unable to sleep in his stuffy cabin, again wandered forward to the wireless-room, where Scriven and Hargrave were both on watch.

"Nothing come through?" he inquired.

Scriven, with a pair of earphones clipped on over his head, looked up. "Nothing yet, sir," he said, with an air of resignation. "The atmospherics are something cruel. Reckon there's thunder-storms about."

"Are you sure you're on the right wavelength?"

"Yes, sir. Quite sure."

Scriven could understand Acton's fretful anxiety—he was anxious himself, knowing all the circumstances. But he wished fervently that the skipper would stop fussing and leave him and his mate to get on with the job. This was the fourth time during the night he had come forward asking questions which served no useful purpose. His visits were only disturbing, and Scriven, like other experts, disliked being overlooked.

Deliberately, he reached out a hand and twiddled a knob. The little room became filled with a harsh crackling. "Listen to that, sir."

Acton listened for a moment, and fled. The mysteries of this wizard's den were beyond him. Scriven winked his left eye at Hargrave, who smiled and nodded. He understood.

It was soon after 4 a.m., when Scriven had almost given up hope, that he heard a faint scratching in his receivers which sounded like the *Eurydice's* call sign. He made an adjustment, and it became clearer. Hargrave, leaning back in his chair with his head bowed, was dozing. Scriven leant over and pushed him by the shoulder.

"Get busy!" he said. "This is it! Stand by to check!"

The younger man snatched at a duplicate pair of earphones and slipped them over his head. Before long both men started to write.

It was a fairly short message, twice repeated and still in cipher. But it came from a different operator and a different source, as they could tell from the touch and the actual note.

Within twenty minutes the groups had been written down and checked. Scriven grunted with satisfaction. "Rush this down to Mister Acton!" he said triumphantly, handing over his own pad.

Once more McInnes and Farnworth were summoned to the captain's cabin; once again they sat at the table wrestling with the deciphering, with Acton looking on.

ANULA TO EURYDICE (the message began). REGRET . . . All three of them groaned in unison.

Dear God! Had something happened? Did the ominous word 'regret' mean that the *Anula* wasn't coming, that their hopes had been raised for nothing? Acton felt himself trembling.

But there was more to come.

. . . UNFORESEEN DELAY (the signal continued). MY *E.T.A. (and their hearts bounded) NOW *2200 TONIGHT TWENTY-EIGHTH. RAISE STEAM AWAIT ME ONE MILE SOUTH OF BAY. WEATHER PERMITTING INTEND COMING ALONGSIDE FOR TRANSFER. HAVE DEMOLITION CHARGES PREPARED. IF EURYDICE UNABLE PROCEED RENDEZVOUS ANULA WILL ENTER BAY. ENDS.

It was 5.30 a.m. "Gosh!" the sub exclaimed, glancing at the clock on the bulkhead. "Sixteen and a half hours!"

"Thank God for His mercies!" Acton breathed, joy singing in his heart. "So now we know!" He felt rather like crying, so great was his relief.

Even the unsentimental, hard-boiled McInnes was overcome with emotion. Staring at the paper in front of him he couldn't trust himself to speak.

* E.T.A. 2200. Expected time of arrival 10 p.m.

Now that the time had come, Acton had a feeling of something like guilt at leaving Beekman and the islanders to whatever might happen. Had it not been for their kindness and generous hospitality the *Eurydice's* people would have been in a bad way, and if the Japanese came to the island and discovered there had been collaboration they were perfectly capable of burning the village and slaughtering everyone they found. Human life meant nothing to them.

Since the islanders, or even a portion of them, could not be evacuated, Acton did not mention this grim thought to Beekman. Nor did he remind him that the enemy *must* be aware that a party of Japanese with their radio set had been parachuted into the island much earlier. Had these men been forgotten? Nothing could have been heard of them for some time. Wasn't it possible that they'd send a ship to the island to discover what had happened, or was the radio party callously regarded as expendable? There was also the matter of the disappearance of the landing-craft and the submarine. Acton was surprised that the island hadn't been visited weeks earlier.

Beekman, when Acton told him the news of the *Eurydice's* imminent departure, was regretful though unperturbed. The Japanese, he thought, had more than enough to think about in fighting the Americans than to find time to visit an insignificant island like theirs. And even if they did come what could they discover, what could they prove?

Acton, hoping he was right, left it at that.

They spent a busy day.

The three Bofors guns, still mounted ashore, with their ammunition, were transported back to the ship by parties of natives and dumped on deck. Some of the lighter contents of the *Eurydice's* storerooms, with tinned provisions, drums of oil, paint, clothing, movable fittings which might be useful in the village, and furniture, carpets, canvas, rope, were carried ashore and handed over into Beekman's keeping to be dealt with as he thought fit. Much else that the Dutchman would have liked to possess had to be left behind as too heavy or unwieldy to move. There was no time really to strip or gut the ship, though as the afternoon wore on the *Eurydice* was thrown open to acquisitive visitors.

Numbers of chattering natives, excited at the prospect of a 'free for all,' flocked on board and were given unwanted clothing and much else. Their women and children came with them. It was the opportunity of a lifetime. In the natives' own interests Acton had given strict orders that no articles of clothing easily recognizable as British naval uniform must be given away or bartered, and put a sentry on the gangway to enforce his edict. There was lamentation when brass buttons and badges were ruthlessly stripped from coats and jumpers. The islanders loved finery.

The upper deck, as Hartopp observed, looked like a glorified jumble sale. As time went on and there were shrill quarrels and even free fights as to what belonged to whom, Acton rather regretted giving the natives the run of the ship, though once started it was difficult to stop. It was an amazing sight to see small children, usually mother naked, proudly strutting around in white shorts or rolled-up, sailors' bell-bottomed trousers many sizes too large for them. Their elders staggered ashore with heavy bundles and came back for more. Cabin mirrors were in eager demand among the younger women, and there were tears when the supply ran out. Cooking utensils, table linen, the officers' sheets, blankets, knives, spoons, forks and crockery went the way of everything else.

Acton soon came to realize that if the enemy did land and took it into their heads to make a house-to-house visitation they would find much that was obviously British. Inevitably there would be awkward questions. He said as much to Beekman, who replied that he'd warn the inhabitants not to parade their finery and to hide their loot if the Japs ever did appear. He seemed quite happy about it.

Towards dusk, when Draycott came up from the engine-room to report 'ready to proceed,' the last natives had been hustled out of the ship. Littered with piles of this and that the cliff-edge alongside which the *Eurydice* lay was still swarming with people.

"It's damned lucky no Jap aircraft came snooping around," the engineer officer remarked. "The place must look like a crawling ant-heap from up topsides."

Acton could but agree, though the ship was still hidden under her camouflage netting and if an aircraft had been seen the natives would have dived into the nearest bush. "I'm wondering," he added, "what the Director of Stores and other Admiralty pundits would think of our free disposal of His

Majesty's property. I'd like to see their faces. Am I liable to court martial, d'you think?" he asked jokingly.

"I imagine so," Draycott laughed. "You've probably broken at least sixteen of the King's Regulations and Admiralty Instructions. But what's the sense of sinking the ship chock-a-block with stuff useful to the unenlightened heathen, poor devils? They've been darned good to us, and after all they are our allies. Oh well, this time tomorrow, George, and we may be on our way to Australia. Just think of that, old boy!"

"We'll be in a pretty sorry sort of mess if she doesn't come after all, Chief. We'll have to pinch a lot of the stuff back again."

"Don't fret, George. She'd have let us know if she weren't coming. Well, everything's all right below. Steam's ready when you want it; but don't forget we've only the port whizzer."

"I propose slipping at nine," Acton told him.

Mr. Blatchington arrived on deck. The demolition charges were ready, he reported—four of them, close to the outer skin and alongside the 'thwartship bulkheads and well below the water-line to ensure rapid flooding. They were fitted with five-minute fuses. To complete the destruction of the ship two depth charges in the chutes aft had been set to detonate at a hundred feet.

By the time darkness came the *Eurydice's* port anchor had been weighed and the camouflage netting unrigged and hauled ashore. They had a final picnic supper, after which the seamen brought their suit-cases and bundles on deck ready for transfer. Saying goodbye to Beekman and his wife and daughters, Acton again thanked them for all they had done. To Beekman he handed a gold half-hunter watch given him by an uncle as a twenty-first birthday present, with a pair of binoculars, the property of His Majesty's Government and clearly marked with the broad arrow. He could think of nothing suitable for Mrs. Beekman and the daughters. The Dutchman was profuse in his thanks. Indeed, in one way and another, he hadn't done so badly out of the *Eurydice*.

The night was dark and clear, with no breath of wind and hardly a ripple on the water. Many natives, some carrying torches, stood in silent, watching clusters on the cliff-edge as Acton climbed to the shattered upper bridge. Everything was ready for slipping.

"Let go for'ard!" he called through his megaphone. "Let go aft!"

A pause was followed by a splash; then Farnworth's voice from the forecastle. "All gone for'ard, sir!"

"All clear aft, sir," from Mr. Blatchington.

"Slow astern port," Acton ordered through the telephone to the searchlight platform. "Port fifteen," to the helmsman.

He felt the old familiar throb of the turbines. A stokehold fan buzzed and a whiff of hot oil-fuel drifted forward over the bridge as the *Eurydice* started to move, gradually gathering way.

"Half astern port! Helm amidships!"

Men on the upper deck shouted their last farewells to friends on shore, and their friends, women among them, called back in reply.

Then, spontaneously, the islanders raised their voices and burst into song. It was not the mournful lament they had sung when the *Fiona* sailed. It was something they had learnt by rote from their friend Donald McInnes, M.R.C.S., L.R.C.P., D.P.H., when, with his ukulele, he had conducted community singing in the village. It sounded strangely incongruous:

> "*Roll out de barrel,*
> *We haf a barrel ob fun.*
> *Roll out de barrel,*
> *We get de blues on de run.*
> *Sing BOOM-TARA-RA-RAREL,*
> *Ring out de song ob good cheer.*
> *Now de time to roll out de barrel,*
> *For de gang all heah.*"

Before the *Eurydice* was finally out of earshot the tune had changed to the chant with which the natives had received the ship on her arrival, the air to which one of the seamen had fitted the words:

> "*Nicky Taylor's long-haired daughter,*
> *I kissed her twice and didn't oughter.*
> *Nicky Taylor's lovely daughter,*
> *Once with her I'll never falter.*

252

Wah!—Wah!—Wah!
Wah!—Wah!—Wah!
Eng-leesh-maan!
Eng-leesh-maan!"

It was to the sound of the blending male and female voices gradually fading away into the distance, with the orange glare of the torches reflected across the calm water, that the *Eurydice* moved rapidly seaward, presently to circle round and steer for her rendezvous with the *Anula*. Then, but for the normal sounds of the ship moving through the water, there was silence. One by one the torches ashore flickered redly and died out.

Acton found it difficult to realize that unless something unforeseen occurred the *Eurydice's* island story was ended. He had become so accustomed to the life that it was hard to imagine anything else. He was happy to get away; glad also to know that the *Eurydice's* departure was regretted. But his most overwhelming feeling was one of sorrow and infinite sadness. In less than an hour his beloved *Eurydice* in which he had served for so long, the first ship he had ever commanded, would be lying fathoms deep, a battered wreck. To him she was much more than an inanimate creation of steel and complicated machinery. She was a living, sentient thing.

The *Eurydice* lay motionless, heaving easily to the slight swell. To the northward the dark shape of the island stood out like ebony against the deep blue of the sky. To the south, where all eyes were searching and straining for the first signs of the *Anula*, the horizon was blotted out in a low-lying layer of mist.

25

NINE-FORTY-FIVE came . . . nine-fifty, and still there was no sight of the *Anula*. It was not until three minutes to ten, by which time Acton's nerves were all on edge, that sweeping his glasses along the clearer horizon to the eastward he suddenly saw what looked like the pale phosphorescent glimmer of a heavy, V-shaped bow wave. Above it, a little later, he made out the slender silhouette of a ship, steaming bows on towards him. She looked like a destroyer. In case of something unexpected happening at the last moment, the *Eurydice's* two 4.7's and the pom-poms were manned and ready for action, and as the oncoming ship had appeared from an unexpected direction there was always the faint possibility that she might be Japanese. Acton was taking no unnecessary risks, and started to turn the ship to bring his guns to bear.

He needn't have worried. The *Eurydice* had already been sighted, for a moment later, when within a mile, the stranger started to flash with a shaded light.

"Answer," he said to the signalman beside him. "Make our number." In almost the same breath he passed the order to stop engines.

The signalman's hand-lamp clicked, and there came the winking reply.

It *was* the *Anula*, and in a few minutes she glided slowly alongside, went astern, and was secured with slip-ropes.

"*Eurydice*. Are you ready for abandoning ship?" someone hailed from her bridge.

"All ready, sir," Acton replied, realizing he was addressing the captain.

"Then get cracking, please, and be smart about it," came the voice of authority. "I've another job to do and am pressed for time."

"What about my scuttling charges, sir?"

"Never mind them. Our depth charges are ready. Now, get busy."

Acton ordered his two men off the bridge and hurried after them. There was no confusion. The procedure had been rehearsed, and the ship's company were already mustering in the waist and passing their belongings to the *Anula*, to be sorted out later. Then the men themselves started to scramble across, and finally the officers. Acton, having made certain of the steel box containing the confidential books and ciphers, was the last to go.

A new White Ensign had been hoisted at the *Eurydice's* peak, for whatever happened the ship must sink with her colours flying. The tattered, smoke-grimed ensign and pendant she had flown in action were safe in one of Acton's suit-cases. Alone on board before leaving he turned aft for a moment and saluted. Now that the time had come he felt strangely wrought-up and

254

emotional. "Goodbye, old ship," he murmured to himself, gulping. "You've done us well."

Turning, he climbed over the berthing rails and held on, balancing himself. The two ships were rolling and surging a little, and watching his chance he leapt. Willing hands helped him on board.

"All clear, sir!" someone shouted. "Everyone on board!"

"Let go forward! Let go aft!" from the bridge.

There was a short pause before he felt the throbbing vibration of the turbines, as the *Anula* went astern. It was dark and the upper deck was crowded with men. Someone came forward and wrung him by the hand.

"George, old boy!" said a familiar voice. "It's damn good to see you again!" It was Melton.

"Pilot!" Acton exclaimed in surprise. "What the blazes are you doing here?"

"They asked me to come along as I knew the local set-up in case things went wrong."

"Good for them! How about your trip in the *Fiona*?"

"Quite a frolic to look back on," Melton told him, "but pretty gummy in spots while it lasted. I can't tell you all the details now; but we got through the straits all right, captured a Jap patrol boat the other end and made some prisoners."

"Lord! What happened to her?"

"We towed her out and let her drift ashore on the rocks after putting in a few rounds. There was heavy surf, so that was that. Well, we went on and had a hellish gale of wind. Then, when we were running short of water, a pint a man a day—believe it or not—by the grace of God we ran into a convoy and were picked up by a cruiser, the *Lincoln*."

"A convoy! What luck!"

"I should say it was," Melton returned. "If we hadn't, I doubt if we'd have made it. You'd have been left stranded here, and we might have drifted about the ocean gradually dying of thirst. There wasn't much hope of rain. But it's too long a yarn for now, George. I'll tell you later. Here we are, anyhow."

"Thank God for that!" said Acton from the bottom of his heart. "How about all our letters?" he went on to inquire. "And have all our names gone home to the Admiralty?"

"Everything's taped," Melton reassured him. "All the

255

names, ours and yours, have been sent home by wireless, and the letters and other stuff in sealed bags, probably by air. Letters, I believe, 'll have to be censored in London, and I gather that all news of us'll probably be held up until the whole crowd are reported safe. It's what they call a security measure."

"Hell!" Acton muttered disgustedly. "It'll take weeks!"

Fiona and his parents were on his mind, as all the other survivors must be thinking of their wives and families in England.

The *Anula* was still going astern, with the *Eurydice* out of sight from where they stood on deck. Then they felt the turbines stop and the whole ship check and quiver as they went 'full ahead'. . . . She gathered headway, moving faster and faster.

The dark hull of the *Eurydice* came into sight again fine on the starboard bow. The *Anula* swerved in towards her, and Acton gasped as for a sickening moment it seemed as though they must inevitably crash into the *Eurydice's* stern.

"God!" he muttered, gazing forward over the ship's side.

Melton sensed his anxiety. "Don't worry," he said. "The skipper's a wizard at handling the ship."

"Who is he?"

"One Greenacre, a commander. Just watch."

It was well worth watching, a breath-taking performance. Travelling at high speed parallel to the motionless *Eurydice*, Greenacre took his ship so close that it seemed as though one might almost have leapt on board, while the wash, surging back from the *Eurydice's* side, splashed over the *Anula's* upper deck. As she drove past four depth charges rolled off their chutes in the stern. Once clear she stopped and went astern to check her way.

There came the muffled, clanging thump of four successive underwater detonations which shook the ship and sounded as though some colossus had struck the hull with a gigantic sledge-hammer. It was not easy to see in the darkness; but Acton and Melton, standing together, had a glimpse of the dome-shaped hummocks of whitened water bursting upwards into spray close alongside the dark shape of the *Eurydice*.

It was a minute, perhaps two minutes, before the end came. The stricken ship rolled bodily over to port, the stern dipped under and the bows began to lift. There were further lighter explosions, and the wreck became enveloped in a cloud of steam and smoke as the water reached the boilers. The vapour dissolved, and with the rumbling crash of heavy weights breaking free from their fastenings the bows rose almost vertically skywards like the point of a broad-bladed spear. Almost at once there were two more heavy detonations as the *Eurydice's* depth charges went up. The bows hung for a moment, and then swiftly disappeared with the rushing, whistling sound of escaping air.

All the survivors were still on deck, watching the end and talking in low voices. There was dead silence, followed by a sort of gasping sigh from them all as the *Eurydice* made her final plunge. What the men thought Acton could only imagine. He only knew he felt unutterably depressed.

It was Mr. Blatchington who came to the rescue.

"Well," he said. "She was a damn good ship, God bless her! What say, lads, do we give her a cheer?"

And they did give three roaring cheers, with three more for 'the Aussies' as the *Anula* gathered way and sped on into the night.

Ten minutes later Acton had been introduced to Commander Greenacre in the charthouse. The Australian was a burly, deep-chested giant of a man with a face tanned to the colour of mahogany, twinkling bright blue eyes, fiery red hair and pointed beard and, Acton judged, a sense of humour. They exchanged the usual civilities, Greenacre half-apologizing for having to sink a good ship, the Englishman trying to express his gratitude.

"Cut it out!" Greenacre broke in. "You're welcome. Now about your chaps. It'll be a tight fit, and they'll have to doss down where they can. As for the officers, we've spare bunks in double cabins for your Sub and Gunner, and the rest of you can use the wardroom and my cabin aft, you in my bunk and the others on camp beds. My Number One's got it taped."

Acton thanked him.

There wouldn't be sleep for anyone that night, the commander continued. He expected and hoped to be in action in about two hours.

Acton stared at him in amazement. "What, sir?"

Greenacre laughed. He was hoping to have a crack at a Japanese convoy coming east from Batavia, he went on to explain. It consisted of about two tankers and two transports or supply ships lightly escorted. According to his latest infor-

mation they ought to be met at one o'clock, he said, pointing
to a spot on the chart. The *Anula* was now steaming thirty
knots; but if and when radar contact was made he would ease
her down to avoid being spotted by the heavy wash.

Acton marvelled. "But . . . but how did you get news of
this convoy?" he asked.

Greenacre grinned, tapped the side of his nose and looked
mysterious. That would be telling, he said; but the Intelligence
people were pretty spry. They had ways and means of discovering enemy fleet or convoy movements in advance, and
the *Anula* was in constant wireless touch with Australia. He
hadn't been 'mucking around' under the Japanese ensign for
close on two days on mere guesswork, no, sir!

"Did you sight anything?"

"Plenty of native craft; but as for Nips, not a sausage, not
even an aircraft. Let's hope it's money for jam tonight. It's
time my chaps were blooded."

Acton asked if the *Eurydice's* people could lend a hand.

Greenacre smiled and shook his head. He thought not at
such short notice. But if Acton himself would like to see the
fun, he might find a free corner somewhere on the bridge.
"Find your way for'ard when you hear the alarm rattlers," he
said. "Meanwhile there's my cabin aft. Ask for anything you
want."

Acton was dozing in an arm-chair when he heard the deep-
toned 'burr . . . burr . . . burr . . .' of the alarm, followed by
heavy trampling overhead. The time, he noticed, was twenty-
three minutes to one, and the ship seemed to be steaming fifteen
knots, certainly no more. Wearing his kapok life-jacket and
slung binoculars he went on deck and groped his way forward.
The night was starlit and not very dark, though after the
lighted cabin it was difficult to see until his eyes adapted
themselves. Finding an unoccupied corner, he watched and
waited. Greenacre, duffle-coated and capless, stood on the
compass platform conning the ship.

"What's going on?" Acton asked a rating huddled over
some instrument.

"Picked up the bastards five minutes ago," the man grunted,
intent upon his own particular job. "Five big 'uns and some
tiddlers."

The convoy was being plotted by radar, that newly-perfected

device of which Acton had heard; but had never seen in use. It had only been fitted in the newer ships.

"Two-five-seven. Eighteen thousand five hundred," he heard someone repeat. There came a pause, and then again: "Two-five-seven. Eighteen thousand two hundred," followed a little later by: "Two-five-five. Eighteen thousand."

The first figures mentioned represented the gyro-compass bearing, Acton realized; the second, the range. Eighteen thousand yards meant nine miles.

An officer, evidently the navigator, was leaning over his dimly-lit chart table on the fore-side of the bridge. "We're closing at the rate of about a thousand yards a minute," Acton heard him say to the captain. "That gives 'em about fifteen knots, sir."

"Okay," Greenacre replied. "I shan't go in until they're closer."

The horizon ahead was clear, and excitement became tense as the distance dropped to sixteen thousand . . . fourteen thousand . . . thirteen . . . twelve thousand five hundred. . . .

Greenacre asked a question down a voice-pipe, and said something to the effect that the blighters seemed to be zig-zagging. He passed an order to the coxswain in the wheelhouse below, and told someone to pass the word for the torpedo-tubes to be trained to port. A man spoke into a telephone, and the message went through.

"Two-five-oh. Twelve thousand," came the calm, impersonal voice of the man repeating the radar readings. "Two-four-eight. Eleven thousand eight hundred . . . Two-four-eight. Eleven thousand six hundred. . . ."

Whoever was speaking might have been a robot. His voice sounded utterly unemotional. Acton, listening and realizing what was happening, was fidgeting with impatience. To get a better view he oozed himself out of his corner and scrambled on to the raised platform abaft the bridge.

He had hardly arrived there when there came a sudden hail —"Ships right ahead, sir!"

Using his glasses he could see them for himself as a cluster of black shapes silhouetted against the clear sky on the horizon. Thereafter time was of no consequence. Event followed event with such startling rapidity that he was left with nothing more than a series of vivid impressions.

To get a clear picture, Greenacre waited until the convoy was within three miles and then passed an order to the wheelhouse. Acton heard the clang and rattle of the engine-room telegraphs, and the *Anula* increased speed. She seemed to bound ahead.

Orders followed in quick succession.

"All guns, load! Train on red-one-oh!"*

From the pair of 4.7's just before the bridge came the sound of men's voices, followed by the thud of projectiles being rammed home and the slam of breech-blocks.

"All guns, ready!" There was a short pause, and then a new voice saying: "Director layer sees the target."

"All guns, follow director!"

There came a sudden diversion. Practically simultaneously with a radar report of a small echo to the left of the main convoy, a man yelled: "Destroyer, bearing red-two-five, sir!"

Acton first saw her as a slim black shape well ahead of the larger ships and distant perhaps two thousand yards. She was steaming on an opposite course to the *Anula* and travelling, from the size of her bow wave, at about fifteen knots. The director was put on to this nearest target. Greenacre gave a helm order, swung his ship slightly towards the enemy and then steadied. At that very moment the Jap woke up and started to flash with a shaded light. With the *Anula* steaming about thirty-three knots the two ships were closing fast.

"Let her have it!" Greenacre shouted.

The director layer was ready and waiting, his finger itching. Acton heard the 'ting-ting' of the firing gongs, and the two foremost pairs of 4.7's crashed into flame.

Where the first salvo fell Acton didn't see. He was shaken by the blast, half-blinded by the flashes and a cloud of acrid cordite smoke driving over the bridge. Then the guns fired again, and a pom-pom or a Bofors joined in. Through the smoke he glimpsed streams of coloured tracer hurtling off into the night.

Whether or not the enemy opened fire nobody could say. The first real view Acton had of her was between the clouds of

* 'Red-one-oh,' i.e. ten degrees on the port bow, reckoning from right ahead. Similar bearings on the starboard side would be prefixed by the word 'Green.'

smoke when the *Anula* swept past at little more than three hundred yards, with every gun in action.

She was a small destroyer or torpedo-boat, already badly hit, blazing fiercely, with her mast and foremost funnel shot away. He could see the men clustered on her deck, and some throwing themselves overboard. At so close a range the guns could hardly miss. Shell after shell drove home into the already battered wreck, to burst in gouts of orange flame and showers of debris. Through gaping holes in her side he saw the red-hot glow of fire. She was down by the bows with the water lapping over her forecastle, heeling over to port and still moving slowly ahead. In the ruby light of the flames he could see floating wreckage and the dark heads of swimmers. Her port propeller, half out of water and still revolving, was inexorably churning its way through a mass of men struggling in the sea. It was a sickening, ghastly sight.

The *Anula* ceased firing and sped on for the larger ships ahead. Before she had gone five hundred yards there came a shattering explosion, and the blazing wreck disintegrated skywards in a great gout of flame and smoke. Her magazine had blown up.

"Mere chickenfeed, she was," a seaman near Acton remarked to a friend. "Can't help feeling sorry for the poor muggers."

"It might 'a been us, chum," the other returned. "An' them Nips isn't hardly human. Fires on chaps in the water, I've heard tell. Fair bastards they are, what with killin' their prisoners an' all. What about them bayonetin' our blokes in New Guinea, the dirty——. Coo!" he broke off. "Look at that!"

A star-shell had burst overhead and was followed by others, to flood the sea in an unearthly bluish-white brilliance as the flares floated downwards. They can have been of no assistance to the enemy, and helped the *Anula*. The large ships of the convoy, steaming in two columns about half a mile apart, were shown up in dark relief against a bright background as if in a chiaroscuro painting. There was no mistaking the leader of the nearest column, an obvious passenger liner with a built-up superstructure, two masts and single squat funnel, probably serving as a transport.

The *Anula* fired a torpedo, which hit and detonated in a great geyser of smoke and water. Almost simultaneously, driving past at more than thirty knots, she plastered the ship with every gun that would bear. The range was no more than six hundred yards, and again Acton saw the bright glow of exploding shell. This time, however, the ship returned the fire. He noticed the flashes, and heard the unmistakable 'wheew . . . wheew . . . wheew' of projectiles passing overhead. One fell short, to raise its usual fountain of spray as it burst. He heard the angry drone of flying splinters; but the *Anula* was not hit.

It was breathlessly exciting to watch. Speeding on, she fired a second torpedo at the ship astern of the leader, another passenger vessel. It apparently missed, though as the destroyer drove past she again opened up with her guns. The enemy, forewarned, retaliated with some vigour with what looked like a couple of 4-inch and some heavy machine-guns. Where most of the heavier shell went no one saw; but anxiety clutched at Acton's heart as he heard a crash from somewhere aft and felt the ship shudder. The enemy machine-guns were more accurate. In the midst of the smoke Acton saw the converging lines of green and yellow tracer shooting towards him. There came a clanging and a series of little popping explosions from somewhere on the upper deck. The *Anula* had been hit again; but still steamed on at full speed.

In another second or two all firing ceased. Greenacre must have ordered a smoke-screen, for a dense black pall was rolling from the *Anula's* funnels as she altered course under the enemy's stern with the obvious intention of attacking the other three ships to the southward. The star-shell had ceased; but the vessels, low-lying with their funnels right aft, were clearly recognizable as tankers. They seemed to have turned away.

Zigzagging, Greenacre took his ship on a wide sweep to the westward before going in to attack. There was a short breathing space. A telephone burred. A man took the message and repeated it to the captain.

"A dud shell's wrecked the wardroom galley," Acton heard Greenacre announce to his gunnery officer. "No casualties from that; but four wounded by those cursed machine-guns."

"Thank God it's no worse. Who were the wounded, sir?"

"They didn't say," came the hurried answer. "They'll be looked after. Stop making smoke," he went on to order. "Keep the tubes trained to port! . . . Guns, stand by for another

262

crack!" He gave a helm order, and the *Anula* swerved to port, steadied, and rushed on.

"Gunfire, red-two-five!" someone shouted.

Acton saw the flashes; but who was firing, and at what, nobody could know. No shell came anywhere near the *Anula*.

"Holy cats!" said a seaman. "The goddam bastards are firing at each other!" He was probably right. The convoy seemed to be in a state of confusion.

And away to the left of the gun flashes could be seen the hull of a large ship beneath an ascending column of dark smoke, its underside tinged with flickering gleams of scarlet and orange. It was the first passenger ship attacked. She was on fire!

From now on it was a destroyer's paradise, and the *Anula* had it all her own way. Steaming all out, she swung to starboard and engaged the nearest tanker at a thousand yards, pumping in shell from every available gun and firing a third torpedo as she drew ahead. In the welter of smoke and splashes nobody saw any results, except that the immediate target seemed to have stopped and to be vomiting clouds of steam.

"Port fifteen!" Greenacre roared down the voice-pipe to the wheelhouse, making himself heard above the roar of gunfire. The *Anula* heeled over as she turned. "'Midships! . . . Meet her starboard! . . . Steady! . . . Guns!"

"Sir?"

"Do your stuff on the next ship!" the captain shouted, pointing. She was another tanker, at a distance of perhaps eight hundred yards.

There was no need to engage her. Greenacre had hardly spoken before they saw the tall white column of an explosion close alongside the long, black hull. By some freakish stroke of luck the torpedo, missing its proper target, had hit the ship beyond. The result was immediate and spectacular. With a thundering concussion the ship burst upwards in a huge gush of golden flame. It rose and spread, to come curving downwards like a fiery waterfall.

"My God!" Greenacre exclaimed. "Starboard twenty! That's petrol or I'm a Dutchman!"

The *Anula* sheered off out of harm's way and left the blazing wreck behind.

She turned, and had already fired three salvoes at the last remaining ship when there came a sudden diversion. The pom-pom had come into action, when between the bursts of gunfire Acton heard a man shouting something to the effect that there was a small ship on the starboard bow, distance about three thousand yards and closing fast. For the moment nothing could be seen against the dark horizon to the south-eastward. The new-comer must have been picked up by radar.

Acton sensed Greenacre's dilemma. The ship was probably a destroyer, one of the escorts, and there were probably others in the vicinity. The last thing the captain must want was a destroyer mêlée at night with the possible chance of being torpedoed. He was too far from home to risk heavy damage. Moreover, there was the time factor, and time was drawing on. Dawn would be breaking in about four hours, and unless the *Anula* was well clear by daylight she ran the grave chance of attracting a swarm of enemy aircraft. In all probability the attack on the convoy had already been reported by wireless, and the Japanese would send out everything they had.

The Australian destroyer, or her gun flashes, must already have been sighted by the oncoming ship. Also she must be silhouetted against the glare of two burning ships astern.

Acton found himself wondering what was the right thing to do. Should Greenacre go in and attack this new enemy, or, having already played havoc with the convoy, should he leave well alone, lay a smoke-screen, turn to the northward and make off? With his thirty-six knots he could easily outrun any destroyer the Japanese were likely to use for the mundane job of convoy work. Whatever the decision it must be taken at once. There was little time for thought. The combined speed of approach must be a mile a minute.

The enemy was in sight now through glasses—a slender, rushing black shape over the white plumes of her heavy bow wave. The gunnery officer, on his own initiative, had already switched the director and the guns on to the new target, and was breathlessly asking if he should open fire.

"No," said Greenacre, his binoculars to his eyes. "Wait! Wait!" He shouted a helm order, and the ship swerved slightly to port, and steadied. All the guns must now be bearing. The range, repeated from the radar, was eighteen hundred yards, and still closing.

"Right, Guns! Carry on!"

Acton saw the bright red flash of a gun from the enemy, then another. He heard the screech of a shell, though where it dropped he didn't see.

Then the *Anula* opened fire—eight 4.7's firing by director, their sweating crews slamming home projectiles and cartridges as fast as they could load. The ship shuddered and seemed to jerk bodily over as each salvo roared out. The noise was deafening.

Acton had a brief glimpse of a forest of splashes leaping one after the other out of the water in the direction of the enemy. Whether there were any hits he couldn't see. There were no signs of any shell bursting.

"Target out of sight!" called the director layer.

"Check! Check! Check!" the gunnery officer shouted.

Firing ceased. The enemy was invisible. In her stead a lengthening layer of rolling black smoke was trailing over the calm water.

"She's thought better of it," Greenacre grunted. "Sugared off under a smoke-screen. Well done, boys! Good work!"

The gunnery lieutenant seemed disappointed. "Aren't you going after her, sir?"

"Heck!" the captain returned. "Don't be so bloody-minded, Guns."

"But, sir, if . . ."

"No, Guns. We'll leave what remains to pick up the bits. It's high time we sugared off ourselves if we're not to be caught with our pants off at daylight. I don't want their goddam aircraft buzzing round like a swarm of hornets! I had enough dive-bombing in the Med. to last me a lifetime, and the sooner we leg it the better. I'm for home, and it's a hell of a long way."

The navigator chipped in with a remark to the effect that they'd singed Hirohito's whiskers, if he wore them, *and* put the fear of God into the convoy.

"You've said it, lad," Greenacre replied. "Now get busy and work out the course for the straits. When you've done that I want to know the distances to King Sound and to Fremantle." He went on to tell someone to telephone down that he wished to see the engineer officer with a tally of what oil-fuel he had remaining.

The first lieutenant, who had been at his station aft, arrived on the bridge. He'd given orders for the ammunition in the ready racks to be replenished, he reported. When that was done, should the ship's company remain at their action stations or could they go into normal night cruising routine?

Greenacre considered the question. "Keep the crews at their guns for the time being," he said. "They can doss down in the gun positions if they want to, provided one chap's awake at the telephone. You can fall out the others. I want everything manned at crack o' dawn in case of aircraft." He went on to inquire about the wounded.

The first lieutenant hadn't heard the latest news of them; but one man, Able Seaman Billings, had a broken arm which might have to be amputated. The others weren't so serious. The doctors, for they had two now with the Scots bloke from the *Eurydice*, were looking after them. The funnels and upper-deck fittings must be a bit peppered with small stuff, and the wardroom galley was a pretty fair shambles. It was lucky the shell was a dud. As it was the petty officer cook was all but in tears. His cooking-range had been knocked for six and his pots and pans sent flying.

"We'll manage," the commander said. "Okay, Number One. Good work all round. You might tell the ship's company from me they've done a damn good job and I'm proud of 'em. I'll tell 'em so myself when I get a chance."

They had indeed done a good job, thought Acton, as the *Anula* steamed off to the eastward at high speed. Away over the horizon astern the sky was aglow with crimson. Two, no, three ships seemed to be on fire. One of them, belching long tongues of red and yellow flame, looked like a ragged, wind-blown tulip.

Now that the excitement was over Acton felt desperately tired. It was time to go below, so he descended to the bridge proper.

"Thank you sir, for one of the most thrilling hours I've ever spent," he said to Greenacre. "And may I congratulate you."

"Nasty business," the Australian returned. "It was rather like murder, particularly when the destroyer and tanker went up. Can't say I like killing people when it comes to the point. All the same, we can call it revenge for what they did to us in the Java Sea battle, which you know more about than I do."

"What's the tally of their losses?" Acton inquired.

"God knows! I haven't had time to sort 'em out, and even then they'll be only approximate."

No one, Australian or British, that is, was to know the full extent of the enemy losses until months later.

But the Japanese knew.

Within eight hours, as the reports came through piecemeal by wireless from the two destroyer escorts that remained, Rear-Admiral Isoroku Yamaguchi, at his headquarters at Surabaya, was in a state of insensate fury. The reports mentioned an 'enemy cruiser'; but what cruiser? Where had she come from, where was she now? In any case he had nothing to send after her. He had no cruiser, nothing but a few lumbering flying-boats. The attack on this important convoy and the growing list of losses was his crowning misfortune. His unfortunate Chief of Staff and some others suffered the full weight of his fury; but he felt himself disgraced and dishonoured for ever. He even contemplated committing hara-kiri in the good old-fashioned method of the Samurai.

Commander Yaichi Tanaka, the irascible, at Batavia, and poor little Lieutenant Kondo, his assistant, though by no means responsible, had also to bear some of the brunt for what had happened.

Telephones rang and the wireless crackled without ceasing. Before many hours had passed both the Commander-in-Chief and the Admiralty in Tokyo were asking awkward questions. How and why had this disaster been allowed to happen? Whose responsibility? What was the name of the senior officer of the escorting destroyers?

The *Anula's* foray had resulted in a ghastly holocaust— valuable ships burnt or blown up and others damaged; many soldiers killed and a greater number drowned; important military stores, ammunition, guns, vehicles, oil and precious petrol and aviation spirit gone for ever.

26

AFTER WEEKS of nervous strain and responsibility Acton was wearier than he realized. It was a blessed relief to know that someone else was now carrying the burden, and he, a passenger, could try to relax while Greenacre did the job and made the decisions.

In spite of the tense excitement of the engagement and the unforgettable sight of those stricken, blazing ships, in spite of the rushing sound of the sea along the thin skin plating within a few feet of his bunk and the muffled churning of the propellers as the *Anula* rushed on through the night, Acton was asleep almost as soon as his head touched the pillow. He had intended to go on deck at dawn when the ship's company went to action stations; but did not wake. McInnes had mixed him a stiff whisky and soda before turning in. He wasn't to know that the thoughtful Pills, recognizing the symptoms of mental and physical exhaustion, had adroitly doctored the drink with a couple of little white tablets.

It was late in the morning when he suddenly came back to consciousness. Someone had shaken him. He sat up, rubbing his eyes and still rather muzzy-headed. It was Jevons, with his morning tea on a tray.

"Oh, it's you!" he said, blinking. The cabin was stuffy. There was a vile taste in his mouth.

"Your tea, Mister Acton," the steward said, balancing himself as he poured.

"What's the time?"

"Well past ten o'clock, sir."

"Ten! Great heavens! What's been happening?"

"Nothing, sir. Nothing since the shemozzle last night," Jevons replied, handing the cup. "Guy Fawkes day wasn't in it. I never thought I'd see a show like that. I'll open your deadlights, sir. It's a fine day with hardly a cloud in the sky and the land nearly out of sight. We're getting along fine."

Acton, sipping, did not reply. The ship was still travelling at high speed; but the motion had changed to a gentle rise and fall combined with an occasional deep roll. Standing on a chair Jevons leant over the bunk, drew the curtains, unscrewed the deadlights over the three side scuttles and hooked them up. Brilliant sunlight came flooding in, to be obliterated now and then by the bright emerald green of bubbling water as the *Anula* rolled to port.

"There's a buzz going around we'll be ashore in about three days' time, sir," Jevons volunteered, stepping off the chair. "Shall we be able to send cables to our wives?"

Acton handed him the empty cup. "I see no reason why not," he said, going on to explain that the names of all the

Eurydice's survivors had probably reached the Admiralty already and that the list only needed final confirmation before the next of kin were informed.

Jevons grinned. "I reckon my old woman'll pass out with excitement at me coming back from the dead," he observed. "It'll give her a shock, it will. Well, sir, your clothes are laid out and the bath ready. I'll be along with your breakfast in twenty minutes' time."

"How are our chaps being looked after?" Acton wanted to know.

"Fine, sir. A la Ritz Hotel. Couldn't be bettered. Eggs and bacon, coffee and marmalade for breakfast, believe it or not. These Aussies know how to look after themselves, and us, I give you my word! Free run of the canteen and all else we like to ask for, and all on the house!" Jevons was enthusiastic. "Their tails are all up and wagging after that show last night, and good luck to 'em, says I."

Half an hour later, when Acton went on deck, the pale blue peak of a distant mountain was faintly visible over the horizon to the northward.

"The last time I saw that was from the *Fiona*," said Melton, pointing. "Gosh! Little did I think how it was all going to end."

"But it hasn't ended yet," Acton objected. "Don't tempt providence."

"Oh heck, George! For heaven's sake don't be such a damn old pessimist!" his friend laughed.

Three mornings later, soon after daylight, the *Anula* steamed in through the narrow gap between two long breakwaters and after taking a local pilot moved on up the river into a basin lined with shipping, where she secured alongside a jetty to fill up with oil-fuel. Acton, with all the other officers of the *Eurydice* and most of the men were on deck watching the arrival. It felt strange to be back in civilization, to see ships and storehouses, cranes and locomotives with long strings of railway trucks, and the buildings on both sides of the river.

The *Anula's* arrival did not arouse any unusual interest. There was no wild enthusiasm, no cheering crowd; but they all knew the reason for that—secrecy.

The previous afternoon Greenacre had addressed his ship's company and all the *Eurydice's* survivors. He knew, he said, they were all very pleased with themselves, as they deserved to be. He congratulated them, and was proud of them. But there was one snag. The news of what had happened mustn't be allowed to leak out. That was urgent, most urgent. They mustn't talk when they got ashore. They must say nothing in their letters, which in any case would be censored. Any mention of what had taken place might prejudice the success of some similar operation in the future. He relied on them, and put them on their honour to say nothing, to write nothing which might be harmful. He knew it was irksome; but there it was. The lives of others might depend upon their strict silence. There was no doubt that when they thought fit the authorities would allow the news of what the *Anula* had done to be made public. That was all.

That evening, after signalling his expected time of arrival and requirements in the way of fuel and fresh provisions, Greenacre had briefly reported having 'smashed up' a large Japanese convoy, and that he had on board sixty-five survivors from the *Eurydice* as per schedule.

A reply had come at about 3 a.m.:

FROM FLAG OFFICER IN CHARGE. YOUR 1943 RECEIVED AND PASSED TO ALL CONCERNED. WELL DONE 'ANULA.' HEARTIEST CONGRATULATIONS. PILOT MEETS YOU ON ARRIVAL. ARRANGEMENTS BEING MADE DISPOSAL OF PASSENGERS. MOST URGENT YOUR ACTION AND RESCUE KEPT SECRET UNTIL RELEASED HIGHER AUTHORITY. ENDS.

As the ship secured alongside, a large black car with a small Rear-Admiral's flag flapping on the bonnet drew up at the shore end of the jetty. Three figures descended, all in naval uniform, the first a short, tubby little man with gold shoulder-straps on his 'British warm' and a double row of gold oak leaves on his cap-peak. It was a cold, overcast morning.

Greenacre had just rung down 'finished with engines' when he saw the visitors. He levelled his glasses. "Holy snakes!" he exclaimed. "It's old Porky Bennett himself, come to welcome us! Suffering Moses!"

He hurriedly left the bridge and went aft, where some seamen were man-handling a wooden brow, or gangway, from the jetty.

"Get a move on, men!" he ordered. "The Admiral's arriving

.and may come on board! We'll have to pipe him over the side! Has anyone got a pipe?" Someone bustled off to find his bos'n's whistle.

Greenacre himself wore a duffle coat, an orange and black woollen scarf, his oldest cap and leather sea-boots, his usual seagoing rig on chillier mornings at sea. The sailors, too, were variously attired, some of them colourful in woollen caps and brightly coloured football jerseys.

'Porky' Bennett, and the nickname suited his appearance, was something of a disciplinarian with a tongue like a whip-lash. He was also a stickler for etiquette and strict uniform, and though it was barely seven o'clock in the morning Green-acre expected a rocket for setting a bad example and allowing his men to be dressed like a gang of pirates. However, it was too late to do anything now.

The seamen placing the brow sucked their teeth and hurried on with their job, wondering why there should be all this fuss and pother because a podgy little man in gold lace had been seen advancing along the jetty with two other brass-bounders astern of him.

"'Strewth!" a man muttered blasphemously. "Is 'e the Lord Gawd Ormighty with two of 'is angels in attendance?"

What followed was as good as a play. Greenacre was half-way ashore intending to meet his superior on the jetty when the Admiral waved him back. "I'm coming on board," the great one said. Greenacre saluted, turned about, caught his foot on a loose tread, stumbled, and all but plunged into the water between the ship and the jetty. Recovering himself and feeling a fool, he returned to the ship and took his place at the top of the gangway. Porky advanced. His rubicund face was wreathed in smiles. It was definitely not one of his bad mornings, thank heaven! Greenacre felt greatly relieved. After many days at sea the ship was dirty and untidy. And the men, oh Lord, the men!

A petty officer and a leading seaman had found their bos'n's pipes. Distending their cheeks they blew and tootled shrilly as the Admiral came over the brow and stepped on board. Everyone sprang to attention and saluted. Porky returned the salute and shook hands with Greenacre.

"Been celebrating, young feller?" the visitor asked, grinning.

"Not yet, sir. I slipped."

"So I observed. It's a long time since I met you, Greenacre," the Admiral said, eyeing him. "It must have been in 'thirty-five, when you were still a two-striper."

"It was 'thirty-six, sir, to be exact, when you were captain of the——"

"No matter," Porky interrupted. "This is just an informal visit, purely informal, so no more ceremony, please. I came to congratulate you. Fine work, my boy! Fine work!" He patted Greenacre on the shoulder in fatherly fashion.

"Thank you, sir."

"Yes, an informal visit, and I've brought my Chief of Staff and Operations Officer," he added, introducing the pair behind him. "We want more details of what happened. I'm being pestered from Sydney for full information of ships sunk or damaged. I gather you gave 'em hell, eh?"

"We did our best, sir."

After sending for the navigator with chart and notebook Greenacre ushered the visitors below to his cabin. Those on deck relaxed and went about their business; Acton, Melton, Draycott, McInnes, Farnworth and Mr. Blatchington to the wardroom for tea and biscuits.

Some forty minutes later, as he was eating an early breakfast, Acton was sent for. The Admiral wished to see him. Greenacre and his guests were sitting over the inevitable eggs and bacon in the captain's cabin.

"This is Acton, sir," Greenacre said. "Have you eaten, Acton, or shall I order?"

"Thank you, sir. I already have."

"Sit down, lad. Sit down," the Admiral said affably, his shrewd little brown eyes on the visitor's. "I've heard something of your story and know all about young er . . . you know, the lad who got away in that schooner and was picked up by the *Lincoln*."

"You mean Melton, sir."

"Yes, yes. Melton, of course. Melton. Now I'd like to hear something of your yarn, straight from the horse's mouth, what? Just tell me what happened in your own words."

Acton mentioned his report, the earlier part of which had already gone off in the *Fiona* with Melton, though of course he had a duplicate. The later part was typed out and ready, and the Admiral could see the whole document if he wished to.

Porky shook his head. He was a busy man and had no time for reports that didn't immediately concern him, he said. He just wanted to hear the high-lights. He was interested, that was all.

So, collecting himself, Acton again described what he had seen of the battle of the Java Sea; the *Eurydice's* arrival at the island; the shooting down of the aircraft; the mopping-up of the Japanese radio party; the sinking of the landing craft and the submarine; the arrival of the schooner; the final sinking of the *Eurydice* and their rescue by the *Anula*; and anything else he could think of. What with the Admiral's frequent questions and interjections it was a long sitting. It was nearly nine o'clock, and Greenacre was fidgeting with impatience and longing to get away for his bath, when Porky congratulated Acton on his safe return and got up to go.

"You'll be wondering about yourself and your people," he said. "I understand your earlier lot are still at Sydney, and that's where I propose sending you. We've a fast convoy sailing at dusk this evening, and your passages'll be arranged. See to that," he added to his Chief of Staff. "Fix up transport, and let 'em know at what time. They'd better all be in one ship."

"Where are we likely to be sent after Sydney, sir?" Acton ventured.

"Back home to England, I imagine. I can't think that the Admiralty'll allow the best part of a destroyer's ship's company to remain out here. I can't tell you details; but there are still ways and means of getting you there."

Acton's heart jumped. "May I tell the others, sir?"

"I see no objection," the Admiral returned. "And I'm glad our good friend here was able to pick you up," he went on, nodding in Greenacre's direction. "If Australia isn't exactly home to you, you'll find it's the next best place."

Acton tried to express all he felt; but Porky was in a hurry and cut him short.

"Goodbye," he said, holding out his hand. "The best of luck to you all, and a safe passage home."

"Thank you, sir," was all Acton could say as he shook hands.

Porky suddenly gave vent to his feelings. "I'm an old 'has-been' stuck in a shore job," he continued, his voice pathetic.

"They won't send me to sea, even after thirty years' service. I'm too ancient, they say. No. You lucky young men can't realize how I envy you your chances of a crack at something," he sighed. "I'd give my right arm to be *really* in the war instead of just looking on." He paused.

"Oh! One more thing, Acton," he added, his mood changing.

"Sir?"

"In case you don't know them, you'll find Australians very hospitable. Warn your boys to steer clear of . . . er too much hospitality in Sydney. Don't be run away with. Keep a tight hand, and no loose talk."

With which rather cryptic words of advice he found his coat and cap and hurriedly left the cabin.

A few minutes later he was being piped over the side.

Little remains to be told.

After calling at Adelaide and Melbourne, with a gale on the way, the voyage to Sydney lasted fourteen days. There, on arrival, nearly all of the *Eurydice's* survivors had cables from their people in England.

Acton's cable from Fiona was characteristic:

HAVE HEARD THE WONDERFUL NEWS FROM YOUR PEOPLE BUT FELT IT IN MY BONES ALL THE TIME. FULL OF JOY DARLING. ALL MY HEART. COME HOME QUICKLY. CABLE WHEN YOU CAN. SEE SONG OF SOLOMON CHAPTER TWO VERSE FIVE. FIONA.

'*Stay me with flagons, comfort me with apples: for I am sick of love,*' he read in the Bible.

He replied in suitable terms.

At Sydney, where they were kitted up and provided with money, the news of their rescue had somehow leaked out, though nothing had been published. They were made much of and entertained, and there was good reason for Admiral Bennett's few words of caution.

Eight days later they embarked in one of the ships of a fast convoy bound for San Francisco, a distance, with a wide detour to the southward, which meant a voyage of eighteen days with never the sight of an island or of other ships, nothing but mile upon mile of rolling ocean until they saw the faint blue ridge of the Californian mountains to the eastward, and finally steamed into harbour through the Golden Gate.

At San Francisco, to his infinite relief, Acton found they were expected. Taken charge of by the United States Navy, he and his men were accommodated and fed on a scale which was generously lavish. Acton himself was summoned to an interview with a most friendly American Admiral, and had again to tell his story. By evoking the Admiralty in London and perhaps rather exaggerating the urgency of their speedy return to England, he managed to avoid the trans-continental journey by railway. The Admiral, with a twinkle in his eye, ordered air passages for the whole one hundred and seventeen of them. After all, he remarked, he had a British grandmother and they were shipwrecked seamen. America was no longer a benevolent neutral. No, sir! She was a formal Ally, and he guessed the bill for transportation would only add a few more dollars to Lend-Lease. Two telephone messages and the thing was done.

And how was the lieutenant off for spending money? He would need more dollars for expenses. Acton, who hadn't really thought about it, supposed he would. The Admiral again spoke into a telephone, authorizing someone to advance dollars. How much? He didn't know. That had better be worked out with the officer concerned. Yes. He was a British naval officer in charge of a party of more than a hundred men on their way back to England. Okay! He'd be sent along.

He pressed one of a battery of bell-pushes on his huge desk and a blue-eyed blonde in uniform came into the room. It was the first time Acton had seen a 'Wave,' the equivalent of a British 'Wren.' He stared in astonishment. She was an extraordinarily pretty girl.

"Sir?" she asked, very much on duty.

"Miss Barton, take this officer to Captain Middlemass in room two one nine, wait, and then bring him back here."

"Yes, sir."

Acton followed Miss Barton along a corridor, up by elevator, and along another corridor, where she halted at a door, knocked and ushered him in.

"I'll wait," she said, smiling for the first time.

"Thank you very much," said he.

"You're welcome."

The officer at the desk, who wore the four stripes of a

captain, rose, shook hands, and inquired how much Acton needed. Acton didn't know; but explained he was in charge of a party of British seamen who had been ordered an air passage to New York. Captain Middlemass made some hurried calculations. Going into the adjoining room he returned with three official forms and a thick wad of notes. "That," he said pleasantly, mentioning the amount and handing them over, "ought to be enough. I've allowed a fair margin."

Acton blinked. The sum in dollars sounded enormous. Reckoning it out later it came to about a year's pay.

"Won't you count it, lieutenant?"

"Thank you, sir. I'll take your word for it."

"Okay. Just sign your full name, rank and official address in England." Middlemass gave him a pen, indicated the printed forms, recovered the notes and put them in an envelope.

Somewhat staggered at the ease of it all, Acton signed on the dotted line, pocketed the money, thanked the captain, and left the room. The war, he had heard, was costing a million pounds a day, or was it two millions? But following Miss Barton back to the Admiral's office he couldn't help wondering what would be the eventual reaction of the Director of Navy Accounts at the Admiralty.

So they flew in lordly fashion across the continent, stopping for two nights on the way. In New York, where their arrival was expected, Acton reported himself to the British Naval Liaison Officer. Comfortably accommodated, they had three days to see the sights of that great city, and then embarked in one of the ships of a convoy bound for Liverpool by way of Halifax, Nova Scotia. It was not so comfortable on board. Their ship was very crowded.

Once away from Halifax in company with twenty-two other merchant vessels, escorted by destroyers and corvettes, with aircraft ranging around during daylight, Acton came to realize that their little adventures on the other side of the world were of microscopic importance in the gigantic picture of the war as a whole. Even the *Anula's* exploit against the Japanese convoy had received no more than cursory mention in the American Press, though according to the ship's officers it had been well 'plugged' by the B.B.C.

At sea, in the North Atlantic, they were back into the war. German U-boats, operating in 'wolf-packs,' were still ranging all over the broad ocean and sinking an average of three merchant ships a day. The enemy's losses were mounting steadily as the counter-measures improved; but new U-boats were coming from the building yards much faster than they could be destroyed. Like every other seaman, Acton knew that the Atlantic supply line was the hinge of the war so far as Britain was concerned. Once severed, the country would be brought to her knees through the starvation of her war industries and population. Her power to continue even a defensive struggle would vanish when the last tons of fuel held in reserve had been expended by her warships and aircraft. Unable to bring in supplies of fuel from overseas, the Navy and Air Force would be fettered and finally immobilized. Disaster, comparable to that of France in 1940, would have stared Britain in the face.

They had two bad scares during the twelve-day voyage home, when the zigzagging convoy had to make sudden wide alterations of course to avoid U-boats reported ahead. Twice some of the escorting destroyers and aircraft went off on hunts of their own, and those in the merchant ships heard the thudding of depth charges in the distance, though with what result Acton never discovered.

They were lucky indeed to get through without attack, and it was a blessed relief when one evening, just before dusk, land was in sight on both sides, Scotland to port and Ireland to starboard. The escorts had been heavily reinforced, and as they steamed on into the North Channel one section of the convoy was detached to the Clyde. Daylight next morning, a grey day with occasional shafts of sunlight, found the remainder passing the red hull of the Bar lightship and entering the Mersey.

The journey was ended—a very long journey for the survivors of the *Eurydice* as they feasted their eyes on the huddle of buildings and docks along the waterfront on both sides of the river. This was England, and home.

Liverpool, as Acton knew, had been badly bombed; but as the ship sidled in towards the landing-stage, the city looked much the same as when he had last seen it. The gilded birds on the top of the Liver Building still regarded the waterway and its traffic with their air of aloof unconcern.

The inevitable crowd of people seemed to be waiting ashore.

There was the usual fuss and flurry of arrival with a horde of officials and others streaming on board when the brows were in place, and passengers milling around asking questions.

Acton was in the process of mustering the *Eurydice's* officers and men on the after end of the promenade deck when a lieutenant-commander appeared.

"My name's Willoughby," he said. "Are you Acton?"

Acton saluted and said he was. Willoughby was grey-headed and nearly old enough to be his father.

"You're from the *Eurydice* and these are your men?"

"Yes, sir."

"I've a message from the Commander-in-Chief. He wants to see you. A car's being sent at nine-thirty. You're to go to London later."

"London!" Acton exclaimed.

"You're to report at the Admiralty."

"What for, sir?"

"I wouldn't know. All we had was the telephone message last night."

"What about the other officers and the ship's company, sir?"

That was all in train, Willoughby said. The men would not be sent to the depots at their home ports. They would be paid up to date and kitted up at the naval base in Liverpool, served out with railway passes and sent straight on leave. Transport was being sent, and with any luck they should get away during the afternoon.

"Can they let their people know they're coming, sir, or do they just burst in on them?" Acton inquired. He was always thoughtful for the men, and already had a bunch of telegrams announcing safe arrival. He didn't know what censorship regulations might be in force.

"There's nothing against it provided they don't mention names or movements of ships or convoys," Willoughby said at once. "They'll arrange it at the base. I take it you and your people have all had breakfast?"

"Yes, sir."

"Then that's all for now, Acton. Congratulations on getting home all right. Transport for your people ought to be alongside soon after nine. It's eighteen minutes to now, so you'd better get busy on getting them ashore. I'll warn the people on the gangway. And don't forget, a car'll be along for you at nine-thirty sharp, and don't keep it waiting. I must be off. I've something else to see to. Meet you later, perhaps."

Acton had talked to the ship's company during a private farewell party the evening before. Though the ship was officially 'dry,' he had managed to wangle a half-pint bottle of beer per man, which added to the conviviality of the proceedings. Draycott and Farnworth alternated at the piano; McInnes played his precious ukulele, and everyone who thought he could sing was called upon to do so. Mr. Blatchington, somewhat surprisingly for one so staid, contributed the well-known ditty 'She was poor, but she was honest,' and was loudly applauded. Petty Officer Hartopp obliged with his farmyard imitations, and Melton with the only song he really knew, 'The waiter shouted down the hall, we don't serve bread with one fish ball.' There were sentimental songs and songs rather ribald, with 'Roll out the barrel' and the 'Islanders' Chorus,' as McInnes called it, otherwise 'Nicky Taylor's long-haired daughter.'

A good time was had by all except Acton, who had to make a farewell speech and nearly broke down, especially when his audience cheered wildly and broke spontaneously into 'For he's a jolly good fellow.' Before they dispersed they joined hands and sang 'Auld Lang Syne,' after which the men pressed round shaking their officers by the hand. They had been together for so long they were almost a family.

"Well, sir," Hartopp whispered throatily in Acton's ear, overcome with emotion. "She was the best ship I ever served in, and that's a fact. And when you go to a new one, sir, I hope you'll remember I'd like to come along with you."

Now, in the clear light of morning when the final parting had come, Acton felt gloomier still. He told the men what arrangements had been made, and wished them goodbye, good luck and a happy leave. He couldn't have wished for a better crowd. He was parting from friends, and one and all he was proud of them.

"That's all I have to say," he ended, "and thank you."

On shore, twenty minutes later, as the last of the charabancs carried his shipmates out of sight, he could almost have wept. He felt dreadfully alone.

The Admiral, whom Acton knew by repute, was kindness itself. Once more he had to tell his story, while the great man listened. He had by no means finished his account of the *Anula's* action when one of the desk telephones buzzed. Sir Robert picked up the receiver and put it to his ear.

"Arrived," he said. "Rather early, isn't it?—Yes.—Good. —In two minutes then.—Yes. All right." He replaced the instrument.

"I must be off," he added to Acton, glancing at the clock on the wall opposite as he rose. "I won't be long. Meanwhile you stay here, Acton. A—er—young friend of mine from London is anxious to have a word with you."

"Sir?" asked Acton in astonishment. "What . . .?"

"Never mind," Sir Robert broke in, taking his cap and gloves and going to the door. "You'll see. Just wait a minute. Good luck to you." There was a smile on the face and a twinkle in his eye as he hurriedly left the room.

What was all the mystery, Acton wondered. What young friend of the Admiral's could possibly. . . .

He heard a door behind him open. It probably communicated with the secretary's office. He turned.

"Fiona!" he gasped, as the door was discreetly shut. "Oh, my sweet, my darling! What on earth. . . ."

The rest was incoherence. They were in each other's arms.

"But what *are* you doing here?" he asked, releasing her when they came back to sanity.

Fiona laughed, the old laugh that Acton knew so well and loved. "Daddy's an old friend of Sir Robert's," she said. "I had your cable from New York and got busy, so here I am. You surely didn't think I was going to have you out of sight for a moment longer than was necessary, you old silly. What else matters?"

"Nothing matters," George Acton murmured, pulling her into his arms and kissing her right ear. "Nothing, nothing in the whole wide world! Oh heaven, Fiona, I can't realize it."

"You'd better," she replied softly. "From now on, or very soon anyway, you'll have me to look after, and I, God help me, shall be looking after you."